THE ATROCITY ENGINE

TIM WAGGONER

aethonbooks.com

Aethon Books
www.aethonbooks.com

Print and eBook interior layout and formatting by Steve Beaulieu. Cover Art provided by Maxim Kostin.

Published by Aethon Books LLC.

Custodians of the Cosmos

The Atrocity Engine

The Book of Madness

The Desolation War

Check out the entire series here! (Tap or scan)

One

Neal Hudson stood at the edge of the playground, watching. Something was wrong here, *very* wrong. He just didn't know what yet.

It was late afternoon. School was out for the day, so the children here were a mix of different ages, the youngest probably around ten, the oldest a pair of high school boys who sat in the grass on the opposite side of the playground from Neal. The teenagers watched the younger children play with studied indifference, likely waiting for them to clear out so they could take over the playground. They'd sit on the swings and talk about whatever teenagers talked about these days. Funny YouTube videos, the latest video games, all the sex they pretended to be having... The majority of kids were middle schoolers, still young enough to enjoy playing on the equipment, but old enough to feel a little embarrassed about it.

It was early September, the day warm and sunny, and most of the kids were in T-shirts and shorts. There were a number of parents present, mostly moms, sitting on the wooden benches positioned around the playground or standing and talking in groups. Neal could always tell new moms from more seasoned ones. The less experienced moms kept their eyes glued to their children, as if worried that someone was going to attempt to abduct their precious darlings at any second. The more experienced moms texted or talked on their phones, chatted with friends, or read books and magazines. They'd only look up if someone screamed bloody murder, and if their child wasn't bleeding to death, they'd return to what they were doing, unconcerned. The majority of the women were in their thirties, with only a couple in their forties. Younger mothers, those with toddlers, would've been here earlier in the day, when their little ones could play without any bigger kids around.

Neal was one of the few men present, and the only one who kept receiving furtive glances from the mothers. He didn't blame them for being suspicious of him. In his line of work, you had to be suspicious of everything all the time. It was the only way to get the job done, and – if you were lucky – still be alive when it was over.

His uniform didn't help, either. Maintenance employees, regardless of rank or position, wore long-sleeved white shirts, black ties, black pants, and black shoes. Those who went out into the field, like him, also wore a pair of black-rimmed smart glasses. Neal wore his sleeves rolled up and his tie loose, both of which were against regulations, not that he gave a damn. But these two nods to casualness and comfort didn't make him look any less like a deranged accountant who was contemplating a new career as a serial killer. His physical appearance only contributed to this impression. He was in his forties, thin, with straight black hair that refused to stay combed and a narrow face that could generously be described as careworn. When any of the women looked at him, he gave them a smile, and they quickly looked away, suppressing a shudder.

He expected to hear Pam Duggan's voice saying something like, *If you keep smiling like that, they'll evacuate the park.*

He sighed. He missed Pam. They'd worked together as partners for seven years before... Well, just before.

One of the women paid more attention to him than the others. She kept looking around the playground, as if watching the children, but her eyes lingered on him a few seconds too long whenever her gaze fell upon him. She was a pretty brunette in her late thirties, around 5'8", slender, wearing blue slacks and a green sweater over a white blouse. She held a rectangular plastic container with a sealable lid in her hands, and her fingernails ended in sharp points. Neal wondered what was in the container. Brownies? Cookies? The woman was smiling, as if enjoying watching the children play, but it was a smile that didn't reach her eyes. They were emotionless, almost calculating.

She appeared not to notice when Neal smiled at her, but he was certain she did. Unlike the other women, though, she didn't seem disturbed by his presence. He supposed he should've felt grateful that at least one woman present didn't find him skeevy-looking, but it struck him as odd.

The woman paid the most attention to one of the boys on the playground. He was eleven, maybe twelve, with blond hair, slightly chubby, and wearing sneakers, shorts, and a T-shirt with an anime character on it that Neal didn't recognize. The woman's son? Maybe, but Neal didn't see any resemblance. Maybe the boy was adopted, or maybe the woman was his caregiver, but not his mother. An aunt, a nanny, a friend of the family?

The boy played on the merry go round, getting it spinning really good before hopping on. He held onto the bars, leaned backward, then pulled himself up and inward, the action increasing the merry go round's speed. There were three other kids on the merry go round, all younger than him, and they held on for dear life as they spun around and around, ashen-faced and on the verge of tears. The boy's laughter had a dark edge to it, and most of the parents – those who weren't terrified their little ones were going to fly off the merry go round any second – scowled in disapproval.

Asshole.

Orchard Street Park was located on the west side of Ash Creek, and as Neal – who was driving solo these days – had drawn near it, the van's dashboard scanner had detected a surge of entropic energy. Not a very large one, but any surge was cause for concern. He'd pulled in, parked in one of the few empty spaces remaining in the lot, and sat for several minutes, engine running, watching the dashboard scanner. The readings stayed in the normal range, though. No more surges.

He'd supposed it could be a glitch of some sort. The van was overdue for an equipment check, and it was possible the surge was nothing more than a normal fluctuation in the entropic field. Entropy by its very nature was chaotic and unstable, after all. On another day, he might've decided the reading meant nothing and left the park. But he'd driven his assigned route since starting work at nine that morning, without a single interesting thing happening – unless you counted the fact that he'd seen not one but *two* albino squirrels in the same neighborhood – and he was bored out of his mind. So, he'd gotten out of his vehicle and started walking into the park.

Orchard Street Park was the largest in the city, with a good-sized playground, black-topped paths for walking and jogging, a duck pond, tennis and basketball courts, soccer fields, and a wooded area with hiking trails. The E-energy surge could've come from anywhere within the park, but Neal decided to check out the playground first because it had the largest concentration of people – and, of course, because there were kids there. The forces of Entropy (with a capital E) weren't picky about who and what they Corrupted, but they were especially attracted to children, so young, so full of life.

The playground was covered with cedar chips and had the usual accoutrements – teeter-totters, a dome-shaped metal climber, merry go round, slides, and swings. He'd been here before, most notably when he'd worked Clean-Up back in 2005. There had been an "incident" at the park then, a nasty one, and the clean-up had been a nightmare. Most of the playground equipment had been replaced and updated since then, but not the swings. The frame was tinged with rust, and the chains creaked loudly as children swung back and forth. But the oddest aspect of the swings were the three heads that sat atop the frame, metal sculptures of Dorothy's friends from *The Wizard of Oz* – the Scarecrow, the Tin Man, and the Cowardly Lion. They'd originally been painted to make them seem more lifelike, but the paint had long since flaked away, leaving them looking cold and sinister. The heads faced the playground's interior, as if this was a prison yard and they were the guards.

Bet a lot of kids have had nightmares about those guys over the years.

Neal's smart glasses did more than send a live feed to the Analysts at Ash Creek's Maintenance office – a feed that would be recorded and studied, not only to determine if there were any signs of Corruption he might've missed, but to monitor and evaluate his job performance.

When you worked for Maintenance, you had to get used to constant oversight. *None of us are ever alone,* his supervisor Deanna had once said during a staff meeting. He'd thought she'd intended it to sound comforting, but he'd found it anything but. Besides providing the Analysts with a constant stream of data, the smart glasses also allowed their wearer to detect entropic energy and the presence of Corruption. Neal had continually swept his gaze across the playground since his arrival, but so far, everything looked clear.

Getting paranoid in your old age.

And then he saw it: a dark shimmer around the blond kid – the one on the merry go round – a translucent shadow superimposed over his body, invisible to the unaided eye but revealed by Neal's glasses.

The unmistakable sign of Corruption.

Cody Pittman was having a *blast.*

His mom had picked him up after school and, since she had an appointment to, *Get my hair done*, she'd dropped him off at the park to play until she was finished. Cody was twelve, and he suspected, *Get my hair done,* was a euphemism for, *Spend an hour having sex with the man I'm cheating on your daddy with.* Not that he cared. After all, his dad was cheating on his mom with a woman who worked at the QwikMart near their home. He liked the woman. She always gave him free slushies. He wondered if his parents actually believed they were fooling anyone other than themselves or if it was all just an elaborate – and silly – game they played. Adults were weird.

Normally, he wasn't all that thrilled with playgrounds. They had one at McKenzie Middle School, but most kids didn't bother using the equipment. That stuff was for babies. Mostly kids stood around talking or staring at their phones, which they were allowed to use during recess. But for some reason, the Orchard Street Park playground was really doing it for him today. Part of it was that there were younger kids around for him to boss.

He might not have been at the bottom of the pecking order at his school, but he wasn't one of the cool kids, either. And while he wasn't all *that* fat, he did get teased about his weight sometimes. He wasn't a dummy, but he also wasn't particularly smart. Bottom line: He was no one special, just another kid trying to get through middle school one dull day at a time.

But it was different today. He felt *fantastic*, filled with energy and confidence, like he could do anything he wanted – anything at all – and no one could stop him. He was the king of this playground, its absolute lord and master, and if he desired it, everyone – kids and adults alike – would bow down to him. He hopped off the merry go round, grabbed hold of one of the bars, and started running, faster and faster, laughing as he increased his speed. There were three younger kids on the merry go round – two girls and a boy, all around five or six – and they sat down, gripping the bars to steady themselves, eyes wide with fear. Cody laughed louder and, when he judged he'd gotten the merry go round spinning as fast as he could, he hopped on, grabbed two bars, and leaned back as far as he could, his head nearly touching the ground.

The three unwilling passengers on this voyage began begging him, sounding on the verge of tears.

"Don't do it!"

"No, no, no!"

"Stop, *please!*"

Their cries for mercy only made him laugh harder. He heaved himself up and into a standing position, the motion causing the merry go round to accelerate. The younger kids screamed as Cody pulled himself toward the merry go round's center, sneakers stomping on the metal floor, making the device go even faster. The centrifugal force proved too much for one of the girls. She lost her grip on a bar, slid rapidly toward the edge of the merry go round, and was flung off. She flew several feet through the air then landed hard on cedar chips. She sat up and sobbed, face tear-streaked, snot running from her nose. It was the funniest thing Cody had ever seen, and he let out a high-pitched ululation that didn't sound quite human.

The remaining two kids huddled together, holding onto each other as much as they were holding on to the merry go round's bars. The merry go round was already starting to slow down, and Cody knew they weren't going to fly off like the one girl had. Well, he'd just have to try harder next time, wouldn't he?

He looked over at Ms. Blackburn and saw her smiling at him. She'd arrived at the park not long after his mom dropped him off, and he'd been surprised to see her. He was in her advisory at school, and it was always weird to see one of his teachers out in the real world. He knew that teachers were people who lived normal lives just like everyone else, but part of him believed that they were like robots who powered down at the end of the school day and waited silently in their classrooms until it was time to activate the next morning.

He liked Ms. Blackburn. She was nice enough, even if she was kind of strange. There was something off about her smile, as if she understood the concept of smiling but hadn't quite mastered the action yet. And her eyes assessed you in a clinical, detached way, as if you were an unfamiliar insect and she was trying to decide if you merited further study. She was a biology teacher, though, so he supposed she looked at everyone like that.

He'd hoped she'd ignore him, but she didn't. She'd come up to him and asked how his day had gone. He'd mumbled something in reply, and then she offered him a treat from the plastic container she was carrying.

"It was Mr. Rhodes' birthday today, and we had a little celebration in the teachers' lounge. I brought some sweets to share with everyone, and I had a few left over. Would you like one?"

Cody had wondered why Ms. Blackburn had come to the park, and why she'd brought her "sweets" with her. Had she hoped to distribute the leftovers to the kids playing here? That seemed kind of creepy. Then again, maybe she didn't have any kids of her own to give them to. Cody *loved* sweets, though – too much, his mother always told him – and he had no reason not to trust Ms. Blackburn. She'd given him another of her not-quite-right smiles, pulled the lid off the container, and held it out to him. He leaned over to peer inside and saw a half dozen greenish-gray objects slathered with a thick mucus-like coating. The odor that came off the things was repellent, a combination of sour milk and rotting meat, and Cody's stomach lurched when he breathed it in.

Go ahead, Ms. Blackburn had urged. *Take one.*

No way in hell was Cody going to eat one of those nasty-ass things.

And yet, the longer he looked at them, the more appetizing they began to appear, and their smell, at first revolting, became enticing, almost irresistible. Before he knew it, he'd picked up one of the slimy things and brought it toward his mouth. He thought he felt it quiver in his grasp, as if it was alive, but he told himself it was just his imagination, and he popped it into his mouth and swallowed.

It wriggled all the way down.

It was *delicious*. It tasted like sunshine, rainbows, and Christmas mornings... Like electricity, fire, and ecstasy... Like *life*. He was young and strong and he was going to live forever! Laughter bubbled up from deep inside him, but when it came out it sounded like the harsh bray of a diseased donkey. He didn't say thank you to Ms. Blackburn, didn't tell her how good her weird-looking treat was. In fact, he forgot all about her. All he wanted to do was play, play, play! He raced onto the playground, ready to release the energy jangling inside him before he burst.

Now he stood on the slowing merry go round, watching the crying girl who'd fallen and grinned from ear to ear. A woman – presumably her mom – ran over and crouched beside her.

"Are you okay, Meredith? Did you break anything?"

The girl was sobbing too loudly to speak, and her only response was to point toward Cody.

The mom looked at him, and her face darkened with anger.

"What the hell is wrong with you?" she demanded.

Cody let out another bray of laughter. "What's wrong with *you?*"

The woman looked astonished, as if he'd slapped her. She stood, her expression one of absolute fury now, and headed toward Cody. The merry go around had almost stopped by this point, and the other two kids trapped on it decided this was an excellent time to make their break for freedom. They dashed off the merry go round and ran in different directions, but they didn't go far. When they reached the edge of the playground, they stopped and turned to see what was going to happen to Cody.

Meredith's mom walked over to the merry go round, but she didn't step onto it. Instead, she took hold of two bars and leaned forward until her face was less than a foot from Cody.

"You think it's fun to hurt kids that are younger than you?" the woman asked. Then, without waiting for a reply, she said, "Is your mother here?"

"My mother is dead. I killed her." It was a lie, but Cody wanted to see how the woman would react. But now that he'd given voice to the idea, it didn't sound half-bad. When this was all over and his mom had picked him up and taken him home, he might really do it, just to see what it would be like.

Part of him – buried deep down inside – couldn't believe what he was thinking. But the rest of him told that part to shut the fuck up, and it did.

Meredith's mother pulled her head back at Cody's words, eyes wide with surprise. Then she scowled.

"That's not funny."

"Maybe not," Cody said. "But this is."

He opened his mouth wide, and a stream of green-gray fluid shot forth to blast the woman's face.

After twenty years working for Maintenance, Neal had a fairly strong stomach. But when the kid vomited on the upset mother, hot bile splashed the back of his throat, and he thought he was going to throw up as well. He'd had White Castle for lunch, though, and the burgers hadn't tasted all that great on the way down, and he certainly didn't want to know what they tasted like coming up. So, he fought his rising bile and managed to keep the contents of his stomach where they belonged.

The woman, face and hair covered with green-gray goo, threw herself backward from the merry go round, stumbled, and fell hard on her ass. She screamed, seemingly from being disgusted and not from pain, but Neal needed to make sure. He took a step forward, then reached up, removed his glasses, and dropped them to the ground.

"Oops," he said.

He kicked cedar chips over the glasses to make sure the Analysts wouldn't see whatever happened next, let alone have a record of it, then he hurried toward the woman. Her daughter had gone to her, and now the two of them huddled together, mother screaming, girl sobbing. He was aware of the other kids and adults on the playground, more than a few struggling to keep from vomiting, but he didn't pay them much attention. It was the woman he needed to worry about – and the boy.

"Are you alright?" he asked her.

"I can't breathe," she said between screams. "I can't breathe!"

"You're probably just having a panic attack," Neal said. Still, whatever had come out of the boy's mouth was pure Corruption – his aura had turned pitch-black the instant he puked – and there was no telling what effect it might have on the woman. Neal bent down, lifted his right trouser leg several inches, then pulled a slim white rod from his sock. It was the same thickness as a pen, but longer, almost nine inches. He pointed the Nullifier at the muck covering the woman's face and thumbed an almost undetectable switch on the device's surface.

Work... Please...

At first nothing happened, but then the Nullifier grew warm in his hand and the muck began to evaporate. The stuff already stank like hell, but the smell got worse as the Nullifier did its job. Neal held his breath, not wanting to breathe in any of the fumes, just to be on the safe side, and watched as the Nullifier finished. The green-gray slime was gone, but unfortunately, it had done a number on the woman's face before Neal had reached her. Her eyes and nose were gone, the skin where the organs had been smooth, flat, unmarked, as if she'd been born without them.

"What's wrong?" the woman said. "Why can't I see anything?"

Before Neal could stop her, she reached up and ran trembling fingers across her face. Then she screamed again. Her daughter looked at her mother through tear-filled eyes, and when she saw what had happened, she screamed, too. Neal knew whatever the crap was that the kid had puked on the woman, he'd stopped it from erasing her entire head, but that didn't make him feel any better about what had happened.

Still gripping the Nullifier, he stood and turned toward the merry go around.

"You little shit, why did–" He broke off. The kid wasn't there.

He looked around and saw children and adults alike fleeing the playground in panic after seeing that the woman's eyes and nose were missing. The boy wasn't among them, though. He'd walked over to the swing set, hopped on one of the swings, and now sat there, watching Neal, a broad grin on his face, madness shimmering in his eyes. The boy wasn't the only person who'd remained. The eyeless woman and her daughter continued sitting on the ground, holding each other and crying, and the brunette woman in the green sweater – the one who'd smiled at him – stood on the edge of the playground, watching. She didn't look upset in the slightest, her expression one of cool detachment. Without his glasses, he couldn't see her aura, but he guessed it was as black as midnight right now, probably even darker.

He stood for a moment, debating his next move. The kid was the more obvious threat, but instinct told him the woman was by far the more dangerous of the two. Neal was alone, with no partner to watch his back, and if he dealt with the kid first, he'd leave himself open to a potential attack by Green-Sweater Woman. Eleanor – the Analyst that had been monitoring his glasses' live feed – had most likely already dispatched an Intervention Team. But it would take them at least five minutes to get here, and a lot of bad things could happen in that time.

Before Neal could decide what to do, the boy turned his face to the sky, opened his mouth, and blasted forth a gout of muck. It shot upward to strike the swing set's top bar and adhered to it like glue. It spread, covering the bar from one end to the other, then slowly flowed into the metal until it was gone.

Not good.

Nothing happened for several seconds, then the swing set began shaking. The boy hopped off his swing, took several steps away, then turned back to watch. The swing set became soft and collapsed, flowing in on itself like liquid until nothing was left but a mound of viscous gray-green. The heads of the *Wizard of Oz* characters remained intact, though, and began to move, eyes blinking, mouths opening and closing. The muck mound separated into three smaller piles, one for each of the heads, and they rapidly formed bodies. An instant later, the remains of the swing set were gone, and the Scarecrow, Tin Man, and Cowardly Lion stood in its place.

. . .

The characters had been brought to life by the boy's Corruption, but as twisted, distorted versions. The Scarecrow's fabric was mildewed and rotted, broken ends of bone sticking out from its seams instead of straw. A skull was painted on his face instead of cartoonish human features. The Tin Man was dented and rusted, his arms and legs bending at wrong angles. His chest was torn open to reveal a swollen black heart, dark blood oozing from the wound and trailing down his abdomen. His features resembled those of an angry gargoyle, and he gripped a two-headed broad ax more suitable to an ancient warrior than a humble woodsman. The Lion stood upright like his movie counterpart, but he looked anything but cowardly. He was broad-chested and thick-limbed, and muscles like those of an Olympic bodybuilder's bulged beneath his tawny fur. His black mane was a wild tangle, framing a feline face with amber eyes and a mouth filled with sharp white teeth. His fingers and toes terminated in long ebon claws resembling small scythes, and he flexed them, growling deep in his throat.

The boy laughed and clapped his hands in delight. The Tin Man raised his ax, joints creaking as he moved, and then with a single vicious swipe, he lopped off the boy's head. Blood jetted from the wound, and the boy's body remained standing for a moment, as if it didn't realize it was dead yet. Then it fell onto its side, blood still gushing from the neck stump to soak cedar chips. The head rolled toward the Lion, and he snatched it up, sinking his claws into the top of the head, and breaking off the top of the skull. He tossed it aside then jammed his mouth into the opening. With loud, wet smacking sounds, he began eating the dead boy's brains. After a moment, he withdrew his blood-smeared face and looked at the Scarecrow.

"You can have the rest," he growled.

He tossed the head to the Scarecrow who caught it easily. The Scarecrow removed his hat and tossed it on the ground. He then raised the boy's head over his own, turned it upside down, and shook out the remaining brains. They splattered onto the fabric on top of his head, some bits sticking while others sliding off and plopping onto the cedar chips below.

"I feel smarter already!" the Scarecrow said, then laughed like a lunatic.

The Tin Man then bent down to the boy's headless body, jammed his metal fingers into his chest, and tore out his heart.

"It's about time I found a replacement," he said in an emotionless metallic voice. He jammed his ax into the ground, then with his free hand, he reached into his chest and removed his swollen black heart. He tossed it aside, then inserted the boy's. Metal cables drilled into the fresh heart, and it began to beat. The Tin Man's rust vanished, his dents repairing themselves, and his metal gleaming in the afternoon sunlight. He stood straighter, turned his head back and forth, flexed his arms and knees. Everything moved easily and silently, as if he'd just been freshly oiled. Neal supposed in a way he had.

"Much better," the Tin Man said. He then gripped the ax's handle and withdrew it from the soil.

"I've seen some fucked-up shit in my line of work," Neal said. "But this is definitely in the top ten. Maybe even top five."

He raised his Nullifier, pointed it at the trio, and activated it.

Nothing happened.

"Goddamn it!" He pressed the activation button several more times, but the device remained cold and lifeless in his hand. But even if the Nullifier had worked, he wasn't certain it would've been strong enough to deal with manifestations of this nature. Corrupting something that was already alive was one thing, but bringing to life something that was unliving took *serious* power.

He glanced nervously toward the park's entrance. Where the fuck was that Intervention Team?

He looked back at the eyeless woman and her child. They still sat by the merry go round, holding each other and crying. *The woman in the green sweater...* He looked around, but there was no sign of her. Whoever she was, he envied her. He would've liked nothing more than to get the hell out of here, too.

The Lion was the first of the Oz characters to make a move. He lunged forward, but instead of attacking Neal, the Lion fell on all fours, bounded past him, and rushed toward the eyeless woman and her daughter. Even if the Nullifier had been working, the Lion moved too fast for Neal to stop him, and with a deafening roar he attacked the defenseless pair and began tearing them apart with his teeth and claws. Mother and daughter screamed in agony, but not for long.

Neal detected movement from the corner of his eye, and he stepped to the right just in time to avoid getting sliced in half by the Tin Man's battle ax. The Tin Man brought the weapon down in an overhead strike, and the blade bit deep into the ground beneath the cedar chips and stuck there. The ax head was embedded much more firmly this time, and as the Tin Man fought to extract the blade, Neal – who was now in arm's reach of the Scarecrow – dropped his Nullifier and grabbed one of the bones protruding from the ragged thing. He gripped the bone, a femur, he thought, with both hands, spun around, and smashed it as hard as he could into the Tin Man's face. Once these creatures had taken shape, they'd become bound to their new forms, with all their strengths and weaknesses. And tin was a soft, weak metal.

Neal had aimed for the Tin Man's gargoyle eyes, and the impact of his strike had caused their metal to crumple, effectively blinding the creature. Neal jumped back as the Tin Man began swinging his ax wildly, hoping to connect with the human that had stolen his eyesight, but the ax kept slicing through empty air, and the Tin Man growled in frustration.

Sharp pain flared in Neal's left shoulder, and he staggered to the side, turned, and saw the Scarecrow standing there, lengths of broken bone gripped in each gloved hand. The sharp end of the bone in his right hand was red with blood, and Neal knew the Scarecrow had managed to cut him with it. He'd been lucky. Distracted as he'd been by the Tin Man's attack, the Scarecrow could've inflicted a fatal blow. The Scarecrow came toward him, moving with rattling-clacking sounds and awkward, jerky motions. At first Neal thought the creature only had a few bones sticking out from his body, but now he realized that the thing was stuffed entirely with bone instead of straw. The Scarecrow carried his own weapons in his body, which Neal had to admit was very efficient, but there was a major drawback to being little more than a cloth bag filled with loose bone fragments. The bag needed to remain intact for you to function.

The Tin Man had continued swiping his ax back and forth as the

Scarecrow had attacked Neal, and now Neal moved toward the metal creature. The Scarecrow followed, laughing his maniacal laugh, bone daggers raised high in preparation for a second strike. Neal kept darting his gaze back and forth between the Tin Man and the Scarecrow, and when the time was right, he fell to his knees.

Neal had lured the Scarecrow in range of the Tin Man's ax, and when the metal man swung his weapon next, it struck his friend in the side, just below his right arm. The Tin Man put so much strength into the blow that the Scarecrow exploded. The top half of his body separated from the bottom, his head came off, and his gloved hands fell away from his shirt sleeves. His laughter died, and when his various pieces hit the ground, they laid there, unmoving.

The Tin Man continued swinging his ax back and forth, grunting from the effort. The bone daggers the Scarecrow had wielded remained clutched in his gloves, and Neal bent down and retrieved one. He stood and turned toward the Tin Man. He watched the creature swing his weapon a couple times, and when he judged the moment was right, he rushed forward and plunged the bone dagger into the Tin Man's stolen heart.

Blood gushed from the penetrated organ, and the Tin Man released his grip on the ax's handle. He staggered backward, stiffened, then froze like a metal statue.

"That's two," Neal said.

The Lion crouched over the remains of the mother and daughter, tearing bloody chunks of meat from their ravaged bodies and jamming then into his mouth, swallowing them without taking the time to chew. Neal gripped the battle ax's handle and worked it back and forth. The Tin Man had almost freed the weapon before he died, and it didn't take Neal too long to pull the ax out of the ground. The ax was heavy as hell, but he managed to lift it and balance the handle on his shoulder. His wound gave a cry of protest at this treatment, but he ignored it.

As he walked toward the Lion, the cat-man must've sensed his approach, for her turned to look at Neal, a slick, red gobbet of meat in his right hand. Neal wasn't sure, but it looked like a woman's breast.

"Want some?" the Lion offered. "There's plenty to go around."

"No thanks," Neal said, stomach turning. "I prefer my meat cooked – and not human." He raised the ax and brought it down on the Lion's head.

Two

Neal sat on one of the park benches, holding a wad of gauze to his shoulder and watching the Interventionists work. His wound throbbed, but he wasn't worried about contracting Corruption from the Scarecrow's attack. The Interventionists had brought a med kit from their van and had immediately sprayed blue Expungent on his injury. He was certain he'd be okay, but when he got back to the office, he'd have someone from Medical Division examine it, just to be on the safe side.

After killing the Lion, he'd retrieved his smart glasses and was wearing them once again. During his debrief, he planned to claim that the glasses had fallen off while he'd been trying to deal with the situation in the park, and he hadn't had time to put them back on until the danger was past. He'd doubted the Debriefer would believe him, but he intended to stick to his story. He'd also picked up the malfunctioning Nullifier before the Intervention Team arrived, and it was safely tucked into his sock and concealed by his pants leg. Surveyors weren't supposed to carry weapons, especially not ones as powerful as a Nullifier, which was why Neal had "accidentally" dropped his glasses – so no one would know he'd used it.

Seven men and women between the ages of thirty and fifty were gathered on the playground, five Interventionists, and two Cleaners. In addition to the usual Maintenance uniform, the Interventionists wore black leather equipment belts around their waists with a holster for their Nullifiers. The belts also had loops and pouches for holding additional equipment, a flashlight, handcuffs, small containers of Expungent, and other odds and ends.

A pair of Interventionists stood on either side of Neal's bench, and he couldn't escape the feeling that they were guarding him, as if he was a prisoner who might try to flee any moment.

"Christ, what a fucking mess," Royce Bigelow said, without looking at Neal.

"You got that right," Sabrina Howell replied. She gave Neal a quick wink and smile. Like Neal, Sabrina wasn't a stickler for rules and regulations when it came to making split-second decisions in the field – unlike her tight-ass partner.

Royce was a white man in his late forties, broad-shouldered and barrel-chested, the kind of person who worked out every day, no exceptions. His head was freshly shaved, black mustache and goatee perfectly trimmed, his clothes spotless and wrinkle-free, shoes so highly polished they gleamed. Sabrina was a petite African-American woman with short hair, fit rather than muscular, and her clothes – while not quite up to the high standards Royce set – were clean and neat.

The others were hard at work. One Interventionist walked the perimeter of the playground, recording energy readings on her hand scanner. The two Cleaners wore cannisters of Expungent on their backs and were spraying the chemical on the remains of the distorted Oz characters. After being destroyed, the creatures had begun returning to the ooze that had birthed them, and the Expungent would complete that process. When it was all over, nothing would remain.

The cedar chips where the creatures had fallen would be collected, bagged, and removed for later analysis and disposal. The biggest problem was what to do about the three human bodies, and that's the question the remaining two Interventionists were pondering. One stood by the boy's decapitated corpse, scanning it, while the other did the same to the grisly remains of the girl and her mother.

Neal let out a long sigh, and Sabrina – as if reading his mind – said,

"It's not your fault you couldn't save them. From what you described, some heavy shit went down here."

"And you're only a Surveyor," Royce added, still not looking at him. "It wasn't as if you were properly equipped to deal with the situation."

Maybe not. But I took care of those three motherfuckers before your sorry ass got here.

Sabrina rolled her eyes at Royce's comment. She and Royce might've been partners, but Neal knew she thought the guy was a dick.

The two Interventionists who'd been assessing the dead bodies finished at the same time and came over to the bench. The one who'd examined the boy – an Asian woman in her early thirties named Nikole Harp – was the first to speak.

"We need to take the boy with us. His body has been suffused with an extremely high amount of entropic energy, and we'll need to study it to determine its exact nature and origin. Plus, it would be far too dangerous to release him to his family."

"We'll have to let them think he disappeared then," Royce said. "Regrettable, but there's nothing else we can do."

"You don't sound too broken up about it," Neal said.

Royce finally looked at him. "If you'd saved his life, we wouldn't be having this conversation, would we?"

Neal started to rise to his feet, but Sabrina put a hand on his shoulder and urged him to sit back down. Royce gave him a thin smile, clearly amused.

"Now, now. Violence only hastens Entropy," he said.

"Maybe," Neal said. "But sometimes it feels so god damn good."

Nikole struggled to suppress a smile and was only partially successful. Royce frowned, but he didn't say anything.

"I'll go get a containment bag," Nikole said.

She hooked the scanner onto her belt and started walking in the direction of the parking lot, where two unmarked white vans were now parked next to Neal's. A pair of police cars were present as well, lights flashing. The officers had parked a dozen yards from the vans, and they remained inside their vehicles, waiting for the Maintenance crew to finish with the scene. Maintenance had an understanding with police; when weird shit happened, they showed up to deal with it, and the cops were only too happy to let them, with few questions asked.

When Nikole was gone, Royce addressed the man who'd examined the ravaged bodies of the girl and her mother.

"What about the other two?" he asked, lips pursed in distaste.

Kenton Seidel was a short white man in his mid-forties, with a round face and curly brown hair. He was overweight, not grossly so, but in Maintenance's culture, the slightest sign of fat meant you were consuming more resources than necessary, and it was looked down on. Hence, Royce's obvious dislike for the man.

"They have only trace amounts of Corruption on them," Kenton said. "There's no need for us to collect their remains, which is good. Given the state of their bodies, we'd need to haul them away in a number of *very* large buckets." Kenton grinned, as if he'd just made the most hilarious joke. None of them – not Neal, Sabrina, or Royce – so much as smiled, let alone laughed.

"Tough crowd," Kenton muttered, then went on. "The damage to the mother's head makes it impossible to tell that her eyes and nose were erased. The biggest problem will be coming up with a believable story to tell the police."

Sabrina and Royce spoke at the same time.

"Serial killer," Royce said.

"Animal attack," Sabrina said.

They looked at each other, then Royce turned back to Kenton and shrugged.

"Pick whichever one you like," he said.

"I'll go with animal attack," Kelton said. "That'll make it easier to explain why the mother's nose and eyes are missing."

He headed toward the parking lot. Most of the time, Maintenance was able to do its work under the radar, but when that wasn't possible, they provided a rational explanation to the authorities, something they could more easily accept than the truth. And more importantly, something believable that they could tell the citizens they served to keep them from panicking.

The last remaining Interventionist – a freckled redhead named Jeanette Willis – had almost completed her scan of the playground.

When she reached the spot where Neal judged the woman in the green sweater had stood, she stopped, and her body went rigid. Her eyes widened, and her already fair complexion paled to chalk-white. "Oh my," she whispered and collapsed to the ground. She thrashed as if in the throes of a seizure, her eyes rolled white, and foam bubbled past her lips.

Neal, Sabrina, and Royce rushed to her side, and the two Cleaners stopped their work to watch, concerned. Neal and Sabrina crouched on either side of Jeanette, while Royce picked up the scanner she'd dropped and examined the information on its screen. Neal pulled his wallet out of his back pants pocket and forced it between Jeannette's teeth so she wouldn't bite her tongue. Then both he and Sabrina put their hands on the woman's shoulders to try to keep her as still as possible.

Royce spoke without any trace of his usual arrogance.

"She encountered a Rift Scar."

Neal and Sabrina looked at him in shock.

"Are you serious?" Neal asked.

Royce nodded. He pointed at a spot not two feet from where Neal and Sabrina crouched. "It's right there. I'd advise you not to go any closer to it."

"No shit," Neal said.

There was nothing obvious to indicate the presence of a Rift Scar. Everything looked normal enough – the ground, the air above it... Neal had never encountered one in the field before, but he knew from his training that Rift Scars were undetectable, even by Maintenance's scanners, until you were right on top of them, and by then it was too late.

"Do you think the woman in the green sweater caused it?" Neal asked. He'd told Sabrina and Royce about her when he'd filled them in on what happened at the playground.

"Maybe," Royce said. "One thing's certain, though. Whoever caused it had to be one of the Multitude."

"Seriously?" Sabrina said.

"Fuck me," Neal said. An already bad day had suddenly gotten a lot worse.

It was after six by the time Neal made it back to the office.

The Hawthorne Office Park was located on the east side of town, and Maintenance was located in a one-level, dark-red brick building. A number of unmarked white vans were parked out front, and a small sign bolted to the wall next to the glass door read MAINTENANCE, and beneath it in smaller letters it said, ASH CREEK DIVISION. Neal parked his vehicle, Surveillance Van Number Seven, and sat behind the wheel for several moments. He'd worked for Maintenance for twenty years, and while he'd seen a lot of awful things in that time, he'd never experienced anything as bad as what had happened at Orchard Street Park today. He kept seeing the Tin Man's ax cut off that poor boy's head, kept hearing the little girl and her mother shriek in agony as the Lion tore them apart.

Royce had not-so-subtly hinted that those three deaths were Neal's fault, and Neal – despite how angry he'd been at Royce – agreed. Sure, he'd stopped the Corrupted Oz characters from killing anyone else, but that was little, if any, comfort to him. He imagined speaking to the families of the victims.

It's a damn shame your loved ones are dead, but on the bright side, I took out those three E-energy manifestations all by myself. I'll probably make employee of the month!

He was tired as hell. Normally after a shift this taxing, he'd go home, put something mindless on TV, and eventually surrender to sleep. But if he slept tonight, he feared he'd dream about what happened at the park, and he couldn't face watching the boy, the girl, and her mother die over and over in his mind, their agony playing on a loop. He considered skipping the Debriefing session and heading over to the Edge to kill his memories, if only temporarily, with cheap booze. But Debriefing sessions were mandatory following an incident, and he knew that he wouldn't be allowed to leave until he'd completed his. Resigned, he opened the front door and stepped into the reception area.

There was nothing remarkable about the office, which was exactly the way Maintenance liked it. All the colors were bland and neutral – beige walls, dark green carpet, gray desks and cubicle dividers, black chairs. Everyone wore white shirts or blouses, black pants or skirts. No piercings or tattoos and very little makeup or jewelry. None of the staff was particularly good-looking, but none of them were ugly, either. Nondescript was the best way to describe them. People who wouldn't attract a first glance, let alone a second.

Anonymity was one of Maintenance's chief weapons, and it was carefully cultivated and fervently guarded. Maintenance was open around the clock, although they didn't post office hours anywhere. They weren't really a business, and they didn't have an online presence or advertise their phone number. They didn't advertise at all, as a matter of fact. They didn't serve customers, and they didn't want any. They served a calling.

The Office Manager – her duties were too numerous and complex for her to be called a receptionist – sat at her desk, her attention fixed on the open laptop before her. Erika Labianco was in her early sixties, rail-thin, with bright silver hair. She didn't look up from her computer as Neal entered and stood in front of her desk. She typed for a few more seconds, slender fingers flying across the keyboard, before at last hitting the enter key. Only then did she raise her head and meet Neal's gaze.

"Deanna wants to see you."

Neal was surprised and a bit dismayed.

"Shouldn't I see a Debriefer first?"

"Not this time," Erika said. "Flavor to the feast." Without another word, she returned her attention to her computer and resumed typing.

Neal knew there was no use in pumping her for further information. Erika was old-school Maintenance, and she believed in avoiding waste of any sort, and that included wasted words.

"Flavor to the feast," he said. He turned away from her desk and started down a narrow hallway that led deeper into the building.

Deanna Nicely was head of Maintenance's Ash Creek Division, and as such, she had one of the few private offices in the building. Deanna did not believe in an open-door policy, and she insisted that everyone knock, even if she was expecting them. So, when Neal reached her door, which had nothing on it, not even her name, he knocked three times.

"Come in."

Neal opened the door and stepped inside, only to discover that Deanna wasn't alone. She had two chairs in front of her desk, and occupying one of them was another Maintenance employee, one he didn't recognize.

Must be someone new.

The woman was in her mid-twenties, Hispanic, with long black hair that reached to her waist. She gave him a warm smile as he entered, and he acknowledged it with a nod. He wasn't a big smiler.

Deanna was square-headed, broad-shouldered, and big-handed. She wore her black hair tied back in a ponytail, and while she had on the same white shirt and black pants as everyone else who worked for Maintenance, her tie – which hung over a mammary shelf of truly epic proportions – was red, a sign of her rank.

"Sit down, Neal," she said, gesturing to the empty chair. She was a big woman, muscular, not fat, but her voice was high-pitched and girlish. Somehow this contradiction gave her even more authority.

Neal sat.

Deanna's office – like the rest of the facility – was almost entirely devoid of personal touches. She had a desk, chairs, laptop, cell phone, a couple filing cabinets, and, of course, her two windows. She always kept the curtains drawn shut, though, and Neal never understood the point of having windows if you didn't use the damn things to look outside once and a while.

A framed picture hung on the wall behind the desk. It depicted a starfield, in the middle of which was a large black space surrounded by a swirl of colors. If you looked closely, you could see several stars stretching and lengthening as they were pulled into the swirl. This was the Gyre. It lay at the heart of all creation, and it was the reason Maintenance did what they did. Neal wasn't sure, because he'd never spent enough time in Deanna's office, but he thought the image in the picture might be moving, so slowly it was almost impossible to detect.

There was one other piece of personal décor: a silver metallic-looking feather displayed in a glass-covered frame on the wall opposite Deanna's desk. Whenever Neal saw the Umbral feather, he wondered if Deanna had placed it there so she could always see it when sitting at her desk. She'd never struck Neal as someone who needed outward motivation to perform her duties, but Maintenance did take a psychological toll on its employees, and if looking at the Umbral feather from time-to-time gave Deanna a boost when she needed it, Neal wasn't about to criticize her for it.

"Neal, I'd like to introduce you to Gina Sandoval. Gina, this is Neal Hudson."

The woman didn't respond right away. She was looking past Deanna at the picture of the Gyre on the wall behind her. Her face was expressionless, but her gaze held awe and, unless he was mistaken, a touch of fear. Then she returned to herself, flashed him a thousand-watt smile, and stuck out her hand. The change in her demeanor was so abrupt that it took Neal a moment to reach out and shake her hand. Her skin was delicate and cool, but her grip firm and confident as they shook.

"Nice to meet you," she said.

"Uh-huh." He was beginning to have a bad feeling about this, and that feeling was confirmed when Deanna next spoke.

"Gina is new. This is her first job with Maintenance, and that means–"

Don't say it. Please...

"She needs a partner," Deanna finished. "And so do you. You've been working alone for almost two months now, but after what happened in the park this afternoon..."

Neal didn't have to ask how Deanna knew about that. Sabrina, Royce, and the others had all been wearing their smart glasses. Everything they saw and heard – including Neal's explanation of the incident – had been transmitted to Analysts who, given the severity of the situation, had no doubt immediately relayed the information to Deanna.

"Are you saying if someone had been there to cover my sorry ass, no one would've died?"

Gina looked shocked by Neal's words, but Deanna didn't show any emotional reaction at all.

"I'm saying that if *two* people had been on scene, things might've turned out differently. I'm not criticizing your performance today, Neal. You did as much as any person could do. Any *one* person."

Neal sighed then turned to Gina. He'd met plenty of over-eager, over-ambitious rookies in his time. He'd been one himself once, hadn't he? Chomping at the proverbial bit, ready to face the forces of Entropy head-on and, if not exactly save the world, at least delay its inevitable end as long as possible.

Working for Maintenance carried significant risks, though, especially if you worked in the field. A lot of rookies didn't make it past their first couple of years. They either died, were Corrupted, or cracked under the mental strain. Hell, Pam had been a veteran with years more experience than him, and looked what happened to her.

Neal turned to Gina. "Nothing personal, but I don't..." he trailed off as something occurred to him. "Your last name is Sandoval, right?"

She gave him an uncertain smile, but she nodded.

"As in *the* Sandovals?"

She looked embarrassed. "I prefer not to rely on my family's reputation."

"That's admirable," Neal said. "I take it that means you're going to start out in Cleaning Division. That's what I did. Or maybe you'd rather begin in Archives. That's a great way to learn about Maintenance's history."

He glanced at Deanna and she gave him a look that said, *You're not funny*.

Gina seemed even more embarrassed now. "Well... Ms. Nicely and I were discussing that before you got here, and I think I'd rather start out in the field. Maybe as a Surveyor. A junior one, of course."

"Of course." *Not relying on your family name, huh? I bet your parents contacted Deanna personally to "suggest" that you be assigned to Surveillance. Can't have a Sandoval getting Expungent on her hands, can we? Too sticky and smelly.*

Neal turned to Deanna. "As much as I'd like to–"

"Good! I'm glad that's settled. Gina will start riding with you tomorrow morning."

Deanna smiled, but her gaze warned Neal not to challenge her on this. He got the message and forced a smile of his own, although he doubted it was very convincing.

Gina looked so excited, he thought she might start jumping up and down.

"This is wonderful! I'm *so* looking forward to working with you, Mr. Hudson. I know I'm going to learn a lot."

She stuck out her hand again, and Neal reluctantly shook. As enthusiastic as she was, he supposed he was lucky she didn't try to give him a hug.

"Call me Neal," he said. "*Mr. Hudson* makes me feel old."

Gina looked at uncomfortable, but she said, "Okay... *Neal.*"

Deanna looked at Gina. "Why don't go out into the main office, find an open cubicle, and review incident reports from the last six months? That'll give you some background on the sort of things we deal with here in Ash Creek. If you need any assistance, just ask Erika for help."

"Yes, Ma'am."

Neal looked at Deanna to see how she responded to being called, *Ma'am*. Her brow furrowed slightly, but she made no comment on it.

Gina stood. "See you tomorrow morning, Mr.... I mean, Neal."

She gave them both a departing smile, said, "Flavor to the feast," then left the office and closed the door behind her.

Neal looked at Deanna. "You have something else you want to discuss with me... *Ma'am?*"

"I know the girl is as green as grass, but she has a lot of potential. I expect you to do the very best job you can training her."

"And as soon as she gets that training, she'll put in for a transfer to a higher-status position," Neal said. "Chicago, L.A., New York, London, Paris, Tokyo..." *And with her connections, she'll probably get it.*

"She *is* ambitious," Deanna admitted.

"Runs in the family," Neal said.

"That it does. Now, let's talk about what happened at the park. At one point the video feed from your glasses was interrupted."

Here it comes. "They got knocked off my face in the confusion."

"So, you're saying it was an accident."

"Yes."

"And you didn't drop them on purpose, then cover them with cedar chips to block the cameras?"

"Of course not," Neal said. "That would be against procedure."

"Mmm-hmm." Deanna held out her hand. "Give me the Nullifier, Neal."

He thought about trying to bullshit her some more, but really, what was the point? With a sigh, he reached down, removed the weapon from his sock, and handed it to her. She took it and placed it in one of her desk drawers.

"How did you know?" he asked.

"Because I know *you*," she said. "You've made it quite clear over the years that you think all field agents should be armed, not just Interventionists."

"And if I'd had a brand-new, state-of-the-art Nullifier with me instead of a broken-down piece of shit that I... borrowed from Tech Division, the events at the park might've turned out very differently."

"Perhaps," she allowed. "But Maintenance Control has made its position on the matter very clear. The fewer personnel who are directly exposed to Corruption, the better. If every field operative carried weapons, they'd feel emboldened to confront a source of Corruption, and I don't have to tell you the results of that could be disastrous."

Neal's jaw tightened. She was talking about what had happened to Pam. But before he could say anything, she moved on to another topic.

"Tell me more about this woman in the green sweater," she said. "What were your impressions of her?"

Neal didn't want to allow Deanna to sidetrack him, but this subject was too important to ignore. Besides, he preferred not to talk about Pam right now.

"Her attention was definitely focused on the boy who caused the disturbance at the park. It was as if she was waiting to see what he'd do, like she was aware that he'd been Corrupted."

"As if she'd caused it?" Deanna asked.

"Yeah."

Deanna nodded. "And you didn't see her create a Rift?"

"No, but the Rift Scar was located in the same place the woman was standing. Who else could've made it?"

"Are you a hundred percent certain of the scar's location relative to where the woman was?"

He considered, then admitted, "Not a hundred percent, no."

"That's a shame," Deanna said. "If you'd kept your glasses on, we could assess the video footage and make a more specific determination of the woman's position."

Neal wanted to protest, but what could he say? Deanna was right.

"Do you think she might be one of the Multitude?" he asked.

"Who else are capable of creating a Rift so easily?"

"True." *A member of the Multitude, right here in Ash Creek. What could one of those bastards possibly want from our little town?*

"Don't tell anyone," Deanna said. "I don't want to any rumors to start until we're certain of what we're dealing with."

Neal didn't like keeping secrets from his co-workers. He believed the more the employees of Maintenance knew, the better prepared they were to deal with the dangers they faced in their work. Still, in this instance, he thought Deanna was making the right call. If people learned a member of the Multitude had come to Ash Creek, they would lose their shit, big time.

"Speaking of the Rift Scar, how's Jeannette?" Neal thought of the way the Interventionist had collapsed after encountering the scar, the way her body had been gripped by seizures, eyes rolling white, mouth foaming.

"She's on her way to the Columbus office. Their medical facility is far superior to ours. With any luck, they'll be able to help her."

Deanna didn't sound hopeful, though, and he didn't blame her. Rift Scars were bad news, and not everyone recovered from contact with one. And those who didn't recover ended up being sent to the Farm.

"I have to be honest, Deanna. I'm surprised you think it's a good idea to partner Gina with me. I'm sure she's well trained, but chasing down one of the Multitude isn't exactly an assignment for a rookie. It's far too dangerous."

Deanna was silent for a moment, and Neal knew he wasn't going to like what she said next.

"You're not going to be following up on today's incident."

It took an effort for Neal to keep his voice calm. "I'm the best Surveyor you have, Deanna."

"That's true. But you haven't been *at* your best lately, have you? Not since–"

"It's been a couple months, and I've kept all my mandated appointments with Psych Division. They've certified me as qualified to return to active duty."

"They did. But it's up to me to determine what type of assignments you're ready for, and you're not ready to go after one of the Multitude. Your recent lapses in judgment testify to that. 'Borrowing' the Nullifier, 'accidentally dropping' your glasses at the park... Either of those are grounds for further suspension of duties. But as you said, you're the best Surveyor I have, and I *want* you to get back to work. I think it will help you heal more, don't you? But it's best if you start with more... manageable goals. Training a rookie is challenging enough as it is. We don't need to make things any harder on you right now."

A dozen different responses flashed through Neal's mind, from, *Are you crazy?* to *I can't believe you're this stupid* to *Fuck you, I quit!* But in the end, he chose to remain silent.

Deanna sighed. "We all loved Pam, and we all miss her. You're not the only one still grieving her loss."

Neal stood. "If that's all, I'd like to go now."

Deanna looked at him for a moment, and when she spoke again, she did so as his boss. "Go talk to a Debriefer and make an official report. After that, go home and get some rest, okay?"

Neal gave her a stiff nod, turned, and started to leave.

"Flavor to the Feast," she said.

He didn't look back. "Yeah."

He managed to not slam the door on his way out.

Three

Neal intended to get the fuck out of there. But as he approached the reception area, he was intercepted by Eleanor Fletcher. She was one of the best Analysts Ash Creek Division had. She was also his ex.

"Are you alright?" she asked.

After his meeting with Deanna, this was the last thing he needed.

"I'm fine."

Eleanor was in her mid-thirties, with short strawberry blond hair and girlish features that made her look ten years younger. Like other Maintenance workers, she wore no makeup or jewelry. Such enhancements were considered a waste of resources.

Eleanor had seemed genuinely concerned when she first approached him, but now her face scrunched up in anger and she punched him on the shoulder.

"What the hell were you thinking, going into a situation without any backup?" she said. "I tried contacting you, but you didn't respond. What's wrong with you? Do you have some kind of death wish?"

"Right now, my wish is to go home and try to forget today ever happened. And you are preventing me from doing that."

She glared at him. "Word is that you're going to be training our new recruit. It's one thing if you want to die, but you'd better get your act together before you get her killed, too."

Before Neal could respond, she turned and threaded her way through the maze of cubicles. Neal saw Gina sitting at one of the workstations, laptop open in front of her, no doubt reviewing incident reports as Deanna had suggested. She turned and when she saw him, she smiled and waved.

Christ help me...

Neal didn't feel like speaking to a Debriefer right now, and he decided he'd do it in the morning. He headed for the door, and when he passed Erika's desk, he didn't look at her. Nevertheless, he had the impression that she smiled with amusement as he left the building.

Sometimes he really hated his job.

It was closing in on eight o'clock by the time Gina made it back to her condo. She would've remained at the office and continued going over reports all night if she could've, but she knew it would be best if she got a full night's sleep so she'd be ready for tomorrow. Too bad employees weren't allowed to view files from home, but Maintenance Control believed the risk of someone hacking into their system was too great to allow off-site computer access. Otherwise, she'd try to get a little more reading in before bed.

She pulled her Toyota Prius Hybrid into the River Loft condominium complex, located on the northwest side of town. This was one of the nicer sections of Ash Creek, not far from the Graywater River, hence the complex's name. She drove through River Loft until she came to her unit, and parked in her designated space directly in front. She grabbed her purse off the passenger seat, got out of the car, and walked to the door, unlocking it and stepping inside. She flipped on the front hall light, then stood for a moment. It was hard to believe that this place was really hers. She'd never had a home of her own before. For most of her life, she'd lived with her parents in South Kensington, Maryland, close to the Maintenance Division in Washington, D.C. where they worked. Aside from her time at the Homestead, where she'd shared a dorm room with another trainee, she'd never lived anywhere else.

But then, this place wasn't exactly hers, was it? Maintenance salaries were hardly lavish. They paid their employees enough to cover food and shelter, but that was it. All part of the organization's ethos of maximum conservation with minimal consumption. But some in Maintenance, her family among them, took a slightly different view. They believed that Maintenance's employees needed to remain psychologically healthy in order to perform their duties effectively, and a big part of this was being able to enjoy life. *Work hard, play hard, live well* was their motto – all in service to the organization's mission, of course. The Sandoval family had been investing money for generations, first in their native Spain, then in businesses around the world, and over the years they'd become quite wealthy. Her parents had purchased this condo for her, as well as her Prius.

It's your first posting, her father had said. *You need reliable transportation and a nice place to relax after work. There's a great deal of stress in our profession, and you have to take care of yourself before you can take care of others, yes?*

That had made sense at the time, but now, standing here on the eve of beginning her first real job with Maintenance, she felt guilty. She doubted Ms. Nicely lived in a place like this, or Neal. They probably lived modestly, the way a Maintenance employee was supposed to. She'd almost turned down her parents' help, but in the end, she told herself that by accepting it, she'd make them happy and they'd worry less about her. But now she wondered if she simply hadn't lacked true conviction in her principles. It was a depressing thought.

She walked into the kitchen, turned on the light, the placed her purse and keys on a countertop. She went to the refrigerator, took a microwave meal of fettucine alfredo with chicken and broccoli from the freezer, heated it, then sat down at the table to eat. As she did, she thought back on her day.

She'd reported to work at nine a.m. sharp, and Deanna had given her a tour of the facility. Afterward, she'd suggested that Gina take some time to drive around Ash Creek and familiarize herself with the town. *A good Surveyor needs to know the territory she's going to observe as well as she knows herself,* Deanna said. *Maybe better.* Gina had been excited to explore Ash Creek because this was where her father had started out. He'd begun as a Surveyor, too, before quickly moving up to Interventionist and then to Administrator. With each of those promotions had come a transfer to a different – and better – location, and he'd only worked in Ash Creek for a little over a year. Still, she was delighted to be following in the footsteps of Amador Sandoval, though she had no illusions about filling her father's shoes.

Her mother Mariana, brother Emigdio, and sister Juliana all worked for Maintenance, too. Her mother in D.C. alongside her father, Emigdio in New York City, and Juliana in San Francisco. As the youngest in the family, she was the last to get started on her career, and she was eager to prove herself worthy of the Sandoval legacy – and more than a little scared that she wouldn't measure up to it.

You'll do amazing things, her mother told Gina before she left home. She wished she could make herself believe it. Right now, she'd just be happy if she didn't embarrass herself.

She wondered what working with Neal would be like. After Deanna had suggested she review case files, Gina had pulled up some recent ones of Neal's in order to get to know her future partner and mentor better. She supposed some people might consider this snooping, and maybe it was, a little. But she hadn't been able to get a very good handle on him during their brief meeting in Deanna's office. He'd seemed a bit cranky – okay, more than a bit – and he hadn't seemed to be very enthused about training a rookie. Certainly, it had been a surprise for him to learn that Gina was going to be his new partner. She wasn't sure why Deanna hadn't given him a heads up, but she supposed the woman had her reasons, although she couldn't think of what they might be.

Gina thought about how her first day at work had gone before she met Neil. She had returned from her self-guided tour of Ash Creek around three o' clock, and she had about an hour to get to know some of the other people in the office. When they learned she was going to be partnered with Neal, their reactions varied quite a bit. Some congratulated her on getting to work with one of the best, while others cautioned her that Neal wasn't exactly a stickler for rules, and that she should be careful not to pick up any bad habits from him. Still, others pitied her, and one – a Debriefer named Marshall Li – had told her that Neal's last partner had died on the job, the implication being that he was at least partially responsible for her death.

She'd tried accessing that case file to learn more, but it was locked. To protect him? Protect Ash Creek Division? Both? Or had Deanna locked the file herself, knowing that Gina would inevitably wish to review it and would discover something that would make her want to immediately transfer to another location? So many questions and no answers – at least not yet. She'd find them out eventually, though, one way or another.

She turned her attention back to her dinner. She finished eating, rinsed the empty cardboard container, and placed it in the plastic bin on the counter for recycling. She washed her fork by hand – no need to waste the electricity needed to run a dishwasher – dried it, then put it in the drawer with the rest of the silverware. She then turned out the kitchen light and headed upstairs to get ready for bed. She took a shower, brushed her teeth, and before long was curled up beneath the plush navy-blue comforter her mother had bought for her. Her parents had purchased all the furniture in her condo, as well as her kitchen utensils, pots and pans, along with a dozen separate uniforms so she wouldn't have to do laundry that often.

I'm spoiled. When she'd been a child, the thought would've made her smile, made her feel lucky to be a Sandoval. Now, she felt uncomfortable, a little ashamed, even. She was Maintenance now, she reminded herself. She should forget about herself and focus on the mission. She almost laughed then. She was a Sandoval, which meant she'd been hearing about *the mission* her entire life. She thought of the picture in Deanna's office, the one of the Gyre, and she couldn't help but shudder. Why would anyone want a picture of that... that *thing* hanging on their wall? It made no sense to her. She remembered when her father had first told her about the Gyre and the true nature of existence. She'd been five and lying in bed, just as she was now, and he'd sat on the edge of her mattress and held her hand as he spoke.

"Do you know what Entropy is?"

She shook her head.

"Do you know how when you spin a top it goes very fast at first, but then it starts to slow down, and eventually it falls over and stops altogether?"

She nodded.

"That's what Entropy is: energy is expended until it's gone. Reality is like that too, sweetie. From the instant of its creation, the Omniverse has been winding down like a top, and one day – so far in the future that it's impossible to imagine – it will stop spinning and fall silent. Do you understand this?"

She didn't, not really, but she nodded anyway to please her father. He smiled.

"Good. Now, this next part might be harder to understand, so pay close attention. The reason reality is winding down is because at the center of the Omniverse lies a great emptiness which we call the Gyre. Since the beginning of time, the Gyre has been draining the Omniverse's energy into itself. It's like a gigantic mouth that's always hungry, and reality is its food."

Gina pictured a dinosaur's mouth filled with long sharp teeth, biting, chewing, swallowing, and never-ever-ever stopping. She shivered, and her father squeezed her hand to reassure her as he continued.

"The Gyre is greedy. If it could, it would gobble up everything all at once. There is no way to stop it, but we can slow it down, make it chew its food more slowly, as it were, help it enjoy its meal more thoroughly, teach it to savor each bite. To take its time. This way, we can delay the inevitable as long as we can, give the Omniverse and all its inhabitants a longer life. This is the goal of Maintenance, the organization that your mother and I work for. This is our mission, and one day, it will be yours as well."

Her father had asked if she had any questions, and she said she didn't, although, of course, she had many. He'd kissed her on the forehead, rose from her bed, turned out the light and left, closing the door softly behind him, leaving her alone with the darkness. And when she looked up at the blackness that was her bedroom ceiling, she imagined she saw a gigantic mouth filled with teeth, opening wide as it came for her.

She'd been terrified of the Gyre ever since and seeing its image on her new supervisor's wall today had shaken her. It reminded her – as if she could ever forget – what Maintenance was fighting for, what it was up against, and that no matter what it did, it would inevitably fail. One of her instructors at the Homestead used a medical metaphor to explain Maintenance's role.

Doctors know that people don't live forever, but they do what they can to help extend and maximize the quality of their patients' lives. That's what Maintenance does for reality.

Gina liked viewing Maintenance's mission that way. It beat the hell out of thinking of herself as a soldier in an army of chefs preparing a gourmet meal for an unimaginably large cosmic mouth.

Flavor to the feast, indeed.

She'd never told anyone of her childhood fear of the Gyre, or how that fear had followed her into adulthood. Her family didn't know, and she'd hidden it from her instructors at the Homestead. She didn't want to disappoint her mother and father, didn't want them to be ashamed of her for not being strong, not being a true Sandoval. But tomorrow she was going into the field for the very first time as a full-fledged Maintenance employee, stepping onto the front line in the battle against the forces of Entropy, fighting alongside a man she knew virtually nothing about – and she was scared.

She told herself to stop this foolishness and get some sleep. She closed her eyes, but she didn't turn out the bedroom light. She hadn't slept in the dark since the night her father had told her about the Gyre. Because she knew, without the light, she'd see the Gyre's mouth in the ceiling's blackness, see its razor-sharp teeth, smell its fetid breath, hear its hungry moans... *You look so beautiful, Gina. I could just eat you up!*

She slept, but not for very long.

Neal sat on his couch, drinking a beer, and watching a true crime show on his laptop. He liked these programs, found them relaxing. Sure, they dealt with awful stuff, but it was *normal* stuff, just humans doing shitty things to other humans. No Corruption-created monsters, no evil godlike beings that traveled through dimensional tears in space. Only murderers and thieves and rapists and terrorists. When he watched these shows, he could pretend, if only for a short time, that the world, fucked up as it was, made some kind of sense.

The current program that was on featured the story of a family of five that mysteriously vanished one night in the middle of dinner. It was pretty good, but he was having trouble paying full attention to it. The scenario was too close to a case he'd worked several years back. That family had become trapped within a dimensional eddy within their own home, and it had taken a lot of work on Maintenance's part to free them. After their release, none of the family members ever spoke again, not even to each other. Within three years, they'd all committed suicide, without any of them ever explaining what they'd experienced within the pocket dimension where they'd been held captive.

"Fuck."

He closed the laptop, and the program turned off. He wasn't in the mood to watch any more of it. Instead, he sat back, sipped his beer, and allowed his mind to wander. His apartment was located in the basement of a house on the southside of Ash Creek, a rundown low-income area that residents unofficially referred to as the "Shithole." Neal found it an apt name.

The owner of the house, a retired woman in her sixties named Yvette Schultz, lived on the top two floors of the building. She was nice enough, if a bit lonely and chatty, and Neal was glad his apartment had its own entrance so that he didn't have to see her every day. His quarters weren't very large – a main space that held his ratty secondhand couch, a cardboard table and folding chairs, a small kitchenette with an oven, stove, refrigerator, and sink, and in a far corner, the cot he used for a bed, although a lot of nights he fell asleep on the couch watching TV shows or YouTube videos.

He also had his own bathroom with a toilet, sink, and shower, but it was so cramped he kept bumping into the walls whenever he used it.

The floor was concrete, as were the walls, and there was a single grimy window that barely let any light in during the day. The air was always damp and cool, regardless of the time of year, and it had the musty smell of a closed-in place that was never aired out. There were no pictures or photos hanging on the walls, and the window had no curtains. The basement was lit by fluorescent ceiling lights whose hum formed a constant, but not altogether unpleasant, background noise. Neal lived like this partly because he believed in Maintenance's prohibition against unnecessary consumption, but also because he simply didn't give a damn.

As he finished the rest of his beer, he reviewed the events of his day, a habit he'd been taught by his mentor when he'd first started working in Ash Creek.

Everything a Surveyor sees and hears is recorded by the Analysts. But we're the only ones who know what we think and feel, what observations strike us as most important, what conclusions we draw from them. But we don't always know these things right away. Often, we need a little time to mull over what we've seen before we can truly clarify our thoughts. It may seem like a contradiction, but sometimes you have to rest your mind to help it work more efficiently.

Neal closed his eyes and began.

He started with the incident at the park, as that was the most important. He avoided thinking about his conversation with Deanna, how she wasn't going to let him be part of the investigation going forward. His anger and frustration would only make it more difficult to recall details clearly. He didn't know how long he did this – he lost all track of time when he slipped into this state of hyper-focus – but he discovered nothing new. He really should've spoken to a Debriefer before he stormed out of the office, but he was confident he'd recall everything just as clearly tomorrow. Still, better to make a record of it now. He opened his laptop and spent the next hour writing a detailed report about the incident at Orchard Street Park that he could deliver to one of the Debriefer's tomorrow. He hoped he'd get to speak to someone other than Marshall Li. The man was great at his job, but he was a tight ass and was hardly Neal's biggest fan.

When he finished with the report, he closed his laptop once more.

He sat there then, not hyper-focusing as he no longer needed to recall specific, vivid details, just thinking. Had Deanna been right? he wondered. Was he reluctant to work with Gina because of what had happened with Pam? The Psych Division therapist he'd seen at the Columbus facility had told him it was only natural that he be hesitant to work with a partner again, and he'd been back on the job for two months flying solo. Deanna had periodically suggested he take on a new partner, but she hadn't insisted – until today. As irritating as that was, he thought he could've dealt with it if she hadn't paired him up with a goddamn rookie. And one of the Sandoval kids, yet.

Deanna knew he had history with the family, so why would she want him to work with Gina of all people? He didn't hold her accountable for anything her parents had done, but partnering with her still raised uncomfortable issues for him. Now he had to deal with that on top of adjusting to a rookie partner, dealing with his frustration at not getting to follow up on the Orchard Street Park incident, *and* trying to overcome his guilt over Pam's death. He remembered what Deanna had said during their meeting earlier.

Training a rookie is challenging enough as it is. We don't need to make things any harder on you right now.

"Not harder," he said. "Right."

He thought of the woman he'd seen at the park, the one who'd been holding the plastic container filled with... what? He thought of how she'd been unafraid to meet his gaze, how she'd returned his smile. It was almost as if she'd known him, but he was certain he'd never seen her before. If she was one of the Multitude, she probably hadn't recognized his uniform and marked him as belonging to Maintenance. That she'd been responsible for the boy becoming Corrupted he had no doubt, but he wasn't sure why she'd remained to observe the ensuing chaos.

The Multitude preferred to work behind the scenes and not draw attention to themselves. And why hadn't she attacked him, or more likely, ordered the boy to do so? If she'd known he was Maintenance, she'd surely realized he'd report the incident at the park, thus alerting his coworkers to her presence. The Multitude were arrogant and believed themselves too powerful to be defeated by mere mortals, so maybe she'd felt no need to hide from him. Maybe she hadn't perceived him as any real threat. And maybe she'd gotten off on flaunting her power in front of a Maintenance worker, a kind of taunt – *Nah, nah, you can't stop me.* Still, her behavior struck him as odd. Then again, he'd never encountered one of the Multitude in the flesh before. Who was to say how one of the dark demigods would act in a given situation?

The Multitude had one goal above all others: to hasten the entropic collapse of the Omniverse so that the Gyre could glut itself on reality. They believed the Omniverse had been created solely to be food for the Gyre, and by spreading Corruption and breaking down reality, they were in essence predigesting the Gyre's food for it, making its absorption faster and easier. Supposedly, they viewed what they did as a mercy. If the Omniverse was fated to die, why draw out its death and make its inhabitants suffer any more than necessary? They regarded what Maintenance did as merely prolonging the Omniverse's misery, and sometimes Neal wasn't sure they weren't right.

Old as his couch was, it was still marginally more comfortable than his cot, and most nights he slept on it. He lay down on it now, rolled over on his left side, and closed his eyes. With everything that had happened today, he thought he was too wound up to sleep, but within the space of ten heartbeats, he was out.

He dreamed of Pam screaming as she died, and when he woke, his face was wet with tears.

Rachel Blackburn stood in her luxury kitchen – hardwood floor, marble countertops, custom cabinets, two double-sided refrigerators, two ovens – pondering the ingredients floating in the air around her. A dying man's last breath, a fleshy mass of stage four tumors, the placenta from a woman who'd died giving birth to a stillborn baby, the abandoned dreams of a heroin-addicted welder who'd wanted to be a singer in his youth, the self-loathing of a child pornographer who eventually killed himself, the enmity between identical twins who despised one another, the agony of a car crash victim embedded in her broken teeth, a knife used by a serial killer that stored the screams of its victims within its metal blade...

She'd used these ingredients, and more, to create the Defilement that she'd given to Cody Pittman on the playground that afternoon, and while she'd been pleased with the results, she thought that if she tinkered with the formula a bit more, she would be able to increase the effect, make it stronger, more stable, and longer-lasting. The Maintenance worker had been able to eradicate the manifestations of Corruption with relative ease. She knew she could do better, that she *had* to do better, not only because she was determined to prove herself to the Multitude, but because the price for failing them was horrifying beyond the imagination.

She was pondering a new combination and proportion of ingredients for a fresh batch of Defilements when she sensed the dimensional fabric within the kitchen begin to strain, as if something was pushing on it from the other side. An instant later came a tearing sound that no human ear could detect, followed by an equally indetectable shriek of pain as space was torn asunder. She turned to see a man step through a Rift and enter her kitchen. Once he was through, the Rift sealed behind him, creating a scar that, while invisible to mortal eyes, looked to Blackburn like a thin obsidian line in the air. She'd have to be careful to step around that scar from now on. Each Rift Scar had its own aftereffect, and this one – she narrowed her eyes as she examined it – would make anyone who stepped through it lose control of their bladder and urinate themselves. Lovely.

The man – if that word could be applied to a being such as him – that had entered her kitchen was tall and cadaverously thin, skin desiccated and leathery, hair like bleached bone. His suit might have been white once, but now it was yellowed with age and mottled with unidentifiable stains. A black bolo tie encircled his too-thin neck, cinched with a metal clasp shaped like a rattlesnake's head. The most disturbing feature about him was his eyes. They were twin pools of darkness enclosed within swirling lines of color – miniature versions of the Gyre.

This was Brother Nothing.

The temperature in the kitchen plunged to freezing, and Rachel's breath misted the air. Brother Nothing's did not, however, and she didn't know if that was because his breath was already cold as arctic air or if he didn't need to breathe at all. She couldn't have said which would be worse.

He didn't look at her at first. Instead, he examined the Defilement ingredients hovering in the air.

"Interesting choices," he said, his voice the sound of old bones being rubbed together. "You might consider adding a strangled puppy to the mix. Gives it an extra kick." Dry lips pulled back from jagged yellowed teeth in a rictus smile.

"Did you come to give me cooking tips?" Rachel asked.

The Multitude had no official hierarchy or leadership, but Brother Nothing was one of the most powerful – and feared – of their dread number, and it was rumored that he might even be an avatar of the Gyre itself. He scared Rachel shitless, but she knew she couldn't allow her fear to show. Like all predators, the Multitude became excited in the presence of fear, and she didn't want to tempt Brother Nothing into attacking her. If he did, she knew the odds of her surviving the encounter, let alone defeating him, were steep, to put it mildly.

Brother Nothing gestured with a hand – fingernails long, sharp, and cracked – and the Defilement ingredients vanished.

"I prefer to have your full attention while we talk," he said.

Her mouth was dry, and it took her several attempts to get a response out. "You have it."

"Good. Let us sit at your dining table."

He turned and started toward the dining room, and Rachel trailed after him like a shivering pet, fearing that it had somehow displeased its master and would now be punished. She resented being made to feel this way, but she immediately shoved the emotion aside. The Multitude were resistant to each other's power, but that didn't mean Brother Nothing couldn't read her mind if he wished. *Resistant* did not mean *immune*, not by a long shot – especially when you were talking about someone as powerful as him.

The dining set was a Grand Classic Edwardian table with six upholstered chairs.

As if by unspoken agreement, they sat at opposite ends of the table. She almost asked Brother Nothing if he'd like something to eat or drink, but she knew this wasn't a social call. Besides, she didn't know if a being like him *could* eat or drink.

"I took a walking tour of your neighborhood before I came here," Brother Nothing said. "Expensive houses, luxury cars, professionally landscaped grounds... Do your neighbors ever wonder how you can afford to live in such a nice area on a teacher's salary?"

The Northside of Ash Creek was home to the town's doctors, lawyers, dentists, financial professionals, and other well-to-do citizens. When Rachel had come to Ash Creek at the beginning of the summer to establish her cover as the new biology teacher at McKenzie Middle School, she'd decided that if she had to stay in this pissant little town for several months, she might as well live in comfort and style. What was the point in having her kind of power if you didn't use it to enjoy yourself? And if Brother Nothing had been in the neighborhood, why the hell hadn't he used the front door to enter instead of walking through a Rift? She didn't know if she'd ever get used to the Multitude's love of theatrics.

"I don't interact with my neighbors much," Rachel said. "I've been too busy perfecting the formula for my Defilement."

"Nose to the grindstone, eh? Commendable."

She found it impossible to read Brother Nothing. His manner was always mocking, with an edge of sinister menace lurking beneath the surface, an apex predator toying with its prey.

"I performed my first field test this afternoon," she said. "It went quite well."

"Tell me the details."

"I chose Orchard Street Park because it has a history of Corruption that would make fertile ground for my Defilement to take hold. I also knew that some of my students go there after school to play, so I'd be able to find a child who trusted me and would accept the Defilement when I offered it with only mild psychic persuasion needed."

"Go on," Brother Nothing said.

She told him the entire story of the trial run, leaving out nothing, including the presence of the Maintenance worker. Either Brother Nothing already knew everything that happened – which was likely – or he would discover the truth later. Either way, she couldn't hope to conceal so much as the smallest detail from him, so why bother trying?

When she'd finished her report, Brother Nothing rested his elbows on the table and steepled his overlong fingers before him. He fixed his black, empty eyes on her, and she could feel the power of the twin vortexes pulling at her. She gripped the armrests of her chair to anchor herself, just in case.

"So, you fled the scene without dealing with the Maintenance worker," Brother Nothing said. His tone was cold now, without a trace of mockery. He'd recruited her for the Multitude himself – a great honor – and had served as her mentor ever since. Even so, she knew no more about him than she had on the day when he'd first approached her, except that he was infinitely more dangerous than she'd understood then.

Rachel resisted an urge to swallow nervously. "I thought it best not to engage with him. Isn't maintaining anonymity one of the Multitude's most important guiding principles?"

"It is," Brother Nothing agreed.

She started to relax, but then Brother Nothing shouted, *"Then why the fuck did you test your Defilement in public in broad daylight?"* He jumped to his feet and brought his fists down on the table. The instant his flesh touched the wood, the table collapsed into dust.

Rachel gripped the arms of her chair even tighter, held her breath, and didn't move a muscle, didn't even blink. She felt an almost overpowering urge to protect herself by erecting a shield of E-energy, but she resisted, fearing that Brother Nothing might see that as a sign of aggression.

The anger drained out of him in a rush then, and when he sat back down, he crossed his legs, put his hands in his lap, and gave Rachel a grimace that – for him – passed for a warm smile.

"So, what are your plans moving forward?" he asked.

The dining table was now a mound of gray dust settling on the floor between them. Rachel imagined Brother Nothing touching her, filling her with E-energy and reducing her to a pile of dust like he'd done to the table. She suppressed a shudder, knowing he'd take it for a sign of weakness, and forced herself to meet his dark, eyeless gaze.

"Once I've tweaked the formula to my satisfaction, I'll create a new batch of Defilements. I'll take them with me to school tomorrow, and I'll offer them to a student in my advisory. The Defilements should transform the child and last significantly longer than the one I gave to Cody."

"Should?" Brother Nothing asked.

"It *will*," Rachel insisted. "Once at home, the child will pass the Corruption on to her family. The infected will then go on to create Chaos for as long as the Defilement's effect lasts, which I hope – I mean, I'm *confident* – will be at least twelve hours, maybe even longer. And I promise I'll be appropriately circumspect while observing the results this time."

This was the crucial moment. If Brother Nothing probed her mind now, he'd discover she wasn't telling him the truth, not all of it, anyway, and he'd destroy her as swiftly and easily as he'd destroyed her table. She worked to keep her expression neutral, not too scared, not too confident.

He looked at her for a long moment, and she thought for certain that she'd failed, but then he clapped his hands together, startling her.

"Sounds like a plan!" he said. He stood and walked over to her, careful to step around the dust mound he'd created, and placed his icy hands on her shoulders. "I've known you since you were a little girl, Rachel, and I've trained you to become one of us. You're like a daughter to me. Fuck this up and I will gut you like a fish and feast on your entrails. Good luck!"

He drew away from her, turned, and the fingers of his right hand became ebon talons. He slashed the air to create a Rift, stepped through, and was gone. The Rift sealed shut behind him, forming a scar. She peered at it. If you stepped through this one it would make you feel like someone was piercing the inside of your heart with dull, rusty needles. She'd have to remember to avoid this scar, too. She didn't rise from her chair immediately. She sat for several moments and thought about her meeting with her mentor.

Failure was not tolerated among the Multitude, and she knew Brother Nothing hadn't been joking about eviscerating her if her plan did not succeed. She wondered how he would've reacted if he'd known what her *true* plan was. This was her first solo project, her test to see if she truly belonged with the Multitude, but despite the stakes, she had refused to take the easy route. She'd chosen to work with children because they we were far more difficult to Corrupt than adults and because she wanted the members of the Multitude to see what she could really do. To that end, she didn't intend to cause a simple outbreak of Corruption, as was required of Multitude recruits. No, she had something better in mind. Bigger and far more awful. Something even a full-fledged member of the Multitude might hesitate to try.

She intended to build an Atrocity Engine.

She'd learned of the device during her studies at the Athenaeum, the Multitude's vast place of learning, located in a distant dark dimension. There, within an ancient tome called *The Promulgation of Nihility*, she found what she was searching for: a device so devastatingly powerful that it would increase her strength a thousandfold, catapulting her into the first ranks of the Multitude. She would become the equal of Brother Nothing, perhaps even his superior. Of course, if the Atrocity Engine failed, the resulting discharge of entropic energy would destroy the Earth, as well as a significant chunk of the solar system. She was confident she could escape the devastation, though, so it was a risk she was willing to take. Once she perfected the formula for her Defilements, she could get started.

She glanced down at the dust mounded on the dining room's hardwood floor.

But first, she needed to order a replacement dining set.

FOUR

"I'm surprised the scanner is showing so many fluctuations," Gina said. She was wearing a pair of smart glasses, as was Neal. The pair she'd been given felt a little tight. She kept reaching up to adjust them, but nothing she did helped. She told herself she'd get used to it eventually. She hoped.

Gina leaned forward in her seat to get a better look at the van's dashboard screen. The readout indicated numerous variances in the area's entropic energy – nothing particularly alarming, but the pattern was more erratic than she would've expected.

Neal was driving, and he took his eyes off the road for a second to glance at the monitor. He then looked forward again, unconcerned.

"That's normal for Ash Creek. Certain places in the world are more susceptible to E-energy and thus more prone to Corruption. The technical term is *entropically vagarious zones*, but usually we just call them Soft Spots. The entire town is one, and so is a good portion of the surrounding area. It's why so much weird shit happens in Ash Creek." He glanced over at her. "I figured you requested a post here because it's a Soft Spot. Makes for a challenging first assignment. Good way to build experience *and* a name for yourself. If you live long enough." He turned his attention back to the road once more.

"I'm familiar with Soft Spots," Gina said. "I've just never been in one before."

She had learned about such places at the Homestead, but she hadn't realized that Ash Creek was one. She'd wanted to come here because this was where her father had started his career. Why hadn't he told her it was an entropically vagarious zone? He or her mother should've warned her. She still would've come here, but she would've felt better prepared knowing what she was walking into. But they'd said nothing. Maybe they'd wanted her to discover Ash Creek was a Soft Spot on her own, maybe they hadn't wanted to make things too easy for her.

Neither of them were the type to coddle their children, at least when it came to matters related to Maintenance. Even so, she felt a little abandoned, like she'd been thrown into the deep end of a pool and was expected to learn to swim on her own or drown. Her parents would stand by, watching and judging her, but they wouldn't help.

You're being overdramatic, Gina, she told herself. *It's first day jitters, that's all.*

"Dad told me to say hi to you, by the way."

Neal looked startled. "I'm surprised Amodar remembers me. It was a long time ago, before you were born. Did he..." Neal trailed off.

"Say anything else? No. Only that you worked together during his time in Ash Creek."

This was a partial lie. When her father had asked her to deliver his message to Neal, he'd added, *And tell him that he'd better have your back or I'll be paying him a visit.* Her father could be overprotective at times, and she hated it when he treated her like a little girl, so she wasn't going to share the second part of her father's message with Neal. Besides, she didn't want to start their morning on a sour note.

Gina had reported for work at six a.m. sharp. Neal didn't get there until six twenty. He didn't apologize for being late, which Gina found both inconsiderate and unprofessional, but she wasn't going to make an issue of it on her first day. Neal had brought a travel mug from home, and he filled it from the office coffeemaker, while a Debriefer named Marshall – who Gina had been briefly introduced to yesterday – tried to convince Neal to sit down with him and go over what had happened at Orchard Street Park yesterday.

Neal said they needed to get on the road and promised to meet with Marshall after his shift. Marshall was not happy with this, and he stomped off to voice his displeasure to Deanna. Neal didn't stick around to see how their supervisor would react to Marshall's complaint. They went outside, got in Surveillance Van Number Seven, and were on the road by six thirty-five. Deanna had assigned them to patrol the suburbs on the east side of town, which rankled Neal. Orchard Street Park was located on the west side, and he believed Deanna was trying to keep him from further investigating the incident that happened there yesterday.

Gina had a basic understanding of what had taken place in the park, thanks to interoffice gossip, but while she was dying to know the specific details of what had happened, she sensed that this wasn't a good time to press Neal to talk about it. Maybe after lunch.

They drove down tree-lined streets, where generic ranch houses sat too close to one another on small sections of land. There were no sidewalks here, and the streets were in dire need of repaving, but the houses – although modest – were nice, and the yards were well kept up. Not nearly as nice as the Maryland neighborhood where she'd grown up, of course, but all in all, a pleasant enough place to live.

"What's it like, being a Surveyor?" she asked. "I mean, *really* like."

"You're looking at it." Neal lifted his travel mug from the van's cup holder and took a long sip. "We drive around our assigned area, monitor the energy readings, and hope we don't find anything out of the ordinary. If we do, we call it in. We might get orders to investigate further, or we'll be told to remain on patrol while another pair of Surveyors are dispatched to observe the area on a longer-term basis. It's Deanna's call. She decides *where* we go, and she decides where we *don't* go."

Gina wasn't sure how to respond to this. It was obvious Neal wasn't happy, but she wasn't sure what was bothering him. Did he resent Deanna saddling him with a rookie for a new partner? She decided to continue as if he hadn't said anything about Deanna.

"So, we could drive around all day without anything happening?" Gina asked. She'd known this, of course, but only in the abstract. To be confronted with the reality of it, with the prospect of long hours riding in the van with Neal, was a different matter.

Neal gave her a cynical smile. "Welcome to the glamorous life of Surveillance."

Gina was about to reply when she saw a flash of movement on the left side of the street. A large lizard-like creature darted out in front of the van, scrabbling across the asphalt on clawed limbs that resembled human arms and legs. Its pebbly hide was covered with a combination of dark stripes and white spots, its eyes brown around big black pupils. Neal slammed the brakes and the van stopped before it hit the monstrous animal. The lizard-thing stopped as well, turned its head to regard them, and a long pink forked tongue extended from its mouth to flick the air. Gina's glasses allowed her to see an aura of dark energy shimmering around the creature, and she knew the thing was Corrupted.

They remained like that for several moments, the lizard and the humans, before finally the creature turned away and continued its dash across the street, long tail trailing behind. Gina watched as it skittered into a yard and passed between a pair of houses.

"What the hell was that?" she said.

Neal sighed. "We call it Teguzilla. The damn thing's been roaming the suburbs for months, feeding on cats and dogs and generally scaring the shit out of everyone."

She frowned. "Teguzilla, as in *tegu?* Those are South American lizards, aren't they? People keep them as pets sometimes."

Neal nodded. "But our friend isn't a normal tegu. You probably figured that because of the way it looks and the aura of Corruption around it, but..." He pointed to the monitor, and Gina saw the readings for E-energy were significantly higher than they should be, even for a creature touched by Corruption.

Neal pulled the van over, parked in front of one of the houses Teguzilla had disappeared behind, and cut the ignition.

"Bring a clipboard and pen," he said. He grabbed a handheld scanner from the glove box, took a long swig of coffee, then got out of the van.

She frowned. "What do we need a clipboard for?"

"People never question someone who's carrying a clipboard. They assume whatever you're doing, it must be official and you have permission to do it."

Before she could ask him where he kept a clipboard, he'd gotten out of the van and closed the door behind him. There was no sign of a clipboard up front, so Gina turned in her seat and looked into the back of the van. The interior of the vehicle was set up like any standard Surveillance van: tables, chairs, laptops, two-drawer filing cabinets – all bolted down to prevent them from moving – fluorescent light strips in the ceiling, no windows, fire extinguisher attached to the wall. She left her seat, hunched over, and moved into the back of the van. The desktops were empty, but she found a couple clipboards in one of the filing cabinets, both holding several blank pieces of paper, along with several pens. She grabbed one of each, then hurried to catch up to Neal.

By the time she got out of the van, Neal was already walking through one of the yards, following the direction Teguzilla had taken. She ran up and fell in stride beside him.

"We're not really sure what Teguzilla is," Neal said. "It might be a mutation of some sort, intentional or accidental, caused by exposure to entropic energy. It also might have slipped into our world from an alternate reality."

"A place where tegus rule the world," she said, attempting to make a joke.

"Could be," he said.

She laughed, but stopped when she realized he was serious.

They passed through the narrow strip of yard between the two houses. The backyard of the house on the left was enclosed by a chain link fence, but the house on the right had no barrier. What it *did* have was a large wooden shed with a black shingled roof and windows on the sides. To the left of the padlocked doors, the ground beneath the shed had been cleared away to make a small space, big enough for a rabbit to pass through but not a human-sized lizard creature. Still, Neal stopped in front of the shed and held out his hand scanner.

The device was silent as it analyzed the E-energy levels surrounding the shed, and Gina leaned closer to Neal in hope of catching a glimpse of the readings. But she found her gaze drawn back to the opening beneath the shed. It was too dark to see inside, which was normal enough, except the darkness was more than the absence of light. It was a thing in and of itself, roiling and swirling as if the small hole was a window onto a vast ocean of living shadow. She couldn't stop staring, felt suddenly dizzy, light-headed.

It reminded her of the Gyre, but instead of being repulsed by it, she wanted to step forward, walk to the hole, crouch down before it, put her hand inside and *feel* that darkness... and let it feel her in return.

A screen door slammed, startling Gina out of her trance, and she turned to see a middle-aged woman coming toward them across the house's back patio, an expression of angry suspicion on her face.

"We're Animal Control," Neal said softly, not looking up from the scanner.

Gina guessed the woman to be in her sixties. Her short hair had been dyed a blond so bright it appeared to be glowing with its own internal power source. She wore a faded red Ohio State sweatshirt a size too large for her, and jeans a size too small. She was barefoot, toenails painted a glossy cherry color.

"What are you people doing in my backyard?" she demanded.

Gina glanced at Neal, but he continued examining the scanner screen, brow furrowed.

Clipboard, do your stuff.

She put on what she hoped looked like a friendly smile.

"Hi. As my partner said, we're from Animal Control."

Gina stuck out her hand for the woman to shake. She'd been taught that this was a social interaction martial art move. It forced the other person to surrender a bit of their power before a conversation truly began. The woman eyed Gina's hand as if it carried the plague, but she overcame her reluctance and shook, although she didn't maintain physical contact for long. Not long ago, the Multitude had released a disease into the world that caused a global pandemic, and it had taken Maintenance Control some time to develop a vaccine. The treatment had worked, but many people were still uncomfortable touching or being touched, especially by strangers.

"Animal Control, huh?" Her eyes narrowed as she took in Neal, and he gave her a small wave without taking his gaze away from the scanner's screen. The woman sniffed then turned her attention back to Gina. Her eyes lowered to the clipboard in Gina's right hand, and when she saw it, she relaxed and smiled.

"What can I do for you?" she asked.

I'll be damned. Gina was so surprised by the woman's sudden change in attitude that at first, she couldn't speak.

"Tell her," Neal whispered.

Gina remembered something she'd learned during her training at the Homestead. The most effective lies are those that are closest to the truth.

"We've had reports of a large lizard roaming the neighborhood," she said. "Probably someone's escaped pet. Have you seen it?"

"You bet I have! It's about goddamn time the town sent somebody out here. I don't know how many times I've called and reported it."

"I'm sorry it's taken so long for us to respond," Gina said. "Can you tell me about the first time you saw it?"

The woman looked at her for a long moment. Gina had the sense she wanted something from her, but she didn't know what.

The woman nodded to her clipboard. "Aren't you going to write this down?"

"Oh. Yes, of course." Gina raised the clipboard, slid the pen off the metal clip, and touched its point to the paper. "Ready."

"My name is Margie Ferguson. My address is 361 Brandywine Drive. My phone number is..."

Gina started to write down the information, but then Neal said, "We should step back from the shed. *Way* back."

"Why? What's–"

A cloud of darkness burst forth from beneath the shed and filled the air, swirling and seething like a mass of silent black hornets. Gina's first thought was the Gyre had finally come for her, and she froze, body rigid, nerves aflame, instincts screaming at her to run-run-*RUN!*

Her worst nightmare was coming true – and on the first day of her goddamned job! And it was that thought that broke her paralysis. No fucking lizard was going to take her out only a few hours after she'd officially began her career with Maintenance. She wouldn't let her family down like that. She grabbed Margie's arm with her free hand and pulled the woman away from the shed. Margie stared at the ebon cloud, mouth gaping.

"What the fuck *is* that?" she asked, sounding on the edge of hysteria.

"Um... gas leak?" Gina said.

Neal drew back from the shed, scanner still in hand, continuing to take readings, although he kept his gaze fixed on the cloud.

"That came from Teguzilla," he said. "The damn thing isn't just a big ugly lizard. It's a Void Breather, too."

Those two words hit Gina like a punch to the gut. Void Breathers weren't real, at least not on this plane of reality. How–

Her thoughts broke off as the dark cloud's swirling began to slow. It drifted toward the ground in front of the shed, settled onto the grass, and began to dissipate. When it was gone, so too was a large chunk of soil that the cloud had touched. If the dark mass had come into contact with one of them...

Teguzilla squeezed out from beneath the shed, humanoid hands clawing dirt, mouth open in a hiss. Once out, it rose onto its hind legs and let out a louder, more aggressive hiss.

It's defending its lair, Gina thought.

Neal was still closer to the shed than Gina or Margie, and Teguzilla started toward him. Gina didn't know much about Void Breathers – Maintenance had little information on them – but she knew they expelled clouds of E-energy that could unmake anything they touched. Hell, she'd *seen* it. If Teguzilla managed to hit Neal with a second cloud, he'd be unmade down to the subatomic level within seconds.

She didn't think. She still held the clipboard in her right hand, although she'd dropped the pen somewhere along the way, and she flung it like a Frisbee toward Teguzilla as hard as she could. The clipboard spun toward the creature, paper flapping in the air, and struck the thing hard on the snout with a solid *thunk*. The clipboard bounced off and landed in the grass, and for a moment all four of them – the three humans and the monster – stood there, as if unsure what to do next. Then Teguzilla's eyes became watery, as if it was crying. It let out a loud bawling sound, spun about, fell onto all fours, and ran toward the line of trees at the back of Margie's property. The large lizard plunged through the brush surrounding the base of the trees and was gone.

Gina, Neal, and Margie stared at the spot where Teguzilla had disappeared, as if they expected it to come roaring back toward them any second. But after several moments passed without a reappearance from the creature, Neal turned to Gina.

"That was fast thinking. Good job." His eyes narrowed, and she had the sense that he was reappraising her.

Gina gave him a shaky smile. "Thanks, but I was aiming for his eyes."

"It worked, and that's all that matters." Neal checked his scanner. "No readings. As fast as that damned thing is, it's probably several streets away by now."

Gina's entire system was jazzed with adrenaline, and she felt like she could run a hundred-yard dash.

"Are we going to go after it?" she asked. She was surprised by how eager she sounded. She felt like running after Teguzilla, and she might have, too, if it hadn't been her first day on the job.

"After what just happened, I'm sure the office is going to make catching Teguzilla a priority."

Neal tapped the side of his glasses, and Gina got the message. The Analysts had watched and recorded their encounter with the lizard, and now that Teguzilla had revealed itself to be a Void Breather, Deanna would dispatch an Intervention Team to find and deal with the creature. She felt disappointed. Sure, it was standard protocol, but she and Neal were here *now*. Yes, they were Surveyors, but by the time an Intervention Team got here, who knows how far away Teguzilla would be and how many people it could potentially harm? But right now, her job was to observe and report, that's all, and until she was promoted to the rank of Interventionist – which she hoped would be sooner rather than later – she would just have to live with it. She didn't have to like it, though.

Margie had continued staring at the spot in the brush where Teguzilla had vanished. Now she turned to Gina and Neal.

"What in the ever-loving hell was *that?*" she demanded.

"In our trade, that's what's known as an exotic animal," Neal said.

Margie looked at Gina.

"*Very* exotic," Gina added.

Rachel stood outside her classroom door as students made their way to their advisories. Teachers were expected to be a "presence" in the halls before and after classes in order to help maintain discipline. They were also encouraged to smile and be friendly.

Think of yourselves as ambassadors for education, Principal Ruben Dixon had told the faculty during a meeting before the beginning of school. Rachel couldn't stand the smarmy fuck, so that night she'd sent him an erotic dream that halfway through turned into a nightmare, ending with his castration. She smiled at the memory. It was little pleasures like that which she enjoyed most about being one of the Multitude. Or at least a candidate.

She did *not* enjoy the cover she'd chosen for her current project, although with her abilities, creating the false credentials and references needed to obtain a teaching position had been simple. Brother Nothing had recruited her as a child, and from that point on all of her learning had been focused on becoming a servant of the Gyre. What the hell did she know about teaching children, especially middle school kids? All they cared about was watching YouTube videos, sharing stupid memes, playing videogames, taking selfies, and experiencing the first stirrings of sexuality. They were loud and obnoxious, and worst of all, *boring*.

She sometimes fantasized about implanting an irresistible compulsion in each one the school's students to gather in the gym and kill each other in the most grotesque ways as she watched. But while she'd enjoy that immensely, it wouldn't do much to raise her status among the Multitude. All living creatures died eventually, and killing off a few hundred children – as satisfying as it might be – wouldn't do much to hasten the Omniverse's inevitable entropic collapse. Besides, the Multitude would find such an action amateurish, lacking in both creativity and vision. Building an Atrocity Engine was definitely the way to go, and that meant she would have to put up with pretending to teach middle-school brats biology, at least for a while longer.

"Hi, Ms. Blackburn!"

A tall, thin girl with an unruly mass of blond curls approached Rachel's classroom. Molly Strickland grinned and waved as she drew near, and Rachel gave the child a smile and raised her hand in greeting. Molly was known for wearing jeans and tied-dyed T-shirts, day in and day out, even in the winter, and today was no exception.

Rachel liked tie-dye, the more colorful, the better. It reminded her of the multicolored ring of light swirling around the Gyre as it slowly devoured reality. Molly wore a backpack as well, a white one which she'd decorated herself with various colors of ink, drawing cartoon characters – some from TV, some original – and writing the names of music and movie stars she liked. Stars and hearts were liberally scattered across the backpack's surface, and they all had little smiley faces on them.

"Good morning, Molly," Rachel said. "Ready for another glamorous day of middle school?"

Molly rolled her eyes. "It's not *that* bad, Ms. Blackburn."

"Just joking," Rachel replied. *Not,* she added mentally.

Molly practically skipped past Rachel to enter the classroom. The girl was perpetually in high spirits, one of those annoying people who never seemed to be sad or depressed – which was one of the main reasons Rachel had chosen her as the prime candidate for her project. Corrupting such a child, snuffing out her light and replacing it with darkness, would be delicious.

Rachel followed Molly into the classroom. Rachel's teacher's desk was in front, in the corner near the row of windows that looked out upon the cemetery, or – as it was officially called – Oak Grove Cemetery. Rachel had no idea who had decided it was a good idea to build a school next to a graveyard, but she loved the macabre irony of it. A school was a place dedicated to helping children get a good start in life, but the cemetery was a stark reminder that it didn't matter where people started; they all ended up in the same place, as food for the Gyre.

When her students were busy taking a test or working on an in-class activity, she liked to gaze out the window at the brick wall surrounding the cemetery, the rows of grave markers– some more than a century old – and the large leafy oak trees that she supposed accounted for the name. She liked to imagine the roots of those trees had wormed their way through the soil, penetrated burial vaults and coffins, tendrils growing into the bodies within, feeding on their organic substance. Human flesh and bone as fertilizer. She found the idea almost unbearably erotic, and she'd touch herself, her hand hidden by her desk. A shudder came over her just thinking about it now.

Her classroom looked little different than most of the others at McKenzie Middle School – desks for students, white boards with dry erase markers, a computer projector and screen, posters on the walls displaying biology topics like the life cycle of frogs or the eight levels of taxonomy: domain, kingdom, phylum, class, order, family, genus, and species. Interspersed with these were posters espousing banal motivational slogans like, *You Were Born with the Ability to Change Someone's Life, Don't Ever Waste It,* and *There is No Elevator to Success. You Have to Take the Stairs.*

Rachel had fourteen students in her advisory, and a quick headcount told her that most of them were here. She glanced at the clock on the wall above the door. The stragglers had less than two minutes to get here before the first bell rang, otherwise they'd be counted tardy – assuming they showed up at all. One child who would definitely *not* be present in advisory today was Cody Pittman. Officially, the boy had disappeared, and that's how the media was reporting it, although they hinted with barely restrained ghoulishness that foul play may have occurred. Principal Dixon had sent an early morning email to faculty and staff telling them that they were to avoid speaking about Cody unless one of their students brought up the subject, in which case they were to say something along the lines of, *We don't know where he is, but we hope he's safe and that he comes home soon.* Rachel had laughed when she read the email then promptly deleted it.

She went to her desk and recorded the names of those who were in attendance in her gradebook to get a head start on things, then she stood and regarded the little shits. A few were frantically doing schoolwork that they should've completed at home last night, but most were talking, animatedly and loudly. She had no idea how they had so much goddamned energy, especially so early in the morning. She found them especially irritating today, probably because she was still on edge after Brother Nothing's unexpected visit last night, so she implanted a suggestion into their minds. All of them would "accidentally" make a mistake this day, one they would find hugely embarrassing and recall with shame throughout the rest of their lives. All except Molly. Rachel had other plans for her.

"Molly? Would you mind coming here for a moment?"

Molly had removed her backpack when she'd sat down and was now chatting with Cathy Symanksi and Marie Goebel. All three were "good" girls – in other words, well-behaved rule-followers – and they kept their voices low when conversing in the classroom. Rachel figured this was so no one would overhear what they were talking (and giggling) about rather than from any real concern over being polite, but she nevertheless appreciated their quiet tones.

Molly looked at Rachel when she called her name, but there was no flash of concern in the girl's eyes. Students like Molly didn't get in trouble, and thus didn't fear being asked to speak with a teacher one on one. Smiling, Molly rose from her desk and came toward Rachel with that bouncy walk of hers that was almost a skip.

"Yes, Ms. Blackburn?"

Molly's expression was relaxed and untroubled. This was a child who'd never known hardship or struggle, whose only experience of pain was a skinned knee or elbow, whose only real fear was losing her phone. Rachel had been a normal girl once, not much different from Molly, and she felt a twinge of guilt over what she was about to do to the child. But she squashed the emotion as soon as she felt it. There was no place for empathy and kindness in the Omniverse. All that mattered was hunger and the sating of that hunger.

"I want to bring a batch of homemade treats for Friday's advisory" Rachel said. "I have a new recipe I want to try out, but I'm not sure if it's any good. I made a few samples. Would you mind trying one for me and giving me your honest opinion about how it tastes?"

Molly's eyes lit up. School might only have been in session for two weeks, but in that time, Rachel had learned that Molly had a sweet tooth, even more so than Cody. Molly always got an extra dessert with lunch, and when Rachel had brought in donuts for her advisory at the end of the first week, Rachel had eaten three, making almost orgasmic sounds of pleasure the entire time. If the girl didn't watch out, she'd be twenty pounds overweight and have a mouthful of fillings by the time she graduated high school. But then, after today, she wouldn't have to worry about graduating, would she?

"Sure!" Molly bounced up and down on her toes, excited.

Rachel's smile was genuine. "Great!"

She went to her desk and removed a plastic container from the top drawer. It was the same container that she'd had with her at the park yesterday, but its contents were, she hoped, new and improved. She'd worked the better part of the night on them.

She popped off the lid, set it aside, and held out the container so Molly could see what lay within: A trio of globs, each roughly the size of a large marshmallow. They were as black as the void itself, their ebon surfaces threaded with yellow-white veins of pus. The Defilements bulged and writhed obscenely on the plastic, looking more like gangrenous slugs than any kind of dessert. Molly didn't see their true appearance, though. To her eyes they looked like little square cakes covered in pink and white frosting with red sprinkles on top.

"Take whichever one looks the–"

Before Rachel could finish, Molly grabbed hold of the biggest one, and tossed the entire thing into her mouth.

"–best to you," Rachel finished.

Molly chewed thoughtfully, not perceiving the agonized screams of the thing her teeth tore apart, but the sound was like sweet dark music to Rachel's ears. Molly had to swallow three times to get the mess down her throat, then she looked at Rachel and opened her mouth to presumably render an opinion on the "treat," but no words came forth. Her eyes glazed over, and a sound like sizzling meat issued from deep inside her as the Defilement began its work. Molly remained like that for the better part of a minute, and then her eyes cleared and her mouth snapped shut. The bell rang, but Rachel barely noticed. Her attention was entirely focused on Molly.

"How does it feel?" Rachel asked.

"Bad," Molly said, her voice hollow. "*Real* bad."

Rachel nodded, pleased. "And do you feel molecularly stable?"

Molly tilted her head in a silent question.

"Does it feel like your physical structure is degrading?" Still no answer. Rachel sighed. "Do you feel like your body is going to collapse into a big puddle of goo?"

Molly considered, then said, "No."

"Excellent." In order for Rachel's plan to work, she needed Molly to remain functional for at least a couple days. The Corruption that now seethed within the child would eventually destroy her body, but if Rachel had gotten the formulation right – and initial results seemed to indicate she had – the process of dissolution would be slow for the girl. Time for the next step. "There are two things I want you to do for me, Molly. Are you listening?"

Molly's eyes were dead, her features slack, but she nodded.

"Good."

Rachel put the lid back on the plastic container and handed it to Molly.

"I want you to take this and keep it with you until you're alone with your parents. Then I want you to open it and offer them each a treat. Will you do this?"

Another nod.

"The second thing I want you to do is easy," Rachel said. "You have something inside you now, something beautiful and deadly. I want you to spread it to everyone and everything you come in contact with. A touch is all it will take. Will you do this, too?"

A third nod.

"When your parents have eaten their treats, I'll be in touch with further instructions. Now go about your day as if everything is normal." She paused, then added, "At least as normal as you can manage."

"Okay," Molly said in a toneless voice. Holding the plastic container tight in both hands, she turned and walked back to her seat. She sat, picked up her backpack, slid the container inside, zipped it closed, and lowered the backpack to the floor once more. She then stared straight ahead.

"Is something wrong?" Cathy Symanski whispered.

"What did Ms. Blackburn say to you?" Mari Goebel asked.

Molly didn't respond at first, but then she turned to the girls and smiled.

"I'm fine."

And then she reached out with her two forefingers and touched the backs of their hands. They stiffened, faces immobile, eyes blank like a doll's. Then the three of them faced front and silently stared at the whiteboard.

Rachel's smile was cold enough to freeze flame.

It had begun.

Five

Molly was one of those rare students who actually enjoyed her classes. After advisory, she had Spanish, then American History, then English, then lunch. Neither Cathy nor Mari shared those morning classes with her – which stunk – but at least they all had the same lunch period. They would go through the serving line together, get their food, find a table just for the three of them, and happily chat while they ate.

That was on a normal day.

This day, Molly had sleepwalked through her morning classes, wide awake but mentally absent. She'd appeared to pay attention to her teachers – sitting up straight, eyes open, gaze directed forward – but their words were meaningless noise to her. Her attention was focused on the dark forces surging inside her, roiling like the waves of some vast shadow-shrouded ocean. And within the crash of those waves, she heard a single word repeated over and over. *Spread, spread, spreeeeeaaaaaad...*

In Spanish class, she obeyed the voice by breathing on Tony Patrick, who sat next to her every day and always tried to cheat off her during quizzes. She felt Corruption flow out of her, could almost see it drift across the space between them, see Tony inhale it. He made a choking sound deep in his throat, his eyes went wide, and his hand shot into the air. Senora Morales – who'd been lecturing about adjectives – stopped and looked at Tony, eyes narrowed, brow creased into a frown.

"Si?"

"May I be excused to go to the bathroom?" His face was pale, his voice tremulous.

Senora sighed. "En español, por favor."

Students were required to speak Spanish at all times in Senora's class.

Beads of sweat gathered on Tony's brow.

"Please, it's an emergency!"

Senora just looked at him. She was a good teacher, and her students liked her, but she was strict as hell.

Tony, trembling now and drenched in sweat, began repeating his request in halting Spanish.

"Puedo... uh... usar el... baño."

Halfway through *baño* his neck muscles tensed, his mouth opened wide, and a gout of blood jetted forth – dark blood, with small worm-like things writhing in it. Senora and the other students in the class screamed, and several vomited in sympathetic reflex. Tony, blood dripping down his chin, sat there crying, crimson splattered on his desk and running to the floor in thick rivulets. Somewhere deep inside herself, Molly was crying, too, but outwardly she smiled.

In History class, while Tony lay on a cot in the school nurse's office, still crying and dry heaving, Molly brushed the tips of her fingers against the back of Mr. Saunders' right hand as she entered his classroom. Fifteen minutes later, Mr. Saunders – who had come down with the most intense migraine he'd ever had in his life – excused himself and left the classroom, eyes squeezed almost all the way shut to block out the light. His classroom was on the second floor, and as he descended the stairs, intending to go the office and ask Principal Dixon to cover his class so he could go home for the rest of the day and lie in a dark room, a wave of dizziness overcame him. He lost his balance, along with his grip on the stairs' railing. His left foot slipped out from under him, and he tumbled the rest of the way down the stairs, hitting the first-floor landing with the harsh crack of breaking bone.

Later at the hospital, he'd learn that he'd suffered almost a dozen different breaks of varying severity in different locations. A day after that – following a number of tests – he'd be informed by a doctor that he had advanced osteoporosis. Saunders was only twenty-seven years old.

Molly didn't do anything strange for the majority of English class. They watched the first part of a 2013 movie version of *Romeo and Juliet* in preparation for reading the play next week. English wasn't Molly's favorite subject, but the film's leads were young and attractive, and they held her attention. For a while, it was almost like she was back to her normal self. But when Romeo killed Tybalt, the Corruption inside her – as if aroused by the violence in the movie – welled to the surface once more.

Obeying the Corruption's urging, she raised an index finger to her mouth and bit off part of the nail. She took the sliver between her thumb and forefinger, and then flicked it into the air as hard as she could. It sprouted wings, multiple legs, and an insectoid head until the thing resembled a small honeybee, save that it was made entirely of keratin. It buzzed through the air, dipping and diving, finally settling on the back of Daria Wingfield's neck.

Daria was a small, quiet girl who struggled with acne, and while her dermatologist had – after some considerable effort – managed to get her skin mostly clear, some of the kids in school still made fun of her, called her Pizza Face and Pimple Farm. She pretended not to hear when they said these things, but she always did, and they always hurt.

When the fingernail-bee lighted on her skin, she reflexively reached back to brush it off. But before she could, it sliced a small opening with one of its sharp little legs and quickly burrowed inside. Daria let out an *eep*, the sound as much one of surprise as pain, and frantically rubbed the back of her neck, but all she managed to do was smear around the blood oozing from her wound. The skin on her face tightened and pinpoints of fiery pain blossomed as zits erupted across her flesh, so many that they merged together, cheeks, chin, forehead, and nose becoming a single swollen red mass. Dots of white emerged in the red, dozens upon dozens of them, growing rapidly larger.

Molly sat two rows away from Daria, but Ms. Tucker had left the classroom lights on while the movie played, and Molly – along with everyone else in the room – had an excellent view of Daria. The sore, swollen flesh stretched, stretched... and then exploded. It wasn't pus that was ejected from Daria's ruined face, but rather a score of tiny fingernail bees.

The insects buzzed around the room while the students and Ms. Tucker screamed and flailed their hands in the air, attempting to keep them away. Daria sat in her chair, tears mixing with the blood running from dozens of small wounds on her face, and Molly – despite feeling a certain amount of disquiet – smiled.

Molly met Mari and Cathy in the hall outside the cafeteria, and the three friends walked inside silently, their motions slow and deliberate, as if they needed to concentrate to make their bodies do as they were told. They kept their gazes focused straight ahead, didn't look around to see what other kids were wearing, who they were talking to, who they *weren't* talking to. Despite her outward appearance. Molly felt good, better than she had in her entire life, actually. But unlike Cody Pittman, Molly was generally more restrained in her day-to-day behavior, plus Rachel's new Defilement formulation had been crafted to last longer than the one she'd given Cody. Cody had always been something of a wild child, and his Defilement had resulted in a kind of hyperactive mania. Molly's Defilement was designed to last.

The atmosphere in the cafeteria was a strange mix of energized and subdued. Many of the kids were talking animatedly about the weird events that had happened that morning, not only those incidents sparked by Molly but those created by Cathy and Mari as well. But other kids, especially those who'd witnessed the incidents, were quiet and withdrawn, and more than a few of them were crying.

Normally, teachers didn't eat lunch in the student cafeteria, preferring instead to go to the faculty lounge where they could get a break from their students. But today they were present in the cafeteria, some standing against the walls and monitoring the kids talking and eating, while others walked up and down the aisles between the tables, pausing now and then to check in with one of their students and see how they were doing.

A handful of teachers sat at tables with students, talking with them, trying to reassure them that everything was okay. Not that they believed it themselves. The adults kept exchanging worried glances, and it was clear that they were just as afraid as their students, if not more so. Principal Dixon had joined the teachers – indeed, it had been his idea that they be present in the cafeteria right now – and he circulated through the room, speaking with both students and teachers. He tried to radiate an aura of calm, but he couldn't hide how nervous he was.

Ms. Blackburn stood against the wall not far from where Molly, Mari, and Cathy sat. She was smiling, and when Molly looked over at her, she gave the girl a thumbs up. After a moment's hesitation, Molly smiled and returned the gesture. They still had half a day before it was time to go home, and she wondered what other dark mischief would occur before the final bell rang. She couldn't wait to find out.

After lunch, Molly and her friends went outside for recess. While other kids played on swings, shot baskets, chased each other in games of tag, or simply stood around laughing and gossiping, Molly, Mari, and Cathy remained motionless and silent.

They stood shoulder to shoulder – Molly in the middle – facing the cemetery, features expressionless, eyes wide and staring. The day was sunny, warm, and windy, and the limbs of the trees bordering the cemetery swayed, leaves rustling, the sound like running water. The three girls heard more than this, though. Thanks to their transformation, they could hear a high-pitched scream that echoed throughout all of space and time.

It was wondrous.

Principal Ruben Dixon stood outside the school, ostensibly to "be a presence," as he so often encouraged his teachers to be, but right now he wished someone would put a gun to his head and blow his fucking brains out. He suffered from seasonal allergies – although in his case *seasonal* meant every goddamn day of his life – and this autumn was already one of the worst he'd ever endured. He was on so many allergy meds that he could barely keep his eyes open, and his head felt like a gigantic snot-filled balloon wrapped in several feet of wet cotton.

His eyes watered so much it was like he was constantly crying, and he'd been asked some variation of *Are you okay?* at least a dozen times today so far. He had a packet of tissues in his pants pocket, and he gripped a sodden one in his left hand, and pressed it to his nose periodically in vain attempts to stop the flow of mucus. He stood near the main entrance so that if it got to the point where it was too hard to breathe, he could duck inside and suck in some sweet, sweet processed air.

Ruben was in his early forties, prematurely bald, with a mustache that looked a little too much like a walrus'. He had a pot belly, although his arms and legs were thin, just like all the men on his dad's side of the family. *Thanks a fucking lot, genetics,* he thought.

He wore a navy-blue suit, a white dress shirt, and a tie covered with small images of Bugs Bunny. He always wore silly ties to work, thought they humanized him, emphasized the *pal* in principal. He had no idea that both kids and teachers made fun of him behind his back because of this sartorial choice. He was single, by preference, he told himself. He was waiting for the right person to come along, that's all. Lately, he'd begun toying with the notion that he might be asexual, but his mother and father periodically badgered him to get married and provide them with grandchildren, so he hadn't explored this idea very far.

It wasn't just his allergies that were bothering him today, though. The school day so far had been one disaster after another – and they'd all been so *odd*. He wasn't by nature a superstitious man. Yes, he bought three lottery tickets every week (three was his lucky number), and he avoided opening an umbrella in the house because his mother had always told him doing so would bring misfortune. But he didn't regard these behaviors as superstitions so much as personal quirks. Harmless idiosyncrasies. But if he *had* been superstitious, he might've thought the school had been jinxed somehow.

What the hell else can go wrong today? he asked himself, and immediately wished he hadn't. No reason to tempt fate into sending more bad luck his way. Not that he was superstitious.

The bell rang to indicate the end of recess, and students began filing toward the main entrance, most of them sullenly dragging their feet. Normally, Reuban might've attempted some banter with the students to cheer them up, but he felt as blah about getting on with the rest of the school day as they did. When the last student walked past him, he swept his gaze around the play area, checking to make sure that everyone had gone inside and there were no stragglers. He didn't expect to see any – he almost never did – so he was surprised when he saw three girls standing shoulder to shoulder, backs to the school, facing the cemetery.

"Time to go inside, girls!" he called out. His throat was sore from all the drainage, and his voice was strained.

The girls didn't so much as glance in his direction.

He pursed his lips in irritation. He wasn't one for throwing his authority around, but he *was* the goddamn principal, and when he spoke to a child, he expected them to respond.

"Girls!" he called out, louder this time.

Still no reaction.

This was beginning to really piss him off. He dabbed the tissue to his nose then started walking toward the girls. He prided himself on knowing the names of every student in his school, but he didn't recognize any of them from behind, although he did have the sense that whoever they were, they weren't children who normally got in trouble.

As he drew near the girls, a cold prickling sensation spread across the back of his neck, and his stomach muscles tightened. Primitive senses that had warned his species of danger long before humans had stood upright began screaming at him, urging him to forget these children, to turn around and go inside the school where the air was fit to breathe. He almost did it too, but as principal he couldn't allow these children to remain outside as classes resumed. Not only would it be a dereliction of duty, there were liability issues to consider – along with the girls' safety, of course.

So, he ignored the warning of his subconscious and when he reached the girls, he stepped in front of them and crossed his arms over his chest and looked down at them with a stern expression. Now that he could see their faces, he recognized them: Molly Strickland, Cathy

Symanski, and Mari Goebel – girls who'd never caused the slightest bit of trouble before.

"Didn't you ladies hear me?" he asked.

The girls' features were slack, expressionless, and they stared straight forward, as if they could see through him.

"We're listening," Cathy said.

"To the song," Mari added.

"The Song of Ending," Molly finished.

Ruben didn't know what they were talking about, but that phrase – *The Song of Ending* – sent a chill rippling down his back.

"It's time to return to class," he said. His voice sounded weak, so in a stronger tone he added, "*Now.*"

The girls still didn't look at him, but Cathy and Mari turned and began walking toward the school. Molly, however, reached out to take his hand before she started to walk, and – surprised and unsure what to do – Ruben allowed her to lead him. This sort of physical contact wasn't appropriate, but he also didn't want to pull his hand away and reject the child. She'd been behaving strangely before he'd reached her and her friends. What if something was wrong and this small gesture was some sort of cry for attention, a signal from Molly that she needed help?

"Is everything all right?" he asked.

"Everything is exactly as it should be," she said. "Would you like to listen to the Song? I can make it so you can hear it."

"I... I would like to learn more about this song, yes."

He assumed she would start explaining it to him, whatever it was, but instead her hand tightened on his, and a soul-deep cold rushed up his arm and infused his entire body. And then, just as Molly had promised, he could hear it. The Song of Ending. It was centered on the cemetery because that was the strongest concentration of entropic energy in the vicinity, but the Song was everywhere. Except it wasn't really a song, was it? It was the death scream of existence itself, a sound which had started with the birth of the Omniverse and which would continue without pause until the moment of its death. He had never heard anything so beautiful.

"You understand now," Molly said. It wasn't a question.

"Yes."

"You know what to do."

"Yes," he repeated.

They continued holding hands until they reached the school's main entrance. When they went inside, Molly released her grip on Ruben's hand, and she continued walking without a backward glance at him. The halls were busy with students rushing to class to beat the last bell, and while ordinarily he would've waded into the chaos and urged the kids to slow down, instead he walked into the central office. There were two people behind the front counter – Anna Wolfe, his administrative assistant, and Darrel Wilson, one of the guidance counselors. They looked up as he came in, and Darrel grimaced.

"Man, Ruben, your eyes are so red and watery they make mine itch just looking at them."

Anna smiled. "Fall allergies. I'm surprised he hasn't turned into a giant ball of mucus by now."

The staff members were teasing him, and normally he might've responded with some good-natured banter. But not today. He stopped at the counter and turned to look at them.

"Mucus is no laughing matter," he said. "It should be respected."

Anna and Darrel looked at each other, as if to ask, *Did we really hear that?*

"Let me show you." Ruben leaned forward, drew in a deep breath through his mouth, and forced it out his nose. Green tendrils of mucus shot forth from his nostrils and whipped through the air toward Darrel and Anna. Before they could react, the tendrils plunged into their own noses, then penetrated their mouths, ears, and eyes. Blood gushed from their violated orifices, and their bodies began spasming. They tried to cry out, but their throats were clogged by Ruben's snot tentacles and all they could manage were muffled sounds of distress.

It didn't take long for the tendrils to worm their way into Darrel and Anna's brains, and a couple seconds after that happened, their bodies went limp and fell to the floor. The mucus tendrils withdrew and slid back into Ruben's head, but not all the way. The blood-slick tips remained outside of his nose, undulating lazily in the air. He heard Molly's voice once more. *You know what to do.*

He surely did.

He exited the office and walked down the hallway, snot tentacles quivering, eager to find new victims to play with.

Deanna was sitting at her desk reviewing recent incident reports on her laptop when Kenny Miles burst into her office. She looked away from the computer screen, prepared to chastise him for not knocking, but when she saw the upset expression on his face, she decided to let the lapse in office protocol slide.

"What's wrong?" she asked.

Kenny – in his fifties, short, long gray hair pulled back in a pony tail – worked in Communications. That department was tasked with monitoring all incoming and outgoing communications in Ash Creek – phone, text, email, and radio – for any hint of the sort of trouble Maintenance specialized in dealing with.

Kenny took a second to catch his breath. *He must've run all the way from his work station to her office,* Deanna thought. Another indication that whatever was going on, it was serious.

"We've intercepted some 911 calls," Kenny said. "Something's happening at the middle school," he said. "Something *bad*."

Deanna didn't ask for more details, not yet. She grabbed her phone and made a quick call. Whatever was going on, she wanted an Intervention Team on scene stat.

Neal and Gina drove around for the rest of the morning and into the early afternoon, hoping the van's scanner would pick up some sign of Teguzilla, but it detected nothing. The initial excitement of their encounter with the creature had worn off for Gina, and Neal could tell that she was bored and frustrated – not to mention hungry – so at 1:00, he decided to break for lunch.

He headed toward the Southland Mall, parked near the entrance to the food court, and they went inside. The Mall had been constructed in the 1970's, and it smelled faintly of must and mildew. The floor tiles were yellowed, and the ceiling panels were splotched with water stains. Despite its age – or maybe because of it – Neal preferred the mall to the newer and far more upscale shopping center called the Village, located on the northside of town. Maybe he liked the mall because, as an employee of Maintenance, he spent most of his time dealing with the effects of Entropy, and an old, rundown place like this was comfortable for him.

This place might be aged, but it kept trucking on, which was the very definition of Maintenance's motto: *Flavor to the Feast.*

He thought Gina might comment on the mall's appearance, but she said nothing. She looked around once as they entered, features scrunched in distaste, but that was her only reaction. The mall was never crowded, even on the weekends, and on school days it was practically deserted. Neal led Gina to the food court, which hosted only five fast-food restaurants: Jeannie's Burger Bar, Chicken Kitchen, A Taste of Italy, Ice Cream Dreams, and Blazin' Tacos.

"Do you have a preference?" he asked Gina.

She eyed their choices dubiously. "Not to get food poisoning."

"No promises," Neal said.

Gina opted for a Caesar salad from A Taste of Italy, and Neal got the especial del dia from Blazin' Tacos: two grilled chicken tacos and a spicy jack cheese quesadilla. They chose a table away from the few other diners present – a couple in their seventies and a harried mother with rambunctious twin girls – where they wouldn't be overhead. The shoulder wound Neal had sustained while fighting the Scarecrow yesterday ached, so he took one of the pain pills the Med Tech had given him, and washed it down with soda.

They talked as they continued to eat.

"It wasn't just Teguzilla underneath Margie's shed," Gina said. "Was it?"

"There was also a massive concentration of E-energy," Neal confirmed. "It was like nothing I've ever run into before. The scanner readings were unclear, but I could tell that whatever it was, it was powerful and dangerous as hell."

"Do you think Teguzilla created that dark energy?" Gina asked. "The creature *is* a Void Breather. Maybe that's its den."

"I suppose it's possible, although I've never heard of Void Breathers being able to do anything like that. We'll have to wait to find out anything until after Deanna sends an Intervention Team to examine the area beneath the shed more thoroughly."

They ate in silence for several moments, and then Gina said, "It's rather galling, isn't it? To discover something and not be able to be part of the follow-up investigation."

Neal kept his tone even as he replied. "Yes, it is. But that's the job." He took a bite of taco, chewed, swallowed. "I was impressed by the way you handled yourself with Teguzilla. You reminded me of..." He trailed off and took a sip of his diet soda.

Gina frowned. "Who? My father?"

"Yeah," Neal said. "He was always good at thinking on his feet." He hoped she would leave it at that. The less they talked about Amador Sandoval, the better, but Gina was naturally curious.

"How well did you know him?"

Neal knew he wasn't going to be able to escape this, and why should he try? Might as well get it over with. But he didn't have to tell her everything.

"Your dad was my partner when I was a rookie."

She smiled uncertainly, as if she thought he might be making a joke. "Seriously?"

"Yep. Only for about six months, before he was promoted and transferred. He'd been working in Ash Creek for only a year at that point, but he'd already distinguished himself, enough so that he was given the responsibility of being my mentor, even though he was only a couple years older than me."

He hoped she would leave it at that, but he knew she wouldn't.

"Did he do a good job?" she asked. "As your mentor, I mean."

Neal carefully considered how to answer this.

"I learned a lot from him," he said. This was true, although it hardly told the full story.

"It must be weird to be working with me then," Gina said.

Neal was glad she'd turned the topic around to herself.

"A little, but there's a certain symmetry to it that I like."

He smiled, but as he did, he wondered just how far this particular apple had fallen from the tree. Gina was Amador Sandoval's daughter. The question was just how much like her father was she – and how much could he trust her?

Before either of them could speak again, Eleanor's voice came from the small microphone embedded in the right arm of his glasses.

"How's the first day with your new partner going? Have you won her over with the patented Hudson charm yet?"

Neal sighed, then touched the side of his glasses to let Gina know that he'd gotten a personal call. She nodded her understanding.

"Everything's going fine so far. What's up?"

Despite Eleanor's opening banter, Neal knew this had to be a work-related call. She never used a Maintenance comm channel for personal reasons, not even when they'd been dating.

"I've been reviewing the video footage of yesterday's incident in the park – at least what little was recorded before you 'accidentally' lost your glasses. The woman who was there, the one who may or may not belong to the Multitude?"

"Yes?"

"Her features are blurred, and no matter what I do, I can't clean up the image."

Neal frowned. "The footage wasn't like that yesterday, was it?"

"No. I saw her face clearly during the live feed, and I saw it clearly again when I checked the video last night. But today, she's blurry. Here's the weird thing, or maybe I should say weirder thing: I can't remember what she looks like."

"That *is* weird."

"Can you? Remember her face, I mean."

"Of course, I..." He tried to picture the woman. He could see how she was dressed, could see the way she moved as she offered the boy something from the plastic container she held. But he could not see her face, and the harder he tried, the more indistinct her features became, until she had no face at all, just an empty space where it should've been.

"No," he said. "I can't."

"This definitely argues for her being one of the Multitude. She must've

recognized you as Maintenance and used her abilities to alter the video evidence of her identity along with any memory of it – both yours and mine. It's going to make finding her a hell of a lot..."

Eleanor trailed off, and after several seconds of silence ticked by, Neal wondered if their connection had been broken.

"Eleanor? You still there?"

"Sorry. Deanna just cut in. I've got to go."

Neal spoke quickly, before she could disconnect. "What's happening?"

"There's some kind of incident taking place at the middle school. Deanna's dispatched an Intervention Team and she wants me to monitor their live feed."

"What's going on? Who'd she send?"

No answer. Eleanor had already switched channels and was now virtually traveling with the Interventionists – Royce and Sabrina, probably. Who else would Deanna send?

"Is something wrong?" Gina asked.

"Yeah, over at McKenzie Middle School. That's where the boy who died in the park likely went to."

"Do you think that whatever Corrupted him might be spreading?"

"I don't know, but I intend to find out." He smiled grimly. "Your first day on the job is about to get a hell of a lot more interesting."

He jumped up from the table without bothering to clear the remains of his meal and sprinted for the exit. After a moment's hesitation, Gina followed.

I'm not going to let it happen again, Neal thought as he ran toward the mall entrance, Gina close behind. *Not this time.*

Six

Maintenance Van Number Three roared into the middle school's parking lot, Royce behind the wheel, Sabrina riding shotgun. Royce always got excited when responding to a report of Corruption, so much so that he had a tendency to drive more recklessly than Sabrina was comfortable with. Normally she'd chastise him for his excessive speed and remind him to slow down, but not today.

Corruption tended to fester in small, out-of-the-way places. Surveyors usually detected it early, and then Interventionists dealt with it before it spread and caused any significant damage. But this was the second incident of Corruption occurring in public within the last twenty-four hours, and this one wasn't confined to a small playground with only a handful of people present. It was taking place inside a school filled with hundreds of students, teachers, and staff. If anything, Sabrina thought that Royce wasn't driving fast enough this time.

A pair of police vehicles was parked in front of the school's main entrance, and Royce brought the van to a screeching halt behind them. He put the van in park, turned off the engine, and he and Sabrina jumped out – Nullifiers in hand – and ran toward the front door.

Sabrina glanced at the police cars as they passed and saw they were empty.

She heard Eleanor's voice come from the mike in her glasses.

"The officers are already inside – in the gym."

Sabrina didn't question how the Analyst knew this. Maybe Eleanor had intercepted transmissions from the officer's radios, or maybe she'd listened in on a 911 call from the school. All that mattered was that in all the time Sabrina had worked with Eleanor, she'd never known the woman to be wrong.

She knew Royce had heard the message as well, and without speaking the two of them entered the school and began running.

"Take a left at the end of the hallway," Eleanor said.

Sabrina and Royce did so. They passed rows of student lockers and closed classroom doors. Sabrina wondered what the students and teachers thought was happening. Did they believe they had an active shooter in the building? If so, good. Like so many students in America, they'd likely drilled for that situation and knew how to shelter in place and stay safe. As tragic as it was for kids to need to prepare for such attacks, in this case, it would save them from something equally as bad as a shooter, if not worse.

As they continued running, Sabrina noted streaks of greenish goo on the walls, along with bits of the same substance on the floor. She wasn't sure what the glop was, but her glasses revealed it shimmered with a black aura, and she was certain it had been produced by the Corrupted person they'd come here to deal with. She didn't know if it was dangerous, but she avoided stepping on it anyway, just to be safe, and Royce did the same. Interventionists had a number of tools to help them deal with Corruption, but they were no more immune to its effects than anyone else.

They came to a juncture, Eleanor told them to turn right, and they did so.

Sabrina registered a body lying on the floor, and at the last instant she jumped to avoid tripping over the corpse. She glanced backward at it as she kept running, so that the image would be transferred to Eleanor via her smart glasses for later analysis. It was a man's body, garbed in a dress shirt, tie, and slacks. At least, she thought it was a man's body. It was difficult to tell since the corpse no longer possessed a head. A large mass of blood, brain matter, and green goo had been splattered on a nearby wall, and grisly chunks of flesh and bone – eyes, ears, patches of hair, fragments of skull – lay scattered on the floor.

"Now *that's* a lovely sight," Royce said.

Sabrina knew her partner cracked jokes in the field as a defense mechanism. Interventionists routinely encountered bizarre shit on the job, and everyone dealt with it in their own way. Royce pretended, even to himself, that nothing got to him, no matter how strange and horrible it was. Sabrina envied him. She'd be able to put aside the sight of the man's headless body and do what she had to, but later – assuming she survived whatever waited for them in the gym – she'd think about the man and the terrible way he died, think about what an awful waste his death was, and she'd wonder why anyone in Maintenance bothered to do what they did, considering how the Gyre took everything in the end.

They encountered no more dead bodies along the way, and with Eleanor's help, they soon reached the gym. The large double doors had been torn off their hinges and lay in the hallway, the glass in the small square windows shattered. From within the gym came the sounds of more destruction, and Sabrina knew that they'd found what they'd come here for. She and Royce passed through the open doorway and stopped just inside to look around and get a clearer idea of what they had to deal with.

A middle-aged man in a suit and tie stood at one end of the gym, next to the wreckage of a basketball hoop and backboard. Long tentacles of mucus protruded from his nostrils and whipped the air wildly, as if they were agitated. A police officer lay beneath the backboard, unmoving and bleeding from a serious head wound. Sabrina couldn't tell if the man was alive or dead. A second officer stood in front of the Snotman, gun held in a two-handed grip and aimed at the man's chest.

"Don't move or I'll fire."

The woman sounded terrified, but she stood her ground, grip on her weapon steady.

Sabrina wanted to shout at the woman, tell her to get the hell away from the Snotman and let her and Royce handle him. But before she could say anything the greenish tentacles shot forward, arced toward the sides of her head, and plunged into her ears. Blood gushed from the wounds, and the officer's body went rigid. For a moment she stood there, not moving, and then the tentacles withdrew and she fell to the gym floor, dead.

There was a third casualty. A man wearing a tracksuit sat on the floor, leaning back against a wall, unmoving. He had bloody holes where his eyes had once been, and Sabrina imagined the Snotman's tentacles lancing forward like a pair of spears, piercing the dead man's eyes and penetrating into his brain. A horrible death for the man, a physical education teacher from the way he was dressed, but hopefully one as swift as the police officer's.

Nullifiers only worked at close range, so Sabrina and Royce needed to get closer to Snotman to use their weapons.

"We need to split up," Sabrina said, "and approach him from two different angles. That way, one of us should be able to get a shot at him."

"Good plan. I'll distract him, and when his attention is on me, you get him from behind."

Before Sabrina could protest, Royce ran toward Snotman.

"Hey, Snotopus!" he shouted. "I know it's allergy season, but this is taking things too far, don't you think?"

The tentacles – ends slick with the police officer's blood – oriented on Royce first, and then the man they were attached to turned his head in the Interventionist's direction, as if following the tentacles' lead. Was the man merely the host for the tentacles? Were they the ones really in charge?

Sabrina wanted to yell at Royce for running off like that before they could finalize their plan, but there was no point. She started running.

Nullifiers worked best when both the wielder and the target were stationary, so when Royce came within ten feet of Snotman, he stopped, raised his right hand, and aimed the device at the man. But before he could activate it, Snotman's tentacles shot toward him. Royce ducked to the side, managing to avoid having his eyes or ears penetrated, but one of the tentacles caught hold of his right wrist and squeezed – *hard*. Bones snapped and Royce cried out in pain. His hand went limp, and the Nullifier fell to the floor. The tentacle lifted Royce's arm above his head and kept lifting until he was dangling in the air. He writhed, struggling to free himself, but the tentacle held fast, and there was nothing he could do.

Sabrina feared the Snotman would use his second tentacle to kill Royce, penetrating his brain as he'd done to the police officer and the gym teacher. She couldn't let that happen. Royce could be a jerk sometimes, but he was her partner. Besides, his death would be a waste, and if there was anything an operative of Maintenance couldn't stand, it was waste. She ran full out, approaching Snotman from behind, but she knew she couldn't reach him before he could kill Royce. She needed to draw his attention away from her partner.

"Leave my friend alone, you Corrupted bastard!" she shouted.

She hoped Snotman would turn in her direction, maybe even forget about Royce and let go of him so he could focus on her. Snotman did turn toward her, but instead of dropping Royce, he whipped him around and hurled him at her. Royce flew toward her, right hand flopping bonelessly, an apologetic look in his eyes. And then he struck her and everything went dark.

"Both Sabrina and Royce are down."

Eleanor's words sent a chill through Gina. Despite her lineage and all her training, she'd never before faced a dangerous situation in the field – not counting Teguzilla earlier that morning – and she was surprised by how frightened she was. In the past, whenever she'd imagined confronting one of the Corrupted, she'd thought it would be exciting.

There's nothing like the thrill of working in the field, her father had once told her. But she didn't feel thrilled now. She felt sick.

Neal had also heard Eleanor's words, and his face was set in a grim expression.

"Are they dead?" he asked.

"Not yet. But they will be if you don't haul ass."

Neal was already driving fast, but now he floored the accelerator and the van picked up speed. Gina recognized this neighborhood from her self-guided tour of Ash Creek yesterday, and she knew they were near the middle school.

"What are we going to do when we get there?" she asked. She did her best to sound calm. She didn't want Neal to know how scared she was.

"I'm sure Deanna's already dispatched another Intervention team, but they won't get here in time to do any good. We'll have to save Sabrina and Royce's asses on our own."

"But how? We don't have any weapons... unless you've got some stashed away in here."

"Sorry, I don't. I did have a wonky Nullifier, but Deanna confiscated it. We'll just have to make do with what we've got."

"What *do* we have?"

"Questionable intelligence, delusional bravery..." He smiled. "And a large container of Expungent."

"You ready for this?" Neal asked.

Gina had no idea if she was or not, but she nodded. They were closing in on the gym, and the only "weapon" they had was a large unmarked plastic container of Expungent which Neal carried. She assumed Neal had a reason for bringing the Expungent with them, but if so, he hadn't shared it with her.

"I have to warn you," Eleanor said. *"It's not pretty in there."*

Gina's stomach tightened. She knew from her training – along with the stories that her family told – that Maintenance operatives regularly encountered disturbing sights on the job, but she'd never seen anyone who'd been injured, let alone killed, in real life, and she wasn't sure how she'd react.

You're a Sandoval, she told herself. *You can do this.*

She glanced at Neal. If he was afraid, he showed no sign of it. His expression was one of grim determination, his gaze sharp and clear. Inwardly, he might have been just as scared as she was, but seeing his game face reassured her that at least one of them knew what they were doing.

When they reached the hallway where the gym entrance was located, Neal motioned for them to stop. The gym doors had been torn from their hinges, indicating that the Corrupted inside was strong. If the thing managed to get its hands on them, it could rip them apart like they were made of tissue paper.

"Eleanor, what's the situation in the gym?" he asked.

"Sabrina and Royce are still unresponsive."

Gina understood the implications of Eleanor's words. The Interventionists were unconscious, perhaps even dead.

"What's the Corrupted doing?" Neal asked.

"Royce's glasses are offline, so I can't see or hear through them. Sabrina's are still working, but the image is hazy. As far as I can tell, the Corrupted is just standing there, not doing anything."

"Maybe it knows we're coming and is waiting for us," Gina said.

"Maybe," Neal said. "But it might be in the early stages of dissolution. If so, that'll work to our advantage."

The negative energy of Corruption was intrinsically destructive by its nature, and it ate away at anyone affected by it, unmaking them bit by bit. The more E-energy a person or object was infused with, the faster they decayed, both on a physical and metaphysical level. There were techniques that could be employed to mitigate this effect, but they required a great deal of time and training to master. The Corrupted inside the gym most likely didn't know of such techniques, which meant it was already in the process of self-destructing. This was probably why it was motionless at the moment. It was attempting to conserve energy and slow its decay as much as possible. So, if she and Neal could get the Corrupted to fight them – which shouldn't be difficult – the dissolution would hasten, weakening it and making it easier to deal with.

Theoretically.

"What about Royce and Sabrina's Nullifiers?" Neal asked.

"I don't know where Sabrina's is, but Royce dropped his while confronting the Corrupted. It should still be lying on the floor where it fell."

"Okay. Thanks."

"What's the plan?" Gina asked.

"We go inside, and while I distract the Corrupted, you grab Neal's Nullifier and use it on the sonofabitch. And try not to get killed. Deanna will be all over my ass if I let you die your first day on the job."

Gina smiled. "I'll do my best. So, what's the Expungent for?"

In response, Neal removed the cap from the container, tossed it aside, then emptied the contents onto his body, making sure to get plenty on his hands. Then he set the empty container on the floor.

"Insurance," he said. "I'll go in first, and you follow right after me. Locate the Nullifier and head straight to it. Don't worry about me. I'll be fine. Got it?"

"Got it."

Neal nodded, then turned and ran toward the gym, globs of Expungent falling off of him as he went. Gina took a deep breath, and then ran after him.

This has got to be the stupidest goddamn thing you've ever done.

Neal ran head-on at the motionless Snotman. Well, not *entirely* motionless. The tendrils of mucus that extended from his nostrils still moved, although slowly, almost lazily, like serpents that remained alert even while at rest. The man's aura was coal-black, indicating he'd been infused with a large amount of E-energy. He couldn't see Gina – she was somewhere behind him – but he heard her footfalls and knew she was running toward Royce's Nullifier. He hoped she managed to get hold of the weapon before Snotman came out of his dissolution fugue and attacked. But he doubted he would be that lucky.

And he was right.

When Neal was within ten feet of Snotman, one of the tendrils shot toward him, aiming for his left eye. He raised his right arm – which was slathered with Expungent – to block the strike, and when the tendril came in contact with the chemical, it sizzled and bubbled, as if it had touched a powerful acid. White vapor curled upward from the tendril, and it swiftly withdrew, shorter now by almost a foot. Neal was still running, and when he drew close to Snotman, the man turned and tried to flee, but it was too late.

Neal leaped toward him, wrapped his arms around the man's middle, and bore him downward. They hit the gym floor hard enough to make Neal's teeth rattle, but he maintained his hold on Snotman. Everywhere the Expungent touched Snotman, vaporous wisps came into being as the chemical interacted with the man's Corrupted body. Snotman shrieked in pain and fury, the sound alien, something a human throat shouldn't have been able to produce. Snotman thrashed back and forth, trying to dislodge Neal, and although the Surveyor tried to maintain his grip, the Expungent made Snotman slippery, and Neal's hands slipped away.

A tendril quickly wrapped around Neal's throat, and while the Expungent on his flesh immediately began to vaporize the appendage, it constricted tight, cutting off his breath. Neal understood what was happening. Snotman was trying to strangle him before the Expungent could reduce the entire tendril to harmless vapor.

Neal clawed at the coils around his throat, smearing more Expungent on them in hope of hastening their dissolution. A cloud of white vapor surrounded Neal's head, making it impossible for him to see anything. His throat burned like fire, his lungs screamed for air, and blackness crept into his vision, obscuring the white vapor, and he knew he was on the verge of passing out.

But then he felt the pressure around his throat slacken, and he was able to breathe again. He lay there for several seconds, gulping air and waiting for his vision to clear. When it did, he found himself looking up at Gina's concerned face.

"Are you alright?"

He started to sit up, but he couldn't quite manage it yet, so Gina helped him. He stood on unsteady legs and smiled weakly.

"I'm going to have a hell of a sore throat for a couple days, but other than that, I'm okay."

He looked around but saw no sign of Snotman. Gina held a Nullifier in her hand, and nearby a patch of greenish goo lay on the floor, white wisps of vapor curling upward from its surface. A stench like spoiled meat crossed with rotten eggs filled the air.

"Good work," Neal said.

"First time I've used a Nullifier in the field." Gina wrinkled her nose.

"The instructors at the Homestead don't tell you how bad it smells when used on something highly Corrupted, though."

"They tend to leave out a lot of unpleasant details like that," Neal said. "Wouldn't want recruits having second thoughts, would we? Come on, let's check on Sabrina and Royce."

"Both of their vital signs remain strong," Eleanor said. *"They're still unconscious, but sensor readings indicate they'll be in considerable pain when they wake."*

Monitoring a Maintenance worker's health was another of the many functions the organization's smart glasses performed. Neal understood the practical reasons for such monitoring, but it always made him feel as if his privacy was being violated. Especially a couple weeks ago, when Eleanor told him that according to his glasses' readings, he needed to get more fiber in his diet.

Gina and Royce lay close to each other, eyes closed. Royce's left arm was bent the wrong way, as was his right leg, and Sabrina's face was bruised, one eye swollen shut, her lips split and bleeding. The two looked like they'd been beat to hell and back, but they didn't appear to have been injured too severely. However, the smart glasses' sensors were only capable of performing basic medical diagnostics. Sabrina and Royce could have suffered internal injuries.

"I've dispatched a medical team," Eleanor said. *"They'll arrive in a few minutes."*

"Good." If Sabrina and Royce's vital signs were as strong as Eleanor claimed, the two should be okay until the med team got there. "Are there signs of any further Corruption in the building?"

Eleanor was quiet for several moments before speaking again.

"I've hacked into the school's security cameras, as well as every computer and phone in the building. There doesn't appear to be any more Corruption. Do you hear anyone screaming in terror?"

Neal listened for several seconds.

"No."

"Then I'd say the building's clear."

"Is it really?" Gina asked, looking at Neal.

He was surprised to see that she – a member of the much-lauded Sandovals – looked scared. He almost said something to this effect, but then he remembered how scared and confused he'd been during his first encounter with Corruption in the field when he was a rookie.

"We should still keep our eyes open, but when Eleanor says a place is clear, it's clear."

Gina smiled and visibly relaxed, though he noticed she tightened her grip on Royce's Nullifier.

Neal glanced at the remains of the Snotman, then requested that Eleanor send a cleanup crew. He wondered what Deanna would do. She'd likely alert Media Relations and tell them to devise at least a semi-plausible cover story for whatever the hell happened here. And she'd send some people from Psych Division to help the staff and students deal with the trauma that had occurred – *and* to reinforce whatever bullshit story Media Relations concocted. She'd also call the police. Some of their own died here today, and they were going to want answers. Deanna wouldn't tell them the whole truth, of course, but she was well experienced at telling just enough when she needed to.

He turned to Gina. "Hopefully, Deanna won't be too angry at us for engaging with the Snotman before another Intervention Team could arrive. If she *is* upset, though, you tell her it was all my idea. No need for you to get in trouble on your first day."

Gina looked uncomfortable, and Neal was afraid the Sandoval sense of honor would make it difficult for her to lie to Deanna.

"It's okay," he said. "When you work in the field, you have to have each other's back. That's what being partners is all about."

"Yes..." Gina smiled. "We *are* partners, aren't we, Neal?"

Neal looked at the still unconscious Sabrina and Royce, the two dead police officers, the dead gym teacher, and Snotman's smoldering goo.

He sighed.

"Yeah, I suppose we are." He reached up and rubbed at the Expungent on one of his cheeks. "I need a shower. This shit's starting to sting."

Rachel stood in the gym's open doorway, watching the two Maintenance workers from the concealment of a small pocket dimension she'd created. She could see and hear them, but they were completely unaware of her presence. If they used their hand scanners, they *might* detect her – especially if they came close enough – but they thought the threat was over, so there was no reason for them to use their scanners. She should be safe enough.

All in all, she was pleased with how her experiment had turned out. Not only had Molly maintained her molecular stability after ingesting the Defilement Rachel had given her, but the child had been able to pass her Corruption on to others – most spectacularly so in the case of Principal Dixon.

Rachel had hated that officious little prick, and his death was a welcome bonus. But the point of her experiment had been to see if Molly could withstand the Corruption inside her, and she had. This meant there was an excellent chance that when she did as Rachel had ordered and gave the Defilements she'd created to her family, they would be able to function with Corruption inside them as well. And then the building of the Atrocity Engine could begin in earnest.

Brother Nothing wouldn't be happy with what she'd done here today. He'd been furious that she'd conducted her last experiment in the park, and he would be beyond livid when he learned that she'd conducted her follow-up test here at school. There'd been more deaths and more witnesses than yesterday, and Maintenance was now on even higher alert than they'd been before. Brother Nothing might be her mentor, but she was far from his only concern, though.

As one of the oldest and strongest of the Multitude, he had many projects going across this world, as well as others. He'd circle back around to check on her eventually, but by then she would have completed assembling the Atrocity Engine, and when he saw what she'd accomplished, he'd be so impressed that he wouldn't care about the way she'd achieved her goal. Who knows? He might even feel proud of her, if a being such as him was capable of the emotion. But in the end, it didn't matter how he felt. She intended to use the Engine to destroy him and prove to the rest of the Multitude that not only was she worthy of joining their dark ranks, that she should be allowed to take her teacher's place as one of the strongest among them.

And if the fools at Maintenance started giving her trouble, she'd destroy them, too.

Neal, Gina, and Eleanor didn't notice the small greenish glob clinging to the underside of Royce's chin. Nor did they see it move swiftly onto his cheek, streak across his skin, and disappear into his left nostril.

Rachel did, however, and – concealed within her pocket dimension where she couldn't be seen or heard – she laughed with delight.

Seven

Neal would've liked to put off being debriefed, as he usually did, but he knew he couldn't get away with it this time, not after such a serious incident as what had happened at the middle school. Thankfully, he was given permission to stop by his basement apartment first, and he grabbed a quick shower and put on a new uniform while Gina waited in the van. He would've invited her in, but he felt self-conscious about how *minimal* his place was.

While it adhered to the Maintenance ethic of living simply with as little waste as possible, he knew Gina's family lived differently. The Sandovals believed in enjoying yourself while you were alive, and they had an appreciation for the finer things in life. He was certain Gina had grown up in a very nice house, and even though he shouldn't be ashamed of what she might think of the dump he lived in, he couldn't help it.

After he returned to the van, it took only a few minutes for them to arrive at Maintenance's Ash Creek HQ. As they entered the building, he expected Deanna to come rushing out of her office to yell at them, but she didn't. Erika, as always, sat behind the front desk, and when Neal gave her a questioning look, she said, "Deanna's on the phone with the Homestead right now."

He shouldn't have been surprised. After all, there had been two incidents of serious Corruption in town in less than twenty-four hours, and there were indications that one of the Multitude might be involved. Of course, Deanna would need to consult with the Homestead. But he was so used to her demonstrating complete and total confidence in everything she did that the idea she would seek anyone's help – even her superiors' – seemed out of character for her. Maybe Deanna was worried, and if that was the case, then the current situation was worse than Neal had thought – and he'd already thought it was pretty fucking bad.

Neal and Gina spoke to different Debriefers. Neal was less than thrilled that he was assigned to speak to Marshall, but he managed to sit in the man's cubicle for the hour the debriefing took without throttling him, so he counted that as a win.

When they were finished, Marshall told him that while he and Gina still had several hours remaining in their shift, it was okay that they take the rest of the day off. This was standard procedure for workers who'd experienced a stressful event on the job – more stressful than usual, that is – and normally Neal might've accepted the offer. But he wanted to get back to work, the sooner the better.

"I appreciate that, Marshall, but if one of the Multitude really *is* involved with what's going on, we need every Surveillance team we have out on the street searching."

Marshall sighed. "You know the rules as well as I do. Probably better considering you've broken most of them during your career. You need to decompress after what happened today so that you'll be a peak efficiency tomorrow, or at least as efficient as *you* ever get. Now go."

Neal glared at Marshall, but he knew there was no use in trying to convince the man any further. He got up and started to walk away, but then stopped when Marshall began speaking again.

"And don't try to take your van back out so you can do some off-the-clock surveilling. After the last time you did that, Deanna had Tech Division install additional trackers on the vehicle. You might be able to locate and disable some of them, but you won't find them all."

Neal hadn't turned to face Marshall as he'd spoken, and when the man finished, he started walking again without comment. He *had* been considering taking the van back out, and he thought there was a decent chance he'd be able to find and disable all the trackers, but he was in enough hot water with Deanna, and he didn't need to make his situation worse.

Gina's debrief finished about the same time his did, and they met in front of Erika's desk once more.

"Any word about Sabrina and Royce?" Neal asked Erika.

"The Med Techs got them stabilized at the scene and took them to the Columbus headquarters. They arrived a short time ago and doctors are currently tending to them. That's all I know right now."

The Med Techs had checked out Neal and Gina at the school as well. Physically, they'd been roughed up a bit, but otherwise they were fine. The medics had some concern about their exposure to entropic energy, but while their levels of E-energy were higher than normal, they were well within the safe range, and they'd been given the go-ahead to return to HQ.

Neal turned to Gina. "Let's go."

After they'd stepped outside, Gina asked, "Are they going to be okay?"

"They should. Columbus HQ has the best Maintenance medical facility in the state. Not only will the docs be able to take care of them physically, they'll also be able to treat them if they were infected by Snotman's Corruption."

"Do you think they were? Infected, I mean."

"Signs of Corruption usually manifest shortly after infection, and neither Sabrina or Royce appeared to have been infected. Hopefully, they'll be fine."

An awkward silence descended upon them then, and Neal figured that, as Gina's superior, it was up to him to break it.

"Sorry you had a rough first day. The life of a Surveyor isn't usually this exciting. Tomorrow things will likely be back to normal, and we'll drive around all day without detecting a single sign of Corruption. Go home and try to get some rest. I'll see you in the morning."

He stepped off the front walk and into the parking lot. He didn't own a car – too much waste – so he usually took the bus. There was a stop a half mile from here, and a bus came by every half hour. Considering how the day had gone, he considered splurging and calling for a rideshare, but he decided against it. The walk would do him good, give him a chance to clear his head.

But he hadn't walked more than a few feet before Gina ran up and joined him.

"I'm too wired to go home right away," she said. "You want to go get a drink? I'm buying."

Neal knew what was happening. Gina needed to process everything that had happened today, and she wanted to go somewhere she could tell him what she feeling and ask him a million questions. He wasn't up for it, but when he turned to Gina to tell her so, he saw the hopeful expression on her face, and he couldn't bring himself to disappoint her.

"Sure," he said. "You got a car?"

She pointed to a Prius parked in the lot. Brand-new, of course.

"Great. Let's go."

Judith Stickland had been showing a two-story house to a young couple over on Henderson Street when she got the call from Molly's school. Something horrible had happened, although the caller – one of the staff, she assumed – wasn't clear as to the exact nature of the incident. The caller assured her that Molly was uninjured, but they were closing school for the day, and Judith should come pick up her daughter.

Judith disconnected, made her excuses to the couple without going into detail, then got in her SUV, and hauled ass to the school. On the way, she called Carlton. Her husband ran his own construction company, and he often didn't answer his phone when he was working. That habit drove Judith crazy at the best of times, but right now it infuriated her. When the tone for Carlton's voicemail sounded, she quickly told him what happened – at least as much as she knew. She disconnected, resisted the urge to hurl the phone at the windshield, and tossed it on the seat next to her.

"Asshole," she'd muttered.

The Mackenzie Middle School parking lot was a scene of absolute chaos. Multiple police cars were parked near the entrance, as well as a couple paramedic vehicles. There were a handful of white vans too, but

Judith didn't know who they belonged to. There was a line of cars moving slowly through the lot, maneuvering around the emergency vehicles as best they could. When one drew close to the entrance – or as close as the driver could get – a man walked up to the car, talked to the driver for a moment, then raised a phone and spoke into it. A moment later, another staff member – this one a woman – brought out a crying child and the man helped the boy get into the car. The vehicle then pulled away and another took its place and the procedure was repeated.

Patience had never been one of Judith's virtues, and by the time she reached the front of the line, she was ready to strangle someone. She rolled down the passenger window and shouted Molly's name to the man – one of the teachers? – standing outside. He spoke into his phone, and a moment later the blond woman came out, Molly at her side. As she ushered the girl to the SUV, Judith asked the man what the hell had happened to close down the school.

"Honestly," he said, "I have no idea."

As soon as Molly was settled in the backseat, he slammed the door closed and headed to the next vehicle in line. Molly buckled herself in and Judith pulled away from the curb.

She looked at Molly's reflection in the rearview mirror. Her daughter stared straight ahead, features flat and expressionless.

"Are you okay, honey?"

No answer.

"Are you okay, sweetie?"

No answer again, not even a flicker of recognition on Molly's face that she'd heard Judith speak.

"Molly? Did you hear me?"

Still nothing.

Molly had never been so cold, so machine-like before, and Judith feared she'd been deeply affected by whatever had happened at the school. Had there been a shooting? God, she hoped not.

The longer they drove, the more Judith's anxiety increased. Molly appeared unharmed physically, but whatever had happened at school seemed to have traumatized her nearly to the point of catatonia. Should Judith take her to a doctor? Or would Molly be better served by going home, to a place of familiarity and safety? Maybe there, once she got settled, she might return to normal. Judith wrestled with indecision. Doctor, home, doctor, home...

"Mommy?"

Judith had been so lost in thought that her daughter's voice startled her. She flicked her gaze to the rearview mirror and addressed Molly's reflection.

"Yes, dear?"

She steeled herself, expecting Molly to start talking about whatever incident had forced her school to close early.

"Ms. Blackburn gave me some treats today. Can we have them for dessert after dinner?"

Molly's request took Judith off guard. It seemed so trivial, so random.

"Uh, sure, sweetie. It was very nice of your teacher to do that."

In the rearview mirror, Judith watched her daughter smile.

"Yes," she said. "Very nice."

Next time, I pick the bar, Gina thought.

She and Neal sat a corner table, mugs of lukewarm beer before them. Neal had already drunk half of his, but Gina had given up on hers after a couple sips. She didn't think she could get any more of the swill down without gagging. She wondered if the beer really was as bad as it seemed, or if she'd been so spoiled by her family's insistence on having the best of everything that she couldn't appreciate a less-than-spectacular brew. She risked another sip.

Nope. It truly sucks.

Grimacing, she put her mug back down on the table and looked around. The Edge was a hole-in-the-wall joint located on the west side of town, with tables, chairs, a bar, and minimal décor. Like, *none*. There were no kitschy pictures on the wall, no neon signs promoting various brands of alcohol, no pool table, juke box, dart board... The walls were bare, plaster shot through with cracks, the paint peeling in numerous places. The floor was wooden – half the boards warped – and the ceiling was stained by water damage. At least, she hoped it had been water. The air smelled musty and stale, like in an attic that had been closed off for a long time. But the most disturbing part were the patrons. None of them were what Gina would've called normal, and most weren't even close.

At the table nearest them, a woman with glittering metallic eyes and skin that looked like polished leather sat talking to a man whose long sharp teeth had grown out vertically, piercing his lips. His flesh tore as he spoke, and thin rivulets of blood ran down his chin and pattered onto the table.

At another table was a man whose entire body was covered by what Gina first thought was hair but soon realized was more like thousands of cilia, the tiny tendrils waving slowly back and forth, as if stirred by a sourceless breeze. His drink was a glass of orange liquid with an eyeball resting on the bottom. From time to time, the eyeball moved, as if shifting its gaze toward something of interest. Sitting across the table from him was a pile of rags arranged in a rough approximation of a human form. The rags remained motionless, and Gina had no idea if they were some sort of strange being or just literally a cloth dummy placed at the table for some unknown reason. She didn't know which prospect was more disturbing.

On the other side of the bar, sitting alone, was an extraordinarily handsome man – broad-shouldered, well-muscled, with curly black hair. He wore a yellow shirt, blue slacks, and black shoes, his clothes tight on his body-builder's frame. He'd nodded to Neal when they'd first entered, and Neal had nodded back. Neal hadn't told Gina who the man was, and she wished he would. He projected intensity and strength, and – to put it bluntly – he was hot as hell.

The bartender appeared normal enough at first glance: a woman in her thirties with long brown hair. But when she mixed drinks, strands of her hair acted as extra limbs, moving of their own accord and helping to grab ingredients, add them to the mixture, then put them back. She'd also nodded to Neal when they'd entered, and she'd given him a beaming smile that made Gina wonder if the two of them had been, or currently were, lovers. Neal hadn't said anything about her, either.

Neal drained the rest of his god-awful beer, then put the empty mug down on the table.

"I know what you're thinking," he said. "Yes, these people are all Shadowers."

"And this place is called Edge because it lies on the edge of Shadow," Gina said.

"That's right."

Shadow was an extradimensional realm bordering on absolute nothingness, where reality was slowly broken down and absorbed by the Gyre, and many strange creatures and beings – including humans – dwelled there. Spend too long in Shadow, though, and it began to change you in unexpected and sinister ways, which is what Gina assumed had happened to most, if not all, of the people present in the bar.

Pockets of Shadow existed throughout the world, but most humans were unaware of them because their minds refused to acknowledge anything outside the comfort zone of their day-to-day lives. Which, considering how dangerous Shadow could be, was good. But some humans had the Eye, the ability to see into Shadow, and were compelled to explore it. Most died quickly, falling prey to the unnatural dangers of the realm, but some were captured and exploited by Shadow's denizens, often in unspeakable ways. Still others found ways to live – and thrive – there.

"Uncomfortable?" Neal asked.

Gina was, but she didn't want him to know that. Up to now, her experience with Shadow had been limited to some training exercises at the Homestead. But being here, surrounded by Shadowers, while still wearing their Maintenance uniforms? Hell yes, she was uncomfortable. But she was a Sandoval, and her family wasn't supposed to be afraid of anything.

"I'm curious," she said. "Why would you pick a place like this to unwind? It's rife with Corruption, and the entropic energy in here must be off the charts. Does Deanna know you come here?"

They weren't being monitored by an Analyst right now. Neal had left his smart glasses in the car before getting out, and he'd insisted Gina do the same. *We're off-duty, right?* he'd said. Gina had agreed and had left her glasses behind as well. She regretted that now. She'd feel safer if she knew someone was watching and could send back-up if they needed it.

"Deanna doesn't need to know *everything* we do. She's stressed out enough as it is."

Strands of the bartender's hair stretched toward their table, their length extending until their ends wrapped around the handle of Neal's empty mug.

"Want another?" the woman asked.

"Yeah. Thanks, Sylvia."

The bartender smiled, and her hair retracted, taking the empty mug with it.

Gina had to admit that some Shadow mutations were more useful than others.

Neal turned to face her. "You asked why I come here. This place reminds me not to look at the world in simple terms of black and white. Order vs Entropy, Good vs Evil. Life's not that simple, regardless of what they teach at the Homestead."

Despite herself, she smiled. "You sound like my father."

Neal looked away, and his tone became noncommittal. "Yeah, well, we shared a lot of similar views... back in the day."

Gina sensed she'd touched a nerve. Something had happened with Neal and her father to create a rift between them, and she wanted to find out what it was. Now wasn't the time, though.

Sylvia's hair deposited a full mug of beer on the table in front of Neal, then it reached up to gently tickle a spot underneath his chin before retracting. Gina raised an eyebrow and was surprised to see Neal blush.

Definitely lovers, she thought.

"Do you get information here that helps with your investigations?" she asked. "Do you have regular informants? I'm surprised they talk to you, given that you're clearly a Maintenance agent."

Ever since they'd entered the bar, Gina had felt the other customers' eyes on them. No one had said or done anything, and while the atmosphere in the place wasn't especially tense, she could feel a certain amount of wariness coming off the Edge's patrons. They might not be overly worried about the two Maintenance agents in their midst, but they weren't comfortable with their presence either.

Neal shrugged. "I don't come here to interrogate anyone, but you hang out in a place enough over the years, people get used to you, and some of them tell you things."

"And some of them become friends?" Gina nodded toward Sylvia, who was now serving a woman covered in porcupine-like quills at the bar.

Neal glanced in Sylvia's directions and blushed again.

"Yeah. This is a relatively safe place as Shadow goes. The people who come here tend to be neutral. They're not fans of Maintenance, but they don't actively hate us, and they're not fans of the Multitude, either."

Neal's words reassured Gina – a little, anyway. Still, she wished she was carrying a Nullifier. Or a gun. Hell, even a knife would be something. She was painfully aware that neither she nor Neal were armed. She told herself she could trust Neal's judgment. He'd lived and worked in Ash Creek for decades, which meant he knew the town far better than she ever would. Plus, despite whatever rift had developed between Neal and her father, her father trusted him absolutely.

So, if Neal had brought them here unarmed, they meant he believed they would be safe enough. Then again, she'd only known him a little more than a day, and in that time, she'd seen him disobey orders and take questionable risks. She wanted to believe that he knew what he was doing, but did he? Then again, she'd chosen to come to the Edge with him, and she could leave any time she wanted, and she was still here.

Maybe Neal wasn't the only one in this partnership who took risks.

"You did bring your last partner here?" she asked. Then, realizing this question was more than little insensitive, she hurried to add, "Sorry. I shouldn't have asked."

Neal looked at her a moment, his expression unreadable, then he took a long sip of his beer.

"That's okay. Yeah, Pam and I used to come here. She was more of a people person than I am and made friends more easily. If we ever needed to get the lowdown on something bad that was happening in town, she could always find someone willing to talk. She had a way of drawing people out so that they'd tell you far more than they intended. And she could be hell on wheels in the field. She was a damn good agent – and a good friend."

He took a longer drink of his beer this time.

"What happened to her?"

"Why ask? I assume you've read the incident report by now. If I was in your shoes, I'd have done the same thing."

"I tried," she admitted, "but I couldn't access it. I think Deanna didn't want me to read it. But that's okay. I'd rather hear the story straight from you anyway."

Neal looked down at the table and several moments passed in silence. When he eventually looked up, something about his expression made Gina think he was going to change the subject. But then he started talking.

"It was a Thursday morning, a couple months ago..."

Eight

"We were on a routine patrol of the southside, and we pulled into the Bargain-o-Rama's parking lot. We cruised up and down the rows of vehicles, scanning for signs of Corruption, and while we received some faint readings, there was nothing definite. Gina thought we should park, go into the store with hand scanners, and walk around a bit, see what we could find. I thought that was a good idea, but I wanted to finish scanning the outside of the building first. That made sense to me, so we drove around to the rear of the building, and as we passed one of the dumpsters in back, the van's scanner went crazy, reporting some of the strongest readings I'd ever seen," he took a drink and then continued.

"You know what Corruption is like, how it finds any small imperfection in reality to infest, and once embedded there, it grows and festers, degrading the environment around it. You can find Corruption anywhere, so we didn't think it strange that a dumpster would be suffused with E-energy, but so *much* of it? That wasn't common at all. With readings that high, we should've immediately called for an Intervention team and guarded the dumpster until they got there. What we should *not* have done was park, get out of the van, and walk up to it with hand scanners to get a better idea of what was going on. But of course, that's exactly what we did..." he paused for a moment, then went on.

"We told ourselves the more information we could gather, the better prepared an Intervention team would be when they arrived, but really, we were just curious. What the hell could possibly be in a dumpster to create readings that high? And our glasses revealed the dumpster had an aura as black as pitch, and that was unusual, too."

"As we drew closer to the dumpster, Pam and I did a quick round of rock, paper, scissors to see who'd get to approach first. Pam won – she almost always did – so she got to walk all the way up to the dumpster, while I hung back."

One partner staying back while the other approached a Corrupted object was standard Maintenance procedure, and Gina was glad that both Neal and Pam had chosen to follow that rule. Doing so had most likely saved Neal's life.

He went on.

"The Corruption in the dumpster was so strong that our hand scanners couldn't accurately record it. It was at that point that I started having doubts about what we were doing. Maybe it *would* be smarter to leave the dumpster alone and call for an Intervention team. I was about to suggest this to Pam, when she gripped the dumpster's plastic lid and threw it open."

"Trash surged upward in a great mass – plastic garbage bags, crumpled paper, dented cans, broken bottles, flattened cardboard boxes, and more – and Pam jumped back. The refuse began moving, rearranging itself, pieces adhering one to another, and within seconds the trash had formed a roughly humanoid shape approximately ten feet tall standing in the dumpster. The creature had a plain cardboard box for a head with no features on it, but I could still feel it somehow sensed us, and our presence did not make it happy. It was, however, *hungry*."

"I started to yell for Pam to run, but before I could get the word out, the trash monster leaned forward and made a grab for her with hands made from twisted wire coat hangers. It wrapped its arms around her torso and lifted her into the air as if she weighed nothing. Pam thrashed around, trying to free herself, and I ran forward, intending to help her. But before I could reach her, the trash monster pulled her tight against its body, and it started to… I guess the best word for it would be *absorb* her. She sank into its conglomerate mass, and at the last instant, she looked straight at me and opened her mouth as if she intended to say something, but all that came out was a scream."

"And then she was gone." Neal took a long pause after this, his emotions overcoming him.

"I shouted something, I don't remember what, and then I ran the rest of the way to the dumpster, intending to somehow free Pam from the trash monster. The creature made a swipe at me, but I was ready for it, and I ducked aside without getting caught. My training took over then, and I backed away and used my hand scanner to try and detect Pam's life signs. All it detected was the trash monster's negative energy. I tried to tell myself that she was in there somewhere, still alive, but I knew better. She was dead." Neal took another long drink before continuing.

"Numb, I turned and walked to the van. I glanced back once to see if the trash monster was following me, but it remained standing inside the dumpster. The thing was probably bound to it somehow, which was good. It would be easier to kill that way. I opened the van's rear doors and climbed inside. Maintenance vehicles always carry a container of extra gas. It wouldn't do to run out of fuel somewhere, not with the kind of advanced tech they have aboard. I grabbed the container, as well as a pack of matches from one of the equipment cabinets, then I returned to the dumpster. Making sure to stay out of the trash monster's reach, I removed the cap from the gas container, and tossed it into the dumpster. I then struck a match, lit the rest of the matches on fire, and tossed the whole book into the dumpster as well. There was an explosive *whump* and flames burst upward. They burned fast and hot, and the trash monster was immediately engulfed. It flung itself back and forth, as if trying to escape the fire, but it was unable to leave the dumpster. A section of the cardboard box head tore open, creating a makeshift mouth, and the creature let out a high-pitched shriek of agony. I stood and watched it burn, dark smoke billowing into the air, giving off a stench like flaming sewage. I don't know how long it took, but eventually, the trash monster's exertions began to slow, and its shriek dwindled to a pathetic whine. It collapsed into the flames then, and I knew it was dead."

"I heard the sound of an engine and headlights washed over me. It was another Maintenance Van. Eleanor had been monitoring both Pam and me, and she dispatched an Intervention team the instant she saw we were in trouble. But they arrived too late to do any good, and Eleanor sent a Cleaning Crew to remove any remaining traces of Corruption. Deanna held a memorial service for Pam in the office the next day. She said a lot of good things about her – all true – and I spoke about what a great partner she'd been. Afterward, people came up to me and told me how sorry they were for my loss, and while their condolences were sincere, more than a few looked at me like they thought I was responsible for Pam's death, that I'd let her down, that because I was a Surveyor, I should've known not to approach the dumpster, and my impulsivity got my partner killed."

Neal downed the rest of his beer, and before Gina could say anything – not that she had any idea *what* to say – he stood.

"Come on. Time to ask a few questions."

Carrying his empty mug, he headed to the bar. After a second, Gina grabbed her mostly full beer and followed.

"That was great, honey."

Judith smiled at her husband. Carlton was appreciative of every meal she prepared for him and Molly, no matter how simple. She was hardly a gourmet chef, but Carlton's compliments always made her feel like one. Molly usually echoed her father's praise, but now she was silent, as had been throughout the meal. Judith had prepared Molly's favorite tonight: ground turkey tacos with avocado and mildly spicy salsa, but the girl had barely touched her food.

She brought the treats her teacher had given her – tiny homemade cakes – and she'd sat with the plastic container on her lap the entire time they'd eaten. Judith wondered if Molly had purposely not eaten much dinner so she had more room for the treats. Maybe. She *was* a kid, after all. Or it might be a result of the trauma she'd suffered at school today, the nature of which remained a mystery.

Judith had monitored the local news ever since they'd come home, and she called several mothers of middle-schoolers that she knew, but no one had any more information on what had happened today than she did. It was beyond frustrating. Maybe the late news would have more details. She sure hoped so. She needed to know what had happened if she was going to help her baby girl.

Judith had told Carlton about the incident – at least, as much as she knew about it – as soon as he got home. He was concerned, but not nearly as much as she was.

She's young and strong. She'll bounce back, he'd said.

Judith knew it wasn't going to be that easy, though. If their daughter continued acting like this, she'd need to talk to Carlton about having Molly see a therapist. He was suspicious of psychologists – *They put thoughts in your head* – but while he'd been resistant at first, she thought she'd be able to bring him around eventually.

"Dessert time!" Judith said.

Like a robot that had been suddenly activated, Molly sprang to life. She pushed her plate of uneaten tacos aside, lifted the plastic container off her lap, and placed it gently, almost reverently, on the table in front of her. She removed the lid, put it aside, then held the container out to Carlton.

"You first, Daddy!"

Carlton leaned forward to examine the little square cakes.

"These look yummy!" he said. "You'll have to thank your teacher for us."

Carlton selected a cake, brought it to his mouth, and took a bite. He chewed thoughtfully, then grinned.

"Delicious!" He popped the remining piece into his mouth and chewed, this time with more vigor.

Judith stared. For an instant, instead of a cake, she'd seen a nasty globby thing, its black surface leavened with yellow-white veins of pus. It bulged and writhed as Carlton brought it to him mouth, and when he began chewing, a thin dark line of drool ran from one corner of his mouth.

"Your turn, Mommy!"

Molly held the container out to her, and Judith saw that the two remaining cakes inside looked perfectly ordinary. *I'm losing it,* she thought. *Maybe I'm the one that needs to see a psychologist.* She then picked up one of the treats and bit into it. A foul taste like liquefied shit filled her mouth, and she almost gagged, but the flavor quickly changed to strawberry-raspberry, becoming not only palatable, but – as her husband had said – absolutely *delicious*. She swiftly ate the rest of the cake, swallowed, and a pleasant warmth spread throughout her body. She looked at Molly, mouth twisting into a cruel mockery of a smile.

"I understand now," she said.

"Me too," Carlton added, his smile also a sinister one.

A vertical line appeared in the air in one corner of the dining room, and a woman stepped out of it. Judith had never seen her before, but she recognized her nevertheless. This was Molly's teacher, Ms. Rachel Blackburn.

The smile Rachel gave them was the cruelest of all.

"Nice to have you on the team," she said.

Neal settled on a stool at the bar, and a moment later, Gina sat next to him. After telling her what had happened to Pam, he felt awkward in her presence. They'd known each other for little more than a day, not long enough for him to share something so personal with her. Plus, this was only her second day on the job. She didn't need to hear about how he'd failed his last partner. It didn't exactly inspire confidence in his mentorship.

Sylvia came over to them, her hair gently waving in the air. It reminded him of sea plants swaying slowly in the current, and he found the effect soothing, almost hypnotic.

"Hey, Neal. Haven't seen you in here for a while." She nodded toward Gina. "Who's this?"

Before Neal could speak, Gina smiled and stuck out her hand.

"Gina Sandoval. I'm his new partner."

Sylvia gave Neal a side look, but he kept his face expressionless. She looked at Gina once more, and shook her hand.

"Good to meet you," she said. "How do you like working with this grumpy bastard so far?"

Gina grinned. "It's been… educational."

Sylvia laughed. Neal frowned, but he didn't say anything. He couldn't tell whether Gina was making fun of him or not.

"You two off duty?" Sylvia tapped the side of her head to indicate their lack of smart glasses.

"More or less," Neal said.

Sylvia looked at Gina. "Don't let him fool you. He never stops working."

"That's something we have in common."

"Then you should get along swimmingly," Sylvia said. "Assuming you both live long enough to get to know one another." She turned to Neal. "You both still have plenty of beer left, so you don't need refills. I don't suppose you came over here to catch up with an old friend?"

Sylvia's voice had a slight edge to it, and Neal felt guilty that it had been so long since he'd stopped in. But he'd come here for information, not to chat.

"You hear anything about a new player in town? Someone who wields a significant amount of power?"

"Like whoever melted that kid in the park yesterday and caused the shitshow at the middle school this afternoon?"

"That would be the one," Neal said.

"There's been some talk among the Shadowers, but nothing concrete. Mostly just speculation and rumor." Sylvia shrugged. "You know how it is."

"What kind of rumors?"

"That whoever it is, they've only recently come to Ash Creek. If someone that powerful had been in town for a while, people would've known about it. And this mystery person keeps to themselves. They haven't interacted with the local Shadowers, at least not that anyone knows about."

Up to this point, Gina had merely listened, but now she broke in.

"If that's the case, how would anyone know they were here at all?"

Before Sylvia could answer, a rich baritone voice spoke behind them.

"Because power that strong is like the blare of a storm siren to those sensitive to the ways of Shadow."

Neal and Gina turned to see the handsome broad-shouldered man had risen from his table and walked over to them.

"Hey, Lenny." Neal looked at Gina. "Gina Sandoval, may I present to you Lenny, also known as the God of Small Things."

Lenny favored Gina with a smile so dazzling, it was like his teeth gave off their own light.

"It's a pleasure to meet you."

Gina's eyes widened, and her lips parted as if she wanted to say something in return, but no words came out. Neal smiled. Lenny had that effect on people the first time they met him. He exuded an aura of power, especially strong when you were near him, and it could be overwhelming until you got used to it.

"Join us?" Neal asked.

"Love to." Lenny slid onto the stool next to him.

"You want me to set you up with another beer?" Sylvia asked Lenny.

"Yes, please."

A couple moments later, Sylvia placed a full mug on the counter in front of him. He turned to Gina then.

"I noticed that you've taken only a couple sips of your beer since you arrived," he said.

"Guess I'm not a big drinker."

"Bullshit," Neal said. "She thinks it tastes like shit – and she's right."

Sylvia glared at him. "If you really think that, why do you order beer whenever you come in?"

"Beer's beer," Neal said. "As long as it does the job, I don't give a damn what it tastes like." He turned to Lenny. "But maybe you could help Gina out?"

"Happy to."

Lenny reached past Neal and stuck the tip of his index finger into Gina's beer. He kept it there for a second, then drew his hand back.

"What did you do *that* for?" Gina sounded equally offended and disgusted by Lenny's action.

"Take a sip," Neal said, amused.

She gave him an incredulous look, and Neal said, "It's okay. Go ahead."

Looking doubtful, Gina raised her mug to her lips and took a small sip. Her eyes widened in surprise, and she took a longer drink. She drained half the mug before putting it back down on the counter.

"That's the best beer I've ever tasted in my life! And given my family's snobbishness about food and drink, that's saying something. How did you do it?"

"Neal told you," Lenny said. "I'm the God of Small of Things. At least, that's what people call me." He stuck a finger in his own beer, then took a long drink of it. He sighed with pleasure, then turned to Neal. "Would you like me to do yours, too?"

"Thanks, but no. I'm afraid that after one sip of your improved beer, I'll never be able to stomach the untouched stuff anymore."

Strands of Sylvia's twisted into a braid and smacked Neal on the shoulder with a whip-like *crack*. He winced and rubbed the spot, which now stung like hell.

"You deserved that," Sylvia said.

Gina drank more of her beer, and then only a quarter was left. She looked at the remainder, as if trying to decide whether to chug the rest of it, but she reluctantly put it down, opting to save the last bit.

"I've never met an actual god before," she said. "I didn't even know they existed. The teachers at the Homestead never mentioned them."

"He's not a god, per se," Neal said. "It's more of an honorary title. He's actually one of the Multitude."

Gina paled.

"Neal's exaggerating," Lenny said quickly. "I was in training to become one of them, but I washed out. Normally they destroy recruits who don't make it, but they thought it would be funny to let me live with only a small fraction of the power I would've possessed if I'd become one of them. I can work minor miracles – like improving the taste of beer – but that's all."

Neal felt sorry for his friend. What must it be like to come close to obtaining unimaginable power only to end up performing mere parlor tricks? Not that he wanted Lenny to be a full-fledged member of the

Multitude. The fewer of them there were, the fewer Maintenance had to contend with. But still, his failure had to sting.

"What do you think about what's happened the last couple days?" Neal asked. "Is one of the Multitude in town?"

"Could be. I'd have to be in their presence to tell for sure. But the chaos that's taken place the last couple days sure sounds like the kind of thing one of them would do, doesn't it?"

Gina had been looking at Lenny with suspicion ever since he'd sat down. Neal understood why. Maintenance recruits were taught that the Multitude were the embodiment of absolute evil, to be opposed at every turn and fought without let or mercy. But when you'd spent as much time in the field as Neal had, you learned that life – even the strange existence of Maintenance workers – wasn't so black and white.

"If one of the Multitude *is* in Ash Creek," Neal said, "do you have any idea why they're here?"

Lenny shrugged. "Why do any of them do anything – to cause chaos in order to speed up Entropy. Ash Creek is as good a place as any to do that." He lifted his beer to his mouth and drained the contents in a single gulp. After putting the empty mug back on the counter, he said, "Whoever it is might be undergoing the Valuation. It would explain why there were two incidents so close together."

"What's that?" Neal asked.

"Before a new recruit can officially become one of the Multitude, they have to go through a period of assessment called the Valuation. During this time, they have to demonstrate mastery of their power, usually through the completion of some kind of project. It's kind of like a final exam before graduation. If your project succeeds, you're in. If it doesn't..."

Lenny trailed off, and Neal wondered if that was what had happened to him, that he'd failed his Valuation and as punishment the Multitude had sentenced him to life as the God of Small Things, a mockery of the powerful being he would've become if he'd passed his trial. He decided it was likely. The Multitude reveled in cruelty.

"Do you have some way of finding whoever's behind the incidents?" Gina asked.

She sounded calm and professional, and Neal was impressed that she'd pulled herself together so quickly after finding out who – and what – Lenny was.

"No. Small things, remember? Tracking one of the Multitude, with all the wards and protections they have, definitely counts as a *big* thing."

The front door opened then, and two new customers entered, both obviously Shadowers. One wore only a pair of black jeans and his body – which stank like rotten meat – was covered with open bleeding sores. The other was a woman with long silver hair, garbed in a long-sleeved blouse and slacks so intensely white they almost gleamed. Her eyes glowed brightly, as if a pair of flashlights had been jammed into her skull.

Everyone in the bar turned to look at the newcomers, and when Neal saw who they were, he groaned. The pair stopped when they saw him, and the man covered with bloody sores scowled, the motion widening the wounds on his forehead and making them bleed more profusely. Then he bared his teeth in a humorless smile, and the wounds around his mouth widened and bled too.

"If it isn't Neal-fucking-Hudson," the man said.

"Hello, Bloodrot," Neal said.

"Remember how I told you I'd kill you the next time I saw you?"

"I do."

"Good. Just so we're clear about that."

Bloodrot released a cry that was more animal than human, then ran toward Neal.

Nine

Judith Strickland walked down a sidewalk not far from her home. She felt different after eating the treat Molly's teacher had sent home with her – a Defilement, Molly had called it, but Judith didn't *feel* defiled. She felt good, better than she ever had in her life. In fact, she felt goddamned *great*.

As she walked, she thought back to what Molly had told her and her husband after the Defilements they'd eaten had changed them.

Ms. Blackburn needs us to find five things: An uncorrupted soul, an extremely corrupted soul, a soul that embodies Life, a soul that embodies Death, and an Umbral's feather.

Judith didn't know what an Umbral was, but at least it was specific. The other four things on Ms. Blackburn's list were far less clear. When she'd brought this up to Molly, the girl had said they'd know what they needed when they saw it. Not especially helpful, but Judith had felt too good to argue. Besides, sometimes you had to take things on faith, right? Carlton had asked what Ms. Blackburn needed the five objects for, and Molly had said, *To construct an Atrocity Engine, of course.* Judith didn't know what that was either, but it sounded impressive.

The family then discussed the best way to gather the items that Ms. Blackburn needed. Since they didn't have clear instructions, they decided to search for each object one at a time, as a group. Hopefully, that would maximize their chances of locating what they needed. So, all three of them left the house in search of the first item on the list: an uncorrupted soul. Judith had turned right onto the sidewalk in front of their house, Carlton had turned left, and Molly had crossed the street to search on that side. They all had phones, so if one of them found something, they'd contact the others to let them know.

Judith marveled at how differently she experienced the world now. The late afternoon sun was shining, but despite that, everything was darker, as if perpetually draped in shadow. A gentle breeze was blowing, but it carried an acrid, sterile scent with an underlying odor of decay, like the smell of a hospice facility. And she was aware of a constant agonizing scream that seemed to come from far off in the distance. It was, she realized, the sound of the universe dying its long, slow death.

The Song of Ending.

It was all so beautiful, so overwhelming, and tears began to slide down her cheeks.

"Are you okay?"

Judith had been so lost in thought that she hadn't noticed the woman coming toward her. She stopped walking, smiled, and did her best to wipe the tears from her face.

"I'm fine. It's been... quite a day, you know?"

The woman smiled. "Aren't they all?"

Now that Judith's vision was clear, she examined the woman. Late twenties/early thirties, short brown hair, medium height, jeans, sneakers, and a T-shirt stretched over a bulging belly. On the front of the shirt, in black capital letters, was the word *BUN,* below that, a black arrow pointing to a second word – *OVEN*. This woman was a mother-to-be. Inside her new life was growing. Fresh. Innocent. But most of all, *uncorrupted*.

Ding, ding, ding! We have a winner!

The woman was *huge*, which meant she was likely close to her due date. Judith was certain she, or rather what she carried inside her, was exactly what Ms. Blackburn was looking for. The issue now was how to get what she needed *out* of the woman and back to the house. Judith hadn't brought any tools with her when she'd left home, so she had no hammer to slam against the woman's head and knock her out, no knife to cut open her belly and pull the blood-slick infant from it. And even if she had the tools, it wouldn't do to perform such an operation out here in the open, where anyone might see.

Judith – this new version of her, anyway – wasn't ashamed by the idea of anyone witnessing her carving up this swollen sow, but she knew that people whom she'd been like before tonight, limited of intellect and blind to the true beauty of darkness and pain, would never understand. They'd try to stop her from finishing her work, either by interfering themselves or by summoning the police. And she couldn't have that. Besides, she wanted Ms. Blackburn to finish her Atrocity Engine and activate it. She wanted to see how it operated, and what, if anything, would remain of the world when it finished doing its dread work.

The woman was alone – presumably taking a stroll to get some exercise – so at least Judith didn't have to deal with a spouse or friend that might have accompanied her. If she'd had any Defilements with her, she could've urged the woman to try one, but she didn't. Besides. Ms. Blackburn had specified an *uncorrupted* soul. If the mother ate a Defilement, Judith felt certain it would contaminate the baby inside her. Judith wasn't strong enough to force the woman to come with her, and even if she had been, the woman would no doubt have screamed for help the entire way. Judith had no mystical or physical means of making the woman accompany her. That left only subterfuge.

"I'd best be going," Judith said. "I hope you enjoy the rest... of your... walk."

She swayed, stumbled forward, and reached out for the woman. Alarmed, the woman instinctively took a step backward, but instead of turning to flee, she reached out, grabbed Judith's arms, and steadied her.

"My god, what's wrong? Are you sick?"

"I don't know, I just felt dizzy all of a sudden. I..."

Judith let her knees buckle, and the woman tightened her grip on her arms.

"Maybe I should call 911," the woman said. She sounded really worried.

Good, Judith thought.

"I live close by. Do you think you could help me get there? If I can just get home and lie down for a bit, I think I'll be okay."

The woman looked uncertain, but she smiled.

"Sure, no problem. Lean on me, and we'll go slow."

The woman put an arm around Judith's shoulders, and together they began to walk. Judith let her feet drag a bit as they went, to maintain her illusion of weakness.

"I'm Brianne," the woman said.

"I'm Judith."

They continued down the sidewalk in silence for several moments, and then Judith – to her surprise – found herself speaking again.

"How far along are you?"

Brianne smiled. "Too far. She was due a few days ago."

She. Brianne already knew the gender of her baby. Judith had opted not to know the sex of her child until it was born. She and Carlton had wanted to be surprised.

"Your first?" Judith asked.

"Yes."

Judith smiled. "The first one is always late."

Brianne laughed. "That's what my mom told me. Do you have kids?"

"A daughter. She's in middle school. Her name's Molly."

Judith was starting to like Brianne – and she was beginning to feel the first stirrings of guilt over what she planned to do to the woman and her yet-to-be-born daughter.

I could let her go, Judith thought. *Once we get to the house, I can thank her for her help, say goodbye, go inside, and forget we ever met. Or I could tell her I'm feeling better and can walk the rest of the way home on my own. We can part ways here, and she can continue on in peace, never knowing how close she came to losing her child.*

Judith opened her mouth to speak, but a sharp pain lanced through her skull, and she drew in a hissing breath. She stumbled and would've fallen if it hadn't been for Brianna holding onto her. A woman's voice – Ms. Blackburn's, Judith guessed – echoed in her mind.

The empathy you're feeling is only a remnant of your former self. It will soon pass. You've been Defiled, filled with darkness, and you cannot turn away from your dread purpose. To put it in simpler terms: I own your ass and you'll goddamn well do what I fucking say.

"That's it," Brianne said. "I'm calling 911."

She continued holding onto Judith's arm with one hand, and with the other she reached into her pants pocket and removed a phone. Part of Judith wanted Brianna to call for help, wanted police and paramedics to show up and prevent her from harming the woman or her baby. But darkness did dwell within her now – cold, remorseless, and without pity. And this darkness wanted to hurt Brianne, *needed* to, and it would not be denied.

"My house is over there." Judith raised a hand, pointed. "Just a little farther."

Brianne looked skeptical, but she put her phone back in her pocket – reluctantly, Judith thought – and continued escorting her. A few moments later, they stood at the front door of Judith's house. She took her keys from her pocket and unlocked the door. Brianne frowned, and Judith thought the woman was wondering how her hand could be so steady all of a sudden. She turned to Brianna and smiled.

"Thank you *so* much. I don't know if I could've made it without your help."

"Go inside and get some rest. If you don't feel better soon, promise me you'll call your doctor."

"I will. I'm sorry I interrupted your walk. I hope you'll be able to enjoy the rest of it."

"No need to apologize. I was happy to help."

Brianne turned to go, but Judith grabbed hold of her arm to stop her.

"There's one more thing you can do for me."

Judith spun Brianne around, gripped the back of her head, and slammed her face-first against the door. She did this three times in rapid succession, and when she was finished, Brianne's nose was pulped and the door was smeared with her blood. The woman was dazed but still semi-conscious, and she groaned in pain.

"Now it's my turn to help *you*."

Judith slipped an arm around the woman's shoulders, opened the door, and steered her inside, blood dripping from her wounded nose onto her bun-in-the-oven T-shirt. Judith thought the bloodstains were an improvement.

Gina could only sit and watch as Bloodrot raced toward Neal. The Shadower's sudden attack surprised her, yes, but her inaction was due to more than that. Before today, she'd never been exposed to violence in the real world, and this was her second time in only a few hours. She hadn't even begun processing what had happened at the middle school, and now here she was, about to be embroiled in another fight. She'd had no idea that being a Surveyor could be so dangerous. Then again, maybe the job was only dangerous because of the way Neal did it.

Neal hadn't drunk much of his beer, and he grabbed the glass mug by the handle and hurled its contents at Bloodrot's face. The Shadower coughed and spluttered, but he only slowed down a little. But a little was all Neal needed. Still gripping the mug by the handle, he slipped off his stool, and slammed the mug into the side of Bloodrot's head. Glass shattered, and several large pieces lodged themselves in the Shadower's bleeding flesh, widening sores already there and causing them to bleed more profusely.

Bloodrot staggered backward several steps and instinctively reached for his new wounds. Unfortunately, he forgot about the glass shards lodged in his skin, and he skewered his palm on them. He cried out in mix of frustration and pain and yanked his bleeding hand away from his head.

Seeing the Shadower wasn't invulnerable broke Gina out of her paralysis. She hopped off her stool and stepped forward, intending to help Neal deal with Bloodrot. But the Shadower's silver-haired companion rushed toward her and blasted her eye-lights full force at Gina's face. She squeezed her own eyes shut, turned her head to the side, and raised her arms, attempting to block the light, but it was too late. Her eyes had been zapped, and even with them closed, she still saw glowing afterimages.

Gina heard the woman's shoes scuff the concrete floor, knew she was coming closer, but it still took her by surprise when she felt the woman's fist ram into her gut. The air gusted out of her lungs and she doubled over, dull, leaden pain spreading through her midsection. She tried to ignore the sensation and draw in a breath, but the woman struck her on the jaw. Gina's head snapped sideways, and fresh pain flared. She tasted blood, and she didn't know if the woman's punch had split a lip, loosened one or more teeth, or both. She was too mad to give a damn which.

She risked opening her eyes, and while the afterimages from being blasted by the silver-haired woman's eye-lights still lingered in her vision, they'd faded to the point where she was able to see. Kind of. So when the silver-haired woman came in for another strike, Gina was ready. She swept her right foot outward and knocked the other woman off of her feet. She fell, an expression of absolute shock on her face, as if she couldn't believe what was happening. She hit the floor and smacked the side of her head on the concrete. There was the sound of breaking glass, the woman screamed, and the light emanating from her left eye went out.

Gina's instinct was to ram her foot into the woman's right eye and shatter it as well. Silver Hair *was* a Shadower, after all, which meant that she'd allowed herself to be transformed by Corruption. Hell, she'd probably sought out her transformation, and eagerly so. Gina was a Maintenance worker, but beyond that, she was a Sandoval. Neither her parents nor her siblings would hesitate to deal harshly and decisively with a foe in the midst of battle.

There's no such thing as a fair fight, her mother had once told her. *When you fight, you fight to win, everything else be damned.* But Gina couldn't bring herself to destroy Silver Hair's remaining eye. Doing so would blind the woman, and while she might be able to get the damage repaired in Shadow, she also might end up sightless for the rest of her life. And Gina wasn't certain deserved she deserved such a fate, not for engaging in a simple bar fight. Instead, she put her foot on the woman's neck.

"Stay down," she said.

A clear viscous fluid leaked from the woman's broken eye, and despite Gina's foot pressing on her neck, she managed a slight nod. Satisfied, Gina looked up to see how Neal was doing and if he needed any help. Her vision was still somewhat hazy after being zapped by Silver Hair's eye-lights but she could see well enough. Neal struggled with Bloodrot, gripping the Shadower's wrists and holding his hands above his head.

The front of Neal's white shirt was smeared with blood, and at first Gina feared it was his, but then she realized that Bloodrot must've brushed up against him. His gaze was fixed on Neal, eyes blazing with fury and hatred, and his lips pulled back from his teeth in a snarl.

"I'm going to fucking kill you, Hudson!"

Neal, teeth gritted, jaw tight, shoved Bloodrot's hands backward. The maneuver caught the Shadower by surprise, and before he could do anything, the back of the man's hands collided with his face – hard. Surprised as much as stunned by the blow, Bloodrot's head snapped back. Neal maintained his grip on the man's wrists for an instant more to prevent him from falling, then he let go.

As Bloodrot's arms fell limply to his sides, Neal made fists, stuck out his index fingers, and began poking them into the Shadower's wounds, moving swiftly. *Poke-poke-poke-poke-poke...* Wounds that were merely trickling blood before now began to gush the stuff, and within seconds, Bloodrot had become a crimson fountain. Blood splattered onto Neal's shirt, pants, and shoes, as well as his hands, face, and hair, but he didn't stop, didn't so much as slow down. If anything, he picked up speed.

Poke-poke-poke-poke-poke-poke-poke-poke...

"Stop it!" Bloodrot shrieked, but Neal ignored him and continued his grisly work.

The fluid pouring from Bloodrot's wounds was thick and diseased, smelling more like sulfurous diarrhea than blood. Soon the Shadower began to pale, and his knees wobbled. He pounded on Neal's chest, attempting to drive him back, but the Shadower had lost too much strength already, and his blows were weak and ineffectual.

Eventually, Neal stopped jamming his index fingers into the man's wounds and lowered his hands. Blood dripped from his fingers like red rain, and his face was stippled with crimson. Bloodrot's eyes were bleary now, and they were having trouble focusing. He swayed on his feet, staggered backward, and then his eyes rolled white, and he went down.

"Damn," Gina breathed. That was some hardcore shit. Obviously,

Neal was tougher – and smarter – than she'd thought after their first meeting, and she felt new respect for him. Her stomach and chin ached, but they were already starting to feel better. This was the first time she'd been struck outside of training classes at the Homestead, but those had been practice fights. The real thing was a lot more… chaotic than she'd expected.

Neal turned to look at Lenny. The God of Small Things had remained sitting on his stool during the entire fight.

"Thanks for your help," Neal said sarcastically.

Lenny shrugged. "I knew you had it under control. Even a lame-ass god like me has to be careful about doling about too much divine intervention."

Slyvia leaned over the bar to examine the mess. She sighed, "I'll go get a mop."

Neal did his best to clean up in the Edge's restroom, but while he was able to wash his face and hands, there wasn't much he could do about the blood on his clothes. By the time he left, the waste receptacle was filled with crimson-soaked paper towels. When he returned to the bar, Sylvia had finished mopping up the blood, and she'd placed a plastic yellow CAUTION sign on the floor. Bloodrot and Ms. Bright were gone. Gina still sat at the bar next to Lenny. Neal took the empty stool on Gina's other side.

Sylvia scowled at Neal, and her hair undulated with menacing slowness in a way that reminded him of a nest of angry snakes. He gave her an apologetic smile.

"Sorry about that. It was the only way I could think of to deal with him."

The woman's scowl eased, and her hair grew still. "Forget about it. It wasn't the worst mess I've had to clean up this month." She paused, then added, "But it was close."

Neal turned to Gina.

"I assume that Bloodrot managed to leave under his own power."

"Barely. His friend had to prop him up the whole way. He left a trail of bloody footprints on the way to the door, but Sylvia mopped them up. As badly injured as he was, I'm surprised he didn't die from blood loss."

"Shadowers tend to heal faster than ordinary mortals," Lenny said. "I'm sure Bloodrot will recover soon enough."

"Too bad," Sylvia said. "That guy causes trouble whenever he comes around. And that infected blood of his really stinks. Like, *bad*."

The stench of Bloodrot's ichor still hung heavy on the air, and it would likely linger for some time.

"I wasn't sure if I should take them into custody," Gina said. "They don't exactly cover situations like this at the Homestead."

"We aren't wearing our glasses, so no one at the office observed what happened, and since *technically* we shouldn't be here in the first place..."

"That's what I thought."

Neal smiled. His new partner was quickly adjusting to the realities of working in the field. But then what else should he have expected from Amador Sandoval's daughter?

"Why does Bloodrot was to kill you so bad?" Sylvia asked. "Don't get me wrong. Lots of people want to see you six feet under, but Bloodrot seems more dedicated than most."

"His real name is Marlon George, used to work as a Clean Up tech for Maintenance. One day Pam and I were assigned to patrol an area a few miles south of town. We detected a Soft Spot on an abandoned farm, and when we stopped to check it out, we discovered an Abysm had opened up there."

Abysms were like sinkholes in the fabric of reality, suffused with Corruption and exceptionally dangerous, as they could increase in size rapidly and without warning.

Neal continued. "Eleanor immediately dispatched a Clean-Up Crew, and they arrived ten minutes later. During that time, the Abysm had almost doubled in size, but when Pam and I tried to warn the crew about it, they blew us off. Marlon was the worst. 'You Surveyors are too paranoid,' he said. 'We know what we're doing.' The cleaners exchanged knowing smiles, then went to work. First, they sprayed a healthy amount of Expungent around the Abysm's circumference to prevent it expanding any further, and then they planned to set off an Occlusion

Charge to seal it up. It was Marlon's job to place the charge, but he went too close to the edge of the Abysm. I yelled at him to stay further back, just in case the Expungent wasn't strong enough to prevent the Abysm from expanding. He laughed and called me an idiot, but before he could get the charge ready, the Abysm suddenly doubled in size, and Marlon was fell in. He was gone so fast, there wasn't anything we could do to save him. The Cleaners got a new charge ready, and this time they were extremely cautious as they placed it. Luckily, the Abysm didn't grow any more, and they were able to set off the charge and close it up. But Marlon was gone. At least, that's what we thought."

"He came back," Gina said.

Neal nodded. "Somehow, he found his way back to reality through Shadow, but the Abysm's Corruption had changed him. He took the name Bloodrot – for obvious reasons – and although his own recklessness caused him to be swallowed by the Abysm, he blamed me for what happened, said I'd distracted him at a crucial moment. He lives on the edge of Shadow now, and whenever we run into one another, he tries to kill me. He's not much of a threat, mostly just a pain in the ass."

"A messy, smelly pain in the ass," Lenny said.

"What about his friend?" Gina asked.

"I don't know much about her," Neal admitted, "other than that she goes by Ms. Bright, and her eyebeams can have different effects on people, depending on how she uses them. Although after today, she might have to change her name to One-Eye, thanks to you."

"Congratulations!" Lenny said.

Gina frowned. "For what?"

"For making your first enemy in town! I'd say that calls for a drink. Sylvia, set us up with a new round, please."

Sylvia went to work refilling Gina and Lenny's mugs. She needed to get a new one for Neal since he'd shattered his on Bloodrot's head.

"Making an enemy seems like a weird thing to be congratulated for," Gina said.

Despite her words, Neal detected a hint of pride in her words.

"It's like that old song says: 'You're nobody till somebody hates you.'"

"That's not how the lyric goes," she said.

Neal shrugged. "In our line of work, it should."

"Fair point."

Once they had their beers, Neal, Gina, and Lenny clinked their mugs together and drank. This time, Lenny hadn't used his powers to enhance the brew's flavor, and Gina nearly gagged. But she got it down and even managed a half-hearted smile afterward.

Yep. She's definitely adjusting, Neal thought.

"So, what do we do next?" Gina asked.

"We should probably call it a day. We could use the rest, and I need to clean my clothes." Neal looked down at the bloodstains on his shirt. "It might be better if I said to hell with it and burned them, though."

"They do look like a lost cause," Gina said. "But we aren't really going home, are we? After all, it *is* still early..."

Neal grinned. "I know another place we could go."

"Our first stop should be somewhere you can take a shower and get a new set of clothes," Gina said. "Not to put too fine a point on it, but you smell like shit."

"Literally," Syvia said.

Neal looked at Lenny. "I don't suppose you could..."

Lenny tapped his chest. "God of *Small* Things, remember? Getting you clean is going to be a big job. Like, *huge*."

Neal sighed.

"I guess we'll have to stop at my place first."

Gina looked suddenly uncomfortable. "Would you mind calling an Uber? My car *is* new, and, well..."

"Fine. I'll text you my address, and you can meet me there."

Neal rose from his stool, then turned back to look at Sylvia. "Good to see you, as always. Sorry again about the mess."

"Don't worry about it. But a word of advice? Maybe you should shower a couple times."

"At a minimum," Lenny added.

Ten

The fading light of dusk painted Oak Grove Cemetery in hues of thick orange, heralding the night to come. Rachel stood in front of a small mausoleum, gaze fixed on the cemetery's entrance, impatient for the Stricklands to arrive. Where the hell where they? It wasn't as if Ash Creek was a bustling metropolis, the streets clogged with traffic. They should be here by now. Then again, after receiving the call from Judith, Rachel had simply opened a Rift to the cemetery inside and stepped through. The resulting Rift Scar hung invisibly in the air behind her, throbbing with negative energy. If anyone accidently encountered it, they'd experience a vision of their own death – complete with full sensory detail – which only seemed appropriate given the location.

The mausoleum, which resembled a small stone shed, contained only a single crypt. It had no windows, and the lock on the rusted metal gate was broken. The mausoleum's gray stone was cracked, crumbling, and covered with strange lichenous growths. A stone cross rose from the roof, leaning slightly to the left, one arm broken off. While the cemetery grounds were well-maintained overall, the grass around the mausoleum hadn't been cut in some time, and spiny weeds grew around the base of the structure. Dead leaves had also gathered around it, despite how early it was in the season. Birds sang in the trees and squirrels scuttled about the grounds, but no animals came near this place. They could sense its poison and knew to stay away.

The mausoleum's sole resident hadn't exactly been an upstanding member of society. Wilbur Rose – who'd died of a cerebral embolism at the relatively young age of forty-seven – had supplied homemade child pornography to clients throughout Southwest Ohio. Wilbur had masqueraded as a respectable businessman, an insurance agent, and he'd been a member of Ash Creek's rotary club as well as the masons. But despite his carefully-constructed façade of a model citizen, he'd been a rancid piece of shit throughout his life, and his evil had followed him into death, suffusing his mausoleum with entropic energy to the point of bursting – a prime requirement for the creation of an Atrocity Engine. Which was, of course, why Rachel had chosen it as the incubator for her dark miracle.

More time passed and Rachel's impatience grew. She considered opening a Rift directly to the Stricklands' home, so she could show them precisely how she felt about being made to keep waiting. But then she heard the sound of an engine approaching, and an instant later she saw the Stricklands' SUV enter the cemetery. The paved access road which wound through the place was narrow, with barely enough room for the vehicle, and the driver – Carlton, she saw – drove slowly.

When she was made a full member of the Multitude, she would be powerful enough that she wouldn't have to work through underlings, unless of course she chose to. Although in this case, she had no choice. Not even a being as powerful as Brother Nothing could construct an Atrocity Engine without human assistance.

Carlton pulled up to where Rachel stood and parked. He cut the engine, and a moment later, the trio of Stricklands got out of their vehicle. They weren't alone, though. They'd brought a passenger, a very pregnant woman whose wrists were bound by silver duct tape. A strip covered her mouth, too, making her unable to cry for help. This meant she couldn't scream, at least not without her voice being muffled. Rachel acknowledged the necessity of the precaution, but she was disappointed nevertheless. She loved listening to screams of terror and pain, found them quite soothing. It was one the main perks of her job as far as she was concerned.

Judith and Molly helped the woman out of the SUV, while Carlton stood by and watched. The woman's nose was bloody and swollen, and she had an ugly bruise on her forehead. The front of her shirt was wet with blood, too. She moved unsteadily, and Rachel thought she might've fallen if she hadn't been propped up. Anger flared bright within Rachel.

The Stricklands had used violence to subdue the woman, and while Rachel usually had no problem with violence – was actually quite of a fan of it, really – if those idiots had harmed the baby... She reached out with her mind and was relieved to discover that, while the baby was stressed, it was essentially undamaged.

The Stricklands brought the woman to her, but Rachel stopped them before they could come too close.

"Keep your distance. If I physically touch this woman, if I so much as breathe on her, I'll Corrupt her, and by extension the child inside her. Then the brat will be useless to me."

The Stricklands did as she commanded.

The woman's eyes were wide with terror, although it appeared they were having trouble focusing. Rachel wondered if she'd sustained a concussion. Tears rolled down the woman's cheeks, and she tried to speak, but the tape muffled her words, making them unintelligible. That was okay, though. Rachel had a good idea what she was trying to stay. *Please, don't hurt my baby... I'll give you anything, do anything, just let us go...*

Rachel's upper lip curled in disdain. Humans were so weak and pathetic. It was difficult to believe that she had ever been one of them.

"What now?" Molly asked.

"We're going to put her into the mausoleum to wait while you three find the remaining objects I need. I must prepare her first, though. When the time comes, I'll need easy access to the child, but I also need to keep it alive and healthy until then. Remove her clothes, and try not to be too rough with her."

The woman struggled and shouted behind the tape covering her mouth. But Molly and her parents eventually managed to render her naked, although they ended up tearing her clothes and giving her more than a few scratches in the process. The woman was shivering now, partially due to the dropping temperature, but also from fear. She raised her bound arms in an attempt to cover her breasts, and the futile display of modesty made Rachel laugh.

"Shy about showing yourself? Then you're *really* going to be uncomfortable with what happens next."

Rachel gestured, and the woman screamed so loud the tape loosened on the right side of her mouth and then peeled away. Judith reached for the tape, clearly intending to reseal it, but Rachel shook her head.

"Leave it. This won't take long."

The woman's body, already shaking, began to quiver violently, the movements intensifying until she was almost a blur. Then there was a wet tearing sound, and the woman screamed as if someone had set fire to her soul. With a single violent motion, she turned inside out, her voice degenerating into a series of moist clicks. Her red-raw muscles were visible now, as were her internal organs, slick and glistening. Her heart still pumped, and her lungs inhaled and exhaled. She was forced to draw in air through the back of her mouth now, making each breath a wheezing, labored effort.

Rachel scarcely paid attention to these details. Her gaze was fixed on the large swollen organ that hung down from her abdomen, and especially on the squirming, living thing within. Rachel was confident she'd be able to access the baby with relative ease when the time came. Once swift cut of the placenta was all it would take.

She looked at the Stricklands.

"Put her inside the mausoleum. The door isn't locked."

The family did as they were ordered, and moments later, the hideous inside-out creature that had been a woman named Brianne was caged inside the mausoleum. Rachel gestured, and the door's lock repaired itself and *snicked* closed. The woman was blind now, and it was debatable what, if anything, she could hear. She milled about for several moments, hitting walls and the door, before finally moving into the shadows at the rear of the mausoleum and sitting on the floor, red hands pressed to her exposed uterus.

The pain she was experiencing had to be excruciating, Rachel thought. She was almost envious. That level of agony would drive the woman insane before long, and Rachel knew that would be a mercy. Not that she wanted the woman to have *any* mercy, but it couldn't be helped.

Molly looked up at Rachel, a hopeful smile on her face.

"Did we do good, Ms. Blackburn?"

"You did *well*," she said. "Now go forth and find the next item on the list: an extremely corrupted soul."

Without another word, the Stricklands got back into their SUV. Carlton turned on the engine, and they drove slowly and carefully through the cemetery until they passed through the main entrance.

"One ingredient down, four more to go," Rachel said. Things were going well so far, and she hoped they'd continue to do so.

She opened a Rift to her home and stepped through. The Rift sealed behind her, creating a Scar that would cause someone to lose control of the left side of their body should they accidently touch it.

Once Rachel was gone, a cadaverously thin man in a yellowed suit that had once been white stepped out from behind a nearby tree. He walked over to the mausoleum and leaned forward to look inside. His mouth stretched into a too-large grin, then he stepped away from the mausoleum and started walking toward the cemetery's entrance. His protégé was playing an extremely dangerous game, and he couldn't wait to see how it turned out.

He thought about the day he'd met Rachel.

He'd been walking down a sidewalk in a small town in central Illinois. He didn't recall the name of it. What was the point? Human habitations – from the smallest shack to the largest metropolis – were all the same to him. It was the people that lived in them which interested him. Their self-doubt, anger, shame, resentment, contempt, hostility, hatred, fear, but most of all, their sweet-sweet *pain*. Brother Nothing considered himself an artist, and these emotions were the dark materials with which he created his masterworks.

It was late afternoon in early August, and the air was stifling – hot, humid, and filled with biting insects. The UV index was dangerously high today, and if he listened closely, he could hear skin cells crying out in agony throughout the town as they burned, some of them already in the early stages of turning cancerous.

It was an absolutely miserable day, and he felt a twisted sense of satisfaction, as close to happiness as a being like him could come.

Praise Oblivion, he thought.

He continued walking, and several minutes later he approached a Cape Cod which literally had a white-picket fence out front. The cliché was too good to resist, so he paused to take it in: red brick walls, black roof, black shutters, well-kept yard, a flower garden next to the house, and an elm tree that provided shade for a young girl, six years old, or thereabout. Straight brown hair, blue T-shirt, yellow shorts, bare feet. She sat in the grass, near the edge of the shade. In front of her – in the sunlight – was a small metal bowl covered by clear plastic wrap. Next to the bowl was a sheet of white paper that looked as if it had some sort of crayon drawing on it, but he couldn't make out the details from where he stood.

As much fun as it was to Corrupt children, he was enjoying his walk too much to pause here any longer. *You'll never know how lucky you were today, little one,* he thought.

He started to go, but instinct told him to take another look at the child, and this time he saw a black aura flicker around her body, just for an instant, then it was gone. Intrigued, he stepped onto the driveway, walked into the yard, and crouched down on the other side of the bowl from the girl. The drawing was a crude representation of a man and woman – her parents? – and inside the bowl was a white mouse. The small creature seemed lethargic, but it was alive.

"What are you doing, my dear?"

The girl had not taken her gaze off the mouse the entire time he'd approached her, and she still didn't look at him as she spoke.

"My mommy and daddy won't take me to Disney World. They say it costs too much money. That made me mad, so I'm going to kill them."

The girl said this so matter-of-factly it surprised him, and that was *not* easy to do.

"And how do you plan to accomplish this task?"

She raised her eyes to meet his, and he waited for her to react in horror at seeing him – the skull-like face, the black-hole eyes... But she didn't so much as blink.

"I put my pet mouse into this bowl and covered it up. Her name is Minnie. I put her in the sunlight an hour ago, and I'm going to keep her there until she gets too hot and dies. And then her death will go into the picture and Mommy and Daddy will die."

The girl's crude attempt at a death-transference spell would never work, of course. But the concept was sound, and if she had the right training... He peered into her mind and discovered that her home life was as close to perfect as it was possible to get. Her parents loved her and did all they could to raise her properly. They never laid a hand on her or used harsh language when talking to her, and they attended to her emotional needs as much as they did her physical ones.

He looked deeper.

Her mind, young and still forming, was already a nest of venomous snakes, and it would only get worse as she got older. There were psychological reasons for this, and there were no organic defects either. He looked still deeper, all the way down to the molecular level, and he could find nothing to account for the darkness that seethed within her brain. It was simply her nature.

She was magnificent.

"I'm afraid that your technique – while sound in its basic theory – won't actually work. *I*, however, can kill your parents for you, if you like. You have but to say the word."

The girl looked at him for a moment, then she smiled.

"The word."

Brother Nothing's dried, cracked lips pulled away from his crooked, yellow teeth in what was more grimace than smile. A few seconds later a gunshot came from inside the house, followed closely by another. Then silence.

"I planted the thought in your father's mind that he should take his handgun, shoot your mother in the head, then do the same to himself. They're dead, as you requested."

He waited to see how she would react. She looked at him a moment, then she grinned and clapped her hands.

"Yay!"

Her aura flared black for a moment then, and it stayed that way for several seconds before fading away.

Brother Nothing nodded to the mouse trapped in the bowl.

"Are you going to release Minnie now that you no longer need her for your spell?"

The girl frowned. "Why would I do that? It'll be fun to watch her die. I wonder how long it will take?"

"Another twenty-three minutes."

"That's not long."

"It isn't. And it will give us time to talk."

The girl frowned. "About what?"

"I want to tell you about a place where you can learn how to make your darkest dreams come true. It's special type of school called the Athenaeum."

The girl tried the word on for size.

"A-thuh-nee-uhm." She smiled. "I like it!"

"What's your name, child?"

"Rachel. What's yours?"

"Brother Nothing."

The girl laughed. "That's a funny name!"

His smile was as cold as death itself.

"I'm a funny guy."

Gina sat on the couch in Neal's basement apartment. He'd been in the shower for twenty minutes now, and she hoped he'd be finished soon. Although given the amount of gore he'd gotten on him, she wouldn't have been surprised if it took another twenty minutes for him to get clean. She'd been the one to dispose of his ruined clothes. He'd left them on the tiled bathroom floor, and although he hadn't asked her to get rid of them, she couldn't stand their stench.

She found a plastic shopping bag – Neal kept a collection of them under the bathroom sink – and wrapped one around her right hand so she wouldn't have to touch the clothes as she put them into the bag. She'd then taken them outside and dropped them in the plastic waste receptacle sitting at the back of the house. She didn't know when trash pickup was in this neighborhood, but for the sake of the residents, she hoped it would be soon. Otherwise, the stench of Neal's clothes would waft through the air and suffuse the area. A stink like that could linger for weeks, months, maybe longer. She was glad she lived miles from here.

She supposed she shouldn't have been surprised by Neal's modest accommodations, but she was. Yes, Maintenance employees were required to live as simply as possible and produce as little waste as they could. But she'd always had the impression that few actually tried to live up to this standard.

People need to be comfortable in their home, her father had once told her. *It's a place of respite, somewhere to rest and recharge. The kind of life Maintenance workers lead can wear you down over time if you're not careful. Living well helps us to do our jobs better and – perhaps more importantly – longer. That more than makes up for allowing ourselves a few indulgences here and there, isn't it?*

Neal wasn't a by-the-book kind of guy, and while she hadn't expected him to be living in luxury, she thought he'd at least have a decent place. But this? This was a shithole.

Neal might not be much for rules and regulations out in the field, but it was clear from his apartment that he believed in Maintenance's mission, and deeply so. Maybe that was the real reason he disregarded rules so often – because he believed he was serving a higher purpose, and he'd do whatever it took to get the job done.

She thought of the condo her parents had gotten her, of the lavish home she'd grown up in. She'd had the best of everything, as had her brother and sister. She hadn't questioned her upbringing at the time, had just enjoyed it, but now she wondered how dedicated her family truly was to the ideals they fought for. When it was all said and done, were the much-lauded Sandovals in fact hypocrites? It was a disturbing thought.

She heard the shower turn off, and several moments later, Neal – a towel wrapped around his waist – stepped out of the bathroom. His hair was tousled from drying it, but he looked clean enough. More importantly, he didn't stink.

"Used more water than I wanted," he said. "But I suppose it couldn't be helped."

No one in her family would've given a damn how much water they used for a shower, *especially* if they'd been covered in the same foul shit as Neal had been.

"I'm going to get dressed, so would you mind, uh... you know."

"Huh? Oh, yeah. Sorry."

Gina turned her head to give Neal privacy. She heard him bustle about, as if he was trying to dress quickly, and a few moments later he said, "All done."

She turned back to look at him. Fresh shirt and tie, slacks, socks, and shoes. No smart glasses, though. The two of them were still working in secret.

Neal walked over and sat on the couch next to her, although not *too* close.

"Back at Edge, you said there was another place we could go," Gina said.

"Yeah. The Stygian Market. You can get almost anything you want there, including information. For the right price, of course."

"I've never heard of it."

"I'm surprised your father didn't tell you about it. The Stygian Market was his favorite place while he was working in town. He used to do all sorts of deals there."

Neal didn't put any special emphasis on his last sentence, but something flashed in his eyes when he spoke the words. Before she could ask him about it, he stood.

"Let's get moving. The Market's a big place, and it's only open until sunrise. Or more accurately, it only *exists* until sunrise."

He headed for the steps and started up. Gina watched him for a moment before rising and following. More than ever, she sensed something had happened between Neal and her father back when they were partners – something bad – and she was going to find out what it was.

One way or another.

When Gina and Neal left Neal's place, she'd thought they would return to the west side, as it was the section of Ash Creek located on the edge of Shadow, but instead, Neal directed her to head out of town. Like a lot of towns and villages in Southwestern Ohio, Ash Creek was surrounded by farmland – open fields where cows or horses grazed or where rows of tall corn grew. It was night, and Gina saw no cows, no horses. She figured the animals were asleep somewhere, maybe in a barn, like in the picture books she'd read as a child. The corn had been recently harvested, and only the stubs of bent and broken stalks remained.

She was by no means a country girl. She'd grown up in the metro DC area, after all. But she found the land here – the animals, the crops, the cute little farmhouses – to be enchanting in its own way. When the sun was shining, that is. But night in the country was a different story. The cornstalks suggested strange shapes, as if inhuman creatures squatted there, hunched over, watching them pass with narrowed, baleful eyes. And the fields where cows or horses should've been seemed filled with thick, living shadows, dark wraiths that twisted and swirled through the air, coming closer to the road with each moment, eager to sink ebon talons into the soft flesh of the two humans driving by.

The farmhouses were shrouded in night, the meager illumination from their porchlights doing little to keep the darkness at bay. The houses no longer looked cute to Gina, but rather sinister and haunted.

Neal spoke then, and his voice startled her.

"It's different out here at night, isn't it? Humans create pockets of civilization to isolate us from the wild, to *protect* us from it, but it's never far away. Some people like living with the wild, though, making peace with it, even befriending it, if they can."

"What about you?"

"I think if outside was so great, humans would never have invented inside. Slow down. We're getting closer."

Gina eased her feet off the gas, and her Prius slowed. On their right was several acres of untended land enclosed within a long length of weathered wooden fence. High grass and weeds covered the ground, and Gina wondered if this was an area a farmer had decided to let lie fallow this year, or if it had been abandoned and gone to seed.

"Turn right at the next driveway," Neal said.

Gina expected to see a mailbox – maybe a metal one affixed atop a thick wooden support, like she'd seen in movies – but there wasn't one. The driveway was unpaved, covered with gravel, and when she turned onto it, the rubber of her tires made soft popping noises as they ground the small stones together.

The driveway was uneven, and the Prius rocked back and forth and side to side as they went, forcing Gina to go slow. It was a single narrow lane, flanked on both sides by high grass. Gina wondered what might be hidden within the grass, but she quickly told herself to stop letting her imagination get the better of her. There was nothing here other than the usual animals one would find in the country – field mice, rabbits, possum, raccoons, fox, coyotes, deer... Nothing to be frightened of. All perfectly ordinary.

Then again, if this place was ordinary, why would Neal bring them here?

She was glad the windows were up.

They drove for what seemed a long time, and Gina wanted to ask Neal if this damn driveway had an end, but she was afraid of what his answer would be, so she kept silent. Before much longer, she saw a pair of dark shapes silhouetted against the night sky, spread apart, one larger than the other.

As they drew closer, the Prius' headlights washed over the smaller of the objects, and she saw that it was an ancient farmhouse that had collapsed in on itself, nothing but a pile of torn shingles and splintered wood. The driveway forked here, and Neal told her to bear right. She did so, and a large black barn came into view. A dozen vehicles were parked in front – cars, trucks, vans, and motorcycles, various makes and models, all from different eras, but still normal. Other vehicles, however, were... different.

A chopper entirely covered with gleaming sharp spikes – seat and handlebars included. An arrangement of crystalline panels fused together at strange angles, randomly flickering in and out of existence. A car with a standard metallic chassis, but instead of having tires, thousands of tiny insect legs protruded from its bottom.

"Park anywhere," Neal said.

There were spaces open next to both the spike-bike and the millipede-mobile. Gina pulled in next to the chopper. She regretted her choice when she saw the spikes were coated with blood.

She turned off the engine and looked at Neal.

"What do I need to know about this place?"

"The Stygian Market never closes, but you can only enter and exit it when the sun's down. If the sun comes up when you're inside, you're stuck until it goes down again. We've got lots of time before sunrise, though, so we won't have to worry." Neal frowned. "Then again, time *does* operate differently inside the Market. We'll keep our visit short just to be on the safe side."

"Is it dangerous?"

Neal looked her a moment before answering.

"*Everything* we do is dangerous, especially when it seems like it isn't."

Was he thinking about how Pam had died? Probably.

Maybe this isn't such a good idea, she thought. Surveyors were supposed to primarily observe and report, only getting involved in a situation if they absolutely had no other choice. Neal didn't so much break this rule as act as though it didn't exist. Had Pam believed the same as he did? Or did she go along with him despite her better judgment, and end up paying for it with her life?

"Something wrong?"

She looked at Neal. She'd only known this man for a little over a day, and now she was trusting her life with him. Was she insane? Her father trusted Neal, though. If he hadn't, he would've insisted she be partnered with someone else, and he had the clout to make it happen. If her father trusted Neal, then she should, too.

"Not at all. Let's go."

Carlton Strickland drove the family's SUV, while Judith sat in the passenger seat, Molly on her lap. He knew their daughter should be sitting in the back seat. Secured with a safety belt, but she'd insisted on riding in front so she could better see out the windows. And since Molly had been the first of them to be claimed by Ms. Blackburn, that meant she was in charge, so she could sit anywhere she damn well pleased.

The three of them had split up the last time they'd gone out searching for the first item in Ms. Blackburn's bizarre scavenger hunt, but this time they'd decided to work as a single unit. Well, *decided* wasn't the right word. They'd followed instinct rather than make a conscious choice.

Carlton was a practical person, had been all his life, which was one of the main reasons he'd gone into the construction business. He liked making a plan and working one methodical step after another to see it through to a desired conclusion. Straightforward, no ambiguity. But now here he was, driving through town at night, searching for a corrupted soul, with nothing more to go on than faith they'd recognize it when they came across it. It was an entirely new way of operating for him, and he was surprised by how comfortable it felt.

Who says an old dog can't learn new tricks?

He felt a deep sense of contentment, but a part of him, a remnant of the man he'd been, knew this feeling wasn't normal, that it was *wrong* and deeply so. An image flashed in his memory, the woman they'd brought to Ms. Blackburn being turned inside out by the witch-goddess, organs – slick and glistening – exposed to the night air. At the time, he'd been proud to have successfully served their mistress, but now the horror of what they'd done, of what they'd helped Ms. Blackburn do, rose within him, threatening to destroy his calm.

Molly, as if sensing his turmoil, reached over and put a hand on his shoulder.

"It's all right, Daddy. Everything is going the way it should."

"Yes," he said, voice dreamy, as if he were only half awake. "It is, isn't it?"

He smiled, and Molly smiled back.

Life was good, and it was only going to keep getting better. His thoughts returned to their work.

"Where should we look first?" he asked.

Judith answered. "It depends on how corrupted the soul must be."

"Rotten and stinking all the way through," Molly said.

Carlton thought a moment.

"I might know a place."

Rachel walked through the cemetery, enjoying the stench of decay and the feeling of profound wrongness in the air. She'd decided to wait here while the Stricklands searched for the next ingredient she needed to construct her Atrocity Engine.

They'd found the first item quickly enough, and while she had no reason to believe they'd find the second just as fast, she wanted to be here when they returned. Besides, opening dimensional portals to travel back and forth from her home was creating too many Rift Scars in her place. It was getting so she had to careful where she walked. If she blundered into a scar without having time to raise a protective shield, she'd experience the full force of its effect, and that was something she'd prefer to avoid.

A being as ancient and powerful as Brother Nothing might be unaffected by Rift Scars, but she hadn't reached that level yet. But if her plans worked out, she'd get there far sooner than any of the Multitude – including Brother Nothing – could ever expect.

Speaking of Brother Nothing, she'd placed a Concealment on both the mausoleum and herself. A being at his level had far more important things to do than constantly monitor his apprentice. He was likely worlds away at this moment, tending to his various schemes and machinations. But while the odds of him dropping in to check on her before she completed the Atrocity Engine were small – especially since he'd visited her recently – they weren't zero. Better to be safe than sorry, especially where Brother Nothing was concerned.

She strolled between gravestones as she wandered the cemetery grounds, ignoring the paved access road that wound through the place. She enjoyed the sound of her shoes *whsssk-whsssk-whsssking* through the dry, dead grass six feet above the cemetery's residents. Occasionally she'd sense a faint spark of awareness deep within some of the corpses – just a few – and when she did, she sent down a tendril of power to fan it into a roaring fire. Dead men and women opened their eyes, and when they realized where they were, they began screaming and pounding frantically on the lids of their coffins.

Rachel smiled. She thrived on the heady sensation of power being one of the Multitude (or nearly so) granted her, but Brother Nothing had never told her how much *fun* such power could be.

She continued walking and began reviewing the day's events. She hadn't gotten as far as she had in her dark apprenticeship without paying meticulous attention to detail. She planned and planned and planned again, only enacting a scheme when she thought every aspect was perfect. And even then, she continued assessing, making any changes necessary to ensure success as events played out.

Overall, things were proceeding satisfactorily – with one exception. Yesterday in Orchard Park, when she'd tested one of her defilements on Cody Pittman, a Maintenance agent had been present. She'd left as soon as the test had gone wrong, escaping through a Rift, but she maintained a low-level psychic bond with anyone who ate one of her Defilements, and she knew that Cody had been killed after she'd departed. She didn't care about the boy's life, of course, and on one level she appreciated Maintenance arriving to clean up her mess. But she'd drawn the organization's attention a day earlier than she'd planned.

She'd expected agents to respond to the chaos happening at the school – which they had – but one of them had been the same agent she'd seen at the park. She remembered hearing his partner say his name in the school gym: *Neal.* At the time, she hadn't thought much about Neal's presence. Ash Creek was a small town, and as such, its branch of Maintenance didn't have many agents. The same one responding twice to incidents she'd set in motion didn't mean anything.

And yet...

She couldn't escape the feeling that it *did* mean something. She supposed it might just be nerves. Creating an Atrocity Engine was a huge – and exceptionally dangerous – undertaking. There were so many ways it could go wrong, each more terrifying than the last, not to mention that building such a device was forbidden by the Multitude.

She knew if Brother Nothing discovered what she was doing, he'd not only stop her, he'd punish her in ways beyond imagining. She'd accepted the risks when she'd first committed to this project, but it was only natural to have some doubts, wasn't it? Except she didn't think that was the reason she felt unsettled. Her instincts were warning her that somehow Neal was a threat, and she intended to heed those instincts.

The safest course of action would be to kill him herself, but she feared that would stir up the Maintenance agents even more than they already were. She was confident she could handle them if they attacked, but the Multitude preferred to work in the shadows, silent and undetected. She was already on thin ice by creating an Atrocity Engine. But if in addition she drew too much attention to herself, she doubted the Multitude would look past her transgressions. So, she couldn't kill Neal directly. But that didn't mean she couldn't have someone *else* do it.

She didn't want to use any of the Stricklands. She needed them to continue gathering the items for the Atrocity Engine. But who else... she remembered the two agents who'd gone into the gym before Neal and his partner. Both had failed to subdue the Corrupted principal and been injured. A small piece of that Corruption survived the principal's destruction and had entered the male agent's unconscious body. At this point, the E-energy had been growing within him for nearly ten hours. If she could reach out and connect to it...

She stopped walking, closed her eyes, and concentrated.

Eleven

"How is he?" Sabrina asked.

She sat in a wheelchair in front of a rectangular window set low enough so she could see into the treatment room. Inside, a quartet of Med Techs encased head to toe in specially-designed protective gear clustered around a large machine resembling a metallic cocoon. Two of the techs monitored screens built into the cocoon's surface, while the other two made necessary adjustments to its controls based on the constant flow of information the screens provided.

Sabrina thought the four techs looked like galactic travelers garbed in white EVA suits who were piloting their ship through interstellar space. They might not be futuristic astronauts, but they were using some of the most advanced technology on the planet.

"Honestly, it's difficult to say."

The woman standing next to Sabrina – tall, white, raven-haired, middle-aged – wore a lab coat over a yellow blouse and black skirt. Sabrina, dressed only in an ill-fitting blue medical gown, felt almost naked next to the doctor. If she hadn't sitting down, her bare ass would be hanging out for the world to see. And she was *cold*. Why did they always keep the temperature so low in hospitals?

She'd sustained multiple injuries during the battle with the Corrupted principal at the middle school. Several of her ribs had been broken when Royce collided with her, and she'd hit her head hard on the gym floor when she landed, fracturing her skull. E-energy was dangerous enough on its own, but if you had any injuries or were ill during exposure, it would exploit that physical weakness, move deep into your body, and suffuse it, Corrupting you down to the subatomic level.

Ash Creek's Med Techs had gotten both Royce and Sabrina stabilized at the school so they could be transported to the Maintenance medical facility in Columbus. Sabrina's treatment had gone well. She'd been cleansed of entropic energy, her chest was wrapped tight with compression bandages, and she'd been given medication to help with the pain from her skull fracture. Luckily, it hadn't been severe enough to require surgery, but the medication only did so much to blunt the pain.

Her head throbbed like a motherfucker, and the medicine made her drowsy. She should've been in bed sleeping, but she'd insisted on seeing Royce, and one of the doctors had finally given in and wheeled her down here – *if* she promised to get some rest afterward.

"You were both exposed to a high degree of E-energy today," the doctor said, "but your partner received a far stronger dose than you did. You only needed ten minutes inside a cleansing chamber to nullify the majority of E-energy in your body. Royce has been inside the machine for over an hour."

"Is it working?" Sabrina asked.

A small intercom was affixed to the wall on the right side of the window. The doctor pressed a button and spoke.

"The patient's partner is here with me. Is there any news about Mr. Bigelow's status?"

One of the techs stepped away from the cocoon, approached the window, and pressed a button on the inside intercom to reply.

"His E-energy level is two percent lower than when we started treatment, but it's been slow going. At this rate, we might have to keep him in the cleanser all night." The tech looked at Sabrina. "Is there anything more you can tell us about what happened to him that might explain the extreme amount of E-energy in his body?"

Sabrina had regained consciousness on the trip from Ash Creek, and she'd been given a new pair of smart glasses by the Med Techs so she could make her report to HQ. Royce had remained unconscious ever since the fight in the gym, and if he knew why he'd become Corrupted to this extent, they'd have to wait until he woke to find out.

"Nothing more than what I stated in my debrief."

Behind his plastic face shield, the tech nodded.

"We'll keep working with him and see if we can do anything to speed up the cleansing process. But I have to be honest. We've never had a patient Corrupted this badly, and I don't know if he's going to make it."

The tech's words weren't unexpected, but they still struck Sabrina like a slap to the face.

"What'll happen if you can't get rid of the E-energy in him?"

The tech and the doctor exchanged a silent look, and that gave Sabrina her answer.

"He'll have to be..." she almost said *put down*, but instead she said, "neutralized."

"Yes," the tech said, "but we're not there yet. There are still a lot of things we –"

A shrill alarm sounded inside the treatment room, and the tech turned and ran back to the cleansing station. The Med Techs were frantically adjusting controls on the machine, and while Sabrina could see their mouths moving, the siren was so loud that there was no way to make out what they were saying.

"What's happening?" she asked the doctor.

"I don't know," the woman said, but she sounded worried.

Sabrina rose from the wheelchair so she could get a better view through the window. She expected the doctor to chastise her for standing, but the woman didn't say anything. Sabrina's head pounded in time with her pulse, and a wave of dizziness hit her, but she ignored the sensations and focused on what was happening inside the treatment room.

The techs became even more animated, and she could hear they were yelling at each other now, although she couldn't decipher specific words. Then something strange happened.

The air above the cleansing chamber rippled and a hand – a

woman's hand – thrust through a tear in space. Bolts of black energy burst from the woman's fingertips, struck the chamber, and coruscated wildly across its surface. The energy – *E-energy*, Sabrina thought – overloaded the chamber's system, and sparks shot into the air as the machine began to malfunction. The woman's hand ceased generating E-energy at this point, and then it slipped back through rift it had created and was gone. The tear in space closed, and while Sabrina couldn't see it, she knew a Rift Scar had been left behind.

The alarm fell silent then, and the lid of the cleansing chamber burst open in a further shower of sparks. The four techs stepped back in alarm as black steam coiled upward from the machine's interior, and Royce emerged. Liquid – a mixture of Expungent and other chemicals – dripped from his body and puddled on the floor around his feet. He was naked, his chest covered with round sensor patches, eyes filled with the same dark energy that had crackled from the woman's fingers. The techs stared at him, unable to believe what they were seeing.

Sabrina pounded her fists on the window to get their attention.

"Run, you dumbasses!" she shouted.

Her warning came too late. Royce raised his arms, stretched out his hands, and bolts of black lightning – exactly like those the woman had emanated – burst forth from his fingers. The bolts struck the tech's face plates, breaking through them as if they were no more substantial than tissue paper. The bolts pierced their eyes, penetrated their brains, and they screamed. Not for long, though. A few seconds later their voices cut out and they fell to the floor. Their protective suits flattened, as if they were suddenly empty.

"My god," the doctor said. She stood next to Sabrina at the window, eyes wide with shock. "He sped up their personal entropic fields, reduced them to nothing. I've never seen anything..."

The doctor stopped speaking as Royce turned to look at them, thick darkness roiling where his eyes had been. He grinned and stabbed a finger toward the doctor. A single bolt of E-energy shot forth from his fingertip, sliced a hole through the window with laser-like precision, forked, and then penetrated the doctor's eyes. The woman screamed, stiffened, and then her body turned to black dust which streamed to the floor with a soft *ssssssss*. Her clothes were unaffected, and they fell onto the doctor's granular remains.

Sabrina had seen a lot of messed-up things during her time with Maintenance, but she'd never seen anything like *this* before. She decided it would be a good idea for her to take the advice she'd given the Med Techs and get the hell out of here, but before she could start running, the door to the treatment room disintegrated into black dust, and Royce, still grinning, stepped out into the hall and trained his shadow-filled eyes upon her.

"Hello, Sabrina. I've something to give you."

"No, Royce, don't–"

He thrust his hands forward and black lightning shot toward her eyes.

When it was over, Sabrina smiled at her partner. She felt fan-fucking-*tastic*. Strong, powerful, and focused in a way she'd never been before. She knew who and what she was and what she needed to do.

"Time to head home," she said.

"We'll need a car," Royce said.

"A fast one."

He grinned. "*Really* fast."

They heard the sound of someone – multiple someones – running down the hall toward them. The alarm that had gone off when their mistress gifted Royce with a portion of her darkness, a measure of which he'd passed on to Sabrina, had doubtless alerted security. No matter. The guards would merely be a momentary distraction, then they'd be on their way.

"I think we're going to have to erase a few people from existence before we go," Royce said.

Sabrina grinned. "Sounds like fun."

They started walking toward the oncoming guards, E-energy crackling to life around their hands.

Gina and Neal entered the Stygian Market through a pair of open sliding doors in the side of the barn. She was surprised to find the entrance unguarded.

"No security?" she asked.

"There are guards – just not living ones."

Gina didn't like the sound of that, but she was too overwhelmed by her first look at the barn's interior to ask for more details. There was nothing about the outer structure's appearance to indicate it was anything but a standard-size barn, but inside it was huge – far wider and longer than it should've been. So large, in fact, that Gina couldn't see where it ended. Any direction she looked, it just kept going and going.

What if she didn't see an end to the thing because it didn't *have* one? What if it kept going in all directions forever? It would be so easy to lose your way in here and never be able to find the exit without help. You might even end up wandering around lost and confused until you died. The market's light was provided by burning effigies that hung from the rafters on the end of nooses made from thick, sturdy rope.

The flames didn't appear to be consuming the figures, and Gina thought it was a clever – if disturbing – special effect. That is, until she saw one twitch a hand. She looked at another, saw its foot kick forward, examined a third, saw it wriggle back and forth, like a burning worm on a hook. Then she heard a sizzling-popping sound, caught the stomach-churning stench of cooking meat, and she knew what she was looking at was real.

She turned to Neal. "Are they alive or–"

"I've never asked. I figure I'm better off not knowing."

She thought that a wise policy.

Stalls filled the Market, so many there was barely room to move between them. The narrow aisles were choked with patrons, far more than could be accounted for by the dozen vehicles parked outside. Neal anticipated her next question.

"There's only one Stygian Market, but it can be accessed from a lot of different places. Some of them *very* different."

A pair of bald-headed, eyebrow-less beings walked past them, both garbed in black tunics, gender indeterminate, looking so alike they might have been clones of each other. In place of eyes, they had smooth patches of skin than pulsed gently in time with their footsteps.

"I see what you mean."

The din of conversation in the market was like an ocean's roar, and they had to shout to hear each other. Gina thought there was a good chance she'd have a hell of a sore throat in the morning if they had to continue yelling like this.

They'd remained by the entrance as they spoke, but now Neal started moving, and Gina hurried to keep up with him. Most of the people they passed appeared normal enough, at least on the outside, although their garb often seemed to belong to a different time. She heard a number of different languages being spoken, some of which she was fluent in – such as Spanish, of course, as well as French and German – and some she recognized but didn't speak – Russian, Japanese, Chinese, Korean, and more. Evidently Neal hadn't been joking when he'd said the Stygian Market could be accessed from many different places.

They saw more people like the eyeless pair that had passed them earlier, although these were less numerous. A trio of people in crimson robes, each with a different alteration to their facial features – fish scales under the eyes, a flattened black bulldog nose, boar tusks jutting upward from the lower jaw – but each with pinky nails painted a deep red.

A woman with writhing snakes in place of fingers. A man wearing only a pair of silver shorts who had extra parts attached to his body – he had three arms, two pairs of ears, a second nose, additional eyes on his shoulders, and a mouth placed on his abdomen.

As Gina walked by, the man ignored her, but the stomach mouth smiled, and said, "How y'doin'?" in a thick New York accent. She shuddered and was glad he didn't stop to talk to her further.

Neal seemed relaxed as they walked, but she'd been around him enough by now to know that he was keeping up his guard. His gaze swept back and forth, taking everything in, alert for any sign of trouble. Gina told herself to quit gawking at everything and to emulate Neal's watchfulness. She was a professional, and she should act as such.

The vendors they passed sold a dizzying and quite often disturbing variety of wares at their stalls. Some of their offerings wouldn't have been out of place at an ordinary flea market – vintage comic books, collectible toys, coin and stamp collections, antique glassware, old videogame systems and cartridges, small home appliances... But there were a number of items of a more esoteric nature, and Neal directed her attention to some of the more interesting ones as they walked.

He pointed to a stall containing jars filled with human teeth.

"Those are dead bites, the teeth of dead people that contain the memories of everything they ever ate. Supposedly if you lick them, you can taste any food the owners ever had in their mouths."

He nodded to a vendor selling what looked like tiny naked people locked in small metal cages.

"Homunculi," Neal said. "They obey your every command – while you're awake. When you sleep, they try to kill you by crawling down your throat and tearing you apart from the inside. So, you need to make sure to lock them in their cages every night."

Gina peered closely at one of the homunculi, and the little bastard flipped her off with both hands.

One vendor sold musical instruments – guitars, violins, lutes, banjos, harps... with barbed wire in place of strings. Another sold grapefruit-sized fruit that resembled human heads, with eyes that blinked at you as you walked by. Yet another sold small canary-like birds sitting placidly on small perches.

"What are those?" she asked.

"Snitchers. Don't get too close to them. They reveal thoughts you want to keep hidden."

"Seriously?"

Without thinking, she stepped closer to the table to get a better look at the birds. A little blue one with a black head fixed its tiny black eyes on her.

"You'll never live up to your family's legacy," it said, the voice sounding self-satisfied and mocking.

Gina stepped back so quickly she bumped into Neal. He put a hand on her shoulder to steady her.

"Told you," he said. "Come on, let's keep going."

Her face burned with embarrassment, and she couldn't bring herself to look at him as they continued walking.

They approached a female mannequin garbed in a gray business jacket and matching skirt. The mannequin didn't appear to be part of a specific display, and now that Gina thought of it, she'd seen similar mannequins, male and female, all dressed in formal business attire, scattered through the Market. The woman's plastic features were cold and immobile, but her eyes seemed alive, and Gina was startled when they moved to focus on her.

"You asked about security," Neal said. "You're looking at it. That's a Manikin." He spelled the word for her. "They keep constant watch over the Market, and if there's any trouble, they deal with it – swiftly and viciously."

Gina had found mannequins creepy ever since she was little, but those living eyes set into an unliving face were a whole new level of disturbing. They continued on, Gina imagining she could feel the weight of the Manikin's gaze on her as they walked away from it.

"So, what are we looking for?" she asked, more to pull her thoughts away from the Manikin than because she wanted the information.

"Information, mostly. And there's where we're going to get it."

He pointed to a stall behind which stood a thin middle-aged man with large round glasses, a pencil-thin mustache, and thinning brown hair. He was dressed in brown suit with a yellow bow tie. He reminded Gina of a small-town librarian, the kind you'd see in an old black-and-white film. The only item on his counter was a thick binder with a single word on the cover: *Essentials*. The man smiled pleasantly as they approached.

"Hey, Creech!" Neal said as they reached the stall. "How's business?"

"Hello, Neal." The man spoke so quietly Gina had to concentrate in order to hear him. "Business has been quite profitable lately, thank you. But then it always is when you sell a product that everyone needs." He tapped the binder to emphasize the word printed on it.

"True enough," Neal said.

Up to this point, the man had ignored Gina, but now he turned to her, his smile broadening.

"And who are you? A friend of Neal's, I assume?"

She wasn't sure how to answer. Officially, she and Neal weren't supposed to be here, and she had the feeling that many, if not most, of the Market's sellers and buyers wouldn't be happy to discover that two Maintenance agents were among them tonight.

"Go ahead and tell him," Neal said. "He knows who I work for."

"I'm Gina Sandoval. I'm Neal's new partner."

"Honored to meet you." He stepped back from his counter and gave her a courtly bow. Performed by anyone else, the gesture might've seemed phony and ridiculous, but he made it seem natural and sincere. When he straightened, he said. "I am Arthur Creech, and it's been my good fortune to sell my wares at the Market for more years than I'd like to admit."

He grinned. He had a mild, easygoing manner, and Gina found herself relaxing around him. After all, how bad of a guy could he be if Neal liked him? Then she noticed a small obsidian pin on his lapel – two clasped hands shaking in greeting. She recognized the pin, had seen similar ones many times before this. She glanced at Neal, started to open her mouth to ask about the pin, but he gave his head an almost unnoticeable shake. The message was clear: the pin wasn't something to talk about, not here and now, anyway.

"Are you by any chance one of *the* Sandovals?" Creech asked.

Gina clenched her jaw. She loved her family, but sometimes she hated being thought of a Sandoval first, instead of as an individual in her own right.

"I am." She quickly changed the subject. "What do you sell?"

"Whatever you need," Creech said, gesturing toward the binder.

"Right. The Essentials. And what exactly does that mean?"

"Take a look," Creech suggested.

Gina glanced at Neal, and when he nodded, she stepped up to the stall's counter and opened the binder. The pages were all laminated, and the first one had a title on it printed in large bold letters: *The Complete Guide to Surviving and Thriving in Maintenance: Everything They Didn't Teach You at the Homestead.*

Surprised – and more than a little intrigued – she started to turn the page. But before she could do so, Creech reached out, gently took the binder from her, and closed it. He then gave her an apologetic smile.

"Alas, my wares aren't free, not even for a friend of a friend."

"Is it real?" Gina asked.

"Oh yes. Neal can vouch for me."

"You can trust him," Neal said. "Creech has the best reputation of any seller in the Market. Everything he sells is exactly what it appears to be."

Creech smiled. "Satisfaction guaranteed."

If the guide was the real deal, Gina was sorely tempted to buy it. She thought of what the snitcher had said to her a few moments ago. *You'll never live up to your family's legacy.* The information Creech's manual contained would decrease her learning curve considerably, giving her a chance to live up to the Sandoval name.

"How much does it cost?" she asked.

Creech considered. "Well, since you *are* a friend of Neal's – not to mention a Sandoval – I suppose I can let you have it for five years."

She frowned. "I don't understand. You mean you'll lend it to me for five years."

Creech laughed. "Goodness, no! It will cost you five years of your life."

She felt a chill on the back of her neck. "You mean that literally, don't you?"

"I do. Whatever the fated length of your lifespan, it will be reduced by five years – if you purchase the information you want."

If this had been anywhere other than the Stygian Market, Gina would've thought the man was joking with her, but she believed he was telling the truth. Even so, she was still tempted. She was young. What was five years to her? If she was destined to live to say, oh, eighty-five, she'd die at eighty instead. That wasn't so bad, was it? Especially if she'd had a long and distinguished career in Maintenance during those eighty years and – most importantly – made her family proud. But what if she was destined to live only seventy-five years? Sixty-five? Fifty-five? Suddenly five years of her life seemed like a steep price to pay. And it went against Maintenance's core belief that maximizing resources and avoiding waste was the best way to slow the inexorable march of Entropy.

"Tempted?" Neal asked.

"Sure, but you know… Flavor to the feast."

He smiled, nodded. "Flavor to the feast," he repeated.

Creech sighed as he placed the binder back on the counter.

"Ah well. Can't win them all, I suppose." He looked at Neal. "How about you, my friend? What can I interest you in tonight?"

"I could really use a Nullifier. Two if you've got them."

"I do indeed."

Creech reached below the counter and brought up a pair of Nullifiers. He placed them on the counter next to the binder.

"Top of the line, never been used," Creech said, smiling.

"Then how do you know they work?" Gina asked.

Creech recoiled as if he'd spit in his face.

"Everything I sell is exactly as advertised!"

Neal smiled at Gina. "Satisfaction guaranteed, remember?"

"Precisely," Creech said.

"Don't mind her," Neal said to Creech. "She's still learning the ropes."

Creech smoothed his hair and adjusted his bow tie to compose himself.

"Of course. No harm done." He smiled. "Is there anything else I can do for you?"

"What do you know about a member of the Multitude operating in Ash Creek?"

Creech's smile fell away and he scowled.

"I was unaware of this. I don't like being unaware of things."

He turned the binder around to face him, opened it, and began flipping through it, increasing speed as he went until the laminated pages flew by at a blur. When he reached the end, he slammed the binder's back cover closed, then turned the book over so its front cover faced up once more.

"I couldn't find anything, not a mention, not a hint, not even a vague *suggestion*. Nothing!"

"Maybe she's used her powers to conceal her identity from you," Gina said.

"You don't understand," Creech said. "When I flipped through the book, it was a detailed history of the Multitude, from their creation to their eventual destruction, with entries on each individual member – deceased, currently living, or yet to be born. There was nothing about any of them ever being present in Ash Creek. Only a handful of the Multitude are powerful enough to block *me* from having knowledge of them. And if one of them has come to your town, Neal, you are – not to put too fine a point on it – in a shitload of trouble."

Neal sighed. "What else is new? Do you have any weapons that are effective against the Multitude – especially really powerful ones?"

Creech gestured to the binder. "Take a look."

Neal began flipping through the binder, and Gina stepped closer so she could see the pages as he turned them. Instead of being a book of information, as it had the last two times, the binder was now a catalogue of strange devices that she'd never heard of, things like gravimetric distorters, E-energy isolators, temporal rippers, etheric retrogressors... texts of forbidden knowledge were listed as well, some of which Gina had learned about during her training at the Homestead – *The Book of Oblivion, The Book of Masks, the Book of Depravity, The Insanitarium*...

Neal looked up at Creech.

"There's some heavy-duty shit in here. Must cost a lot."

"Sadly, yes. Almost everything in that catalogue costs an entire human lifetime, sometimes more."

Gina was horrified by Creech's words.

"Neal, surely you're not considering..."

He smiled. "Relax. I'm not exactly the self-sacrificing type." He turned to Creech. "Is there anything in here we can afford?"

Creech thought for a moment, then he took the binder, and flipped pages back and forth as he searched. When he found what he was looking for, he placed the binder on the counter so Neal and Gina could see. The page displayed a gray metal sphere beneath the words *Expungent Grenade*.

"And this is supposed to be effective against one of the Multitude, let alone one of the most powerful?" Neal asked.

Creech shrugged. "You asked for affordable, and that's what this is."

"How much?"

Before Creech could answer, Gina said, "Let me pay. I'm younger."

Neal smiled. "Thanks, but I've told him about the Multitude member operating in Ash Creek. That was information he didn't know, so it's worth something."

"It'll pay for one of the Nullifiers," Creech said.

"Both," Neal countered.

Creech sighed. "Fine. Both."

"Can we see the grenade?" Neal asked.

Creech reached beneath the counter, brought up a metal sphere the size of a tangerine, and handed it to Neal. Neal held it up to his face to examine it.

Gina wondered exactly where Creech's wares came from. Whatever you wanted, it seemed he always had it within reach. It was a cool trick, but more than a little creepy at the same time.

"Heavier than it looks," he said. "How is it activated?"

"Whoever held it last can set it off telepathically," Creech said.

"How much Expungent does it contain?"

"A hundred gallons, give or take."

Gina looked at the gray metal ball and tried to imagine a hundred gallons of pressurized liquid inside the thing. Maintenance had access to the most advanced technology on the planet, but she didn't think even they had the ability to create such a thing as this grenade. Who'd made it? she wondered.

Neal placed the sphere on the counter next to the binder.

"Exactly how affordable *is* affordable?"

"The price is twenty years of life. For you, I could make it fifteen."

Gina supposed that was better than an entire lifetime, but it was a hell of a price to pay for what was – to her eyes, at least – a particularly unimpressive weapon.

Creech went on. "But I'm afraid I can't take a lifespan portion of payment from you in this situation."

"Why not?" Gina said. She turned to Neal, suddenly uncomfortable. "Not that I *want* you to give up fifteen years of your life..."

"It's because one of the Multitude is involved," Neal said. "The odds that I'll live fifteen more years aren't especially high." He looked at Creech. "Anything you'll take in trade?"

Creech pondered the question for several moments.

"If you come up against this woman and manage to triumph, I want you to come back and tell me everything you learned about her. I *despise* having gaps in my knowledge."

"And once you have the information," Neal said, "you'll be able to find a way to monetize it."

Creech grinned.

"Of course."

Twelve

"What are we going to do with an Expungent grenade?" Gina asked.

Neal carried the device in his front pants pocket. Creech had told them it wouldn't go off unless the last person to touch it – which was him – telepathically willed it, but he couldn't stop thinking about what it would be like if the grenade *did* activate. He kept imagining a hundred gallons of Expungent shooting out of his pocket and flooding the area around them. It was like telling someone not to think of something, say a black cat, but no matter what you did, you couldn't avoid thinking about one. The grenade didn't explode, though, so it appeared he didn't have to keep that tight a rein on his thoughts, which was a relief.

He realized then that Gina had spoken.

"Honestly, I don't know. But it's one more weapon we had than when we came in here."

They were heading toward the exit, but Neal wasn't in a hurry. He kept looking around at the various displays they passed, hoping to find something else that might be useful against one of the Multitude. While it was unlikely that he'd find anything, this *was* the Stygian Market. Just about anything could be bought here. *If* you could find it – and pay the price, of course.

"No offense, Neal, but it seems like our trip here was kind of a waste of time. We didn't learn anything we didn't already know, and we've got a weapon that we're not sure is going to really *do* anything – at least against one of the Multitude."

Neal was surprised to find himself feeling like he'd let Gina down. He'd hoped that at least she'd be impressed by the Stygian Market, and maybe she was, but if so, it wasn't enough to offset her disappointment at how their shopping trip had turned out.

"We *did* get a couple Nullifiers, too," he pointed out.

Neal carried his tucked into his right sock, hidden by his pants leg. Gina had concealed hers the same way, but he knew she wasn't comfortable having a Nullifier since she wasn't officially authorized to carry one.

When Gina didn't reply, he went on.

"Creech didn't know anything about the woman from the Multitude, and Creech knows *everything*. She must be extraordinarily powerful, even for one of her kind, in order to conceal her presence and activities from him."

"It's strange that she would go to such lengths to hide herself when she's been operating so openly in Ash Creek," Gina said. "Aren't the Multitude supposed to work in secret for the most part, just like we do?"

"Yes. The woman we're up against is likely a rogue, acting on her own, and that makes her doubly dangerous. The Multitude prefer to operate with a certain amount of restraint, but this woman doesn't seem to have any."

"When we were talking with Creech, why didn't you want me to ask him about the pin he wearing?" Gina asked.

Damn it! Neal had hoped she'd forgotten about that.

"I don't remember you saying anything about a pin. I don't even remember noticing Creech was wearing one."

"You noticed, and when you saw me looking at it, you gave a slight shake of your head, like you were telling me not to bring it up. So, I stayed quiet about it while we were talking with Creech. But now I want to know why it's such a big deal that you didn't want me even mentioning it to him."

Neal didn't answer right away. He was stalling for time so he could figure out how to tell her the truth without telling her too much of it. While he thought, she continued talking.

"I've seen my mom and dad wear the same pin. Not all the time, but sometimes when they went out to have drinks or dinner with friends. My sister and brother have the same pins too. Once during my training at the Homestead, I asked Dad why I didn't have one. He said I needed to graduate and work for a few years first, then – if I proved myself ready – I'd learn what the pins were for and be given one of my own. So what hell are they? And why don't you want to talk about them?"

"Are you *sure* your family's pins are the same kind Creech has?"

"*Neal...*"

"Okay, fine." He looked around to make sure no one was listening, and when he spoke, he kept his voice quiet. "The pin Creech was wearing identifies him as a member of the Black Trust. Members usually only wear it when they get together in private, but here it lets customers know they're dealing with someone vouched for by the Trust. It lends credibility."

"That's why the hands are shaking, isn't it? They're showing trust."

Neal nodded. "At the Homestead, we were taught that the Black Trust doesn't ally itself with either Maintenance or the Multitude, that they only care about themselves and whatever pleasures they can grab hold of while they live. Is that true? And if it is, does that mean *my* family wears those pins because *they* belong to the Black Trust?"

Neal knew he had to tread carefully here.

"In many ways the Trust is like an exclusive club. Its members are ruthless businesspeople who come from different backgrounds, all united in a single purpose: to squeeze as much money and power out of existence as they can before the Gyre finally swallows everything in the end. They'll do anything to get what they what, and they never, ever play fair."

"So, you're saying my family are what? *Mobsters* and *spies?*"

Yes, I am, Neal thought.

"Of course not. Most likely they were doing some deep undercover work for Maintenance, and they just *pretended* to belong to the Black Trust."

Gina's eyes shone wetly and Neal knew she was fighting tears. "Do you really believe that?"

Neal didn't want to lie to her, but he didn't want to hurt her, either, so he was almost relieved when three sinister-looking individuals stepped into their path before he had time to answer Gina's question.

The first was a tall lean figure garbed in a black hat and black trench coat, face and hands formed of living shadow, glowing yellow eyes set in a dark featureless face.

The second was short and stocky, thickly muscled body covered with bristly hair. It possessed porcine features – broad flat nose, beady pig eyes, floppy pig ears, and it wore dirty ragged overalls, no shoes on its hooved feet.

The third was a pale yellowish-white blob that only vaguely resembled a human. It had no fingers or toes, its limbs ending in rounded-off stumps. It was naked – not that it mattered, as it didn't have any apparent genitals to cover – and there was only a suggestion of features on its lumpy face, shallow depressions where eyes, nose, and a mouth might've been.

Trench Coat stepped forward and spoke, a man's voice issuing from somewhere in the shadowy mass that served as a face.

"A good evening to you both. My name is Grimwell, and these are my associates, Squeal and Jane Dough."

He gestured to his companions, and they inclined their heads in silent greeting.

"Jane Doe?" Neal said, and then it came to him. "Oh, Jane *Dough*. I get it. Very cute."

Jane Dough's hands formed five-fingered fists, as if his comment angered her, but otherwise she didn't react. Grimwell went on as if Neal hadn't spoken.

"The three of us are entrepreneurs, and we have a business proposition for you."

"Whatever it is, we're not interested," Neal said. "So, if you don't mind..."

He tried to step past the three, but they spread out to block his path.

Grimwell reached into one of his coat pockets and removed an object formed from pieces of bone bound by leathery strips of dried muscle. It was a gun of some kind, and the shadow-faced man leveled it at Neal and Gina.

"I really must insist that you hear us out," Grimwell said.

Neal had never seen a weapon like this before, but he had no doubt it would prove just as deadly as a normal gun, likely more so.

"I suppose it wouldn't do us any harm to listen," he said.

Grimwell's yellow eyes blazed brighter, and there was a smile in his voice as he replied.

"Excellent! We were standing close to Creech's stall when the two of you spoke with him, and we couldn't help overhearing."

Neal didn't recall seeing these three nearby when he and Gina had spoken with Creech, but his attention had been fully focused on the man at the time, so it was no surprise he hadn't noticed them, especially with so many other strange patrons in the Market.

Squeal spoke for the first time then, her voice so low it was almost a growl. Her pig eyes focused on Gina, and she said, "You're a Sandoval."

A line appeared on the bottom half of Jane Dough's face, and it opened, revealing itself as a rudimentary mouth. Her voice was thick and wet, as if she spoke through a mouthful of pancake batter.

"One of *the* Sandovals."

Gina sighed softly, and for the first time Neal wondered what it must have been like for her to grow up bearing the Sandoval name. He remembered what the snitcher bird had said to her. *You'll never live up to your family's legacy.*

Grimwell spoke next. "Word is that your family has money."

"A lot of it," Squeal added, grinning to reveal sharp yellowed teeth.

"A whole *big* lot," Jane Dough said.

"We inherited it," Gina said, sounding more than a little defensive.

"You work for Maintenance, yes?" Grimwell said. "Your outfit gives you away, I'm afraid. Your organization is known for its ascetic ethos, is it not? It seems contradictory – if not hypocritical – for your family to hold on to its fortune, regardless of how it came by its money."

"We can help with that," Squeal said.

"By relieving your family of its financial burden," Jane Dough added.

"And how do you think you're going to get the money?" Gina said. "Ask my family politely?

"No," Grimwell said, all trace of good humor gone from his tone. "We intend to abduct you and demand a ransom for your return."

"A *significant* ransom," Squeal said.

"*Monumental*," Jane Dough added.

"We intend to make a significant dent in the Sandoval bank account," Grimwell said, "although not enough to plunge your family into complete financial ruin. We're businesspeople, not monsters. Now, if you'll accompany us, we'll get started. The sooner we begin, the sooner the matter can be settled to the satisfaction of all parties, and we can all go on with our lives."

Now it was Neal's turn to sigh. He looked at Gina.

"This is why I wish Maintenance let us carry actual guns."

He quickly glanced around at the tables nearest them to see what he had to work with. Three displays were within arm's reach, each offering very different wares. A collection of life-sized crystalline organs, rows of clay jars with strange runes etched on their sides, and stacks of ancient books, leather covers edged with gleaming metal.

He decided to start with the organs.

His hand darted out to his right and took hold of a crystal heart. Despite its appearance, it was soft and warm, and beat in his grasp like the real thing – *lub-dub, lub-dub*. He felt an instant wave of disgust, accompanied by an almost overpowering urge to hurl the damn thing to the floor. But he fought the impulse and instead threw the heart toward Grimwell, or rather, toward the bone gun held in the would-be kidnapper's shadowy hand. The heart struck the gun dead on, the impact snapping the strips of dried muscle that served as bindings, causing bone pieces to break away from each other and fly through the air, leaving Grimwell holding only the weapon's hard white handle.

Neal didn't intend to give Grimwell or his two companions time to react. He reached out to his left, and his hand found one of the rune-covered clay jars. The booth's proprietor shouted in protest, but Neal ignored him and threw the jar at Squeal. The pig-woman's reflexes were faster than Grimwell's, and she swiftly turned to the side in order to make herself a smaller target – not that it did her any good. Neal hadn't been aiming for her body, but rather at the floor near her feet.

He had no idea what the jar might contain – the runes on its surface were incomprehensible to him – and he hoped he hadn't just attacked Squeal with a jar full of dried herbs or something equally as ineffective. The jar shattered, releasing a mass of white mist that quickly separated into a half dozen small wraith-like beings.

They began circling Squeal, slowly at first, then with increasing speed. Intense cold emanated from the wraiths, and Squeal began shivering violently. She tried batting the wraiths away, but her hands passed through them harmlessly, and they continued swirling around her. Some kind of elementals, Neal thought. Powerful ones, too.

While the bulk of the elementals' power was focused on Squeal, the temperature around them all dropped swiftly, and they began shivering. How far would this cold spread? Neal wondered. Would it come to fill the entire Market, the air becoming so frigid that eventually everyone present froze solid? He hoped not. Talk about the cure being worse than the disease!

Gina had been caught off guard by Neal's actions, but once she realized what he was doing, she stepped in to do her part. She grabbed a pair of ancient tomes from the book display, and hurled them like shuriken at Jane Dough, first one, then the other. But instead of striking the blob-woman, the books took to the air, their covers flapping like birds' wings. Neal feared the books would simply fly away, maybe toward the exit and the freedom that awaited beyond. Instead, they flew toward Jane Dough and began circling her, just as the cold elementals had done to Squeal. They flew so close that the metal edges of their covers – which were razor sharp – sliced through Jane's skin, or whatever the surface of her body was made out of. Wounds opened, much like the line that had appeared on her face to become a mouth. But blood – crimson and thick like syrup – oozed from the injuries, and Jane cried out, half in pain, half in fury.

Neal grinned. This was working better than he'd hoped. If he and Gina hauled ass, there was a decent chance they'd get away unscathed. He grabbed hold of Gina's hand, intending to lead her toward the exit.

But before they could take a single step, Grimwell stretched out his hands, one toward Squeal, the other toward Jane Dough.

His shadowy fingers grew, lengthening into long tendrils that snatched the flying books out of the air, and – despite Squeal's inability to touch them – grabbed hold of the wraiths. The fingers withdrew, pulling the wraiths and the flying books toward Grimwell. The shadow hands retracted into Grimwell's sleeves, bearing the books and wraiths with them. A moment later, the hands emerged from the sleeves to return to their rightful place, only now they were empty.

Grimwell fixed his glowing yellow gaze on Neal.

"Nice try, but did you really think that would stop us?"

"I wasn't trying to stop you," Neal said. "I was trying to do this."

Nothing happened for an instant, and then the proprietors of the three displays Neal and Gina had taken objects from began shouting.

"Thieves!"

"Vandals!"

And then the one word Neal was hoping to hear.

"*Security!*"

A pair of nearby Manikins – one male, one female – swiveled their heads toward the disturbance. Their immobile features showed no expression, but their eyes turned a baleful red, sharp metal spikes slid out of their fingers, and their mouths opened wide to reveal twin rows of serrated metal teeth. With a whirring sound, the teeth began sliding sideways, moving faster and faster, as if the Manikins had twin buzzsaws installed in their heads.

Vendors and customers in the vicinity shouted in alarm and fled, knocking over displays and each other in their panic. The Manikins ignored them as they strode purposely toward Neal, Gina, and the trio of would-be kidnappers, clawed hands raised, teeth saws spinning away.

Grimwell, Squeal, and Jane Dough looked at the oncoming Manikins with undisguised fear, and Grimwell spoke for all of them when he said, "Oh shit."

The three fled, running in opposite directions. The instant they started running, the two Manikins coming toward them released deafening shrieks, alerting other Mannikins in the area. These came to life – red-eyed, clawed, and saw-toothed – and began pursuing the kidnappers. The first two Mannikins didn't join the others, and instead continued toward Neal and Gina, running now as if they thought the two humans would also attempt to escape them.

Gina's eyes shone with terror, but she held her ground, and Neal was impressed. If a couple Manikins had come running toward him when he'd been a rookie, he would've probably soiled his pants and start running in a blind panic. That, or freeze in place, unable to move, just standing there until the Manikins reached him and began tearing him to pieces.

"Nullifiers?" Gina said, her voice shaking slightly.

"Useless. The Manikins aren't Corrupted."

Neal did his best to project a calm that he did not feel, partially to put up a front for the Manikins, but also to try and reassure Gina that he knew what he was doing and wasn't desperately making things up as he went along. As the Manikins approached, Neal removed his wallet from his back pocket, flipped it open, and held it out before him, showing a white card held within a clear plastic insert. Except for a tiny lowercase black *m* in the middle, the card was blank.

The Manikins didn't slow as they drew near, and Neal thought his ploy wasn't going to work. But at the last moment the Manikins came to a sudden stop less than three feet from him and Gina, claws out, teeth whirring, eyes blazing red.

Neal's mouth was desert-dry as he spoke.

"My partner and I apologize for the disruption in commerce. Please bill Maintenance Control for any damages."

The Manikins remained absolutely still, then their eyes returned to normal, claws retracted, teeth slowed. When their tooth-saws stopped, the Manikins' mouths closed, and they stood there, motionless and serene.

Neal let out a breath he hadn't realized he'd been holding. He closed his wallet and returned it to his pants pocket.

"I think I'd like to go home now," Gina said.

"Me too."

They turned and slowly began making their way through the Market toward the exit, everyone giving them a wide berth, just in case the Manikins should change their minds and come after them again.

"Do you think they'll get away?" Gina asked. "Grimwell and his friends?"

High-pitched screams of agony cut through the air.

"No," Neal said.

Neither he nor Gina looked back as they departed.

Thirteen

It had been slow night for business – at least for Paul Romero – so when he saw the white Mercedes Benz pull into the parking lot of American Travel Center, he felt a surge of hope. Sure, the driver might be pulling off the highway to gas up, maybe get a cup of coffee to help him stay awake. But ATC wasn't a modern travel center, the kind of place where everything was well-lit, clean and inviting, with a dozen gas pumps outside, and inside anything that a weary traveler could want, from soda, water, and beer to prepackaged snacks to CD's, DVD's, rotisserie hotdogs, and a do-it-yourself coffee bar where you could make lattes and cappuccinos. ATC was a dump.

Two gas pumps – one of which was usually out of order – in a dimly-lit parking lot, a small building no larger than a basic convenience store, with a limited number of items for sale. The snacks were usually stale, the milk sour, and the coffee tasted like battery acid. No movies or music for sale, but there was a decent selection of porno magazines. Paul's favorite was *Cum-Covered Jugs*.

To say that ATC was not the kind of place that owners of expensive cars normally patronized was an understatement. They preferred to stop at the Pilot a couple exits farther down the highway. Most people who came to ATC didn't come for the overpriced gas or the meager supply of shitty products on the store's shelves. They came because of the other wares on offer, far darker ones sold in the thickest shadows of ATC's parking lot.

Sold by people like him.

Paul stood on the short walkway in front of the store, leaning against a brick wall, smoking his thirteenth cigarette of the day. He held a Styrofoam cup of lukewarm coffee in his other hand, but he'd only managed to choke down a couple sips so far.

As he watched the Mercedes pull up to one of the gas pumps – miracle of miracles, both of them were working tonight – he heard a bell tinkle as someone exited the store. He kept his gaze fixed on the car as Sunny walked over and stood next to him.

"What do you think? We got ourselves a live one?"

She nodded toward the Mercedes. The driver got out, and Paul saw that it was a middle-aged man, balding and paunchy, wearing a blue windbreaker.

"Could be." He took a drag on his cigarette, exhaled the smoke slowly.

Sunny Flowers – he'd never asked if that was her real name, and honestly, he didn't care – was in her late twenties, but she looked ten years older. She was skinny, almost to the point of appearing malnourished, and she wore too much makeup to try to make herself seem younger. Paul thought she looked like an emaciated clown, especially given the red wig she always wore. She did have a nice pair of tits, though, he had to give her that. On the smallish side, maybe, but proportionate to her body. The night air was chilly, but Sunny wore only a halter top and tight, skimpy shorts, the kind that showed a little ass cheek, and chunky heeled open-toed sandals. She had to be freezing, but she held a large cherry slushy and sipped from the straw as they both watched the Mercedes' owner fuel his vehicle.

Paul wore a long-sleeved flannel shirt untucked, jeans, and cowboy boots, and he wished he'd brought a jacket with him tonight. A hat, too. He didn't know how Sunny could stand the cold dressed like she was. Had she grown up in goddamned Alaska or something?

Now that Sunny had come out, the only person left in the store was Brett Hale, ATC's owner and proprietor, a man so old Paul wouldn't have been surprised if he was nearing his second century. Brett didn't approve of the underground entrepreneurs like Paul and Sunny who conducted their business on his premises, but they all paid weekly "rent" to him, so he ultimately didn't give a fuck what they did, as long as they left him out of it.

The driver of the Benz was the only person at the pumps, but the parking lot was far from deserted. Cars, pickups, and vans – a dozen or so vehicles altogether – were spread throughout the lot, with at least one empty space between them. One of the vans, a copper-colored one, belonged to Paul, and Sonny's was an old Chevy that, although it had seen better days, was still in fairly decent shape. The other vehicles weren't empty, though. Only Paul and Sunny were stupid enough to stand outside in the cold.

Tonight, their associates were working from inside their transport, selling whatever goods and services they specialized in, primarily drugs and sex. Paul would've been in his van if he hadn't seen Sonny finish up with a customer, get out of the man's car, and go inside the store to use the women's restroom to wash up a little. His night had been slow so far, and he thought he might ask her if she'd give him a discount on a hand job, seeing how they were essentially co-workers and all. But now that the driver of the Benz had shown up, Paul had forgotten all about getting jerked off by Sunny.

No one stumbled on ATC's open-air sin market by accident. The people who came here did so because they'd heard about it during conversations with past customers, either face to face in dive bars and crack houses or in chat rooms on the dark web. They came to buy, and they knew exactly what they were looking for.

The Benz's driver finished gassing up and paid at the pump with a card. The next few moments would tell the tale.

"Wanna make a bet?" Sunny asked. "Twenty says he doesn't like the look of this place, so he gets back in his car, hits the highway, and never looks back."

Twenty would be enough to get him that hand job he'd been contemplating.

"You're on. I think he'll stay, although I don't know what he came for yet."

The driver did climb into his Benz, start the engine, and turn on his headlights. The car started moving, but instead of curving around the gas pumps and heading onto the street, the man drove slowly toward an empty parking space, pulled in, and killed the engine and lights.

Paul grinned at Sunny. "Pay up."

Sunny sighed, "Take it out in trade?"

His grin widened. "I hoped you'd say that. But later, okay? Let's see what he does next."

When the man stepped out of his car again, Paul could feel the atmosphere in the parking lot change from alert watchfulness to predatory anticipation. He was certain everyone had been keeping eyes on the man since he pulled up to the pumps, but now he'd *parked*, and that meant he could be a potential customer for any of them.

Car windows rolled down, and several people – young women, mostly, but a few guys, all of whom were Sunny's competition – stepped out of their vehicles to give the driver a look at what was on the menu tonight. Paul felt an urge to go over and stand next to his van, but he resisted it. The man didn't *seem* like a cop, but given the special nature of what Paul sold, he preferred not to take any chances. Cops might ignore pushers and prostitutes. They might buy or rent their wares or demand "a small fee" to ensure they looked the other way, but they usually didn't bust them, not here, anyway. But it would be a rare cop indeed who could overlook what Paul had stored in his van.

The man walked a few yards from his car, then stopped and looked around, as if unsure how to find what he'd come here for. People began to call out to him, trying to attract his attention.

"Make you cum so hard, it'll take a week for your balls to fill up again!"

"Got some absolutely mind-blowing shit. I'm serious, man, it'll help you see motherfucking God!"

"I got pills that'll make your pecker so hard you could use it to drill through a goddamn brick wall!"

A couple of the more aggressive girls – both, like Sunny barely dressed – hurried over to the man. One slid her arm around his waist while the other decided to get right to the point and started massaging his crotch. They both spoke to him, so quietly that Paul couldn't hear their words, but he didn't need to. He'd heard their sales pitches, or ones like them, a hundred times before.

Sunny laughed softly.

"He's not interested, but those kids are too dumb to realize it."

Sure enough, the man pushed the girls away from him, gently but firmly. He said something to them, and with twin looks of disgust, they pointed toward the store – toward Paul and Sunny.

The man started walking toward them, and when his back was turned to the girls, they flipped him off. The girls headed back to their cars, and Paul and Sunny watched the man approach.

"You or me?" Paul said.

"You. I can tell by the look on his face. He doesn't want sex – he's hungry for something else. See you later."

Sunny stepped off the walkway and headed toward her car. The man didn't so much glance at her as she departed. He kept his gaze fixed solely on Paul. For his part, Paul tried to look cool and unconcerned, but inside he seethed with excitement. He hadn't made a sale in over a week, and the current item he had in his van – fresh when he procured it – was starting to look a little wilted. That didn't mean he couldn't sell it, course. He'd sold plenty of items in far worse condition. But in his line of work, if you wanted to get top dollar, the fresher the product, the better.

The man stepped onto the walkway and stood next to Paul, close enough that they could talk without being overheard, but not so close that he couldn't make a run for it if Paul tried to attack him. A sensible precaution.

"I heard there's no security cameras here," the man said.

"You heard right. The people who... *shop* here would rather not have their visits recorded, you know?"

"I do. So are you, uh..." The man looked around quickly, then spoke in a whisper. "The Grabber Man?"

Paul had to fight to keep from rolling his eyes. He had no idea where the dumbass nickname had come from, but that's how most of his customers referred to him. Probably some fucker on the dark web had called him that in a post, and the name caught on. Sunny once told him she thought it made him sound scary, like he was some boogeyman out of an urban legend. Paul thought it made him sound like some kind of idiotic kids' toy.

Let's go, Grabber Man! We have to save the world! Out of all the people who plied their trade at ATC, only Sunny called him Paul. Everyone else called him *The Grabber Man* or sometimes just plain *Grabber.* He supposed it was a better nom de crime than he could've come up with on his own, and if it helped draw customers to him, he could live with it. That didn't mean he had to like it, though.

"Yeah."

"And is it true what they say... about what you sell, I mean."

"It is indeed. Come with me."

Paul stepped off the walkway, and after a moment's hesitation, the man followed. Paul hadn't asked his name, and he didn't intend to. In his business, it was better to avoid using names. When they reached the back of the van, Paul stopped and turned toward his customer.

"Before I let you take a look, I want to make sure we're clear on the price. One thousand, and it's not negotiable."

Paul lied about that last part. In business, everything was negotiable, but he didn't want this guy to know that.

"No problem." The man didn't look at Paul as he spoke. His gaze was fixed firmly on the van's rear door. Despite the coolness of the night, beads of sweat had formed on the man's forehead.

Paul mentally kicked himself for only asking for a thousand. As excited as this guy was, he probably would've agreed to pay twice that, maybe more.

"Let's take a look and see what you think."

Paul reached into his front pants pocket, removed the van's key remote, and pressed a button. The door clicked open and then began to rise. Paul liked this bit, the slow reveal. It added a little showmanship to the proceedings.

Paul always parked in an unlit space – the kind of transactions he engaged in needed to take place in darkness – but he carried a flashlight in his back pocket. He returned his keys to his front pocket, removed the flashlight, turned it on, and shined its beam into the back of the van. A preteen girl lay on the floor, hands and feet bound with zip ties, a ball gag in her mouth. Her brown hair was pulled back in a ponytail, and she wore a T-shirt and shorts, no shoes. At first her eyes were closed, but she opened them when the light hit her face. She blinked slowly, then squinted, as if she was having trouble getting her vision to focus.

"I keep them drugged," Paul said. "Makes things easier. She got her last dose a couple hours ago, so she should stay groggy until you get her wherever you plan to take her."

He had no idea what the man intended to do with the girl, and he honestly didn't care. Some of his customers took the kids home and kept them for a while so they could play with them at their leisure. Others couldn't contain themselves and used and disposed of them almost immediately. The kids he abducted were only commodities to him, and once he got paid, they ceased to exist for him. As far as he was concerned, they'd fulfilled their purpose in life, which was to add money to his bank account.

"Like what you see?" Paul asked.

"Yes. Very much."

The man spoke in a hoarse whisper, and Paul thought he was going to splooge in his pants right then and there.

"What's her name?" the man asked.

Paul had no idea. She was just some kid who'd been unlucky enough to meet the Grabber Man while riding her bike on a sideway in a suburban neighborhood.

"Her name is whatever you want it to be. If you want her – and it seems like you do – all I'll need is the money. Once that's taken care of, you pull your car over here, we load her up, and you're on your way. Sound good?"

The man didn't answer. He kept looking at the girl.

"I think I'll call her Sarah... Sarah Smile, like in the old Hall and Oates song?"

Paul didn't know the tune, but he said, "Yeah, sure. Sounds good."

They both fell silent after that, and Paul knew The Moment had arrived. This was the part of the transaction when he learned what his customer was going to do: buy the merchandise, pussy out and leave, or draw a weapon and attempt to get what he wanted without paying. Paul carried a 9mm between his pants and the small of his back, concealed by his untucked shirt. He reached around now and took hold of the grip, ready to draw the weapon and fire if he had to. His pulse sped up as he waited. He liked this part – everything teetering on the edge, no way to know which way it would ultimately fall. It was a rush better than any drug or any sex he'd ever had.

The man continued staring at the girl, dark desire dancing in his eyes. Finally, he reached into his front pocket and pulled out a number of bills. Paul's business was strictly cash only. Paul let out a slow breath, removed his hand from the gun, took the money from the man, and quickly counted it. One thousand dollars exactly. He folded the bills and tucked them into his front pocket.

"Like I said, pull your car over here, and we'll–"

"One last thing." The man turned toward him, an apologetic expression on his face. "I hate to ask this, but she's... I mean, you haven't..."

Paul knew what the guy was trying to say.

"I can't promise you that she's pure as the driven snow, but I haven't done anything to her."

It was true – at least in this case. Paul wasn't above sampling his wares from time to time, and occasionally he'd keep one for his own private pleasure, holding onto them for days, even weeks, before tiring and disposing of them. But he was running low on money this month, and he really needed to sell this one.

"Good, good." The man sounded relieved. He clapped his hands together and rubbed them vigorously. "Okay, let's do this. I'll go get my car."

Paul turned off the flashlight and tucked it into his back pocket.

"You do that."

The man started walking away from the van, but before he got more than a few yards, an SUV approached the travel center, headlights slicing through the night like a pair of high-intensity lasers. The vehicle slowed, pulled into the lot, and then stopped, as if the driver wanted to take a look around before selecting a place to park.

As they had when Paul's customer had arrived, prostitutes – including Sunny – stepped out of their vehicles to show themselves off, and drug dealers called out their sales pitches. The SUV remained where it was a moment, then it began to slowly edge forward, heading directly for Paul.

Just his fucking luck. It had been days since he had a customer, and now he had two in one night – and he'd already sold his one and only item. Maybe he could get the driver of the SUV to agree to return in a couple days so he had a chance to resupply. He could even find out what exactly the driver was looking for, and then he could shop around and see if he could find a match. He felt confident in his ability to do so. He was the Grabber Man, wasn't he?

He turned to his current customer. The man looked nervous, and Paul knew he wouldn't want to complete their transaction while the SUV was present. What if the driver was a cop?

"Go wait in your car," Paul said. "I'll talk to them and see what they want. When they leave, you and I can finish up. All right?"

The man nodded and hurried across the parking lot toward his Benz, looking down at the ground, trying his best to hide his face from the newcomer. When the man was safely inside his vehicle, Paul started toward the SUV. As he drew near, he saw three people sitting in the front seat – a man and a woman in their thirties, and between them a girl no older than the one bound and gagged in the back of his van. Had this couple come to sell instead of buy? It wasn't common, but it did happen sometimes.

The driver's side window lowered as paul approached, and the driver leaned his head out and spoke in a cheerful voice.

"I've heard about this place, but I've never been here. I run a construction company, and sometimes the guys talk about ATC and the things you can get there. Before tonight, I thought they were lying, or at least exaggerating. But now that I'm actually here it looks like this place is everything my employees said it was – and more." The man sniffed the air like a dog, then grinned. "There's so much Corruption, the air absolutely *reeks* with the stench of it."

Alarm bells started going off for Paul. There was something more than a little strange about this guy, and while he didn't know what it was, he knew he wanted no part of it.

"Whatever you heard about this place, you're not welcome here. Leave, before things get ugly."

His right hand twitched with the urge to draw his gun, but he resisted the impulse. He had no idea if the man was armed, and he didn't want to turn the parking lot into a shooting gallery unless he had other choice. He took a quick glance around to see what the others were doing, and he wasn't surprised to see that the prostitutes had gotten back into their cars, and everyone else had rolled up their windows. He imagined people hunkering down in their seats in case bullets started flying, and as angry as he was that no one intended to help him, he couldn't blame them. He'd have done the same thing if their roles had been reversed.

His customer had gotten into his Benz and was hiding, too, although he hadn't started the car yet. Paul guessed the man wanted the girl too badly to leave unless serious trouble started. Besides, he'd already paid for the bitch, hadn't he? He wouldn't want to lose her, not unless he had no choice.

The driver of the SUV opened the vehicle's door and stepped out. He didn't close the door behind him, and he'd left the SUV running. The passenger side door opened then, and the woman got out, followed by the preteen girl. None of them appeared to be carrying weapons, but they still exuded an aura of danger, and Paul instinctively recognized them as a threat.

I should go. Right now.

He almost did, almost turned and ran like hell. But he stayed where he was. These three looked like a stereotypical suburban family. Why should he be afraid of them? He was the goddamn Grabber Man! He was a motherfucking *monster!* These fuckers should be scared of *him!*

He drew his gun and pointed it at the SUV's driver, surprised to see how badly his hand shook.

"I'm warning you... Come closer and I'll shoot. That goes for the girl, too. I've killed kids before, and I'll do it again if I have to."

The woman... no, the *mother* grinned and clapped her hands in delight.

"You were right, Carlton. This *is* the perfect place to find we what need. *He's* perfect."

The little girl, the *daughter*, spoke next, smile growing wider with each word.

"His soul is a gangrenous wound, a cluster of swollen tumors, a mountain of shit and piss drenched in poisoned blood..."

The daughter frightened Paul far more than her parents did. Who the hell talked like that, especially a kid?

The family had walked toward him as they spoke, spreading out as they came. Paul wasn't sure who to aim at, so he moved his gun from mother to daughter to father. Still, they came, seemingly unconcerned that Paul held death in his hand. They didn't even look at the gun, kept their gazes fixed on his eyes instead.

"I. Will. Shoot."

"Sounds like he's trying to convince himself, doesn't it?" the father said.

"Let him try," the mother said.

"He might manage to hit one of us," the girl said, "but not all three."

The family rushed toward Paul then, teeth bared, hands stretched out before them, fingers curled like claws.

He fired.

Fourteen

Rachel was too anxious to wait at home for the Stricklands to return with the next ingredient, so she remained at the cemetery and passed the time by telepathically exploring the shriveled brains of the interred. She examined the memories they were most ashamed of – not simple everyday incidents of embarrassment or guilt, but deep, soul-twisting events that made them wish they'd never existed. In these scenarios they were victims or perpetrators. More rarely, they were sometimes both.

Rachel had never laughed so much in her life.

She was enjoying herself thoroughly and was actually a bit disappointed when the Stricklands' SUV pulled into the cemetery. Still, there was a time to play and a time to work. She walked to the mausoleum and met the Stricklands there.

"Did you get it?" Rachel asked.

"In the back," Carlton said.

Rachel walked to the rear of the SUV, waved a hand, and the liftgate opened. The rear seat of the vehicle had been folded down to make more storage room for the man lying there. He was quite alive, struggling against the silver duct tape binding his wrists and ankles. He was trying to shout, too, but the tape over his mouth muffled his voice, so all that came out was a wordless *mm-mm-mmm*.

LikeCarlton, the man's eyes were wide, but his were filled with terror. His left temple was swollen and bruised, and a thin line of blood ran from the wound down past his ear. But none of these details mattered to Rachel compared to the overwhelming aura of Corruption radiating from the man. It was so strong that it actually knocked her back a step, and she felt dizzy, as if lightly drunk.

Molly, Carlton, and Judith joined her at the rear of the vehicle.

"Did we do good, Ms. Blackburn?" Molly asked. "I mean, did we do well?"

"Yes, you did *very* well."

Curious about her new captive, Rachel reached into his mind and sifted through his thoughts and memories. She pleased to discover that he was just as depraved as his aura indicated. He would make an excellent addition to the Atrocity Engine. But there was one thing...

She turned to the Stricklands.

"He keeps wondering what happened to the girl in his van."

Carlton smiled. "We found her, and then we used the man's gun to shoot her in the head."

"It seemed the only humane thing to do," Judith added.

"I suppose so," Rachel said. "All right you three, let's get our new friend installed in the mausoleum. When we're finished, I want you to get back on the road and start searching for the third ingredient: a soul that perfectly embodies the essence of Life."

By the time the Stricklands left the cemetery, Paul Romero had been reduced to a malodorous black mass of sludge that covered the floor of the mausoleum. The substance was Corruption in its basest form, and the inside-out abomination that had been a pregnant woman named Brianne writhed in agony as the black muck began to slowly crawl up the exposed muscles of her legs. Rachel nodded with satisfaction, then closed the mausoleum door with a sharp hand gesture.

It would be hours before the Corruption had suffused every cell in the woman's body, but the process had gotten off to a good start. Well, *almost* every cell. The child she carried would remain untouched by the Corruption that claimed its mother – for now, at least. The baby needed to be pure and unharmed for the activation of the Atrocity Engine to succeed.

Rachel had ceased being a normal human the moment Brother Nothing had taken her away to be trained for the Multitude. She didn't need to sustain her physical form with food or drink. She didn't even need to breathe if she didn't want to. She had no need of sleep, either, but while her body didn't grow tired, her mind did, especially when she'd been using her powers a great deal, as she had in the last couple days.

Once she reached Brother Nothing's level of power, she would have no weaknesses. But right now, going home and lying on her bed for several hours – not sleeping, but resting – sounded good. She was about to open a Rift to her apartment when she heard the sound of a car approaching. Had Molly and Judith found the third ingredient this fast? No, the vehicle didn't sound like their SUV. The engine was louder, more powerful.

She saw headlights approach the cemetery entrance, and she waited to see who it was that felt the need to visit Oak Grove Cemetery so late at night. Someone with a day job who had no time to come here during the day? Maybe, but that didn't *feel* right.

A moment later, a red Camero entered the cemetery, and Rachel could sense the presence of her two new servants in the vehicle. Royce sat behind the wheel, and he drove recklessly through the cemetery, the Camero's ties edging off the access road at times and churning up grass and soil. Despite the Multitude's absolute devotion to Entropy, she found Royce's carelessness distasteful. Hastening the end of existence was one thing, but there was no need to be so barbaric about it.

Royce parked the Camero near the mausoleum, front tires on the grass, of course, and then he and Sabrina stepped out. Their eyes were pools of seething shadow, and their hands crackled with dark lightning.

She smiled as the pair walked toward her.

"It's about time you two got here."

—

Gina sat on the couch in her living room, dressed in her coziest pair of pajamas, hands wrapped around a mug of warm milk. She hadn't drunk any of it yet, but she found the temperature soothing. The 85-inch flat screen TV on the wall was tuned to a nature documentary on cheetahs, sound muted, closed captions on. It was late, and she didn't want the television's noise to disturb the neighbors. She was too lost in thought to pay much attention to the program, though.

After leaving the Stygian Market, Gina drove Neal back to this place. Before he got out of her car, he asked if she was doing all right, and she assured him she was. They said goodnight, and she drove off, heading to her condo to catch what sleep she could before having to report for work in the morning. Gina was too wired from the evening's events to sleep, though, so here she was, wide awake, staring at the television screen, trying not to think about how much it had cost.

After seeing Neal's apartment earlier that evening, she felt ashamed of her condo and its nice furnishings, and she wished she hadn't let her parents purchase them for her. She understood her parents' philosophy about how living comfortably in your off hours helped you recharge for the next day's work, making you a better agent overall. Hadn't she lived that way her entire life up until the day she went to the Homestead to begin her training? She'd believed it too, even after she graduated, but now – after knowing Neal for even a short time – she was beginning to suspect her parents' philosophy was self-serving bullshit.

The visit to the Stygian Market had been eye-opening for her. She'd known in the abstract that there were many different realities than the one she been born into, but seeing the vendors and patrons at the Market had given her a deeper understanding of the Omniverse's vastness. It also had driven home the fact that regardless of how much training she'd had, she still had much to learn.

But was Neal the right one to teach her? She'd learned so much from him already, but his indifference – if not outright disdain – toward official procedure could be dangerous, even life-threatening, as their trip to the Market proved. But it also could damage her career in Maintenance before it had a chance to really start. She might find herself saddled with the same reputation as Neal – a rebellious rule-breaker and troublemaker. Not the best way to rise in Maintenance's hierarchy.

Neal himself was proof of that. With his years of experience, he should hold a higher rank than Surveyor, but he'd never be promoted if he continued behaving the way he did. Still, she couldn't help admire him for his refusal to conform to anyone's expectations but his own. As a Sandoval, she was expected to consider how everything she did or said reflected on her family, and it had been this way her entire life. She found it stifling sometimes, and she wished she could be more like Neal, someone who did what he thought was right without worrying how other people would react.

She was also scared. She'd never imagined that during her first couple days on the job she'd be dealing with one of the Multitude. Even her parents – who'd experienced so much in their careers – had never gone up against a member of the Multitude directly. She was supposed to start out as a Surveyor, damn it! Someone who observed and reported and let other people deal with the dangerous stuff. She was no coward, but she *was* a green-as-they-come rookie, and she simply didn't have the skill and experience to go up against one of the dark folks.

Someday she might – *might* – be ready to take on such a challenge, but that day, if it ever came, was long off. As things were going, there was a good chance she might die before completing her first week on the job. And while she was willing to die for Maintenance's cause, she wasn't ready to do so yet.

She finally took a sip of her milk. She'd waited so long that it had cooled to room temperature, so she went to the kitchen and put it in the microwave for forty seconds to warm it up again. As she watched the mug slowly spin inside the oven, she mentally chastised herself.

There's something you're avoiding thinking about.

There was indeed, but she wasn't sure she wanted to deal with it tonight – or any night, for that matter.

I thought you weren't a coward.

Maybe she was... a little.

When her milk was finished, she removed the mug from the microwave and took a tentative sip. Much better. She returned to the living room and sat on the couch once more. On the TV, a cheetah was running flat out after a small antelope. Whenever she watched nature documentaries about predators, Gina never knew who to root for. On one hand, she wanted the antelope to escape, but on the other, she didn't want the cheetah to starve. In this situation, there was no such thing as right or wrong, good or evil, just nature doing its thing. Ultimately, all creatures behaved according to their nature. This included Neal, as well as her family.

The cheetah caught up to the antelope, tripped it with a dew claw, then fastened its mouth around its neck, bit down, and held on tight. Cheetahs killed their prey by closing off their airway and suffocating them. It seemed a horrible way to die, but who was she to argue with millions of years of evolution?

She was stalling again, and she knew it.

What she didn't want to think about – but which she desperately needed to – was the obsidian pin that Creech had been wearing, the one shaped like a pair of hands shaking. The symbol of the Black Trust. Every member of her family had a similar pin, except her. She'd asked Neal if those pins indicated her parents and siblings belonged to the Black Trust, and Neal had theorized that her family used those pins as part of some kind of undercover operation that they never told her about. She supposed it was possible, and the reason no one in her family had told her was because they'd all been sworn to secrecy by Maintenance.

Maybe.

Or maybe there was another, much darker reason. Maybe they really were full-fledged members of the Black Trust, and they used their positions in Maintenance to get their hands on rare and exotic items for the Trust to sell, receiving a substantial cut, of course. Her father had always said the family's wealth was inherited, but he'd been light on the details. What if her family's money – *her* money – really came from the Black Trust? She looked around her living room, took in the TV, the expensive couch, the crystal coffee table, the new carpeting, the recently painted walls...

She wanted, no, *needed* to talk with her parents.

Her cell phone lay on the coffee table, within easy reach. She glanced at the wall clock and saw that it was 3:52 in the morning. Was it really *that* late? Her parents tended to be night owls, but that didn't mean they'd still be awake at this hour. And if she did call – and they answered – what would she say?

Neal took me to the Stygian Market tonight, and I saw something there that's got me wondering if our family is somehow mixed up with the Black Trust.

She might as well directly accuse her parents of being criminals. It came down to the same thing, didn't it?

She was sorely tempted to call, if for no other reason than to relieve her anxiety, but all she had for evidence right now were a few memories. She'd need more – a *lot* more – before confronting her mother and father.

You just want to avoid talking to them, she told herself, *because you're afraid of what they might say.*

And if *that* was the case, didn't it mean she already believed her parents were guilty?

Her milk had become lukewarm again, and she put it down on the coffee table next to her phone.

Screw warm milk, she thought. As stressed as she was, she needed something else to calm her down, something a lot more powerful than milk. She headed to the kitchen. There was a pint of peppermint ice cream in the freezer, and right now it was calling her name.

Neal lay on his battered couch, hands behind his head, gazing up at the ceiling. His TV was off, but Yvette was an insomniac so she often watched television late into the night until finally falling asleep in her recliner. She was also a bit hard of hearing, so she kept the volume up loud enough that Neal could almost make out the dialogue on the programs she watched. Normally he found this soothing, like white noise, and it helped him get to sleep. But not tonight. She was watching a western, or maybe a cops-and-robbers movie, something with a lot of yelling and shooting. Whatever it was, it was hardly conducive to sleep. But he knew the TV noise wasn't the real reason he was still awake. He couldn't stop thinking about what Gina had said before Grimwell and his two hench-monsters had attempted to abduct her.

At the Homestead, we were taught that the Black Trust doesn't ally itself with either Maintenance or the Multitude, that they only care about themselves and whatever pleasures they can grab hold of while they live. Is that true? And if it is, does that mean my *family wears those pins because* they *belong to the Black Trust?*

He also kept thinking about how he'd told her that her family had needed those obsidian pins because they were working undercover, helping Maintenance against the Black Trust.

He'd lied, of course, but how could he tell her the truth? It would devastate her, just as it had him, all those years ago.

"Getting sleepy?" Amador asked.

Neal's eyes snapped open. He *had* been about to nod off, but he wasn't going to admit it.

"Wide awake," he said, but then ruined it by yawning.

Amador laughed.

"Don't feel bad. It takes a while to get used to all-night stakeouts. You learn quick that caffeine is your best friend."

He nodded to a large take-out coffee in one of the van's cupholders. Neal picked it up, took a long drink, then shuddered. Gas station coffee was the worst. Amador had brought his own in a large thermos resting at his feet. *I'm very picky about my coffee,* he'd told Neal earlier. *I roast the beans and grind them myself.* Neal didn't know what brand of beans Amador used, but whenever he opened the thermos to pour himself some coffee, the rich smell filled the van and made Neal dislike his own coffee even more. He would have to start bringing his own, too. He'd make sure to ask Amador where he got his beans – and how to roast them.

The two men sat in Surveillance Van Number Twelve, Amador in the driver's seat, Neal in the passenger's. A panel on the dashboard was open, revealing several small screens, along with various dials, buttons, and switches. Information flowed across the screens at a fast rate, and Neal struggled to make sense of it all. Amador had no trouble, though.

"E-energy readings are still a bit high, but stable," he said. "Probably the result of natural fluctuations in the local entropic field. We'll have a better idea once the Analysts have a chance to go over the data."

Both Amador and Neal wore their smart glasses, which relayed a constant flow of information to the Analyst assigned to work with them tonight. Neal still hadn't gotten used to the idea that someone was always looking over his shoulder, metaphorically speaking, whenever he was working. He wondered if he'd ever become accustomed to it.

The van was parked on an upper middle-class suburban street several houses down from a white two-story house with a large oak tree in front and an immaculately kept yard. Not exactly a site suffused with entropic energy – at least at first glance. But earlier that afternoon, he and Amador had been making the rounds, driving through Ash Creek and trying to detect any unusual E-energy readings, when they'd discovered a spike in this neighborhood. It took them several minutes to determine which house the E-energy was centered on, and Deanna had ordered them to park and continue scanning the house, as well as keep an eye on anyone coming and going. That had been nearly twelve hours ago, and aside from a couple quick trips for food, coffee, and restroom breaks, they'd been here ever since. In all that time, the E-energy readings hadn't changed, and they'd seen no signs of life in the house. The porchlight wasn't on, and the windows were dark. No sign of life at all. But on the other hand, the entire neighborhood looked dead. There were no streetlights here – the residents of upscale areas in Ash Creek thought they spoiled the *natural ambience* – and few houses had their porchlights on. Overall, it was a dull, depressing area for a stakeout.

"How much longer do we have to do this?" Neal asked.

"Until Deanna tells us we can stop," Amador said. "Which will probably happen when she comes to work, so around six or seven."

Neal groaned. That was still several hours away.

Amador clapped him on the shoulder, the impact almost causing Neal to drop his coffee.

"Cheer up! You wanted to live the exciting life of a Maintenance agent, right? Well, here you are, defending reality against the scourge of Entropy itself!"

"By sitting on my ass and staring through a windshield for hours and hours."

Amador laughed.

"Whatever it takes, my friend!"

Amador was only a few years older than Neal, but he was far more experienced, not only as an agent for Maintenance, but in life overall. He'd grown up in Spain and had traveled the world before going to the Homestead for training. His family had served in Maintenance for generations, all the way back to the days of the Romans, when the organization was known as the Servi, which was Latin for servants. Neal had grown up in Ohio and had never been out of the country before going to the Homestead for his training. Amador's and Neal's paths in life couldn't have been more different, and Neal admired his partner tremendously. He'd learned so much from him during the short time they'd been working together, and while they'd become friends, they weren't close. He hoped one day they would be.

A light came on in the house's front window, and the E-energy reading on the dashboard screen jumped. Not a lot, only a few degrees, but when it came to E-energy, even a small increase could be serious.

Amador tapped the side of his smart glasses to speak directly to the Analyst working with them tonight.

"What do you think, Eleanor?"

"Hard to say. The E-energy increase is minor but still significant. And while the van's sensors don't indicate that there's anything unnatural about that light, the color appears a bit strange, don't you think?"

Neal tapped the magnification control on the side of his glasses and the house seemed to rush toward him. He focused on the front room, saw that the curtains were closed, but the fabric must've been thin, for light shined through them, almost as if they weren't there. And the light had a slight greenish tint to it.

"Maybe the curtains are green?" Neal suggested.

"Maybe," Amador said. "This calls for a closer look."

"Agreed."

"Neal, would you get me a hand scanner from the glove box?"

Neal did so and handed the device to Amador. It was designed to look like a cell phone, but its sole purpose was the up-close detection and analysis of entropic energy. Amador checked to make sure the scanner was in working order, then placed it on the dash.

Neal was about to ask Amador if he could go too, but before he could say anything, Amador said, "I need you to stay in the van. There's less chance that I'll be caught if I go alone."

Neal was disappointed – he *hated* hanging back when there was work to be done, even if it was dangerous work – but he didn't protest.

"Let me tell you something you don't know about late-night scanning runs," Amador said.

He removed his glasses and set them on the dash next to the scanner, then removed his tie and placed it on the dash, too. He then unbuttoned the first two buttons of his shirt.

"Our uniform works well in most situations. It looks just professional enough for people to take us seriously, but it's anonymous enough that people don't remember us. But late at night, someone sneaking around a house wearing glasses and a tie is more conspicuous. Especially if whoever is in the house is Corrupted. Many of them know who we are and how we dress. But if someone sees me tonight, I'll just be a man in a shirt and dress pants. I could be anyone, including another of the Corrupted who's been attracted by the house's E-energy and has come to check it out and perhaps claim it for myself."

"That sounds just as dangerous as being identified as a Maintenance agent," Neal said.

"It is," Amador admitted. "But if something happens to me, the Corrupted person in the house won't be on the alert against Maintenance. They'll be worried about other Corrupted coming after them."

He took hold of the scanner, gave Neal a grin, and got out of the van, making sure to close the door quietly behind him. Neal watched as Amador moved silently down the sidewalk toward the house. When he drew near it, he stepped into the yard, slipped into the shadows, and was gone.

Neal kept his gaze fixed on the spot where he'd last seen Amador.

"Eleanor, they never told us about this technique at the Homestead. How common is it?"

A moment passed before she replied, *"It's not. Amador likes to do things his own way."*

"And Deanna's okay with that?"

One of the first rules of working for Maintenance: you never removed your glasses while on the clock.

Another pause from Eleanor.

"Amador comes from a very prominent family, and because of that, he's given a lot of leeway – as long as he gets results."

Neal supposed he shouldn't have been surprised that personal politics played a role in Maintenance. Despite the organization's cosmic purpose, it *was* made up of human beings, after all.

"From your tone, I take it you don't approve?"

"I'm an Analyst. I'm not supposed to allow personal feelings to interfere with my assessments. But yes, I think it stinks."

Eleanor fell silent then, and they both waited for Amador's return. It felt like it took forever, but when Neal saw Amador reemerge from the shadows, he saw by the dashboard clock that he'd only been gone ten minutes.

As soon as Amador got back into the van, he put on his glasses. Eleanor spoke over both their feeds then.

"How were the scanner readings?"

"No different than what the van picked up. I'd say what we're dealing with is a normal fluctuation of E-energy. Something to keep an eye on, but nothing to warrant any intervention."

"Can you transmit the readings to me so I can verify?"

Amador frowned. "The scanner was set to automatically send the readings to you. Didn't you receive them?"

"I wouldn't have asked you for them if I had."

"Well, they should still be in the scanner's memory, so I'll..."

He fiddled with the hand scanner's controls for a moment, then said, "Weird. There's no... Wait, there it is! Transmitting now."

A moment passed, then Eleanor said, *"Got it. I'll take a look and get back to you."*

There was nothing to indicate that Eleanor was no longer monitoring them, but although Neal had only been working in Ash Creek for a short time, he'd gotten used to her rhythms. He could feel that she was no longer "present." That didn't matter, though. The feed from their smart glasses was constant, as long as they were wearing them, and everything they saw and heard was recorded, whether it was monitored in real time or not.

Amador handed the scanner to Neal, and he put it in the glovebox. The van's dash sensors were still active, and while their lights were dim, they emitted enough illumination for Neal to notice the outline of a circular object in Amadon's right front pants pocket – something he was sure hadn't been there before.

"What's that?" Neal asked, pointing.

"Hmm?" Amador looked down at his pants and realized what Neal was pointing at. "Oh, *that*. It's a bracelet. I picked it up at lunch, a surprise for my wife. Since we're not currently stationed in the same town, I like to send her little presents every once and a while, to let her know I'm thinking about her."

Neal and Amador had stopped at the mall for lunch that day, and Amador *had* gone off on his own for several minutes, but he'd said it was to use the restroom. When he returned, he'd said nothing about buying a bracelet. That didn't mean he hadn't bought one, of course. And just because Neal hadn't noticed it in his pocket before now didn't necessarily mean anything either, just like the fact he'd gone on his reconnaissance run without his glasses. Neal had no reason to suspect that Amador had gotten the bracelet during his excursion to scan the house up close.

He remembered what Eleanor had said.

Amador likes to do things his own way.

For the first time, Neal was beginning to wonder if there was more to Amador's way than his colleagues at Maintenance suspected.

Neal didn't report his suspicions to Deanna, but several days later, when their shift was done, Amador gave Neal a ride home in his new Lexus.

"It's pre-owned," he said, as if that meant the vehicle wasn't a wasteful indulgence. "Do you mind if we make a stop on the way? I need to pick up something."

"Sure, no problem."

Amador drove to an optometrist's office located on the edge of town that verged on Shadow.

"This won't take long," he said.

He ran in, and true to his word, returned a few minutes later, carrying a small wooden box with a metal clasp held closed by a tiny padlock. When he got back in the car, he sat the box down between them, started the engine, and pulled back onto the road. Neal had already rented Yvette's basement apartment, and her house wasn't far from the optometrist's. They'd be there in five minutes. Neal looked down at the box and saw strange markings carved into its surface, symbols he didn't recognize.

"What's in the box?" he asked.

"Eyeballs," Amador said.

Neal expected him to laugh and say he was joking. But he didn't.

They were both silent for a minute, and then Amador said, "Maybe they're *not* eyeballs, but for the moment, let's pretend they are, and they're in a box with weird markings on it. If you see a fellow agent with something like this – something odd they seem reluctant to explain – what do you do?"

Is this some kind of test? Neal wondered.

"Uh, ask them again?"

"And what if they're still evasive?"

"I don't know. I can't open the box and look for myself since it's locked. I suppose I'd get the hand scanner and test the box, see if it's emitting any E-energy."

"And what if the other agent refuses to let you scan the box?"

Neal thought for a moment. "Are we wearing our glasses?"

"No, this is off the clock. No one else is watching or listening."

"Then I guess I'd let the matter drop."

"Would that be the end of it? Or would you report the incident to Deanna?"

"I *should* report it, but I guess it would come down to how well I know and trust the other person. If they were a friend, I'd probably give them the benefit of the doubt."

Amador smiled, as if this answer pleased him.

"And what if this person told you that they were going to get a good sum of money for delivering this box to someone, no questions asked – *and* that if you went along with it, you'd get a share of the money? It's not like Maintenance pays much."

Agents' salaries were enough to cover the cost of living simply, with a tiny bit more – emphasis on *tiny* – for recreational spending, as a certain amount of fun was deemed psychologically healthy by Maintenance's higher ups.

"Then I'd have to report them. It would be obvious they were trying to bribe me to do something wrong, something that might even be dangerous and end up hurting people in the end."

Amador's smile fell away.

"Good. That's exactly the right answer." He turned to Neal and smiled again, but this time it seemed strained. "This is a test all rookies are put through, and you passed."

"So... there's nothing in the box?"

"No. It's only a prop."

Neal looked at the box. He was tempted to pick it up and shake it in order to see if it really was empty, but he didn't. Instead, he said nothing more the rest of the way to his apartment.

Neal didn't report this incident to Deanna. He did, however, tell Eleanor about it when Amador wasn't around, and *she* informed Deanna. Neal didn't know if Deanna called Amador into her office for a chat, but he began acting different around Neal, quieter, more closed off, as if he no longer trusted him. And then a week later, Amador received a transfer to another post, and Neal hadn't seen the man since.

He later learned that Deanna did have a talk with him, but since she had no evidence that he'd actually been testing Neal to see if he was willing to do shady work on the side, there was nothing she could do about it. Neal had kept tabs on Amador throughout the years, and while, from time-to-time, he heard rumors the Sandoval family had dealings with the Black Trust – might even be full-fledged members – Maintenance Control never charged them with any crime. Neal was certain the rumors were true, though. He'd felt it that day in the car, when Amador had *tested* him. Amador was dirty.

Neal sat up, sighed, got a cup from his kitchenette, and filled it with tap water from the bathroom sink. Then he returned to couch, sat down, and slowly sipped the water.

Gina wasn't dirty, he was sure of that. Well... mostly sure. Neal's problem wasn't whether he could trust Gina or not. They may have only worked together a couple days, but he had a good sense for people – one that had been honed by his years on the job. His problem was whether to tell Gina the truth about her father. Did he have a moral and professional duty to do so, as both her mentor and partner? She could help Maintenance bring the Sandoval family to justice, assuming they could get her to cooperate with them.

But she wasn't a weapon to use against her family. She was a person, and she would be emotionally devastated by betraying them. How could he do that to her? But if she one day found out the truth about them – *and* she discovered he'd known about it all the time and kept it from her – she might not ever forgive him.

Neal sat there, taking small sips of water and thinking, until the sun rose.

Fifteen

"I can't believe this shit," Neal said.

This morning, Gina drove Surveillance Van Number Seven, and Neal rode in the passenger seat. They were driving through the neighborhood where they'd encountered Teguzilla yesterday, supposedly searching for the mutated lizard, as Deanna had assigned them to do. But Neal didn't give a damn about the fucking thing, even if it *was* a Void Breather, not after the news Deanna had relayed to the agents and support staff before the morning shift began.

Something had gone wrong with Royce's medical treatment at Maintenance's Columbus HQ yesterday. The entropic energy he'd been infected with during the battle in the middle school gym yesterday had taken him over completely, transforming him into something as powerful as it was murderous. He'd broken free and infected Sabrina, turning her into the same foul thing he'd become, and the two of them escaped the building, killing a dozen medical staff and guards along the way. Columbus agents had been searching throughout the city for them, but so far there had been no sign of the Corrupted pair. No one had any idea where they were or what damage they might be causing.

"I understand how you feel," Gina said. "I don't really know either Royce or Sabrina, but what happened to them is terrible. I wish we were more directly involved in the search for them too. After all, we were at the gym yesterday when they were hurt. But Deanna *did* order all agents to keep an eye out for them in case they return to Ash Creek."

The dashboard monitors were active, sensors set to their highest level, in the hope that if Royce and Sabrina were in the area, they'd give off enough E-energy to register on the instruments. But so far, readings had remained well within the normal range.

"It's scary, isn't it?" Gina said.

Neal kept his eyes on the monitors as he responded. "What is?"

"We were there yesterday... We fought the Corrupted principal, and we could've been infected with E-energy just like Royce and Sabrina were."

Neal turned to look at Gina. She was trying to sound calm, but he could tell from her tone that the thought upset her.

"One of the things you have to deal with when you work in the field is that there's always a chance you could be exposed to Corruption. Surveyors, Interventionists, Cleaners... any of us could be infected by E-energy at any time. We take precautions, and there are treatments if we do get infected, but they don't always work. Every agent has to find their own way to make peace with the risks associated with the job. It's not easy, though."

"No, it isn't. The instructors at the Homestead tell us about the risks, but hearing about them is a hell of lot different than experiencing them firsthand."

"It gets easier," Neal said.

"How much easier?"

"Not a lot," he admitted. "But you learn to live with it somehow. That, or you transfer into Administration."

"Have you ever thought about it? Going into Administration, I mean."

"And give up the thrilling life of a Surveyor? No way."

Neal smiled, and he was glad to see Gina at least make an attempt to smile back. Her first couple days on the job had been rough as hell so far, a veritable baptism by fire. He wouldn't have blamed her for using her family connections to get transferred to a safer position. Hell, he wouldn't have blamed her for quitting Maintenance altogether. But here she was, doing her job despite her misgivings, and he respected her for that.

Eleanor – always present when they were working – cut in.

"You could consider becoming an Analyst, Gina. We get to be part of the action, but from a safe distance. It's the best of both worlds."

"True," Neal said, "but it comes with its own drawbacks."

"Yes. It's hard, watching and wanting so desperately to help, but ultimately being unable to."

Eleanor didn't say so directly, but Neal was certain she was thinking about the day they'd lost Pam. The pain and guilt had to be just as fresh for her as they were for him.

"How do you think they're coping at the middle school today?" Gina asked.

"I checked with Deanna before we left HQ. She said classes are canceled today, and likely would be for the rest of the week. Psych Division decided to blame the attack on a school shooter, and Media Relations fed the story to reporters yesterday. A few details about a snot monster might leak out, but Media Relations will do their best to discredit them. They shouldn't have much trouble. Who'd ever believe in something as ridiculous as a snot monster? Psych Division will make therapists – posing as civilian counselors, of course – available to help staff, students, and families deal with the trauma."

"It doesn't seem like enough," Gina said.

"It isn't, but it's the best we can do."

Neal noticed a slight uptick in E-energy on the monitors then. Nothing too dramatic, but worth keeping an eye on. "Don't Fear the Reaper" began playing from his pants pocket then, and he knew someone was calling his cell phone. Not many people had his number, and of those who did, only Deanna and Eleanor ever called him. He pulled his phone from his pocket and checked the display to see who was calling. *Probably just some goddamned sales call*, he thought. Then he saw the name on the screen, and he felt like he'd been smacked in the gut with a sledgehammer.

It was Sabrina.

He answered it.

"Thanks for coming to our rescue yesterday," she said. "Too bad you didn't show up sooner, though. You might've been able to save us from becoming horrible monsters."

She laughed then, and Neal heard Royce laugh with her.

Neal knew that Eleanor could hear Sabrina's voice via the smart glasses, and the Analyst was no doubt already informing Deanna about the call. He had to keep Sabrina talking in order to give Eleanor time to trace the call and pinpoint her location.

"I hear you and Royce made a spectacular escape from the med center yesterday. How many people did the two of you end up killing in your bid for freedom?"

"Thirteen," Sabrina said. "But who's counting?"

This time her laughter held an edge of mania, and Royce let out a creepy high-pitched giggle.

"Where are you?" Neal asked.

"We *could* be lots of places. Las Vegas. Amsterdam. Cabo San Lucas... But as it turns out, we're right on your ass."

There was a sudden jolt as something rammed the back of the van. The impact caused Neal and Gina's heads to snap forward then back, but their seatbelts prevented them from smacking their heads on the dashboard or steering wheel. The dash's sensors went wild then, and an alarm sounded, a shrill *eeee-eeee-eeee*, announcing the presence of dangerously high elevations of E-energy.

A little late, Neal thought.

"Get out of this neighborhood!" Neal said to Gina. "We need to find somewhere we can maneuver!"

Before Gina could respond, they heard the roar of a car engine, followed by another impact, this one much harder than the last. The van swerved, and Gina fought to keep it on the road. Neal looked in the side-view mirror and saw a red Camero close behind them. He couldn't tell if Sabrina was driving or Royce, not that it mattered. From the way they'd sounded on the phone, they were equally insane.

The phone.

He hadn't realized that he'd managed to hold onto his phone during the two collisions. He held it away from his face, but he could still hear the faint sounds of Royce and Sabrina's dark laughter.

Gina got the van under control and slammed her foot down on the gas pedal. Maintenance's vans didn't appear to be anything special on the outside, but inside was an entirely different matter. A deep thrumming sound came from the engine, and then the van leaped forward as if shot from a catapult. Ranch houses, neatly-trimmed yards, and green-leafed trees blurred past them on both sides.

"Turn left when you reach the next stop sign!" Eleanor said.

Neal pictured her, sitting in her cubicle at headquarters, wearing her smart glasses, map of Ash Creek displayed on her computer monitor.

Sabrina's voice came over the phone.

"Neee-aaalll, where are yooouuu?"

He looked in the sideview mirror once more and saw that Gina had managed to put several yards between them and the Camaro. He could now see that Royce was driving, and Sabrina sat in the passenger seat, holding her phone to her ear. Black threads of E-energy coruscated across the Camaro's surface in a way Neal had never seen before.

Neal raised his phone to talk.

"What do you want?"

"The same things everyone else does, I suppose. A loving partner, meaningful work, financial security, the hot blood of my prey splashing the back of my throat..."

"Neal..." Gina said.

Neal looked out the windshield and saw they were fast approaching a stop sign. Unfortunately, it was part of a four-way intersection, and there were cars sitting before each of the stop signs, as if none of the drivers was sure which was supposed to go first.

"Start honking the horn, don't slow down, and try not to hit anyone," he said.

"Being an Analyst sounds pretty damn good right now," Gina said.

She laid on the horn as they sped toward the intersection. Neal didn't know if the drivers heard Gina's warning, but three of them stayed where they were. One – who was driving a Honda Civic – began moving forward. Neal was about to shout a warning, but Gina yelled, "I see it!" and yanked the steering wheel to the left as they entered the intersection.

Neal pressed his hands against the dashboard and gritted his teeth, preparing for impact. The Civic's driver must've caught sight of the white van barreling toward them, and they slammed on the brakes just in time. Gina missed the vehicle as she executed a left turn, moving so fast they were up on two tires for a couple seconds and in danger of tipping over. The van bounced and juddered as the tires came down on the asphalt, and Gina accelerated again.

Neal didn't know where the rookie had picked up her driving skills, but he was damn glad she had them. He looked to the sideview mirror in time to see Royce and Sabrina's Camaro race into the intersection. Instead of trying to avoid the Civic, Royce angled right just enough to clip the vehicle's front end. There was a loud *whump*, and the Civic spun toward an Altima sitting at the stop sign on the opposite side of the street.

The Civic collided with the Altima in an explosion of window glass, and the momentum sent both vehicles sliding into the yard of what would no doubt be one very surprised homeowner. Eleanor would call 911 and report the accident, and paramedics would arrive soon and tend to any injuries the drivers had sustained. Neal hoped they'd be okay.

The Camaro fishtailed after the collision, but Royce quickly got the vehicle under control and continued pursuing Neal and Gina, that weird black lightning flowing back and forth across the body of the vehicle.

"We need to get them out of the neighborhood before they kill someone!" Neal said.

"Working on it!" Eleanor replied. *"Gina, take the next right!"*

Gina did so, and Eleanor continued giving them directions. Gina drove like a pro, swerving around vehicles without hitting any of them – although she had more than a few near misses. Royce and Sabrina went out of their way to hit as many cars as they could, damaging their Camaro in the process. The front end was dented and steam issued from the hood, indicating a damaged radiator. Neal expected the Camaro's engine to overheat and stall out, but Royce and Sabrina didn't so much as slow down. Was the black lightning doing something to keep the car running? Maybe.

Neal had the sense that Royce and Sabrina could drive them off the road any time they wished and were merely toying with them. He was okay with that, though. The longer they waited to make their move, the more time there was for backup to arrive. And Gina and he were going to need all the help they could get against their Corrupted coworkers. They'd managed to escape the Columbus medical facility, killing over a dozen people in the process. What could a pair of Surveyors – even if they were armed with unauthorized Nullifiers – do against beings as powerful as Royce and Sabrina had become?

"Why are they chasing us?" Gina asked, keeping her gaze focused on the road ahead of them.

"What do you mean?"

"After escaping the med facility, they could've gone anywhere, done anything. So why come back to Ash Creek and hunt us down?"

"They're Corrupted and don't think like normal humans anymore. Maybe they blame us for not protecting them from becoming infected, and they're out for revenge. Besides, Royce and I aren't exactly besties."

"Maybe," Gina said. "But you and Sabrina got along. And they're risking a lot by attacking us like this, directly and in broad daylight. They're agents – or at least they were – so they know that we'd call in backup. It would be smarter and safer for them to set a trap for us."

"Like I said, they're not thinking right. They're basically insane now."

"It's possible they aren't thinking for themselves at all," Eleanor said. *"They weren't Corrupted by random E-energy. The Corruption came from one of the Multitude. Maybe not directly, but that's likely where it originated, based on the Med Techs' analysis. If that's true, then whoever's ultimately responsible for their Corruption could be pulling their strings. They wouldn't hesitate to carry out any commands they'd been given, even if those commands led to their destruction."*

"So, you're saying whoever controls them has purposely targeted us?" Gina asked.

"Based on the currently available data, that's my guess."

"Why would one of the Multitude give a damn about us?" Gina said.

"Because she sees us as a threat," Neal said. "Or at least an annoyance. That's good."

"Hard left!" Eleanor shouted.

Gina followed the Analyst's direction, cutting the turn so close that the van's right tires bounced over a curb.

Gina picked up the conversation where they'd left off.

"How the hell is that *good?*"

"It means she doesn't like us investigating what she's up to. We may not be a true threat to her plans yet, but we've definitely become an inconvenience, and she's willing to take direct action to deal with us."

"Investigating? Neal, have you been working without me again?"

"Uh... No comment."

Eleanor released a long-suffering sigh.

"You'll be coming up on an abandoned shopping center in a minute. There's an Intervention team already there."

"Sounds like a good place to make a stand," Neal said. He was relieved that Eleanor wasn't going to push him about investigating without Deanna's authorization, but he knew he'd hear about it later. He turned to Gina.

"Ready?" he asked.

She smiled grimly without taking her eyes off the road.

"Sure," she said. "Just another day on the job, right?"

Neal couldn't help grinning.

"Right."

Judith Strickland drove the SUV this time, while Connor rode in the passenger seat, Molly between them. They'd been driving through the streets of Ash Creek since leaving the cemetery last night, but so far, they'd had no luck locating the next item on Rachel's shopping list: a soul that represented Life.

It would be helpful if Rachel was more specific about what she wanted. Hard to find a thing if you don't know what the hell you're looking for exactly.

As soon as Carltonthought this, he felt an overwhelming sense of guilt. Rachel was their goddess. She had made them what they now were, gave them special abilities, made them strong. They were her avatars, carrying her great darkness into the world. Questioning her in even the smallest of ways was heresy.

Is it? Or are you starting to fight off her control?

The thought was his, and yet it wasn't. It came from another part of him, one that Rachel's power had pushed far down into the depths of his psyche and imprisoned there. It was the thought-voice of the man he used to be, before *she* had changed him.

This realization was at the same time both exhilarating and terrifying. Their goddess was a wrathful deity, and if he wavered in his devotion to her, she would punish him swiftly and without mercy. But he was also excited that his former self was still inside him somewhere, fighting to be free. He'd been a servant of Rachel's for less than twenty-four hours, but already he found it hard to remember what it was like to be a free man, able to think his own thoughts, feel his own emotions, and make his own choices. He would like to be that person again.

No! I have no identity of my own anymore. I am a servant of my mistress, a tool for her to use however she sees fit. That is my purpose, my honor, and my joy.

He waited to see if that other part of him – the Old Carlton– would protest this thought, but he remained silent, and New Carlton was relieved.

One of the benefits of serving their mistress was that the Stricklands no longer needed to eat, drink, or sleep. The only stop they'd had to make since leaving the cemetery was to refuel the SUV. In many ways, they'd become machines themselves, designed to perform a specific function and do nothing else. But even changed as they were, there remained enough remnants of humanity within them to feel frustration.

"It seems like we've been driving forever," Judith said. "What if we never find a soul that represents Life? Our mistress' glorious plan will never be fulfilled."

Carlton was a bit vague on the details of Rachel's plan, but since she was the one who'd originated it, he knew it had to be wondrous. The idea that his family might fail in their mission to serve their mistress filled him with almost unbearable shame. They couldn't let that happen! They had to succeed!

Do you? Old Carlton asked. *Or is that the Corruption inside you talking?*

New Carlton had no answer to this.

"Events will unfold in their own time," Molly said. "Have faith."

Since she'd been directly Corrupted by Rachel, the Corruption in her was the strongest of them, which made her the de facto leader of this twisted version of their family.

Chastened, Judith said, "Yes, dear," and concentrated fully on her driving once more.

Another twenty minutes passed, and the Stricklands found themselves on the north side of Ash Creek. As they approached an intersection, they saw the flashing lights of two police cruisers, a fire engine, and an EMT van. The vehicles had gathered around a pair of cars that looked as if a giant had picked them up and hurled them to the ground with all its might. Metal bent and twisted, window glass shattered and spread across asphalt, black tire marks indicating the drivers' failed attempts to avoid a collision. Two police officers – one man, one woman – were directing traffic, while the firefighters hung back, waiting to see if they'd be needed.

A pair of EMTs knelt next to a woman lying prone on the ground. face and arms streaked with blood. One of the EMTs – a blond women in her thirties – was giving the accident victim CPR, while her partner – a silver-haired man in his fifties – held the woman's wrist and monitored her pulse. From the unhappy expression on his face, it looked like he doubted the woman could be saved. The driver's side door of one of vehicles was open, and a broken, bloody body hung halfway out, held in place by a seatbelt. There was so much blood on the driver's face that it was difficult to make out the person's gender, but his/her/their eyes were open and unblinking.

"Too bad we didn't get here a few minutes earlier," Molly said. "That accident would've been something to see."

The sliver of his former self that still existed within Carltonfelt a pang of sorrow upon hearing the genuine regret in his daughter's voice.

When she'd left for school yesterday, she'd been a normal kid, eager to see her friends and worried about an upcoming math test. Now she was a monster, as were her parents. The thought saddened him.

Vehicles were backed up on all sides of the intersection, but the two police officers were keeping traffic moving. Drivers gave the accident scene a wide berth, but they passed by slowly, gawking at the wrecked vehicles and the victims, no doubt feeling grateful that it wasn't them lying bloody on the street fighting for life or hanging halfway out of their car, dead.

"Find a place to park," Molly said, smiling. "I think we've found what we've been looking for."

SIXTEEN

Don't give up on me! Don't you dare!

Gretchen Fleming continued chest compressions. When she reached thirty, she leaned down, gave the woman two breaths, then started the process over again, counting compressions under her breath.

"One, two, three, four, five..."

"I'm not getting a pulse anymore," her partner said.

Gretchen had worked with Lamar Weber for the last six months, and while he was good at his job – and she genuinely liked the guy – she thought he had a tendency to give up on patients too easily. It wasn't that he was lazy or anything like that, and it wasn't that he was heartless. He was one of the most caring people she knew. He just accepted death too readily.

Not her. Not *ever*. As far as she was concerned, death could fuck right off.

She reached thirty, gave two breaths, started compressions again.

"One, two, three..."

The muscles in her arms and shoulders felt as if they were on fire. She didn't know how much longer she could keep this up.

"You got to take over for me," Gretchen said.

Lamar removed his hand from the injured woman's wrist and lay it gently on the ground. He made no move to take over CPR from Gretchen, though.

"It's over, Gretchen. You need to accept it."

"What I *need* is for you to get your ass in gear and help me save this woman's life!"

She reached thirty again, gave the woman two more breaths, started counting. One, two, three...

"Get the cart," she said.

She would keep the compressions going as Lamar got the woman onto the cart and into the ambulance, and she'd continue them until they reached the hospital in Waldron regardless of how loudly her arms and shoulders screamed in protest. Lamar might be right – this probably was a lost cause – but Gretchen wanted to give the woman every chance possible to survive, no matter how slim.

Lamar sighed. "You're crazy. You know that, right?"

He smiled, taking the sting out of his words, then stood and ran toward the ambulance.

...fifteen, sixteen, seventeen...

The day Gretchen became aware of death was the same day her hatred of it was born.

She'd been five, and it was the hottest summer of her young life. She lived with her mother in a small, rundown house in a crappy neighborhood on the south side of Ash Creek. She was an only child, and while she figured she had a daddy like most of the other kids she knew, she had no memory of one. She once asked Mommy where her daddy was, and Mommy said, "Who the fuck cares?" Gretchen had never asked again.

They didn't have air conditioning, but even with all the windows open, they were miserably hot. They both wore only underwear, and Gretchen couldn't stop staring at Mommy's breasts, fascinated by the way they jiggled, bounced, or swayed, depending on how Mommy moved. Gretchen couldn't imagine growing up and having things like *that* growing out of her body. The thought made her queasy. Or maybe that was just the heat.

Both of them lay in the living room, Mommy on the ancient couch held together by voluminous amounts of duct tape, Gretchen on a grimy throw rug on the floor in front of their broken TV. Sweat covered them like a second liquid skin, their hair was a sodden mess, and their underwear – which neither had changed for days – was damp and uncomfortable. Gretchen had never been in a pool before, but she'd seen them on TV (back when it worked), and she closed her eyes and tried to imagine what it would be like to jump into the water and sink down, letting the coolness envelop her. She'd bring her knees to her chest, wrap her arms around her legs, and float, suspended in water, without need for air. She'd remain like that for hours, days, maybe forever.

It sounded like heaven.

"I don't feel so good."

Gretchen opened her eyes and turned her head to look at Mommy. Mommy was sitting on the edge of the couch, one hand on her forehead, the other on her stomach. She was sweating buckets, and her skin had taken on a sickening gray cast. Her throat spasmed as she lurched forward once, twice, and Gretchen jumped up from the floor and took several swifts step back from the couch. Mommy fell onto her hands and knees and vomit gushed from her mouth onto the rug, right on the spot where Gretchen's head had been. Now it was Gretchen's turn to feel sick. If she hadn't moved...

"Mommy? What's wrong? Are you alright?"

She felt stupid asking this last question – it was obvious Mommy *wasn't* all right – but she couldn't think of anything else to say.

Mommy pushed herself into a kneeling position, then smiled weakly, a thick line of saliva hanging from her chin.

"I'm... okay, sweetie. I think the heat just... got to me, that's all."

Mommy's voice was halting, as she was having trouble catching her breath. She lifted a hand and started rubbing the space between her bare breasts.

"Got some... real bad heartburn... too. Don't know... what the hell I ate to..."

Her jaw clenched tight then, her eyes went wide, and the cords of muscle on her neck went taught. Then her face relaxed and she pitched face-first to the floor. There was a horrible crunching sound and blood squirted from both sides of her head. Gretchen would later learn that

Mommy's nose had been reduced to a pulp when her face collided with the floor.

Gretchen stood for a moment, frozen with shock. But then she rushed to Mommy, knelt, and began shaking her shoulder.

"Mommy? Wake up! Please, wake up!"

Tears streaked down Gretchen's face, mingling with the sweat on her cheeks and chin. She kept shaking Mommy's shoulder and calling her name, but her mother didn't respond.

"It was a heart attack, honey," her aunt explained to her a couple days later. "Came on real sudden, right out of the blue. Nothing anyone could do for her. Doctor says she was probably dead before she hit the floor."

Gretchen loved her aunt and was grateful she'd stepped in to take care of her, but she thought she was wrong. Something *could've* been done to save Mommy's life, and Gretchen should've been the one to do it, only she hadn't known how. But she would, she promised herself. One day.

Lamar pulled the cart out of the ambulance and was wheeling it toward her at a run. But before he reached her, three people stepped out of the crowd that had gathered to watch – there was always a crowd – and walked toward her. A man and a woman in their thirties, and a young girl. Gretchen assumed they were a family. Did they know the woman Gretchen was trying to save? Is that why they were approaching? They didn't seem upset, though. In fact, all three of them were smiling.

When Lamar saw the family, he began shouting.

"Get back on the sidewalk! What the hell's wrong with you people? Can't you see this is an accident scene?"

The girl stopped and looked at Lamar.

"I can't see a lot of things. Can you?"

She made a rough wet sound in the back of her throat, as if she was going to spit phlegm at him. But what jetted out of her mouth was mass of coal-black gunk. It struck Lamar eyes, covering them both, and he screamed as his flesh began to sizzle like meat on a grill. He clawed at his eyes, but all he managed to do was get some of the black gunk on his fingers, and then they began to burn. He fell to the ground, rolled back and forth, and continued screaming as he scratched at the black substance over his eyes with fingers which were no little more than bone. The cart he'd been pushing rolled several more feet before coming to a stop.

Shocked as she was, Gretchen continued chest compressions on the injured woman. She wanted to run to Lamar and see what she could do for him, but if she did, that would mean abandoning the woman and leaving her to die. But if she didn't go to Lamar, *he* might die. For Gretchen, who had despised death since that summer day when her mother fell to the floor in front of her, a hunk of lifeless muscles, bones, and organs, this was her ultimate nightmare. She had to choose who would live and who would die.

The police officers – alerted by Lamar's screams – stopped directing traffic and ran to confront the bizarre family. They drew their guns from their holsters. They stopped when they were within ten feet of the family and raised the weapons. Lamar had ceased screaming and was lying still and moaning softly. Both of his hands were nothing but bone now, and Gretchen had a horrible thought. If the black gunk ate through flesh so thoroughly, what would happen when it devoured his eyes? Would it stop there or would it continue on, burning twin holes into his brain?

The woman officer spoke first.

"I don't know what you did to that poor man, but you're not going to have a chance to do it to us! Put your hands on the top of–"

The girl spit black goo at the officer's face. Just as with Lemar, the gunk struck her eyes, and the woman began immediately screaming. The safety on her gun was disengaged, and as she stepped back and flailed her arms, her finger tightened on the trigger and the weapon discharged. The round went wild, struck the father above his left eye, and the back of his head exploded in a shower of blood, bone, and brain matter. He staggered back a couple steps, then collapsed to the ground, dead.

Neither the mother nor the girl seemed particularly broken up about his demise. They both looked at his corpse a moment, and then the girl said, "Sorry, Dad, but Entropy can be a real bitch sometimes."

The male officer stared at his partner who thrashed back and forth, clawing at her eyes as Lamar had done, still screaming. Lamar was still and quiet now, and Gretchen feared he was dead. She realized that sometime during the last several moments she'd stopped giving her patient CPR, but the fact barely registered on her consciousness. All she could do now was kneel next to the dead woman – she could admit to herself now that there'd never been a chance to save her life – watch, and wait for whatever would happen next.

The female officer had dropped her gun before starting to frantically attempt to remove the black gunk from her face. The mother walked over to it now, bent down to retrieve it, then turned, aimed at the male officer's face, and fired. The round struck his nose, obliterated it, and a millisecond later, exited the rear of his skull. He went down, and the mother put two more bullets in his chest – not that there was any need. The cop had died as swiftly as Gretchen's mother had on that long-ago day. Probably faster.

The mother and daughter turned to look at Gretchen now. They smiled, and the mother pointed the officer's weapon at her. She thought the woman would shoot, and she squeezed her eyes shut. She wondered if she'd have time to hear the gun fire before the final blackness rushed in to claim her.

"Don't be so dramatic," the girl said. "We're not going to kill you. You're too important."

Gretchen opened her eyes.

The girl's mouth was stretched in an inhumanly-wide grin.

"Come with us. We've got a friend who can't wait to meet you."

"This is it," Eleanor said.

The shopping center was on their right, and Gina executed a hard turn. The van's tires squealed and the back end swerved, but she kept the vehicle under control, grateful for the offensive driving class she'd taken at the Homestead. She'd thought it useless at the time. How often would she realistically end up in car chases in her career? Obviously more than she'd expected.

True to Eleanor's word, the shopping center – a strip mall next to a larger building that had once housed a popular hobby and craft supply store – was deserted. The various businesses had failed or moved to better locations, which made this a perfect place to confront Royce and Sabrina. No innocents would get caught in the crossfire.

Also, as Eleanor had promised, a pair of Maintenance vans were already there, and the Interventionists who rode in them, four in all, had disembarked and were holding weapons. Two of the agents held Nullifiers, while the other two held Absorbers. The latter looked like futuristic rifles, but they weren't designed to fire projectiles or energy blasts. Their job was to pull E-energy out of a target and channel it into containment chamber built into the weapon.

"Park behind them," Neal said.

Gina nodded and headed for the vans. She checked the sideview mirror and saw that the Camaro was right on their ass, black lightning still crackling across its surface. Whatever that stuff was, she was glad the vehicle didn't seem capable of weaponizing it. If Royce and Sabrina had been able to project the ebon energy and zap their van, surely they would've done so by now. As Gina raced by the four Interventionists, she caught a quick glimpse of them stepping forward and aiming their weapons at the oncoming Camaro. Then she and Neal were past, and she didn't see what happened next.

She did as Neal directed and parked behind the Interventionists' vans.

"Now what?" she asked.

Neal grabbed a hand scanner from the glove box and then pulled the Nullifier he'd purchased at the Stygian Market from his sock. He gave her a grim smile.

"Now we go earn our paychecks."

"Where did you get another Nullifier from?" Eleanor asked. *"More importantly, did you get one for Gina, too?"*

"He did." Gina drew her weapon from her sock, and she and Neal got out of the van and ran to join the battle.

The Camaro had skidded to a stop, its passenger side facing the four Interventionists, but Royce and Sabrina remained inside the vehicle, engine still running. The four interventionists – two men, two women – trained their weapons on the Camaro and began advancing toward it.

Veins of black lightning shot from the vehicle toward the agents holding the Absorbers and entered the barrels of their weapons. *It was like watching an attack in reverse,* Gina thought.

Instead of firing energy, the Absorbers were sucking it in, like rifle-shaped vacuum cleaners. At the same time, the other two agents activated their Nullifiers. At first there was no visible sign the devices were working, but then the Camaro's passenger-side door began to slowly melt as the E-energy suffusing the vehicle was processed into nonexistence. E-energy, but its very nature, could only last so long before burning itself out. It was, after all, *entropic* energy. Nullifiers sped up the process of energy decay until it simply was no more, a case of fighting fire with fire, using Entropy to counter Entropy. Working in concert, Nullifiers and Absorbers were a devastating one-two punch for any Corrupted person or object, and even one of the Multitude might have trouble withstanding the combination.

Gina and Neal joined the Interventionists and directed their Nullifiers at the Camaro. As a result, the passenger door began to melt faster, but not as fast as Gina would've expected, not with the combined power of *four* Nullifiers hitting it. Neal kept one eye on his scanner, monitoring the energy readouts. The information was being automatically relayed to Eleanor back at the office, where she could analyze it more thoroughly.

Gina had been introduced to three of the Interventionists during her orientation at the Ash Creek HQ, but she'd met so many people that she wasn't sure of their names. One of the women – Bahisa? – glanced at Gina and Neal and scowled.

"You guys aren't supposed to have Nullifiers!"

"You want to argue about rules right now," Neal said, "or do you want to get this fucking job done?"

Bahisa's scowled deepened, but she said nothing more. The other three Interventionists were too busy to pay attention to the exchange, and for the next few moments, all six agents concentrated their weapons on the Camaro's passenger door. Even with two Absorbers and four Nullifiers trained on it, the door was taking a stubbornly long time to liquefy. It was only partially dissolved when the black lightning surrounding the car became less intense, and then it faded altogether.

Sabrina called out, "Stop firing! We surrender!"

One of the male Interventionists – Gina thought his name was Rudy – said, "Do you think it's a trick?"

"I–" Gina began.

"I wasn't talking to *you*," Rudy snapped. "You're not an Interventionist, are you?"

Gina was about to go off on the asshole, but Neal leaned close to her ear, and in a soft voice said, "This isn't the time."

She gritted her teeth, but she nodded. He was right.

The other female Interventionist, whose name Gina definitely didn't remember, held a hand scanner, just like Neal. She checked the device's small display, then said, "E-energy levels are way down now, almost to normal background readings. If it's a trick, it's a damn good one."

Gina glanced at Neal, but all he did was shrug.

"All right," Rudy said. "Shut down your weapons, but be ready to use them again." In a louder voice, he called out, "Royce, Sabrina… step out of the vehicle and keep your hands where we can see them!"

According to Maintenance procedure, Surveyors were supposed to defer to Interventionists in the field. A couple days ago, Gina wouldn't have thought to question this, but now she looked to Neal once more. He nodded, but he didn't look any happier than she was.

The six agents lowered their weapons, and a moment later, Sabrina and Royce exited the Camaro – without turning off the vehicle's engine. When Sabrina opened the half-melted passenger door, it fell to the ground and liquefied the rest of the way. She ignored it and held her hands out to her sides to show that she was unarmed, as did Royce. Once out of the Camaro, the two stood by the vehicle, advancing no further.

"What do you want us to do, Rudy?" Royce said. "Get down on our knees and beg forgiveness?"

"*That's* not going to happen," Sabrina said, and she and Royce laughed.

Both agents spoke in slow, measured cadences. They were unhealthily thin, eyes set deep within hollow sockets, cheeks sunken in, skin sallow and lined with wrinkles. Gina knew what had happened to them, what was *still* happening. The entropic energy that filled them was taking a toll on their bodies, eating away at them from the inside.

"You know the drill," Bahisa said. "Put your hands behind your backs, and we'll cuff you."

Interventionists used Suppression Cuffs to negate the power of the Corrupted so they could be brought safely to a holding cell. They remained imprisoned until agents from the state HQ took custody and escorted them to Rehabilitation Division, otherwise known as Summerhill. Despite its name, Summerhill – whose precise location was known only to those at Maintenance's highest levels – was reputed to a less-than-pleasant place. Trainees at the Homestead often referred to it as Summer*hell* when their instructors weren't around.

"I'm afraid that's not going to happen either," Sabrina said.

The hand scanners' alarms went off, indicating a sudden massive surge in E-energy. Black lightning erupted around Sabrina and Royce's hands, and their eyes became pools of darkness. Moving slowly, as if they were underwater, they both gestured at the Camaro, reigniting the ebon power that had coursed through the vehicle only moments before. Then they pointed at the Maintenance agents. The Camaro's engine roared like an angry beast, and the car surged forward, heading straight for Gina, Neal, and the others. Neal grabbed Gina's arm and yanked her out of the car's path, but the other four agents stood where they were, gawking at the oncoming vehicle, as if they couldn't process what they were seeing.

"Run you fucking idiots!" Neal shouted.

They did not run, and the Camaro – which had accelerated at an impossible rate – swerved and slammed broadside into the four Interventionists, crushing them against the backs of their vans with a sickening *whump*. As if that wasn't awful enough, a portion of the Camaro's black lightning transferred to the agents, covering their bodies like a mass of insects made of solid shadow. The Interventionists began to age rapidly as their personal entropic fields were sped up, and within seconds they and their clothes had been reduced to piles of gray dust resting on parking lot asphalt.

Gina wanted to turn away from the awful sight, but she knew she couldn't afford to take her eyes off Sabrina and Royce. She expected them to direct the Camaro to attack her and Neal next, but instead they stretched out their hands, and the black lightning surrounding the car flowed toward them and into their fingers. When they'd absorbed it all, the Camaro's engine began to sputter, its red paint lightened to a washed-out pink, and the tires grew brittle and gray, bits of rubber flaking off them and falling to the ground. And then, just like the Interventionists, the Camaro collapsed into a large dust mound.

"They invested the Camaro with their own power," Neal said. "Now that they don't need the car any more, they took it back."

Royce and Sabrina turned toward the two remaining agents. Their eyes were pools of roiling darkness, and when Gina looked into them, intense despair settled upon her like a cold heavy blanket. What was the point of trying to fight the creatures that Royce and Sabrina had become? Despite the advanced tech she and Neal had, in the end they were nothing more than human. They couldn't hope to stand against the dark might of these creatures. Better to accept the inevitable and wait for death.

She heard Eleanor's voice then.

"Gina, your bio-readings indicate that your dopamine and serotonin levels have taken a serious dive! You've got to stop looking into their eyes!"

"Why?" Gina mumbled. "We can't stop them. Nothing can."

"I hate to do this to you..."

Gina heard a sharp *zzzttt* as her glasses delivered an electric shock.

"Ow! Fuck!"

"Sorry."

Gina was pissed, but that was much better than the way she was feeling a few seconds ago. She didn't have time to thank Eleanor, though. Royce and Sabrina were coming toward them slowly, arms at their sides, black lightning crackling around their hands. Gina made certain to avoid their gazes this time.

"You're working for *her*, aren't you?" Neal said. "The woman I saw in the park, the one who belongs to the Multitude."

Gina knew he was trying to stall them, and it worked. Both Royce and Sabrina halted their advance. Neal had dropped his hand scanner when he'd pulled her out of the Camaro's path, but he'd managed to hold onto his Nullifier. She'd dropped hers, but it lay on the ground only a couple feet away. If she dove, she could get hold of the weapon before the two Corrupted Interventionists could blast her with their black lightning. Maybe.

"Her name's Rachel," Sabrina said. "And she's sent us to kill Gina and you – the fresh-faced, wide-eyed new agent and the cynical, burned-out veteran."

"You mean one of the Multitude is frightened by Gina and little old me?" Neal said. "In a weird way, that's kind of a compliment."

Royce snorted a laugh. "As if. You two are merely annoyances, a pair of bothersome flies buzzing around our mistress' heads. Minor distractions, but distractions nevertheless. Our mistress needs her full concentration to complete her great work. So, we're going to remove you."

"Permanently," Sabrina added.

Neal whispered something then, so softly that Gina couldn't hear it – which meant neither could Royce nor Sabrina. But Eleanor did, and she passed the message along to Gina.

"Neal said when he hands you his Nullifier, go for one of Sabrina's eyes."

What the hell? Gina wanted to ask either Neal or Eleanor for further explanation, but she couldn't, not without alerting Sabrina and Royce.

"What's so *great* about Rachel's *work*?" Neal asked.

Sabrina grinned. "Nice try, but you're not going to be able to get any information out of us like that."

"Oh well. It was worth a shot."

Neal thumbed the button on the end of his Nullifier to activate it, then thrust it into Gina's hand. For an instant she stood frozen, unsure what to do. Thoughts flashed through her mind. *Go for one of Sabrina's eyes,* Eleanor had said, but what did that mean? Aim the Nullifier at her eye? What good would that do? As powerful as Sabrina was, she'd kill her before the Nullifier had any effect. It would take a massive dose of the nullifier's power, delivered directly into... her... system.

Oh god. She understood now, but she didn't know if she could go through with it.

Neal dove for the Nullifier Gina had dropped to the ground earlier. He grabbed the weapon as he executed a somersault, came up on his feet, and ran toward Royce.

"Fuck..." Gina breathed.

She raised the Nullifier as if it was a knife and started running.

If Sabrina and Royce had been able to move at normal speed, they would've easily killed both Neal and Gina. But their Corrupted bodies had decayed to the point where they moved like barely ambulatory corpses. The agents were still in the process of raising their hands to unleash bolts of E-energy when Gina and Neal reached them. Gina gritted her teeth and rammed the Nullifier into Sabrina's left eye. The orb popped easily, and foul-smelling gray muck splattered outward.

Gina felt her stomach flip, but she ignored the sensation and shoved the Nullifier in as far as it would go. Gina released her grip on the Nullifier, and Sabrina let out an inhuman shriek and stumbled backward. The black lightning surrounding her hands died away, and – still moving slowly – she reached for the rod jutting out of her eye, fingers trembling. She managed to get hold of the device, but she no longer had the strength to dislodge it. Her entire body shook violently and then collapsed into a pile of muck, clothes and all. The Nullifier lay atop the viscous mass, wisps of white vapor curling upward from its tip.

She looked to her side and saw Neal standing over a second mass, which also had a Nullifier laying on top. She hadn't heard Royce scream. Maybe Neal had hit him so hard and fast the agent hadn't had time to make noise. Or maybe she'd been so focused on Sabrina that she'd blocked out all other sights and sounds. She was glad to see that Neal appeared uninjured.

Neal looked at her. "Are you okay?"

She nodded. "As far as I can tell."

"I mean are you okay with what we just did?"

She looked at the wet, blobby mass that had been Sabrina.

"She was a Maintenance agent," Gina said. "She wouldn't have wanted to continue serving one of the Multitude, and neither would Royce. We did the right thing."

She turned to the side and vomited.

Seventeen

Rachel stood in front of the mausoleum that housed her masterpiece-in-progress, Molly and Judith Strickland close by – but not *too* close. Servants had to know their place, after all. Within the mausoleum, the inside-out-mother stood up to her shins in a cesspool of liquid Corruption, while the new addition – a woman named Gretchen – stood before her, hands gripping the exposed muscles of the mother's shoulders, fingers digging into red, raw meat, her mouth fixed tightly to the mother's backwards oral cavity.

Gretchen's chest expanded as she breathed in through her nose, then expelled the air from her mouth, passing it from her body to the mother's. Gretchen did this repeatedly – in, out, in, out – rhythm steady and unvarying, as if she was an unthinking, unfeeling oxygen pump. A flesh machine.

There's a reason they call it the Breath of Life, Rachel thought, amused.

She cocked her head to the side then, as if listening to something, but the cemetery was silent – no birds, squirrels, or insects. The Atrocity Engine, while only partially complete, was now giving off more than enough entropic energy to drive the small creatures away. But she'd heard *something*… Felt it, too. She was sure of it.

She allowed her awareness to expand beyond her body, and an instant later, she understood what she'd sensed – or rather, didn't sense. She could not touch Sabrina or Royce's mind, and this could only mean one thing. Her two servants were dead. Not that she'd mourn their loss. They were tools, after all, and tools were only useful until their job was finished. The big question was, had they completed the task she'd given them? Were those two irritating Surveyors dead as well? She didn't know, and she didn't like not knowing. In fact, she *loathed* it.

"Is something wrong, Ms. Blackburn?" Molly asked.

She smiled at Molly. Rachel never had children of her own, but if she had, she wouldn't have minded if one of them had been like this girl, intelligent and forthright.

"It's nothing for you to concern yourself with, dear."

Outwardly, Rachel appeared calm, but inside she was raging. Not only had Carlton died acquiring the latest ingredient, she'd lost Royce and Sabrina too. She was three servants down and only had two left. The child and her mother had done well so far, and there was no reason to think they wouldn't be able to procure the fourth item needed to build the Atrocity Engine – a soul that embodied Death.

But the fifth and final item – an Umbral feather – would not be so easy to obtain. There was only one in the region, and that hung on the office wall of the head supervisor in Ash Creek's Maintenance Division headquarters, miles away from the cemetery. Even from here, Rachel could feel the raw power emanating from it like a dark beacon. As with the other items for the Atrocity Engine, she couldn't touch the feather herself without risk of contaminating it. Or – and while it galled her to admit this, it was the more likely scenario – the power contained within the feather would destroy her.

When Royce had become infected with Rachel's Corruption, and in turn passed it on to Sabrina, she'd decided she'd send them to get the feather, *after* they'd dealt with Neal and Gina, of course. As Maintenance agents, Royce and Sabrina's knowledge of their HQ's layout would be invaluable in obtaining the feather. It had never occurred to her that the pair would die while attempting to kill Neal and Gina. She knew the Corruption inside them would eventually result in their physical dissolution, but they should've had enough power to kill a couple of damn Surveyors before collapsing into puddles of goo!

She'd investigate and learn precisely what had happened to Sabrina and Royce, and if the two Surveyors still lived, she'd find another way to take them out, even if she had to do it herself. By acting directly, she'd risk attracting Brother Nothing's attention, and if he discovered she was building an Atrocity Engine, it wouldn't go well for her. But she'd deal with that when the time came. She still had two more items to acquire.

"Molly, Judith, you've both done well so far. Now I need you to find me a soul that embodies Death. Do you think you can do that for me?"

Rachel examined mother and daughter with a critical eye. They hadn't been expending energy as rapidly as Royce and Sabrina had, and so far, it appeared the effects of Entropy on them were mild. Skin an unhealthy color, eyes cloudy, some lost some hair, but they should be good to go for another day, maybe two.

Molly and Judith grinned at the same time, and even Rachel found it a little creepy.

"Consider it done," Molly said, then she and her mother started walking toward their SUV. They got in the vehicle and drove out of the cemetery.

Rachel turned back to the mausoleum and gazed upon her masterpiece-in-progress. It really was quite beautiful, and when it was complete, it would be magnificent. But before that happened, she needed to deal with Neal and Gina. After Royce and Sabrina had become Corrupted, Rachel had been able to touch their minds, and she'd learned a great deal about the two agents who'd proven to be especially irritating thorns in her side.

"What to do, what to do..."

It took some time, but an idea came to her, and when it did, her smile was that of a predator imagining sinking fangs deep into the flesh of its prey.

A Clean-Up Crew arrived to deal with the remains of Sabrina and Royce, as well as collect the bodies of the agents they'd killed. While the

Cleaners worked, Neal and Gina were ordered to return to the office for debriefing. When they arrived, Eleanor met them in the lobby, gave them both hugs, said how glad she was that they were both unhurt, and then they were hustled off to speak with Debriefers.

Neal was assigned to Marshall – again – but while the man usually irritated the piss out of Neal, today he performed the debriefing with numb detachment. Neal understood. It wasn't uncommon to lose an agent. Hadn't Pam died only a couple months ago? But today they'd lost not only Sabrina and Royce, but also the four agents they'd killed. And it wasn't just Marshall. The entire staff was in shock, going about their duties with quiet, almost robotic efficiency, struggling to come to terms with this afternoon's tragedy.

Neal was having more than a little trouble with that himself.

After their debriefings, Deanna summoned Neal and Gina to her office. Once inside, Deanna asked Neal to close the door. He did, and then he and Gina sat in front of Deanna's desk.

"I've reviewed the video Eleanor recorded," Deanna said. "First, let me say how glad I am that you're both still with us. Second, I want each of you to make appointments to speak with a therapist in Psych Division as soon as possible. You've been through a hell of a lot today, and you're going to need to help to process it. Third, I want to commend you. Your bravery and quick thinking stopped a deadly threat and prevented further loss of life as well as further spread of Corruption. I can't imagine how difficult it must have been to... deal with colleagues the way you had to. Normally, Surveyors aren't supposed to engage directly with threats, but Sabrina and Royce targeted you, and you had no choice but to defend yourselves. In my judgment, you acted appropriately given the circumstances." She paused and let out a long sigh. "That's the good stuff. Now for the not-so-good."

Neal held up a hand to forestall her.

"I know what you're going to say. Gina and I shouldn't have been carrying Nullifiers. Especially me, since you'd already warned me about using unauthorized equipment. And since you viewed Eleanor's video, you heard her ask me if I've been investigating on my own, outside of working hours. I admit to everything, but I ask that you don't punish

Gina or put anything in her permanent file that might damage her career. It's not her fault she got stuck with me as a mentor."

"I knew what I was doing," Gina said. "I'm a big girl, and the choices I make are my own."

Neal wanted to tell her to shut up before she got in real trouble, but he couldn't help admiring her strength of character. She could easily blame him for encouraging her to break the rules, and she'd be right to do so, but she wasn't going to throw him under the bus, even when she probably should've.

Deanna looked at them for a moment before saying, "I have no idea what either of you are talking about."

Neal and Gina exchanged puzzled looks.

"You mean you didn't review the entire video?" Neal asked.

"I did," Deanna said. "And I have no idea what you're talking about. That's my final word on the matter. Understood?"

Neal did. Deanna knew exactly what he and Gina had done and was going to let it slide, *and* she hadn't asked them to turn in their Nullifiers. It wasn't official permission for them to use the weapons, but it was the next best thing.

He nodded. "Thanks."

Deanna continued as if he hadn't spoken.

"Because we're dealing with one of the Multitude – and because of how much damage she's caused – Control has decided that they need to take a direct hand in the matter."

"You mean take *over*," Neal said.

"Yes. I'm not any happier about it than you are, but that's the way it is. Control dispatched an agent earlier today, and he should be arriving soon. In the meantime, because you've both become targets for this woman – Rachel – I'm afraid I'm going to have to place you in protective custody."

"I thought we weren't going to be punished!" Neal said.

"You aren't. The key word is *protective*. We have defenses here that even one of the Multitude would have difficulty breaching. And keeping you here will not only protect you, but it'll also reduce the chance for collateral damage. Four agents died today, not to mention the staff that died at the Medical Division facility in Columbus yesterday when Royce and Sabrina escaped. If Rachel has other servants to send after you, better they come here, where there won't be any risk to civilians, and where we have the tools and staff necessary to deal with them."

Neal didn't like it, but he could see the logic in Deanna's position.

"And *custody* doesn't mean you need to be placed in holding cells. As long as you stay in the building, you should be fine."

"How long will we have to say here?" Gina asked.

"As long as necessary," Deanna said.

A thought occurred to Neal. "By keeping us here, you can also make sure that we're not doing any after-hours investigating."

Deanna smiled. "When have you ever known me to be that devious?"

Neal scowled. "Only on days that end in Y."

Deanna's smile widened for a moment, and then she became serious.

"There's one more thing I need to tell you. The agent Control is sending?" She directed her attention to Gina. "It's your father."

Judith drove and Molly rode in the passenger seat. The SUV seemed so much emptier without Carlton, and not only because he wasn't there physically. She wished they hadn't left his body at the accident scene. At the time, it had seemed the natural thing to do, but now if felt wrong, monstrous even. His death had created a large hole at the center of Judith's being, one that would never be filled. She wanted to cry, scream, rage against the unfairness of it all, but these emotions were held in check by the Corruption that had transformed her.

Years ago, when Molly had been an infant, Judith had found herself having panic attacks. A therapist suggested she was experiencing them because she was a new mother and felt overwhelmed by the responsibility of caring for an infant. What if she did something wrong? What if she unintentionally hurt her baby? The therapist assured her these feelings were normal and put her on anti-anxiety medication. The drug helped, but not in the way Judith expected it to. She could feel a panic attacking coming on, but when it reached a certain intensity, it just stopped, like there was a wall inside her that the panic couldn't break through. The anxiety was still there – she could feel it – but it was held at bay. What she was experiencing now was similar. She didn't like it, but that wasn't important. This emotional barrier allowed her to serve her mistress to the best of her ability, and that was her only reason for existing now. Still, she couldn't help wishing Carlton was here.

She glanced at her daughter. Molly stared out the window, a serene expression on her face. Judith wondered what, if anything, Molly felt about her father's death. Molly had been the first in the family to receive the blessing of Corruption, and it appeared to have transformed her so thoroughly that almost none of her previous self was left. Maybe that was because Molly was a child, her personality still developing. Judith didn't know, but if Molly wasn't experiencing grief over her father's loss, that was good. It would allow her to remain fully focused on their mission. In a distant corner of Judith's mind, she felt sorrow over her daughter's inability to grieve for her father, but that sadness was muted and easily ignored.

"Where should we go this time?" Judith asked.

Molly didn't take her eyes off the road ahead as she answered.

"A hospital? A funeral home? It can't be a cemetery, since the Atrocity Engine's already in one. If all Rachel needed was dead bodies, she has lots there. She needs something else."

Judith wasn't certain their mistress knew what she needed, not specifically. If she did, she would've given them explicit instructions: *Drive three miles on Northwood Drive, then turn left at the stoplight. Continue for five more miles until you see a building with a sign out front that says Death R Us.* She supposed even someone as powerful as their mistress had *some* limitations, although she would never speak this thought aloud, for fear that Rachel might somehow learn of it. She knew their mistress would never forgive such blasphemy.

Judith was a real estate agent, familiar with Ash Creek's various neighborhoods and businesses. Was there a place in town that embodied death more than any other, that was absolutely suffused with it? It came to her then, and her mouth stretched into a wide grin.

"What is it?" Molly asked.

"I know where we need to go," Judith said.

"How are you feeling today, Debra?"

Jonathan Fitzgerald sat next to the woman's bed, holding her ancient hand, which was little more than thin sticks covered with tissue paper, taking care not to put any pressure on it. Even a gentle squeeze might hurt her, and he was here to relieve her suffering as much as he could, not add to it.

She tried to smile, but all she could manage was a tired grimace. "I'm hurting. Real bad."

Debra's room was small – a bed, a dresser, a wall-mounted flatscreen TV, a pair of chairs for visitors (one of which Jonthan was currently using), a tiny bathroom . . . There was a single window to the left of the bed, which provided a view of the grounds behind the building. Green grass, trees whose leaves were just beginning to take on fall colors, cloudless blue sky above.

Jonathan knew Debra preferred to lay in the dark, but the morning nurse always opened residents' curtains in the morning, whether they liked it or not. *Dying people have an eternity of darkness ahead of them,* she'd say. *They need to get sunlight while they still can.*

The walls and ceiling were painted a light blue to create a feeling of soothing tranquility, but Jonathan thought the shade was too cool. It made him think of the arctic in wintertime. It didn't help that the director insisted on keeping the temperature low in the building. He said it was to make the residents, most of whom were elderly, more comfortable, but to Jonathan, it felt like rehearsal for ending up in a funeral home refrigerator. An IV stand stood next to Debra's bed, tubing descending from a bag of saline solution and stretching to a port inserted into the back of her left hand. The skin around the port had bruised a dark purple.

Of course, you're hurting, Jonathan thought. *Stage Four pancreatic cancer will kick anybody's ass.* Aloud, he said, "Have you been doing the visualization techniques we talked about?"

"What?" she said, and Jonathan repeated his question louder.

Debra's brow furrowed slightly, the closest to a frown that she could manage.

"Vis... visu... vislation? I don't think I remember those. "

Jonathan suppressed a sigh. It was common for residents to have memory problems, especially when they were close to the end. He smiled and forced himself to speak slowly and clearly.

"Try to imagine a place from your life where you felt the most peaceful, the most relaxed. Can you remember a place like that?"

Debra 's brow furrowed a bit more as she attempted to concentrate. "I don't know. I..." She winced, and her features contorted in pain. Her hand – suddenly surprisingly strong – clamped so hard around Jonathan's fingers that he thought a couple of them might break. He didn't pull free of the woman's grasp, though. He didn't want to startle or accidentally hurt her by yanking his hand away too fast.

Tears began to roll down her wrinkled cheeks, and she squeezed her eyes shut. Her lips began to tremble, and she pressed them together tight. This continued for almost a minute before the tension left her disease-wracked body and she wilted against the bed.

Debra still had hold of his hand. It ached from how hard she'd squeezed it, but he left it where it was. What was his small pain when compared to the agonizing amount she suffered? He felt foolish for suggesting she try to ease her pain with visualization techniques. Her condition had progressed beyond the point where such methods could help. Nothing could help her now, except for high doses of morphine administered around the clock. And as bad as she was, that would likely only blunt the pain, not take it away.

And it wasn't as if physical pain – as intense as it was – was Debra's only problem. Her husband had preceded her in death, but she had three middle-aged children, and they had sons and daughters, most of whom were teenagers. All of them alive and healthy. Her family was paying for her stay in Caring Hands Hospice, but they rarely came to visit her. Debra's room had a phone, but they never called.

Caring Hands was a good facility, but not a large one, and Jonathan was its lone counselor. He worked with residents, their families, and even staff who found their jobs emotionally difficult at times. He'd reached out to Debra's children on numerous occasions, and during those few times he managed to get hold of them, they promised they'd come visit soon. And once or twice they had, but they clearly felt awkward and hadn't stayed long.

Jonathan understood that death was the hardest thing for humans to face, and most people did everything they could to avoid dealing with it. They tried to pretend that it didn't exist, that they and everyone they loved would live forever. But they could feel death's presence all around them, and no matter how hard they tried to deny it, they knew that one day – sooner than they expected – they would feel its cold touch.

Not all relatives avoided contact with their dying family members, of course. As difficult as it was to be with residents, especially in the later stages of their illnesses, families came and did what they could to eased their loved ones' suffering and, to the best of their ability, ensure they didn't die alone. Not families like Debra's, though. As far as Jonathan was concerned, they were selfish cowards, and by giving in to their fear, they only increased Debra's pain.

There was only one way to help Debra now, and only one person who could do it.

Him.

Jonathan gently slid his hand out of Debra's, rose from his chair, and walked to the door. He locked it, doing so slowly so there wouldn't be a loud *snick*. The other staff were usually so busy that even if they heard the sound, they most likely wouldn't investigate, but Jonathan couldn't take that chance.

He next walked over to the small closet in Debra's room and opened the door. She had several outfits on hangers, none of which she'd worn the entire time she'd been here. There were three pairs of shoes on the floor, which likewise hadn't been worn. Jonathan wasn't interested in any of these. He reached up, took hold of the spare pillow that rested on the closet's upper shelf, and pulled it down.

Each resident room at Caring Hands had at least one extra pillow. The healthier residents would use the extras to prop themselves into a sitting position so they could watch TV or chat with visitors. Others used them to alleviate pain, depending on what their issues were, putting a pillow underneath their lower back or their legs. Jonathan used them to alleviate pain as well, but when he was finished, the pain was gone – forever.

He gripped the pillow in both hands, knuckles tight, and slowly advanced toward Debra.

He'd first used this remedy three years ago, on a resident named Ben Delaney. Fifty-seven-year-old Ben suffered from an inoperable brain tumor that not only kept him in constant excruciating pain, it caused him to experience the most horrific hallucinations. When he wasn't crying and praying aloud for death, he was screaming at the top of his lungs because he believed some nightmarish thing was attacking him.

One evening, Jonathan had been trying to calm Ben, but without success. Ben was in one of his screaming fits, and Jonathan doubted the man was even aware of his presence. What good were his words if someone couldn't hear them? And even if his words *could* be heard, how effective were they really? All the words he'd even spoken in his entire life couldn't take away one second of Ben's pain.

Something changed deep inside Jonathan at that moment, and the next thing he was aware of was pressing a pillow down on Ben's face. The man thrashed and screamed, but Jonathan held the pillow in place with a strength he hadn't known he possessed. It seemed to take forever, but eventually Ben's exertions began to lessen, and soon he stopped moving altogether and fell silent. Jonathan kept the pillow on his face for another minute or so, just to be sure, and then removed it. He expected Ben's features to be twisted into a mask of pain and terror, but they weren't. For the first time since Jonathan had met him, the man looked peaceful, happy even. Jonathan had discovered his true calling.

He discovered something else as well. When a resident was in a bad state, like *really* bad, no one looked into their death very closely. Everyone – family, staff, other residents – was just relieved the person's torment was over. A doc had filled out Ben's death certificate after barely glancing at the man's body, and that was it. Jonathan had gotten away with murder. Although it wasn't truly murder, was it? Ben had already been dying. All Jonathan had done was help him on his way a little early so he wouldn't suffer needlessly. Jonathan hadn't *killed* Ben. He'd *freed* him.

Since that night, Jonathan had "freed" five more residents without once drawing any suspicion to himself. Debra would be Number Six.

He reached the side of her bed and was lowering the pillow toward her face when someone knocked on the door.

Jonathan froze.

A moment, passed, then another knock came.

Debra's eyes were closed, and she moaned softly with each exhalation.

A third knock, this one louder, insistent.

Jonathan's paralysis broke. He knelt, shoved the pillow under the bed, straightened, then went to the door, unlocked and opened it. He expected to see a nurse or a doc standing there, frowning, ready to ask him why the hell Debra's door had been locked. Instead he saw a woman in her late thirties and a preteen girl. Mother and daughter, he assumed, given their resemblance. He doubted they were relatives of Debra's as he'd met most of them. They were family members of another resident, he decided, and they'd gotten lost trying to find their relative's room. He smiled.

"Can I help you?"

It was then that he noticed something odd about the pair. Their skin was an unhealthy shade of gray, dry and cracked in numerous places, their eyes bloodshot and set deep within dark hollows. They smelled rank, too, like raw meat on the verge of spoiling.

His smile faltered.

The girl grinned, displaying gray teeth and black gums.

"Hello, Jonathan. You are exactly the person my mother and I are looking for."

The girl's demeanor was strangely adult, and there was dark amusement beneath her words. Then he realized something.

"How do you know my name?"

The mother smiled then, baring teeth and gums as unhealthy-looking as her daughter's.

"The Song told us, of course."

"What?" Jonathan was beginning to suspect that these two weren't visitors but rather residents who'd left their rooms unsupervised. They certainly looked unwell.

"The Song of Ending," the girl said, her tone irritated, as if she was speaking to an idiot. "It's the death wail of Existence, and when you learn to hear it, it tells you many things."

"When we got close to this room, the Song told us who you were." The mother's smile widened, stretching so far her upper lip split. Blood welled from the wound and dripped onto her chin, but she didn't appear to notice. "And it told us what you were doing."

"I... was doing my job, sitting with a resident and trying to, to *comfort* her."

The girl smirked. "Yeah, comfort her right into a pine box."

"Don't get us wrong," the mother said. "We understand completely. Why don't you finish your work, and then we can talk further?"

Jonathan was stunned. Somehow these two knew his deepest, darkest secret, and not only didn't it seem to bother them, they wanted him to finish killing Debra.

"Are you... demons? Have you come to take me to Hell?"

Jonathan had never been a particularly religious man, but while he'd told himself that what he did to relieve the residents of their pain was a good thing, he feared that in reality it was evil, that he actually killed solely for the thrill of it, and one day he would be punished for his terrible sins.

The mother and the girl laughed.

"There's no such thing as Heaven and Hell," the girl said. "Just the Gyre and its endless hunger."

Jonathan had no idea what she was talking about, but if these two weren't demons – and really, it had been ridiculous of him to entertain the thought even for a moment – they were clearly insane. He needed to report them to the director, and if they told her that he'd attempted to kill Debra, she wouldn't believe them. His secret would remain safe, and these two would be somebody's else's problem.

"We don't have time for this," the girl said.

She made a sharp gesture with her hand, and Jonathan heard a harsh *crack* from behind him. He turned and saw that Debra's head was bent at a sickening angle, her eyes wide and staring.

"That's a lot faster than a pillow, isn't it?" the girl asked.

Jonathan began trembling uncontrollably. He turned back to the mother and daughter, head lowered, back curved, as if he was instinctively trying to make himself a smaller target.

"You *are* demons," he whispered.

"Oh no," the mother said.

"We're much worse," the daughter added.

And then they rushed toward him.

A dimensional Rift opened in the air behind Bargain-o-Rama, the trees and headstones of Oak Grove Cemetery visible on the other side. Rachel stepped through the Rift, but she didn't close it behind her. She wasn't going to be here long.

She stood in front of a dumpster filled with trash, mostly discarded paper and flattened cardboard boxes. She was glad to see there was no separate bin for recycling. As a disciple of Entropy, she approved of waste, for it fed the Gyre faster. She stretched a hand toward the dumpster, closed her eyes, and concentrated.

She knew from Sabrina and Royce's memories that Neal had lost his previous partner Pam Duggan here, and that her death weighed heavily on his conscience because he hadn't been able to save her. Poor Neal! Rachel might've felt sorry for him if she was capable of it, but she'd lost the ability to experience positive emotions when she began training to become one of the Multitude. Hatred, rage, hostility, loathing, repugnance... these emotions were as natural to her as her own heartbeat, and she had experienced no others since Brother Nothing had taken her to the Athenaeum. There, her teachers had spent the first two months torturing her to drive out any vestiges of humanity that might hinder her growth.

Rachel was grateful for her instructors' tutelage. Feeling even the smallest measure of empathy was a weakness, and if she intended to become one of the most powerful members the Multitude had ever known, she couldn't afford a single iota of weakness. It would be like blood in the water to a school of hungry piranha.

She found only residual traces of E-energy in the dumpster, or rather, around it. No doubt Maintenance agents had removed the

Corrupted dumpster after Pam's death and replaced it with a new one. That would make her task harder, but by no means impossible.

Eyes still shut, she focused on gathering the faint threads of entropic energy that lingered in the vicinity of the dumpster and weaving them together. It took some time, but when she was finished, she opened her eyes, and saw a blond woman dressed in a Maintenance uniform standing in front of her. Rachel lowered her hands and smiled.

"Hello, Pam. There's something I'd like you to do for me."

EIGHTEEN

Gina and Neal sat at a round white table in the employee lounge. So far, "protective custody" for them had consisted of bad office coffee, half-stale donuts, and mind-numbing daytime television.

Not exactly a high-security environment, Gina thought.

She and Neal were alone. None of the other staff had entered the lounge since Deanna had sent them here. Evidently even Eleanor wasn't permitted to contact them. Both Gina and Neal had tried to contact her via the comm feed on the smart glasses, but she hadn't responded.

"Why are being isolated?" Gina asked. "It's like we're the ones being punished."

"The situation we're in isn't exactly a normal one," Neal said. "I doubt there are any established procedures for us. Deanna is probably just making things up as she goes. My guess is she thinks it's too dangerous for anyone to be near us right now. She also probably wants to keep anyone from asking us questions."

"But she told the entire office what's going on," Gina said.

"She had to make sure everyone was on their toes in the event of an attack. Sabrina and Royce's deaths hit the staff hard, but if they found out that one of the Multitude has targeted you and me, *and* they're stuck in the same building as us, people would start to lose their shit. Not everyone here is a field agent, remember. Most of them haven't dealt with Corruption up close and personal. Deanna probably figures most of the staff will assume that you and I are in trouble for acting outside the parameters of our job. I doubt any of them – with the exception of Eleanor, of course – think that Deanna's warning of a possible attack has anything to do with us."

"Will Eleanor tell anyone?" Gina asked.

"No. Analysts are careful not to share information with a supervisor's permission." He smiled. "At least, they're very careful not to get caught. But Eleanor won't want to make things worse for us, so she'll stay quiet – unless something changes and she feels she has no choice but to talk."

"I can see why the two of you work together so well," Gina said. "You both prefer to act based on what happens moment to moment rather than reflexively follow rules."

"More me than her, but yeah." Neal took a sip of coffee from a small paper cup then grimaced. "I know Control doesn't want field offices to waste money on luxuries, but would it kill them to increase our operating budget by a few dollars so we could afford some half-decent coffee? Your dad used to bring in his own, you know. Roasted and ground the beans at home, brewed it, then brought it in a thermos. Sometimes he'd share it with me. Best coffee I ever had."

Gina had been wanting to talk about her father, but she hadn't known how to bring up the subject. But now Neal had given her an opening.

"How do you feel about seeing him again?" Gina asked. "It's been a while, hasn't it?"

"Longer than you've been alive. He's an excellent agent, and he'll be a big help."

"That doesn't answer my question. How do you *feel?*"

"It's... complicated," Neal said. "I'm still trying to sort out my feelings."

"Feelings about what?"

A rich baritone voice interrupted their conversation, and they both turned to face the newcomer. Amador Sandoval stood in the lounge entrance, smiling. Gina tried to imagine how Neal must see him. Her father was a tall, athletically-built man in his fifties, with thick black hair and a neatly-trimmed mustache and goatee that had just the right amount of white in them to look distinguished. He was handsome, not in the unearthly way that Lenny the God of Small Things was, but if he ever decided to retire from Maintenance, he could have a second career as a model or movie actor.

He wore the standard Maintenance uniform for someone of high rank – red tie, white shirt, black pants, black shoes – and at first glance his clothes looked no different than those of any other agent. But a closer look revealed that they were all of a finer quality, and thus more expensive, than usual for a Maintenance employee. Gina was certain Neal noticed the higher quality of his clothes, and she felt embarrassed by her father's obvious disregard for Maintenance's ethos of living simply and consuming as little as possible.

Neal rose to his feet, and Gina quickly did the same.

"My feelings about seeing you," Neal said.

"And what feelings would those be exactly?" Amador asked.

Neal didn't answer. Instead, he walked to Amador, stood toe to toe with him, and looked him in the eyes without blinking. For a moment, Gina thought Neal was going to take a swing at her father, but then he grinned and held his arms out to his sides. Amador returned the grin and hugged him. The men patted each other on the back several times before parting.

"Been a long time," Neal said.

"It has indeed. It's good to see you, my friend, but I wish it was under better circumstances." He turned to Gina and gave her a warm smile. "It appears you had a rough introduction to the life in the field. I've had the chance to go over the Analysts' reports, and I'm proud of the way you've handled yourself. You bring honor to our family name."

"Thanks, Dad."

Gina was uncomfortable being praised by her father in front of Neal. She wanted Neal to see her as a full-fledged partner, not as a child who needed Daddy's approval.

Amador nodded toward the coffeemaker on the counter.

"Coffee still as bad as ever?"

Neal nodded. "And the donuts just as stale."

Amador poured himself a cup, but he passed on a donut. Gina thought he got the coffee to be companionable, not because he was actually going to drink the sludge, but he surprised her by taking a sip and only slightly grimacing. Then the three of them sat down to talk.

"I came with a squad of Exemplars," Amador said. "They're well-armed, and they've taken up defensive positions around the building. If there's an attack, they'll be able to handle it – even if it comes from one of the Multitude."

Gina was relieved to hear this. The Exemplars were Maintenance's elite operatives, the equivalent of special forces in the military, and there was nothing they couldn't handle.

She hoped.

"I know I just told you I read the reports," Amador said, "but I'd like to hear what happened in your own words, if you don't mind."

Neal glanced at Gina, then turned back to Amador.

"Sure. Gina and I were on patrol yesterday..."

Gina only half listened while Neal spoke. She thought about the Black Trust pin Creech had worn at the Stygian Market, thought about the times she'd seen her parents and siblings wear similar pins. Looking at her father now, she had a hard time believing that he or any of her family members could belong to what essentially was a criminal organization.

But she didn't entirely *dis*believe it, either. If she got the chance to speak to her father alone, she'd ask him directly about the Sandovals' connection to the Black Trust. Would he tell her the truth? And if he lied to her, how would she know? She felt guilty for doubting her father, but the fact that she *did* doubt him said a great deal.

"Almost there."

Rachel stepped back from the mausoleum and admired the latest addition to the Atrocity Engine. The inside-out mother and her child – the Innocent soul – stood in the center, the liquefied remains of the Corrupted soul pooled around her feet. The soul representing Life stood next to the mother, breathing into her reversed mouth, and the man who represented Death stood behind the mother, his hands wrapped tightly around her throat.

With his addition, the Engine's strength had quadrupled, and the air hummed with its power. The grass around the mausoleum was already beginning to turn brown and die, and this blight would spread slowly outward until the entire cemetery grounds were as lifeless as the corpses buried in them.

This was the moment when the Engine was at its most vulnerable. The amount of entropic energy it generated was enough to draw the attention of any being in the vicinity with the power and skill to sense it, and if Brother Nothing returned to Ash Creek – hell, if he appeared anywhere on Earth – he would sense the nearly-completed Engine and realize what she was up to. He would come for her, and without the full power of the completed Engine, there would be no way she could hope to stand against him. He would obliterate her and claim the Engine for himself.

She reached out with her mind and checked the wards she'd placed around the mausoleum to conceal the Engine from detection. They remained intact and strong, and she would just have to hope they were enough to keep Brother Nothing from sensing the Engine until it was too late for him to do anything about it.

Satisfied for the moment, Rachel turned to Molly and Judith. They'd stood quietly since delivering the Engine's fourth component, and as Rachel faced them, they became excited, eager to serve their mistress one last time. Rachel wasn't certain they'd hold up long enough to get the job done. Their skin was gray now and drawn tight against their skeletons. They were missing most of their hair and a good portion of their teeth, and – not to put too fine a point on it – they stank. Her doubt must've shown on her face because Molly said, "Is something wrong, Mistress?" except the girl's voice was as degraded as the rest of her, and her words came out as "Z'thin ong, Ztrzz?"

"The final ingredient we need is an Umbral feather, and the only place to get one in Ash Creek is at the local Maintenance headquarters. Since this time, I know exactly what we need and where it's located, I could open a Rift, send you there to retrieve it, and bring you back again. But Maintenance buildings are equipped with technology to guard against dimensional incursions. Brother Nothing could probably get through their defenses – especially since it's a smaller field office – but such a feat is beyond my current power level. If the Engine was finished... But then, if it *was* finished, that would mean I already had the feather, wouldn't it? I've sent my new servant ahead of you, and she's in place and waiting. I'd originally intended the two of you to walk into the Maintenance building and fight your way to the feather, but it's clear to me that you can't succeed given your current condition. You'd probably be destroyed before you could get past the lobby. There has to be a way, though. I just need to think..."

Brother Nothing once told her why he'd chosen her to be his apprentice.

You're cruel, sadistic, and power hungry. All admirable traits in one of the Multitude. But you've got an additional quality that takes all the others to a higher level – imagination. It's the most formidable weapon of them all.

And it was that imagination which gave her the solution she needed. Molly and Judith could not obtain the feather on their own; therefore, they needed help.

"Go big or go home," she said.

Even incomplete, the Atrocity Engine gave off vast amounts of entropic energy, and Rachel drew upon this power now. She raised her hands high above her head and spoke a series of words in a language so foul and blasphemous that the leaves on nearby trees curled up, blackened, and died.

For several moments nothing happened, but then the ground began to shake and rotting, skeletal hands thrust their way upward from the soil and into the light of day. Fingers dug into the ground as the residents of Oak Grove Cemetery pulled themselves out of their graves and shuffled toward Rachel – or rather, toward Molly and Judith.

When the first of the ambulatory corpses reached the mother and daughter, it wrapped its decayed arms around them, and they embraced it in turn. The three bodies merged, becoming one mass of flesh, with four heads and twelve limbs. Then more corpses arrived and joined the conglomeration that was forming, and the mass grew and expanded, and still more corpses came...

More...

And more...

Rachel gazed upon the great abomination that was in the process of being born and laughed like a madwoman.

For Gina's sake, Neal had done his best to make it appear as if he was glad to see Amador again, but he was surprised to find that part of him truly *was* happy. He'd forgotten how charming the man could be, and how he always gave you his full attention when you spoke, as if you were the only person in the room with him. As if you *mattered* to him. His presence was also calm and reassuring, which was exactly what Ash Creek Division needed after the last couple days.

The addition of a squad of Exemplars was a hell of a bonus. What did it matter right now if Amador was in bed with the Black Trust? All that was important was he was here to help with the current situation. Maybe because his daughter was stationed here, but so what? Help was help, and Neal was too pragmatic to look any gift horse in the mouth.

As the three of them were talking, Gina caught his eye, and nodded her head almost imperceptibly toward the lounge's door. Neal got the message. She wanted a few minutes alone with her father. He wasn't sure it was a good idea for him to leave. Most likely, Gina wanted to talk to Amador about his connection to the Black Trust, and while he could understand her wanting to do so, now wasn't the best time. But Amador had noticed as well. Gina *was* his daughter, after all.

"Neal, would you mind stepping out for a bit? I'd like to speak with Gina alone."

Neal couldn't think of a good excuse for staying, so he rose from his seat.

"Sure. See you both in a bit."

And, worrying he was making a mistake, he walked out of the lounge and left Gina and Amador to talk.

As he headed down the hall toward reception, he was struck by how deathly quiet it was – emphasis on *deathly*. The arrival of the Exemplars should've had everyone talking, but the office was silent. When agents were at HQ, they normally removed their smart glasses. None of the employees wanted to feel as if they were being spied on, their actions recorded for later viewing and judgment by Administration. But Neal needed information. He stopped walking and removed his glasses from his front shirt pocket. He slipped them on and tapped one side with his index finger.

"You there, Eleanor?"

There was no guarantee Eleanor would be sitting at her computer console, glasses on, waiting for him to contact her. After all, he and Gina weren't out in the field patrolling. There was no need for her to be monitoring him. Thinking about patrolling made him wonder where Teguzilla was at this moment, and what kind of trouble the Void Breather might be causing. Had it really only been a day ago that the mutated lizard was the biggest problem he and Gina had to worry about? It seemed so much longer.

"I'm here. How was the visit with Amador?"

He frowned. "How did you know about that? Don't the glasses deactivate when you take them off?"

"Technically. But if someone is extraordinarily brilliant, they can find ways to access a signal even when the glasses are supposed to be offline. The inside of your pocket is really boring look at, by the way."

Neal wanted to chastise her for ignoring Maintenance procedure and spying on him, but he knew all she'd do was laugh and tell him that he had some nerve lecturing someone about *following procedure*. And she'd be right to do so. He started walking toward the Analysts' area as he spoke,

"If you were listening in, you know how it went. So why ask?"

"I heard the conversation the three of you had, but there's no way for me to know how you feel about it unless I ask you. So, I'm asking."

"It was weird."

"Good weird or bad weird?"

"A mix of both. You know the rumors about Amador and his family?"

"I do. You think Gina may be asking Amador some uncomfortable questions right now?"

He reached Eleanor's desk and she smiled at him. They both tapped their glasses to close the comm link. He continued the conversation from where they'd left off.

"I don't know. Maybe?" He considered for a moment. "Probably?"

"I could open a signal to her glasses and listen in," Eleanor said.

Neal was tempted. He'd be better able to counsel her after the conversation if he knew exactly what she and Amador said to one another. He didn't mind Eleanor occasionally spying on his feed. They'd developed a good working relationship which over the years had evolved into a close friendship as well as an on-and-off, ill-defined romantic relationship. But he and Gina had been partners for only a couple days. Their working relationship had only started to form. Did he want to risk ruining it by spying on her? If she found out, she'd likely never forgive him. Oh, she might *say* she forgave him, might even believe it, but deep down, the bond of trust between them would be broken before it had a chance to fully develop. It was easy to lose someone's trust, but hard as hell to get it back again.

"Thanks for the offer, but no. She'll tell me when she wants to, if at all. But *you* can tell me something. Why is everyone so damn quiet? The office feels like a morgue right now."

Eleanor glanced around to see if anyone else was listening. The other Analysts were all busy, mostly reviewing data as far as Neal could tell, and none sat directly next to her. Even so, she kept her voice low as she answered Neal's question.

"Deanna sent an email informing us of the Exemplars' arrival. You know the mixed feelings people have about them. Some admire – even revere – them as heroes, while others see them as hard-assed cops ready to report agents to Control at the first sign they even come close to breaking a rule or not strictly adhering to procedure. The admirers are whispering quietly about the Exemplars, while the more paranoid workers are keeping their mouths shut and going about their business like it's a normal day. Others are still upset after what happened to Sabrina and Royce, and the fact Control felt it necessary to send Exemplars here only underscores how much danger we're all in."

"I think I'll go outside and check out the Exemplars. I've never met any before, and I'm curious to see if they live up to their reputation."

"Bullshit. You want to see where they're deployed and how they're armed. You always want to know what you're dealing with, and you don't trust people you haven't worked with before."

"You make me sound paranoid."

"If the straightjacket fits..."

Neal smiled. "Do you mind staying close to your console in case Gina and I need you?"

"No problem. What else am I going to do? It's not like I've got a hot date tonight to get ready for." She grew more serious then. "You think something's going to happen?"

"I don't know for sure, but I have a feeling."

"I hate it when you say that. Did you know I calculated how often your 'feelings' prove to be correct? I am an Analyst, after all. Your success rate is 49.8 percent."

"So, no better than random chance. Look on the bright side. That means there's a 50.2 percent chance I'll be wrong and nothing bad will happen."

"And an almost equal chance something bad *will* happen."

"I suppose it all depends on how badly Rachel wants to kill Gina and me. You know how hard it is to predict what one of the Multitude will do. They're Chaos personified."

"Rachel isn't a very intimidating name for an entity of ultimate evil, is it? She needs something darker, like Lady Dread or Misericordia."

"I'll be sure to tell her that the next time I see her."

He gave Eleanor a parting wave and left the Analysts' area. He didn't remove his smart glasses, though. He wanted to stay connected to Eleanor in case anything happened. When he reached the lobby, he saw Erika sitting at the front desk, fingers on the keys of her laptop. The office manager wasn't typing anything, though. She wasn't even looking at the screen. Instead, she was scowling at a pair of agents – one male, one female – who flanked the office entrance. Neal didn't recognize either of them, which in itself would've been enough to tell him they were Exemplars, but while they wore the standard Maintenance uniform, they projected an aura of superiority.

Most agents cultivated an innocuous appearance so they wouldn't stand out, but not these two. They were in their late twenties or early thirties, fit, trim, and strong. Their gazes took in everything, as if they were human-shaped security cameras, and in case it wasn't obvious enough who they were, their ties had the letter E embroidered on them in white thread. They were also better armed than even Interventionists usually were. They each had two holsters, one for each side. On the right they carried gleaming chrome pistols that resembled cartoon ray guns, and on the left, they carried more prosaic Glocks. The Null Guns were more powerful versions of Nullifiers, designed to deal with the deadliest forms of Corruption, while the Glocks were for more mundane threats.

He looked at Erika.

"Busy day," he said.

She didn't take her gaze off the Exemplars as she answered. "*Too* busy, if you ask me."

Erika kept the facility running at peak efficiency at all times and couldn't stand changes to her established routine, even minor ones. The presence of the Exemplars had to be driving her absolutely apeshit. Normally, Neal might've been amused by Erika's discomfort, but there was nothing funny about the situation they were in.

"I'm going to go out to Number Seven and give it a once-over, make sure its oil and gas are good, run a performance check on the computer system, see if we're low on any supplies."

Now Erika's gaze slid toward him, and her lips pursed in irritation.

"You mean you want to go sit in your van where you can get away from everyone and have a few minutes of peace and quiet."

Neal knew he shouldn't have been surprised that Erika knew about his occasional rest breaks, but he was. He'd thought only Pam was aware of them, and that was because she'd often joined him. The life of an agent could be a stressful one, to say the least, and it helped to have someplace to decompress once and a while. Sometimes he and Pam would go sit in the van, drink coffee, and talk. Other times they'd sit quietly, not needing to speak. He hadn't taken a break in the van since Pam died, but the events of the last couple days had worn him down to the point that he was desperate for a little me time.

Not knowing how to respond to Erika's statement, he stood there silently for several moments, smiling in a way that he hoped didn't make him look too much like an idiot. Finally, Erika sighed.

"I'll have to unlocked the door from here. We're on total lockdown." She jerked her head toward the Exemplars, then in a quieter voice said, "*Their* orders."

Neal nodded slowly, hoping Erika would take this for solidarity. *All of us working slobs are in it together, sister. It's us vs. the Man.*

Erika tapped key on her laptop and the entrance's lock clicked open.

"I'll need to do the same thing to let you back in. Call Eleanor through your glasses, tell her your *once-over* of the van is finished, and she'll inform me. Don't take too long. You never know when Deanna will need you."

"Or Gina."

"Her, too."

Neal turned and started toward the door. He debated whether to make eye contact with the Exemplars as he approached them, maybe say something like *Looking good* or *Big fan*. He settled for a single nod as he passed between them. He half-expected them to draw one of their weapons – the Glocks, most likely – aim them at his chest and demand he show them written permission from Amador before allowing him to step outside.

They did neither of these things, but the female Exemplar held a small E-energy scanner, and she checked the readout as he walked by. Evidently, he passed the test, for the agents permitted him to go by. Trying not to look like he was hurrying, he opened the office door, stepped outside, and walked into the parking lot. When he was far enough out to get a decent view of the roof, he didn't see any Exemplars. He knew they were there, though, hiding somewhere, whether they were using some advanced technology to conceal their presence or if they were just *really* good hiders. Maybe a bit of both.

He decided to trust that the Exemplars were there and watching for any sign of attack. After all, if Amador said his people were in place and ready, then they were. Amador never said anything unless he was absolutely sure of his words.

It was afternoon by now, and the air – while still warm and comfortable – held a hint of coolness, an indication that winter was right around the corner. He'd have to start wearing his navy-blue Maintenance jacket to work soon. Did Gina have a jacket yet? He'd have to check.

They'd parked Number Seven away from the building, beneath an old oak whose leaves were starting to edge toward brown and red. Neal liked parking in shade when it was warm out. Sure, you ended up with bird poop on your windshield sometimes, but it helped keep the van's interior – and the computer equipment inside – from getting too hot. It was a trick he'd learned from Amador.

He reached into his left pants pocket, removed the key fob, and unlocked the driver's side door. He climbed in, shut the door behind him, and slipped the key into the ignition and turned it halfway so the radio would work. He found a station that played classic alternative music from the 90's and 2000's, and he turned the volume up just loud enough that he could make out the lyrics. Any louder, and it would've ruined the peaceful vibe he was going for. The Pixies' "Here Comes Your Man" was on, and he hummed along. This was the kind of music he'd listened to when he'd started working in Ash Creek, back when Amador had been training him.

Seeing his former mentor had impacted him more profoundly than he'd expected. Which was weird, considering that they'd worked together for only a short time before Amador transferred to a higher position in another town. It had been a formative period for Neal, though. He'd been young and impressionable. just starting his career, and Amador had seemed like the perfect agent – confident, poised, knowledgeable, and fearless.

Looking back now, Neal supposed it was no wonder his younger self had put Amador on a pedestal. That's why it had hurt so much when he began to suspect his mentor was dirty. The man he was now would try to prove his suspicions, or at the very least report them to Deanna. But he'd been so unsure of himself back then that he'd never said a word about Amador to anyone, and the man had gone on to become one of Maintenance's most lauded agents. He, along with his wife and two older children, had done a lot of good work over the years, and maybe that made up for them also working for the Black Trust. And maybe it didn't.

His big problem now was what, if anything, he should say to Gina. She began to have her own suspicions after their meeting with Creech and seeing the Black Trust pin that he wore – the same pin she'd seen her family wear at times. Gina was smart as hell, and she believed deeply in Maintenance's mission. There was a good chance she'd discover the truth about her family on her own. But what would she think of him if she learned he'd known about the Sandovals' connection to the Black Trust and said nothing to her? She'd lose trust in him and likely never want to work with him again. More, she might become disillusioned about Maintenance and begin questioning her role in the organization. She might resign, and Maintenance would lose a good agent who had the potential to be great one day. He didn't think that she'd follow in her family's footsteps and start working for the Black Trust. She seemed to have more integrity than that, but in her anger and disappointment, who knew what she might do? People could make regrettable choices when they were hurting.

That settled it. He had to talk to Gina and tell her what he knew about her family. They were partners, and partners didn't hold back important information from each other. He'd wait until the current crisis had passed, though. Gina needed a clear head so she could perform at peak efficiency, and – more importantly – so that she wasn't distracted at the wrong moment and ended up dead.

Now that he'd made his decision, he felt better. Time to go back inside the office and see if there were any new developments. He reached for the ignition key to turn the van off, but before his hand reached it, a voice came from behind him.

"I never told you this, but I always hated your taste in music. I'm more of a country gal, myself."

Neal's guts turned to ice water. He recognized that voice, knew it almost as well as he did his own.

It was Pam.

Nineteen

"You know I hate country music."

Neal was surprised at how normal his voice sounded. After all, it wasn't every day that your dead partner returned from the dead to talk about music with you – not even when you worked for Maintenance. He should be freaked the fuck out, and he supposed he was on some level, but he remained in control of his emotions, at least for the moment.

Maybe I'm in shock, he thought.

He wanted to glace up at the rearview mirror and see if Pam really was behind him. Maybe he'd see nothing and he'd realize that he was having an auditory hallucination, probably brought about by a combination of guilt and the stress of the last couple days. But he was afraid that Pam might be reflected in the glass, and since she'd been dead for two months, he didn't think she'd be looking her best. He kept his gaze focused straight ahead as he spoke.

"How did you get in?" he asked. "The van was locked."

"I don't need keys anymore."

"Why? Because you're a ghost and can pass through solid objects?"

"Something like that." Neal could hear the amusement in her voice. "Why don't you turn and face me while we talk? Afraid of what you'll see? I'm not a rotting corpse if that's what you're worried about. If I was, I'd be stinking up the van something fierce, wouldn't I?"

She's got a point.

"Come sit in the passenger seat," he said.

He continued looking forward as she slipped by him, but he caught a glimpse of her in his peripheral vision, and she seemed normal enough. She sat, and with an effort, he turned his head to face her.

She looked exactly like he remembered her: long blond hair tied back in a ponytail, no makeup, wearing a regulation Maintenance uniform. Her smile was different, though. Colder, crueler. And her eyes, of course. Instead of the bright blue he was familiar with, they were twin pools of darkness.

"Sorry about the eyes. It's just... how they turned out."

"Can you see with those things?"

"Yes, but it's like the whole world is draped in shadow."

"Weird."

Neal couldn't believe that his former partner had returned from the dead, and they were chatting about her fucked-up eyes.

"Are you really Pam?" he asked.

"I'm an echo of her."

Now that he was facing her, Neal could see that the movements of her mouth didn't quite match her words, as if they were a split second out of sync. It was an eerie effect, and it made his skin crawl.

"I assume Rachel brought you back for some reason."

"Yes. She sent me to kill you. Gina, too. I'm looking forward to meeting your new partner, Neal. I have to say I'm touched it took you two months before you were ready to start working with someone else, but I'm glad you moved on. It's unhealthy to remain bound to the past."

"Yeah, well it's unhealthy to get mixed up with one of the Multitude, but what can you do? Occupational hazard, right?"

"True."

"Honestly, I'm surprised Rachel's gone to this much effort to kill me. Creating you couldn't have been easy, even for her. I didn't realize I was that much of a threat to her."

"You're not. But you *are* an irritant, and you've interfered with her plans. You've only managed to slow them down a little, but that was enough to piss her off."

Neal's Nullifier – thoroughly cleaned after having been jammed into Sabrina's eye – was tucked into his right sock and concealed by his pants leg. He didn't know if Pam, or rather, this *echo* of her, could sense he carried the weapon, but even if she couldn't, there was no way he'd be able to reach down, draw it, and fire before she attacked him.

"Why use you to kill me?"

"To psychologically torture you before you die. Plus, you know how theatrical the Multitude can be."

"Yeah."

Neal remained statue-still, aware that the slightest movement might set Pam off.

"I'm really sorry that I wasn't able to save you," he said. Part of him was stalling for time to think of a plan, but another part believed this *was* Pam – at least some remnant of her – and he needed to say these things while he had the chance. "I know you were taken by a creature of Corruption, but if I hadn't wanted to stop and check out the dumpster, that trash monster never would've gotten hold of you."

"That's right. It was an indescribably agonizing death, Neal. My body was torn apart, but that was the least of it. My consciousness – what some people might call my soul – was dismantled piece by piece. What only took seconds for you lasted a lifetime for me. Can you imagine what it's like having your body and soul shredded over the course of what feels like decades? That's the death you sentenced me to, Neal."

The shadows in her eyes seemed to grow darker, if that was possible, and small tendrils extruded from them, as if she was having trouble containing the Corruption that seethed inside her.

"It was pure chance which of us approached the dumpster first," he said. "We played rock, paper, scissors to decide, remember? You won, so you got to check out the dumpster."

"Did I win? Or did you *let* me win so you wouldn't have to go first?"

Neal opened his mouth to reply – No way in hell would he ever have done that – but then he realized what Pam, or this distorted version of her, was trying to do.

Why use you to kill me?

To psychologically torture you before you die.

"I appreciate what you're trying to do, but to be honest, the real Pam would never be so clumsy about it."

The ebon tendrils extending from her shadow-filled eyes flailed in agitation.

"What do you mean?"

"For one thing, she would never have said she was going to psychologically torture me. She was too smart to ever give an opponent a warning like that. And she wouldn't use such an obvious tactic as trying to get me to believe that I secretly wanted her to die. She'd know I'd already blame myself for what happened and that I've been beating myself up about it ever since, going over and over the incident in my mind, always trying to think of what I might have done differently to save her. You can't possibly make me feel worse about her death than I already do."

Pam frowned, but her eye tendrils' undulations slowed.

"What *would* she have said?"

Neal pretended to think about it for a minute.

"She'd probably remind me of different experiences we shared to break down my defenses before she went for the guilt trip. It would be more effective that way."

"What sort of experiences?"

"Not big ones, like the time we found a temporal acceleration vortex in a junkyard, or when a herd of Durg wandered out of Shadow and began crawling down Main Street. She'd remind me of smaller things, times when we weren't dealing with some crisis, when we could interact as friends instead of coworkers. She'd tease me about how whenever I order anything hot – a sandwich, coffee – I always take a bite or a sip before it's cool enough and burn my mouth. She'd talk about my hatred of squirrels. They're just rats with fluffy tales, and those black, beady eyes... Ug!" He shuddered and continued.

"She'd remind me of how whenever it rained, we'd park the van, and eat lunch inside, listening to the rain hit the roof and talking about whatever random topics came to mind. Most of the time they were silly things, like why do pigeons bob their heads when they walk, and whether daylight savings time was created by the Multitude as a way to fuck with people's minds. But sometimes we'd talk about serious stuff, too. She got married young, to a guy who didn't work for Maintenance. He could never understand her job, and eventually it became a source of contention between them, and they split up. It was the biggest regret in her life, and she often wondered if she'd tried hard enough to save her marriage. I'd tell her she did more than enough – which she did – but she always had a hard time believing me. We might even talk about the time we thought about dating but decided not to because we didn't want to ruin our friendship. I could go on, but you get the idea."

Pam looked at him a moment, thoughts unreadable, and then she smiled slowly, and Neal saw more tendrils of darkness squirming behind her teeth.

"Thanks for talking about all that shit so I didn't have to. Seems to me you've been psychologically tortured enough, so we might as well get on with it."

Her eye tendrils shot toward him, lengthening and thickening as they came. They encircled his throat, their touch so cold it burned, and then they tightened, cutting off his air. He instinctively wanted to reach for the tendrils and try to pull them off him, but he forced himself to remain still. He kept his gaze fixed on Pam's face – he couldn't look into her eyes the way they were, but he hoped the effect was the same – and even though he didn't possess the slightest bit of telepathy, he tried to reach out to her mind with his thoughts.

Come on, Pam... I know you're in there somewhere...

But the tendrils continued to tighten, and Pam – or the thing that resembled her – continued smiling. Neal's lungs burned, and black haze circled the outer edges of his vision. His pulse thudded in his ears, and sharp pain lanced through his head. The field of black began to widen, moving in toward the center of his vision, threatening to obscure it. When it occluded his vision entirely, would that mean he was dead?

His lungs screamed now, and the pounding in his head was so intense, he thought the top of his skull might pop off, and his brains would spray across the van's ceiling.

Pam... Please!

And then, just as darkness completely filled his vision, he felt the tendrils unwrap from around his neck and pull away. He drew in a heaving gasp of air, and his head throbbed with pain. He continued drawing breath for several more moments, and soon the darkness retreated and his vision cleared. He looked at Pam. At first, she was blurry, but then his eyes focused, and he saw that the shadows in her eyes were gone. She now looked perfectly normal, her expression one of mingled horror and disbelief.

"Oh my god, I'm so sorry, Neal! I don't know what could've made me do such a thing! I mean, like I *literally* don't know. Were those little tentacles that were coming out of my eyes?"

Neal felt nauseated, and his throat hurt like a bitch, but he smiled.

"I knew you couldn't kill me." His voice was raspy, and it hurt to talk. "If there was a spark of you left in there somewhere, I hoped it could be fanned into a flame. I'm glad I was right."

Pam scowled. "What the flying fuck is happening?"

Neal intended to explain the situation to her, but before he could speak, he saw movement in the parking lot outside the passenger window. He pointed.

"Do you see that or am I hallucinating due to oxygen deprivation?"

Pam shifted in her seat so she could look out the window.

"I definitely see it, but I have no idea what the hell it is."

A dozen yards away from Number Seven, something shaped like a gigantic serpent was slithering across the parking lot, heading straight for the Maintenance building. But this was no overgrown reptile. The creature's body was formed from hundreds of men, women, and children holding onto each other. Most were dressed in formal clothing, skin discolored, flesh rotted away to expose bits of bone. Some looked fresh, while others were only skeletons, but they all had one thing in common, Neal realized.

They were all dead.

"Are you and Mom members of the Black Trust?"

Gina hadn't planned on being so direct, but the words came out on their own. Her father didn't respond right away. His eyes narrowed and he frowned slightly, and she had the impression that he was considering his reply carefully.

"Did Neal tell you that we were?"

"No."

"Then what makes you ask?"

She told him about visiting the Stygian Market with Neal, their encounter with Creech, and seeing the Black Trust symbol that he wore – the same symbol she remembered seeing her other family members wear on occasion. When she was finished, Amador laughed, surprising her.

"Neal's certainly giving you an education, isn't he? He's the perfect mentor for you. He'll teach you things you could never learn from the instructors at the Homestead." He grew serious then. "For example, he's shown you that rigid adherence to Maintenance's rules can be... counterproductive at times. Who do you think taught him that?"

"You did."

"That's right. There can be a vast gulf between theory and practice, especially for agents in the field. Sometimes you must think fast, improvise, be ready to do whatever is necessary to get the job done. And sometimes you find yourself making unexpected alliances."

Gina's stomach twisted upon hearing her father's words.

"Is that a confession?"

"You need to learn not to think in simplistic binary terms. Good and Evil are meaningless concepts in the real world. There is only the Gyre and its insatiable appetite, and no matter how hard we fight to slow its feeding, we're only delaying the inevitable. In the end, the Gyre will devour everything, even itself."

"So, there's no point in even trying?"

"Of course, there's a point. We must do what we can while we live. And if working with the Black Trust from time to time – as distasteful as it might be – can help us in our mission, then so be it."

She remembered something Neal had said in the Stygian Market, after they'd finished their deal with Creech, about her family's connection to the Black Trust.

Most likely they were doing some deep undercover work for Maintenance, and they just pretended *to belong to the Black Trust.*

At the time, she'd sensed that Neal wasn't telling her the truth, at least, not the *entire* truth. But before she'd been able to ask him about it, Grimwell, Squeal, and Jane Dough had confronted them, and she hadn't had a chance to return to the subject yet.

"Neal said something to me along those lines."

"See? You know your mother, brother, sister, and me as family, but Neal knows us as agents. If there were any rumors about us being profiteering mercenaries, don't you think he would've said something to you?"

She'd only known Neal a brief time, but it was clear he was a good man who cared deeply about the cause he'd pledged his life to, someone who would do whatever it took to combat Entropy and to hell with everything else. Someone who wouldn't want to do or say anything that might hurt his new trainee.

The Black Trust didn't care about anything except enriching themselves in order to live the best life possible during their short time on the planet. Her parents had always told her that their money had come from a family inheritance, but she was beginning to doubt this was true, and it made her feel sick.

Amador changed the subject then.

"I didn't want to say anything while Neal was here, but I noticed you're not wearing any makeup today."

She wanted to remind him that needless waste was against the ethos of Maintenance, and that included the use of makeup. But he knew that.

"I didn't feel the need for any," she said.

"And Ash Creek *is* your first assignment. I suppose it's a good idea to toe the line for a while. But you're a Sandoval. No one will question you if you decide to look pretty once in a while. They let you wear makeup while you were training at the Homestead, didn't they?" A coldness came into his eyes then. "Why do you think that was?"

Because you and Mom made sure of it.

Before she could answer aloud, a loud crashing sound came from the direction of the lobby, and a tremor juddered through the building. Deanna's voice came over the office's intercom system.

"All employees, initiate defense protocols! We're under attack!"

As if to underscore her words, there came a much louder crash, followed by a more violent tremor.

Amador's expression became grim as he put on his smart glasses.

"I have to go, my love. Head to the Bunker with the others. Stay safe."

He got up from his seat, gave her a quick kiss on the forehead, and ran out of the room, no doubt to direct the Exemplars. Every Maintenance office had an underground Bunker where employees could take shelter when needed, and as a Surveyor, that was where she should go. Is that what Neal would do, though? She smiled.

"Like hell he would."

She put on her glasses and tapped the side to open a comm channel.

"Eleanor?"

"I'm here, Gina."

"What's happening?"

Eleanor hesitated. *"We're under attack by a giant wormlike creature that appears to be made out of dead bodies – hundreds of them."*

A couple days ago, Gina would've found this impossible to believe. Now it was just one more goddamned thing to deal with.

"Where's Neal?"

"He went outside to think. He's in Number Seven."

Outside – where this corpse-thing was.

Gina quickly reached down and drew the Nullifier from her sock. Then she jumped up from her seat and bolted out of the room.

Rachel stood in front of the mausoleum, luxuriating in the feel of the Atrocity Engine's power washing over her. It was almost complete. All it needed was an Umbral feather, and then power beyond comprehension would be hers. Power greater than that wielded by any single member of the Multitude, perhaps even greater than that wielded by Brother Nothing himself.

If the Engine worked, that is. If it failed... well, the universe would hardly notice the destruction of such a small and insignificant planet, would it?

Although her own eyes were open, she wasn't seeing the Atrocity Engine in front of her. She was seeing through the hundreds of eyes that belonged to her new creation as it slithered into the parking lot of Ash Creek's Maintenance division and headed swiftly toward the building.

She grinned. This was going to be fun.

TWENTY

Neal had seen some pretty weird things during his career with Maintenance, but a giant serpent made out of corpses was definitely among the strangest.

He'd gotten out of the van and stood near it, Pam at his side. It was bizarre how natural it felt to have here there with him, as if she hadn't been dead herself for the last two months. Then again, in his line of work, you had to quickly adjust to changing circumstances, no matter how strange they might be. And it was Pam. They'd worked together for years, and more than that, they'd been best friends. So why wouldn't it feel normal – normal-*ish*, anyway – for her to be here now?

The two of them watched as the corpse-serpent slithered toward the Maintenance building, heading straight for the entrance, as if it intended to smash its way inside. Had Rachel sent the thing to kill Gina and him? If so, talk about overkill. The Multitude preferred to work quietly behind the scenes, their plans not revealing themselves until it was too late to do anything to stop them. It seemed that Rachel hadn't gotten the memo, though, because there was nothing subtle about what was happening here.

The Exemplars stationed on the roof of the building spotted the monster – there was no way they could miss the damn thing – and they began firing at it. Bright beams of energy shot forth from the barrels of Null Guns, Null Rifles, and Absorbers and struck the Death Worm. The two Exemplars who'd been guarding the door inside, rushed out and began firing their weapons at the undead beast as well. The Death Worm reared back, hundreds of dead mouths crying out in pain, but otherwise the Exemplars' weapons appeared to have no effect on the creature.

"That's impossible!" Neal said. "Those weapons should've reduced that thing to a pool of Corruption!"

"It's protected," Pam said. "Rachel's infused it with some kind of power I don't recognize, insulating it from the effect of the null beams. Whatever it is, it's strong."

Neal looked at her. "How do you know that?"

"I'm not sure. Maybe because I'm technically dead? Or maybe because Rachel created me too? I'm . . . linked to her somehow. Don't worry – she's not seeing or hearing through me, and she isn't reading my thoughts, although I suppose she could do those things if she tried."

Interesting, Neal thought. *Maybe we can use that.*

The Exemplars had continued firing as Neal and Pam spoke, and while the Death Worm screamed in pain, the energy beams didn't appear to be inflicting any real damage. The creature swayed back and forth as it writhed in pain, but at least it hadn't gone any closer to the building. The Exemplars were managing to hold it off, and if they could keep up the barrage, they might be able to break through whatever protection the creature had and finally destroy it.

But then the front end of the Death Worm – what would've been the head on another creature – pulled back, paused a moment, and then whipped forward. A dozen bodies detached from the main mass of the thing and flew through the air toward the roof. The Exemplars trained their fire at the oncoming corpses, but while they managed to hit a few – which probably dissolved into Corrupted goo – they missed most of their targets. The surviving corpses landed on the roof and immediately attacked the Exemplars.

The elite agents managed to destroy a couple more. Obviously, whatever force protected the conglomerate creature wasn't effective when its components were separated from the main body. But the

Exemplars still didn't get them all, and the remainder tore into them like a pack of starving wolves. The agents screamed as skeletal hands tore at the flesh and dead teeth sank into the soft meat of their throats. The screams didn't last long, though. Streams of blood poured from the roof and slid down the front of the building like crimson rain.

"Jesus," Neal whispered.

The two agents on the ground looked at each other, then turned around and hauled ass back inside. Neal didn't blame them one bit.

Now that it was no longer under attack, the Death Worm moved closer to the building. The undead monsters that had killed the Exemplars leaped off the roof and rejoined the main mass, then the Death Worm turned, lowered its front half to the asphalt, and slithered rapidly away from the building.

"Is it retreating?" Neal asked. "That doesn't make any sense."

But the Death Worm wasn't leaving. Once it reached the rear edge of the parking lot, it turned back toward the building and streaked forward, aiming at the main entrance. Neal understood then what the creature was attempting to do. It intended to ram the entrance and force itself into the building. Pam had the same thought.

"It wants to get inside," she said.

The Death Worm's "head" slammed into the entrance's glass door, but while the door shattered and its metal frame bent, the Death Worm bounced back, as if it had struck an impenetrable barrier.

"It can't," Neal said. "The building's Corruption-proof. No significant amount of entropic energy can enter, and that thing is practically nothing *but* E-energy."

The Death Worm was not deterred by its lack of success. It quickly slithered back to its starting position and tried again. Once more, it was unable to enter the building, and it backed up and tried a third attempt. This time the creature hit the broken door so hard, it flew off its hinges. Now there was nothing barring entrance to the building. Nothing physical, anyway. The E-energy barrier remained intact.

Neal pictured Erika abandoning her desk after the creature's first strike, and the image of the normally stiff, proper, and always-in-control office manager running like a madwoman through the corridors of the building almost made him smile.

"Neal, if the door's down, doesn't that mean the protective barrier in the spot is down too?"

"It's weakened, sure, but there's enough energy in the building façade around the entrance to cover it. The Death Worm can't get in, no matter what it does."

The creature rushed toward the entrance once more, but this time instead of slamming into it, it stopped short. Two bodies separated from it – a woman and a young girl – and they ran toward the open entrance. When they reached it, they passed through easily, as if the energy barrier no longer existed.

"But it might be weak enough for one or two of them to get inside," Neal said.

The rest of the Death Worm curled up like a snake in front of the entrance and rested there, clearly intending to prevent anyone from entering or leaving that way. Neal knew the people inside weren't trapped. There were other exits they could use to escape. The problem was that two of Rachel's servants had gotten in, and he had no idea what they intended to do. Eleanor was still in there, as was Deanna – and Gina. Hopefully, Amador would be able to protect his daughter. He might've been a two-faced profiteer, but Neal knew he loved his daughter, and he was damn good in a fight.

He turned to Pam.

"You said you have a connection to Rachel. Do you know what she wants here?"

"I..." She scowled, concentrating more deeply. "I'm not sure. She's... building something. Something important. And the last piece she needs to complete it is inside."

"Do you know what the piece is?"

Pam shook her head. "All I know is that it's something powerful."

"Do you know what Rachel's building?"

Again, Pam shook her head. "No. I only know that it's unimaginably dangerous. Like, end-of-the-world dangerous."

Neal felt like he'd been punched in the gut. He was used to dealing with localized threats, not planetary ones. This was *way* above his pay grade.

"Where is she building this thing?"

"In a cemetery, the one by the middle school." Sweat beaded her brow, and she looked drained. "That's all I can get. Sorry."

Neal thought fast. He was used to improvising in the field, but he'd never before had to deal with anything as serious – or complicated – as this situation.

"I need to get inside and try to stop Rachel's servants from getting whatever it is they came here for. But if that doesn't work – and assuming I'm not dead – I'll have to confront her at the cemetery. Take Number Four. Bob always leaves the keys in the ignition. Meet me at the cemetery."

"Okay, but I don't know if I'll be able to fight her. She did make me, you know. She might even try to turn me against you, and if I'm close to her, I might not be able to fight her."

"I'll take my chances. But can you do me a favor a make a quick stop on the way?"

Neal did not watch Pam – he was still having trouble believing she was really back – as she turned over Number Four's engine. Instead, he watched the Death Worm. It had settled in front of the building's entrance, as if asleep, but the bodies still held onto one another, maintaining the creature's conglomerate form.

The instant Number Four's engine came to life, the Death Worm's head rose, like an animal suddenly on the alert. It remained that way for a second, as if waiting to see what happened next. And when Pam put the van into gear and began backing out of its parking spot, the Death Worm shot forward. It streaked toward Pam, obviously intending to make sure she didn't get of the parking lot alive.

Neal reached into his pants pocket and withdrew the spherical Expungent Grenade. He'd intended to save it for Rachel, but no way was he going to let Pam die again. He recalled Creech's instruction for activating it.

Whoever held it last can set it off telepathically.

He was already holding it, so he had the first step completed. Time for step two.

He hurled the grenade toward the Death Worm, and he watched as the device arced up, then began to come down. When it was within a foot of touching the creature, he thought a single word.

Boom.

The device exploded and the blue chemical – a hundred gallons of it, Creech had claimed – sprayed out in all directions and then the deluge rained down onto the Death Worm. The creature's howls of pain when the Exemplars were firing on it were nothing compared to the shrieks of absolute agony that tore from the throats of the living corpses that made up the Death Worm. Dead flesh began to liquefy immediately, followed quickly by the bone it encased. The Death Worm's cries faded, the creature fell silent, and its body collapsed into large puddles of viscous goo. The Death Worm was dead – again.

Pam finished backing up, then put the engine in drive and started forward. She honked the horn once to say goodbye to Neal, and then she hit the gas and roared out of the lot and onto the street. As Neal watched her go, he wondered if she'd be able to retain control of her mind or if Rachel would reclaim it and once more use her against him. He hated to think of his former partner becoming Rachel's puppet again, but he knew it was a possibility. He decided he'd better hedge his bets.

He still had his Nullifier in hand, although so far, he hadn't used it, and he gripped it tight as he ran toward the entrance. As he went, he tapped the side of his glasses with his free hand.

"Eleanor, I need you to make a phone call for me."

Gina ran down the hallway, headed for the main entrance, hoping she'd be able to reach the parking lot in time to help Neal fight the giant corpse-thing that was attacking the building.

She saw Erika running toward her, and she wanted to stop and ask the clearly terrified woman what was happening, but she merely hooked a thumb over her shoulder as if to say, *It's that way* as she raced past. Gina heard a second crash this time, and the floor vibrated beneath her feet.

"That worm monster really wants in bad," she said.

"And it might be able to do it," Eleanor replied. *"It killed the Exemplars guarding the building., and it shrugs off Null beams as if they're little more than flashlights."*

Gina didn't like the sound of that. She was about the ask the Analyst if she knew how Neal was doing, but she reached the lobby and saw her father and two Exemplars standing in front of the entrance, Null Guns in hand and firing at the glass and metal door.

When Amador saw her, Gina thought he would chastise her for disobeying him, but he didn't.

"Help us reinforce the door!" he shouted.

Gina did as her father commanded. She took up a position next to him, aimed her Nullifier at the door, and added its relatively meager power to that of the Null Guns. Nullifier beams were only visible as half-seen ripples in the air, but the concentrated energy Null Guns put out was a glowing white. Gina had a hard time tracking the location of her beam due to how bright the Null Gun's discharges were, but she'd aimed at a spot where none of the other the beams was trained on and hoped for the vest. Null tech was designed to counter entropic energy, but she'd never imagined she'd ever have to deal with so damn much of it in any one being. This goddamned corpse-thing was like the entropic energy equivalent of Moby-fucking-Dick – on steroids.

The door wasn't in good shape. The metal frame was bent and the glass was cracked in numerous places. Shards had broken off and lay scattered on the floor. The door looked as if the mildest of breezes could knock it down right now, and Gina didn't see what the energy from their weapons could do to shore it up. But that didn't mean they shouldn't try.

She saw the corpse-thing come slithering at them, moving faster than should've been possible for something of its bulk. As it drew closer, she could easily make out the separate bodies that comprised the monster – their features slack, eyes glowing baleful red.

"Stop!" Amador shouted. But if the creature heard the command, it simply didn't choose to comply. It continued coming at the door like a locomotive, and this time when its head collided with the entrance the sound was louder than either of the two previous times. The door finally gave under the impact, tore free from its hinges, and flew straight toward Gina. Her instincts screamed at her to run, but all she could was stand there, frozen with fear and wait for the mass of twister metal to slam into her. But before it did, her father was suddenly at her side. He shoved her as hard as he could, and she stumbled, lost her balance, and fell to the floor.

The glass flew through the air, striking one of the Exemplars full in the face. The woman screamed as the shards violated her flesh, but her voice was cut off as the bent and twisted door frame clipped her head. Blood gushed from her cuts and head wound as she fell backward onto the floor, unconscious or dead. The male Exemplar was standing next to the woman, and after the door frame struck her, it hit his right shoulder, and her spun around, arm flopping as if it was boneless. Amador tried to leap out of the way, but he was too slow. The door frame hit his chest, and he flew backward, landing on the floor several feet from Gina. The door frame continued on, smashing into Erika's desk and reducing it to kindling before finally coming to a stop.

It had all happened so fast that for a moment, all Gina could do was lie there, stunned. But then she remembered – the corpse-thing! She turned her head so she could see the entrance, expecting to find the monster squeezing its bulk through the empty space. Something did come through, but it wasn't the corpse-thing. Two bodies detached from it – a woman and a girl – and they hurried inside.

"We made it!" the girl said. Her flesh was mottled gray and rotting, her voice a harsh dry rasp.

The woman was in no better condition.

"Come on, we have to–"

Before she could finish, the male Exemplar rose on shaky legs. His right arm was useless, but he now held his Null Gun in his left hand. He aimed it at the woman, squeezed the trigger, and a beam of white light struck her right between the eyes. It had to be pure luck, Gina thought, but whether due to chance, skill, or some combination of the two, it was a hell of a shot. The woman shrieked briefly, then her body began to come apart, disintegrating into dust-like particles. But before they could fall to the floor, they vanished, leaving not a single trace of her behind.

The girl stared at the spot where the woman had been, then she turned toward the Exemplar and fixed him with a hate-filled gaze.

"You killed my mother!" she screamed and ran at him.

He fired, but this time he missed, and the girl leaped onto him, grabbed his shoulders, fastened her teeth on his throat, and began tearing. The man let out a gurgling cry as blood sprayed the air, and then he went down, the girl continuing to savage his throat for several more seconds. When he was dead, she stood, her mouth smeared with blood, his clothes soaked with it.

Gina had lost her Nullifier with she'd fallen, otherwise she'd have fired at the girl. She could try to fight her hand to hand, but the truth was that after seeing what she did to the Exemplar, she was too afraid. She squeezed her eyes shut, held her breath, and hoped the girl would think she was dead and pass her by.

She listened, waiting to hear the girl's footsteps, but there was nothing. She imagined the girl standing there, looking at the three of them, trying to decide whether they were still threats. The woman Exemplar who'd been struck in the face by the door frame was silent, as was Amador. Gina didn't know if they were unconscious or dead, but right now all that mattered was that neither of them moved or made a sound.

She imagined what her father might say if he could see what she was doing.

A Sandoval doesn't hide like a coward! Get up and fight!

Then she imagined what Neal might say.

Stay down and stay quiet. Don't throw away your life performing idiotic heroics. Wait until the odds are in your favor again.

A few more seconds passed, and then Gina heard the girl start to walk away. Soon she was running, her footfalls becoming quieter as she moved deeper into the building.

Gina opened her eyes, jumped to her feet, and rushed to her father. She touched her fingers to side of his neck and was relieved to find his pulse strong. She then checked on the Exemplar who'd been struck by flying glass along with the door frame. The woman's face was a bloody mess, and her pulse was as strong as Amador's. She didn't bother checking on the other Exemplar. There was no question he was dead.

The undead girl had mutilated him so severely that his head remained attached to his body only by a few thin strips of meat.

She grabbed one of the Exemplars' Null Guns, reconsidered, then grabbed another. She then reached up and tapped the heel of her hand to her glasses.

"Where's she at, Eleanor?"

"She's headed toward Deanna's office."

"Is Neal okay?"

"He's fine, now haul ass!"

Gina, a weapon in each hand, starting running.

Twenty-One

"I don't care what it takes! We need reinforcements now!" Deanna paused, listened. "Yes, I *know* we were assigned Exemplars. They've all fallen!"

She kept her gaze fixed on her laptop as she spoke. The screen was divided into four squares showing images from the building's security system. As soon as the snake-zombie creature – whatever the hell it was – attacked the building, she was on the phone to Columbus Division to report what was happening. Columbus was almost an hour and a half away from Ash Creek, so as soon as she'd informed the state office, she contacted Cincinnati Division.

They were much closer, only forty-five minutes away, but they might as well on Mars. There was no way they could get here in time to help. Still, she had to try. She wasn't worried about her people overmuch. The first time the creature slammed into the entrance, she'd given the order to evacuate the building. Aside from Eleanor – who insisted on remaining at her computer station to aid Neal – and several Security guards, everyone was in the process of getting to safety. Her concern was what the creature would do after it destroyed the building. Would it move on and continue its rampage through the town? There was no way she could let that happen.

A thought occurred to her.

"You've got helicopters, right? At top speed, they can reach 160 miles per hour. That means they should be able to get here in twenty minutes, maybe faster if the pilots really push it."

She listened again.

"Good! I'll have one of my Analysts send you all the data we have."

Deanna disconnected without bothering to say goodbye. On her computer screen, in the upper right quadrant, she saw Amador and two of his Exemplars confronting a woman and a girl, both of whom looked as if they were on the verge of rotting away to nothing. She tapped the side of her glasses.

"Eleanor, send security footage of the attack to Cincinnati Division and connect them to a live feed as well. They're coming to help us." She glanced at the lower left quadrant of her screen. This one showed the parking lot, where Neal was preparing to throw something at the creature. Standing next to him was...

"Who is that outside with Neal? It looks like Pam."

"It is. Kind of. It's hard to explain."

"I bet. Just send the data and keep helping Neal. Contact me if you have something to report."

"Will do."

Deanna returned her attention to her computer. Two quadrants showed Amador and Neal, while a third showed Gina running down a hallway toward the main entrance, Nullifier in hand. Deanna admired the kid's guts. She'd make a hell of an agent someday – assuming she survived the next several minutes. Deanna sat and continued to monitor events as they transpired. The thought of evacuating herself never occurred to her. She was this facility's Director, and she would remain at her post until the crisis was over or she was dead. There were no other options for her.

She watched as Neal used an Expungent Grenade to deal with the snake creature. How the hell had he gotten hold of one? The damn things were highly dangerous and illegal as far as Maintenance was concerned. She decided she was better off not knowing. She then watched as Gina arrived to help her father and the Exemplars fight the decaying woman and girl. In the end, they managed to take out the woman, but the girl survived, and all the agents, including Gina and Amador, were down. Whether they were alive or dead, Deanna didn't know. The girl ran out of the lobby and down the hallway. A moment later, Gina rose from the floor, grabbed a pair of the Exemplars' Null Guns, and headed off in pursuit.

The nearly-dead girl was heading in Deanna's direction, and that meant it was time for her to take a more direct hand in matters. She opened a desk door, took out a Nullifier, and walked to the door. She opened it, stepped out into the hallway, and starting running toward the girl. She didn't know what the little Corrupted bitch wanted, and she didn't care. She was going to terminate her with extreme prejudice, and she intended to enjoy every moment of it.

Deanna was tense, but she wasn't frightened. Before becoming Director, she'd been an Interventionist, and she'd seen her fair share of action in the field. It had been a number of years since she'd been in a real fight, but she was ready.

It didn't take long to encounter the girl. Deanna turned a corner, and there she was, less than three feet away and closing fast. Deanna stopped running, slid to a stop, and raised her Nullifier. Unfortunately, her reflexes had been dulled from years sitting behind a desk, and she was a fraction of a second too slow. That was all the girl needed. She increased her speed, and before Deanna could fire, she grabbed hold of her arm with inhuman strength, and bit down on her wrist – hard. Deanna screamed, blood flowed, and her hand sprang open, releasing the Nullifier. When it hit the floor, the girl stamped on it, breaking it in two. She then pulled her face away from Deanna's wrist, taking a chunk of meat with her. She swallowed it, grinned at Deanna with blood-slick teeth, then shoved her into the wall and started running again.

Deanna slumped to the floor, her back against the wall. Her wound hurt like hell, and she was bleeding like a motherfucker. The girl had likely torn tendons as well as broken bone, meaning her hand was useless now. She'd probably need surgery, but she could worry about that later. First, she needed to stop the bleeding. She gritted her teeth. This was going to hurt.

She gripped her wounded wrist with her left hand and squeezed tight to slow the bleeding. She screamed behind closed lips and tears streamed from her eyes. She heard pounding footfalls then, and looked up to see Gina running toward her, Null Guns in hand. Gina stopped, her eyes widening in shock when she saw how badly Deanna was wounded. Deanna appreciated her concern, there was no time for it.

"I'll be okay. The girl ran past me. Go stop her."

Gina hesitated.

"That's an order!"

Gina didn't look happy about it, but she nodded, ran around the corner, and kept going.

Deanna couldn't reach up to activate her smart glasses, but there was no need. Eleanor came over the channel.

"A couple Med Techs have volunteered to re-enter the building, and they should reach you shortly. Hold tight – literally."

Deanna groaned at Eleanor's awful joke. She rested her head against the wall, closed her eyes, and waited for help to come.

Gina hated leaving Deanna like that, but she knew the Director had made the right choice to order her onward. The Corrupted girl had entered the building for a reason, and she had to be stopped before she could accomplish her goal, whatever it was.

Gina turned the corner and ran as fast and hard as she could, but before she was halfway down the hall, she saw the girl step out of Deanna's office, holding the Director's framed Umbral feather in her hands. Gina stopped, confused. *That* was the reason for the assault on the building? So, the girl could steal a *decoration*?

Gina's hesitation cost her. The girl hurled the frame as if it were a Frisbee directly at Gina's head. Gina saw it coming and started to raise her arms to block it, but she was too late. The frame struck her forehead, bright light flashed behind her eyes, and then everything went dark.

"Come on, Gina, wake up! I know you're not dead – Eleanor told me!"

It was Neal's voice, but it seemed to come from far away. She was distantly aware of a physical sensation, but she couldn't pinpoint what it was. A couple seconds later, she realized that someone – presumably Neal – was patting the back of her hand. She became aware of pain next, a great pounding in her head, like something was trapped inside her skull and was desperately trying to batter its way free. She knew she should probably open her eyes, but she really didn't want to. If the pain was *this* bad here in the darkness, what would it be like if she let light in? Better to go back to sleep until the pain was gone.

She felt Neal patting her cheek then, each contact sending bolts of white-hot agony shooting through her head.

"Stop it," she mumbled.

Neal patted her cheek harder.

"I said stop it!"

"Not until you wake up."

Fine.

She opened her eyes, and as light flooded in, she instantly regretted it. The pain in her skull increased tenfold, and she felt as if she was going to throw up. She squeezed her eyes shut tight and vowed that she would never open them again as long as she lived.

Neal stopped patting her cheek.

"I know where Rachel is," he said.

That got her attention. Her eyes sprang open, and she sat up straight. Her head still hurt, but she no longer cared about the pain.

"Let's go," she said.

Neal grinned.

Rachel breathed a sigh of relief as Molly stepped through the Rift she'd created, the Umbral feather – or rather, the frame containing it – clutched in her small decaying hands. Judith had been destroyed during the assault on Maintenance headquarters, as had the conglomerate creature that Rachel had sent, but they were acceptable losses. All that mattered was the feather was here.

The glass was broken, and the frame was bent, but that was unimportant. The feather was intact. Not that this came as any great surprise. No force in the Omniverse aside from the Gyre itself could harm an Umbral feather. Even Brother Nothing, with all the great power at his command, couldn't so much as scratch one. The Maintenance building was too well warded against the Multitude for Rachel to be able to create a Rift inside the building, but once she sensed Molly was out in the parking lot, it had been child's play to open a Rift and bring her back to the cemetery.

The Rift closed behind the girl, leaving an invisible scar that, if someone were unfortunate to walk through the space where it was located, would cause their genitals to attain sentience. One of the more amusing Rift aftereffects Rachel had ever caused.

Molly tried to smile as she held the frame out to Rachel, but her facial muscles were nearly dead now, and all she could manage was a partial grimace. The girl wouldn't last much longer. Soon she'd collapse into dust, as her Corrupted friends – Cathy and Mari – most likely had by now. Rachel hoped the two girls had managed to cause some chaos before being forced to shuffle off this mortal coil.

Rachel reached for the frame and was surprised to see her hands were shaking. She'd never been in the presence of so much raw power before, and she couldn't help thinking that the moment she touched the frame, the feather would destroy her. She told herself she was a fool and gripped the frame anyway.

In order for the Atrocity Machine to work, she couldn't touch any of its components, but she wasn't touching the feather, was she, merely the frame that held it. She brought the frame closer to her face and examined the feather. She'd never seen one before, and it was larger than she'd expected, nearly a foot long. It was made from a silvery metal that had no name – at least none that anyone currently alive in the Omniverse knew – and it shined with a soft inner glow that most people would mistake for reflected light. You couldn't tell from looking at it, but its edge was so sharp it could cut subatomic particles in half.

It was the single most beautiful thing she'd ever seen, and she knew that everything she looked at from this moment on, no matter how glorious, would pale in comparison.

She knelt and gently placed the frame on the ground. Then she stood, held out her hand, and an obsidian dagger appeared in her palm. She gripped the hilt tight, the knife so cold it burned, and she reveled in the pain.

"Get the feather," she ordered Molly. "Be careful to hold it by the shaft, unless you want to lose your fingers."

The girl got down on her knees next to the frame and began pounding on it with her fists, causing more fissures to appear in the already-broken glass. She then pulled shards away, tossing them aside, until she'd uncovered the feather. Now that it was exposed to the air, the feather gave off a soft humming sound. Rachel didn't know if this was something the feather normally did or if it was reacting to the proximity of the nearly-completed Atrocity Engine. Molly, following Rachel's warning, carefully took hold of the feather's shaft between her thumb and forefinger, then stood.

"Follow me," Rachel said. She led the way to the mausoleum, and Molly dutiful trailed after her. Once there, Rachel paused a moment to gaze upon her work – the inside-out mother, the pool of Corruption she stood in, the life-giver who breathed into her inverted mouth, and the killer with his hands wrapped tight around her throat.

Only one final task remained, and the Atrocity Engine would be complete, and power beyond comprehension would be hers. But now that she stood on the cusp of victory, she hesitated. This was the most dangerous moment for her, for once the Engine was activated, she knew Brother Nothing would sense it. She'd managed to shield it from his perception so far – at least she'd managed to avoid drawing his attention to it – but there would be no way to conceal it from him once it began working.

If, or rather *when*, he appeared, she could use the Engine against him, but she had no idea how long it would take her to fully connect to the device so that she could wield its full power. It might only take a few moments for the process to be completed, but that would give Brother Nothing more than enough time to deal with her, assuming he appeared right away. She'd have to hope that he was many universes distant right now, and that when he sensed the Atrocity Engine's power, it would take him some time to make his way back to this world. Enough time to allow her to claim the full power of the Atrocity Engine as her own. She knew it was a gamble, but for ultimate power, she'd risk everything.

"Here we go."

She pressed the tip of the obsidian blade to the inside-out mother's placenta and with a swift, deft motion made a two-inch-long cut. Amniotic fluid flowed from the wound, and a small arm thrust its way out, hand open, tiny fingers working as if trying to grab hold of something. Rachel stepped back, the obsidian blade – its work done – vanishing from her hand.

"You may do the honors," she said.

Molly stepped forward, awe on her undead face. She carefully placed the feather in the fetus' hand, and the tiny fingers snapped closed on the silvery shaft. Power exploded from the now-complete Atrocity Engine in waves too strong for Molly's decayed body to withstand. She disintegrated so completely that not an atom remained of her remained.

Rachel was too overwhelmed by the power surging to notice the girl's destruction, not that she would've cared if she had noticed. All that mattered to her now was increasing her strength as fast as she could before Brother Nothing arrived. She let the Engine's power flow into her, the sensation more intense than anything she could've imagined, and she now knew what it felt like to be a god.

She laughed in delight as she grew stronger and stronger.

"I didn't see the girl leave the building," Neal said, "and I didn't encounter her inside. It doesn't matter how she got out. She's with Rachel by now, and so is the Umbral feather."

Neal drove Number Seven like a madman, racing through the streets of Ash Creek as if the end of the world was upon them. Who knows? Maybe it was. They came to a busy intersection where the light was red, but he didn't slow down. Instead, he laid on the horn and prayed they wouldn't hit another vehicle as they ran the light. Drivers honked their horns, slammed on their brakes, tires squealed, and Neal heard a *krump* as two cars collided. Neither vehicle struck *them*, though, and right now that was all that he cared about. Number Seven roared through the intersection unscathed.

In the passenger seat, Gina groaned. Her forehead wound was covered with a large surgical bandage, and she held a gel cold pack to the side of her head.

"Go easy on the horn, I'm begging you."

"Sorry."

Before they'd left HQ, Neal had quickly bandaged Gina's wound and gave her some powerful painkillers from the van's med kit. Hopefully, the meds would kick in soon and she'd get some relief. He had no formal medical training, but as far as he could tell, she didn't have a concussion, at least not a major one, so she should be all right eventually.

"So let me get this straight," Gina said. "Rachel is in Woodgrove Cemetery, which is located next to the middle school. She's building something there – we don't know what specifically, just that it's dangerous – and the Umbral feather was the last item she needed to complete her project. *And* you learned this from your dead partner who Rachel resurrected to kill you."

"That's about the size of it."

"That frame must've hit me harder than I thought, because that almost makes sense. So what is she making?"

Eleanor answered.

"I've searched the archives for any sort of ritual an Umbral feather might be used in, and the most likely candidate I found is an Atrocity Engine."

Eleanor sounded scared, and Neal didn't blame her.

"Oh fuck," he whispered.

"I don't remember learning about that at the Homestead," Gina said. "How bad is it?"

"*Really* bad," Neal said. "Like, end-of-the-world bad."

"An Atrocity Engine is a massive generator of E-energy. It connects directly to the Gyre itself and absorbs the excess power given off as it feeds. One of the Multitude can use it to increase their strength exponentially, but in doing so, they become highly unstable. If they lose control of the power..."

"The world goes boom," Neal finished.

"Along with a sizeable chunk of the solar system," Eleanor added.

"Okay," Gina said. "Consider me thoroughly terrified. So, what can we do to stop Rachel before she explodes?"

"We might not have to do anything. The vast power given off by an Atrocity Engine should catch the attention of the Multitude, and they'll step in to stop her."

"And claim the Engine's power for their own," Neal said. "Which could also result in a big boom if *they* can't control it."

"True."

"So, our best bet is to shut down the Engine before the boom," Gina said. "Any idea how we do that?"

"I haven't found anything in *the archives yet, but I'm still looking."*

"I'm working on it," Neal said.

"So, we're heading for a confrontation with one of the Multitude who has access to unlimited power, and we don't have the faintest idea how to stop her," Gina said. "*And* we don't have the Expungent Grenade because you used it to destroy the corpse thing."

"I call it a Death Worm, but yeah. Deanna's called for backup."

"But they won't get here in time to help us, will they?"

Neal didn't answer. He didn't have to.

Gina nodded, then winced as the motion set off a fresh wave of pain in her head. She settled back against her seat, cold pack still pressed to her bandaged wound.

"Just another shitty day in paradise, right?" she said.

"We need to have that printed on T-shirts. We can wear them on casual day."

"I'll put in an order for them. I already know your sizes."

"Thanks," Neal said. "If nothing else, we can wear them to be buried in."

"In that case, I'll put a rush on them."

"Good idea," Neal said.

"Remind me why we're doing this?" Gina asked.

"Because there's no one else."

Neal fell silent and concentrated on driving.

Twenty-Two

It was bad enough Gina had been hit in the head by a frame thrown by an undead child, but did Neal have to hit *every* goddamned pothole on the way to the cemetery? Despite the painkillers he'd given her before they left HQ, she felt like her head might explode at any moment.

Once during her first-year training at the Homestead, she'd gone to a bar with some other students, and they'd decided to have a competition to see who could down the most Jello shots and still be able to walk a straight line. Gina had come in third, but the hangover she'd had the next day had been so severe she'd prayed for death. That was nothing compared to how she felt now, but she had one thing going for her. She didn't need to pray for death this time as there was an excellent chance it was coming for her soon, whether she wanted it to or not.

As they entered the cemetery Gina saw the graves had been disturbed. Fresh earth was scattered atop them, as if something – *many* somethings – had dug their way out.

"Now we know where Rachel got the raw materials to make her Death Worm," Neal said.

Gina tried to nod, but her head hurt too much.

The cemetery was deserted except for an SUV parked near a small mausoleum. The mausoleum's rusty gate was open, and a middle-aged woman stood in front of the structure, arms held out to her sides, head thrown back, as if she was in the throes of ecstasy.

"Rachel, I presume."

Gina tossed the cold pack on the floor and picked up the two Null Guns that had been resting on her lap. There had been one more Null Gun lying on the lobby floor of HQ, and Neal had grabbed it on their way out. Null Guns were devastating weapons when used against Corruption, but Gina doubted they'd do much more than irritate one of the Multitude. Still, the guns were all they had.

"Yeah, that's her," Neal said. "She's the woman I saw at the park the other day. I figured she was one of the Multitude then. Guess I was right."

As Number Seven drew closer to the mausoleum, Gina felt the fine hair on her arms and the back of her neck rise, as if the atmosphere was thick with static electricity. She also heard a sound, something that was both melodic and discordant, beautiful and terrifying. It seemed to come from all around her, from inside her too, and it felt comfortable as the presence of an old friend and as dangerous as a malign spirit invading her body.

"It's the Song of Ending," Eleanor said. *"The death scream of existence."*

Gina didn't know whether she could hear the Song because the Atrocity Engine had been activated, or if it was always present, and she'd just managed to ignore it until now. Both prospects were equally disturbing.

Neal pulled the van up next to the SUV, parked, and got out. He ran around the front of the vehicle and opened the passenger door for Gina and helped her out. She was a bit wobbly on her legs, but overall, she felt much better than she had back at HQ. Her head pounded less now that she was no longer in a moving vehicle, and her nausea was beginning to subside. She still felt like shit, only not as much as before. But all she needed to do was remain conscious for a few more moments to help Neal stop Rachel. After that, it didn't matter what happened to her.

The two agents raised their weapons into firing position and approached Rachel. The woman didn't turn to face them, and Gina wondered if she was too overwhelmed by the power of the Atrocity Engine to not notice them. She hoped so. She and Neal needed all the advantage they could get.

Rachel stood directly in front of the mausoleum's open gate, blocking their view of whatever was inside, and Gina was grateful for this. She didn't want to see what was in there, could happily live the rest of her life without ever seeing exactly what an Atrocity Engine looked like. Bad enough that she could smell the damn thing. It stank of decaying flesh and raw sewage, the stench so strong, her gorge rose and it took all her self-control to keep from throwing up.

When she and Neal were with five feet of Rachel, he gave her a nod, and they stopped.

Eleanor spoke softly then so she wouldn't be overheard by Rachel.

"Concentrate all your fire on the same spot. That'll give you the best chance to hurt her."

Neal turned his back to Gina, and with his free hand reached up to touch the spot between his shoulder glades. When he turned back around to face her, she nodded. Message received.

Neal aimed his one Null Gun at Rachel's back and Gina aimed her two. Gina felt no guilt whatsoever at attacking Rachel from behind. The woman was a deadly threat that needed to be taken out as swiftly as possible. Her family wouldn't have approved. *It goes against the Sandoval code of honor,* she imagined her father saying. Well, fuck honor and fuck him, too.

They fired.

Beams of white light lanced forth from the Null Guns' barrels and struck Rachel's back. The woman screamed and spun around to face them, features twisted into a mask of fury. She stretched out her arms, fingers curled into claws, as if she intended to rake their flesh, but they continued firing their Null Guns, now concentrating their beams on her breastbone. Rachel continued screaming for a moment, arms flailing, eyes rolled back in her head, and then her voice cut off and she fell limply to the ground, and lay there, eyes closed, silent and unmoving.

Gina and Neal continued firing their Null Guns at her for another moment before taking their fingers off the triggers. The beams died out, and the two agents peered at Rachel's body.

"Is she dead?" Gina asked hopefully.

"Null Guns didn't stop the Death Worm she created," he said. "Why should they work on her?"

Rachel opened her eyes and smiled.

"Why indeed?"

She rose to her feet and brushed a few bits of dirt off her clothes.

"I was hoping to fool you for a few more moments," Rachel said, "but it was still a good joke, wasn't it?"

"Maybe we'd appreciate it more if we were psychopaths like you," Neal said.

Gina expected Rachel to stab her fingers toward them and unleash bolts of E-energy that would reduce their bodies to nothing. Instead, the woman laughed.

"Maybe so. If it makes you feel better, if you'd shot me before I completed the Atrocity Engine, you might've have hurt or even killed me."

"It doesn't," Neal said.

"You're the agent I saw in the park a couple days ago, when I was testing out one of my Defilements. Your name's Neal, right? At least, that's what your former partner told me when I brought her back to life and sent her to kill you. Obviously, she failed."

"What can I say? I'm tougher than I look."

Rachel sniffed. "*That* wouldn't be hard."

"Ouch," Neal said. "Coming from someone who's given herself over to Corruption, that really hurts."

"To *power*," Rachel said. "Don't the two of you get tired of being human sometimes? You have so little control over anything in your lives. You're at the mercy of genetics, upbringing, culture, hormones, desires, fears, doubts, self-loathing... You spend your lives running around blindly, trying to grab hold of whatever you can before you die – sex, money, material possessions – and in the end it all adds up to nothing. Oh, you two might think you're different, that you're working to slow the death of the Omniverse. *Flavor to the feast*, and all that. But even if you manage to succeed – and that's a damn big *if* – how long do you think you can deny the Gyre its food? Years? Months? Weeks? Days? Minutes? Seconds? What does it matter? In the end, the

Gyre will be fed. But the Multitude will go on, and when the Gyre vomits a new Omniverse and the cycle of life and death begins anew, we will be there to rule over all existence and shape it as we see fit. *That's* power."

"She's insane," Eleanor said.

No argument there, Gina thought.

"Speaking of power..." Neal pointed to the mausoleum. Now that Rachel had stepped away from the entrance, Gina could see inside, and she wished she couldn't. The Atrocity Engine was obscene, an affront to everything good and decent in the Omniverse.

Neal went on. "I can't imagine your people are going to be too fond of you building one of those things. From what I understand, they're not very stable."

"And I doubt they'll be happy to learn you're seeking to make yourself stronger than they are," Gina added.

"What's your ultimate plan?" Neal asked. "To take over the Multitude and be its queen? Or do you want to kill the rest of them and have the entire Omniverse for yourself?"

"I'd be content with either outcome. We'll just have to see how things shake out, won't we? Now, I could kill the both of you with no more effort than blinking an eye, but I was in the process of absorbing the Engine's power when you arrived, and I'd like to finish. If you're good, you can both watch. Who knows? Afterward, I might transform you into my servants. That could be amusing."

She then turned her back on them as if they meant nothing and returned to her position in front of the mausoleum. This pissed off Gina. She'd had enough of people – namely her family – behaving high and mighty, as if they were better than anyone else. She aimed her Null Guns at Rachel one more time and prepared to fire. But before she could squeeze the triggers, Rachel made a sharp gesture with her right hand, and the guns turned to dust in her grasp, filtered through her fingers and drifted to the ground. The same thing happened to Neal's weapon.

"And don't bother going for your Nullifiers," Rachel said without turning to look at them. "If Null Guns couldn't harm me, those little things certainly can't."

"She's right," Eleanor said. *"As powerful as she is right now, they'd only tickle her."*

The woman held her hands out to her side once again, and while Gina couldn't see any visual sign that she'd resumed absorbing E-energy from the Atrocity Engine, she could sense it. It was like standing on the edge of an ocean while a storm raged in the distance. You could feel its power in the air.

Gina looked at Neal. Her head still hurt, but she didn't care. She had bigger concerns at the moment.

"Now what?"

Before Neal could answer, Gina heard the sound of a vehicle approaching the cemetery. A moment later, a Maintenance van drove through the entrance and headed toward them. Neal turned to look at it and smiled. Then he jerked his head to the side, as if something had suddenly caught his eye. He pointed, and Gina looked in the direction he indicated. She thought she saw someone duck behind a tree, but whoever did it was so fast, she wasn't sure she'd seen anything at all. But Neal's smile widened into a grin. He held it for a moment, and then his face grew serious.

"Goddamn it!" he said. "I thought I'd given her the slip!"

Rachel lowered her arms and turned around.

"What are you babbling about now?" She saw the van approaching, and her face darkened, as if she was anticipating another attack. But then her expression relaxed. "It's Pam, isn't it? And here you tried to make me believe that you'd killed her. That was naughty of you. If I was still posing as a teacher, I'd give you detention for that. But seeing as how I resurrected Pam with the express purpose of killing you, I think it's only right that I allow her to do so – and she can kill your plucky apprentice while she's at it."

"I hope you know what you're doing, Neal," Eleanor said.

Me too, Gina thought.

The three of them – four if you counted Eleanor – watched as Pam backed Number Four onto the grass next to Number Seven and parked. Pam exited the vehicle, and Gina was surprised by how rundown she looked. Stringy hair, bruised-looking skin beneath bloodshot eyes, dry, cracked lips... Then she realized: the woman's body had been fashioned from E-energy, and she was beginning to decay. She looked at Neal to see what his reaction was. His features were impassive, but she saw the pain in his eyes. It hurt him to see his friend like this. She felt an impulse to reach out and take his hand to comfort him, but she resisted. She didn't know what was going to happen next, but there was every chance she'd need both hands free to fight soon.

Pam stopped when she reached the back of Number Four.

"I can't say I'm pleased by your tardiness, but better late than never, I suppose," Rachel said. "Fulfill your purpose. Kill them both, and be quick about it. I have a task to finish."

Pam paid no attention to the woman. Instead, she looked at Neal.

"How's it going so far?" she asked.

"About like you'd expect," he replied.

"That bad, huh? Well, I've brought something that will cheer you up. It wasn't easy to find him and get him in the van, but I've always been good with animals."

"Better than me, that's for sure," Neal said.

Rachel frowned. "What are you two going on about? Stop talking to this idiot and kill him!"

"Neal's not an idiot," Pam said. "He might not be a genius, but he knows the most important thing about being an agent for Maintenance."

"And what's that?" Rachel said.

Pam smiled grimly. "Whenever you can, stack the deck in your favor."

She opened the van's rear door with a single swift motion and then jumped out of the way. A large humanoid form with pebbled hide covered with dark stripes and white spots shot out of the van, landed on the grass, and paused, head turning rapidly this way and that, forked tongue tasting the air, tail swishing back and forth.

It was Teguzilla.

Rachel frowned, puzzled.

"What the hell is *that* thing?"

Gina felt Neal take hold of her upper arm. He then slowly pulled her to the side so the two of them no longer stood between Rachel and Teguzilla.

"That's a Void Breather," Neal said. "It's a creature made of pure entropic energy, and since you're full of E-energy, too, I'm betting he'll see you as a rival predator."

Teguzilla's beady black eyes focused on Rachel, its muscles tensed, and it opened its clawed hands wide. It let out a loud angry hiss and starting running toward her, feet tearing up the earth as it went.

Startled, Rachel raised her hands, as if intending to blast the mutant lizard with E-energy. But before she could do anything, Teguzilla stopped five feet in front of her, opened its mouth, and released a cloud of pure darkness. The black mass engulfed Rachel completely, swirling around her like a miniature tornado, and she screamed as if she'd been plunged into the fires of Hell.

Gina remembered how Teguzilla's void breath had destroyed a large chunk of ground in front of the shed it had been using as its lair. No, not destroyed. *Unmade*. And now that power had been unleashed on Rachel. Could even one of the Multitude survive it?

Rachel continued screaming as the black cloud spun around her. Teguzilla crouched in front of the woman, watching and waiting. Her screams cut off abruptly, the cloud began to shrink, and when the darkness had fully dissipated, they could see Rachel was still there. She was on her hands and knees, head hanging down. Most of her hair was gone, and her clothes hung on her in tatters. She remained in that position for a moment, then she slowly stood, swaying, unsteady on her feet. Her skin was covered with holes of varying sizes where the black cloud had unmade portions of her. Her left eye was missing, as was her right ear and several of her fingers. Her lower lip was gone too, revealing her bottom teeth. She looked hideous, like something that had crawled out of one of the dozens of empty graves around them. But injured as she was, she still lived.

"It'll take more than a lizard with bad breath to stop me," she said.

She closed her remaining eye, held out her hands, and then her injuries repaired themselves. She opened her eyes – both of them – and smiled with, both of her lips whole and healthy.

"She's drawn on the power of the Atrocity Engine to heal herself," Eleanor said.

Even so, it was obvious the void had taken its toll on her. She was thinner and paler than before, and her hands shook slightly. Still, she was alive, and that was nothing short of a miracle. A dark one, maybe, but a miracle nonetheless.

Teguzilla stared at the woman for a moment before turning tail and racing away at top speed. Rachel paid it no attention, and within seconds, the creature had left the cemetery and was gone.

"I have to hand it to you," Rachel said. "That *hurt*, and I didn't think anything could hurt me anymore. But as you can see, it didn't work."

"Then it's a good thing I brought along a friend for backup," Neal said.

Gina didn't know what he was talking about, but then a man stepped out from behind a nearby tree and started walking toward them. It was Lenny, the God of Small Things.

Rachel fell into a defensive crouch, hands out, ready to hurl E-energy at the newcomer. But then she cocked her head to the side, as if truly seeing him for the first time. Then she laughed.

"Your aura says you're one of the Multitude, but your power level is so low it is almost nonexistent. What are you?"

Lenny reached Gina and Neal and stood beside them.

"I'm Lenny. People call me the God of Small Things. I was in training to be one of the Multitude, but I washed out. Wasn't evil enough."

Rachel laughed again, then she looked at Neal.

"*This* is your backup? He's less of a threat to me than the lizard was!"

Lenny's face remained calm, but when he spoke, there was steel in his voice.

"The problem with the Multitude is they have access to so much power, they're not really skilled in its application. They're like huge sledgehammers, and it's difficult for them to do fine, detailed work. The Omniverse may be unimaginably vast, but it's made of small things."

"That may be," Rachel said, "but you can't seriously believe you can do anything to hurt me. I may still be recovering from my exposure to void energy, but I'm more than a match for you."

"You think so?" Lenny said. "Let's see how you handle an aortic dissection."

He gestured and Rachel gasped. She pressed her right hand to her chest and doubled over in pain. Her breathing became rapid, and the left side of her body drooped, as if she was having a stroke. She took a step toward them, swayed, and then fell to the ground. She lay there, groaning, eyes wide with fear.

"You can't heal yourself," Lenny said. "As soon as you try, I'll renew the injury. We can keep going round and around like that until you die from internal bleeding – which shouldn't take long."

Lenny's voice was cold, his words matter of fact, and Gina thought that maybe he was a bit more evil than he let on.

"She's powerful," Lenny said, "but she's not a full-fledged member of the Multitude yet. If she was, I might not be able to maintain the injury. It's still taking all the power I have, but she's done for. Just a few more moments..."

Rachel tried to chuckle, but it came out as a wheeze.

"You morons may have killed me, but you haven't won. I'm still connected to the Atrocity Engine, and I can cause it to release all its power in a single burst. The energy release with destroy the planet and likely most of the solar system. I may never get to be a true member of the Multitude, but they'll remember my name because there will be one less world in the Omniverse for them to worry about. Your deaths will happen so swiftly, you won't feel them, which is a damn shame, but what the hell? You can't have everything."

Rachel sank her fingers into the Earth and slowly turned herself around until she was facing the Atrocity Engine. She stretched a trembling hand toward it, and instantly the Song of Ending became so loud it was deafening. Gale force winds erupted in the cemetery, and Gina and Neal grabbed onto one another to steady themselves. Lenny's hair blew in the wind, but he had no trouble resisting its force and stood firm.

Pam had stood silently by Number Four since releasing Teguzilla, but now she ran toward Rachel.

"You're going to regret bringing me back!" She had to shout to be heard over the Song and the roar of the wind.

Rachel glanced back over her shoulder.

"I already do," she said and snapped her fingers.

Pam stopped, a stricken look on her face. She began to disintegrate, her body slowly turning into gray dust.

"No!" Neal shouted. He tried to go to her, but Gina held him back.

"What happened to me at the dumpster wasn't your fault, Neal. Stop blaming yourself." Pam gave him a sad smile, then turned to Gina.

"Take care of him," she said.

And then her body collapsed into granular particles, and she was gone.

"Goddamn it!" Tears of sorrow and anger streamed from Neal's eyes, to be dried almost instantly by the wind.

Gina pulled Neal closer to her and hugged him tight.

"I'm so sorry," Eleanor said, and from the sound of her voice, Gina thought she was crying.

"Is there anything you can do to stop Rachel?" Gina asked Lenny.

The God of Small Things shook his head.

"There's too much entropic energy flowing from the Engine. My powers are useless."

"Rachel has been severely weakened," Eleanor said. *"Nullifiers might work on her now."*

Neal looked doubtful, but he nodded. Still holding on to each other for support against the wind, they bent down, removed their Nullifiers from their socks, and straightened once more.

"If this doesn't work," Neal said to Gina, "I want you to know that you're a hell of an agent, and it was my honor to be your partner."

Gina smiled. "Flavor to the feast," she said.

"Flavor to the feast," Neal replied.

They aimed their weapons at Rachel and activated them, but they were too late.

The Atrocity Engine exploded in a burst of dark light.

Twenty-Three

"That'll be quite enough of that."

Everything was suddenly quiet and still. No wind, no Song, no darkness. Neal looked around, trying to understand what had happened. Where they dead? He didn't *feel* dead, but since he'd never died before, how would he know?

The two Maintenance vans and the SUV remained parked where they'd been, but the graves in the cemetery had been restored to their previous state. Were their occupants back in their proper places too? He had no way to know for certain, but he suspected it was so. Gina and he were still holding onto each other, and – both feeling awkward now – they released each other and took a step back.

Lenny still stood next to them, but he didn't seem to be aware of them. He was staring forward, mouth open and face pale, as if he was looking at something that terrified him. Rachel still lay on the ground in front of the mausoleum, and the Atrocity Engine was still housed inside. But someone new stood next to Rachel – a thin man in a yellowed white suit and bolo tie – and Neal realized it was he who had spoken.

"Holy fuck," Lenny whispered. "It's Brother Nothing."

The name didn't mean anything to Neal, but he saw the man's eyes were miniature replicas of the Gyre – black holes with multicolored event horizons swirling slowly around them. More, Neal could sense the vast power emanating from the man. It was like standing next to a giant generator throwing off great bolts of electricity. The atmosphere crackled with energy, and Neal's entire body tingled.

As frightened as Lenny seemed, it was nothing compared to Rachel's fear. She looked up at Brother Nothing with an expression of absolute terror on her face.

"Guys, I just looked up Brother Nothing on our database," Eleanor said. *"He's the biggest and baddest of the Multitude. You need to be extremely careful."*

No shit, Gina thought.

Brother Nothing looked down at Rachel and smiled, displaying yellow, cracked teeth. Small dark things squirmed behind those teeth. Insects? Something worse?

"You came *so* close, Rachel. Pity you came up short in the end."

He turned and walked to the mausoleum.

"You did an excellent job on your Atrocity Engine, though. Really top-notch."

He held his right palm up, and the Atrocity Engine disappeared from the mausoleum and reappeared – much smaller – in his hand. He regraded it for a moment, and then opened his mouth wide and tossed the mini-Engine inside. His mouth snapped shut and he chewed for a moment, considering. Then he swallowed.

"And it's *delicious*! Very impressive."

He gestured and the mausoleum's rusty gate slammed shut. He then turned and walked over to Neal, Gina, and Lenny. He reached out and put a hand on Lenny's shoulder, and the God of Small Things shivered.

"Nice work on the aortic dissection. Inspired choice, really. We might've made a mistake sending you home."

Brother Nothing removed his hand and Lenny let out a sigh of relief. If Brother Nothing noticed, he said nothing. He then stepped in front of Neal and Gina.

"Sorry you had to lose Pam a second time, Neal. But that's the way the reconstituted lifeform crumbles, eh? But you're a tough guy – you can take it." Brother Nothing trained his black-hole eyes on Gina. She shrank back a bit but held her ground. "Building an adult relationship with parents can be difficult. Especially when one's family is corrupt as yours."

Gina's jaw muscles bunched as she gritted her teeth, but she didn't reply. That was good, because Neal was certain Brother Nothing could destroy all of them with a single thought if he wished, and if he felt like it, he could surely do far worse things to them. Best not to piss him off.

"You two intrigue me," Brother Nothing said. "You appear to be nothing special as Maintenance agents go, but there's something about you both... I'll think I'll keep my eye on you. If nothing else, it should prove amusing."

He turned away from them and looked at Rachel once more.

"Please," she said, tears in her eyes. "Forgive me."

"For what? Attempting to betray me? For going rogue and constructing an Atrocity Engine so you could make yourself one of the most powerful members of the Multitude? There's nothing to forgive. You did exactly what I hoped you'd do. I was always aware of what you were doing, watching you in secret, cloaking my presence so you couldn't detect me. What do you think the final test for admission to the Multitude is? An apprentice must always attempt to destroy their master. That's why Lenny failed. He couldn't bring himself to harm his mentor."

Neal looked at Lenny, but the man refused to meet his gaze. Brother Nothing continued.

"What I'm angry about is that you *failed* to betray me. Worse yet, you failed to fulfill the promise I saw in the little girl you once were. The girl had such potential for wickedness. She could've been *magnificently* evil. Now look at you, groveling in the grass, begging for your pathetic life . . . You're no better than one of them." He gestured toward Neal, Gina, and Lenny. "Worse, really. All three of them are pants-wettingly terrified of me – which they should be – but none of them have begged for my mercy."

He broke off for a moment, and tapped his lips with an index finger as he thought. His fingernail was overlong and jagged, and it cut his lip, drawing a bead of black ichor instead of blood. Finally, he lowered his hand and sighed.

"Your Valuation is over. It is time for the Reckoning. You may have failed, but as I said earlier, you *did* come close to succeeding. So how about this? I'll send you to a place where you'll have a few thousand years to think about what you did wrong. I'll check back with you then, and if you've learned your lesson, perhaps – just *perhaps* – I'll allow you to start over. How does that sound?"

Neal saw a glimmer of hope in Rachel's eyes.

"Where?" she asked.

"I was thinking the core of the sun. Don't worry. You may burn but you won't die." He grinned. "I'll make sure of it."

Rachel shook her head in denial.

"No, please, don't, I'll–"

Brother Nothing made a sharp gesture and Rachel was gone.

"My god," Gina breathed.

Brother Nothing faced them once more.

"I appreciate the offer, my dear, but I really don't have time for worshippers. I'm much too busy."

As he stood there looking at them, his black-hole eyes seemed to grow larger, until they merged into one mass of darkness so huge it blotted out Brother Nothing, blotted out the entire world. Neal felt a tidal pull coming from the center of the mass, attempting to catch hold of him and draw him inward. But just as the Gyre – for surely that's what this awful thing was – started to suck him in, Brother Nothing said, "Being see you."

Then darkness was gone, and so was he.

Neal, Gina, and Lenny stood there for a moment, struggling to process what had happened. The cemetery had been silent when they first got here, but now they could hear birds singing. The Corruption that Rachel had brought to this place had been neutralized, and life was returning to Oak Grove. Neal figured there was a metaphor in there somewhere, but he was too tired to figure out what it was.

"So..." Lenny said. "You guys want to go get a drink?"

Neal looked at a Gina.

"No," she said. "I want to get several. Really strong ones."

Neal smiled wearily.

"The student has become the master," he said.

Twenty-Four

A week later, Neal and Gina were having lunch at the food court in the Southland Mall. Gina had ordered a grilled chicken salad from the Chicken Kitchen, and Neal was chowing down on a double bacon cheeseburger from Jeanie's Burger Bar. They both were wearing their smart glasses. After everything that had happened recently, they didn't feel comfortable taking them off while working, not even during lunch.

"If you don't start eating healthier, I may end up having to look for a new partner a lot sooner than I'd like," Gina said.

"I got a diet soda. That has to count for something, right?"

Gina held up her bottle of water.

Neal sighed. "Okay, tomorrow I'll get a salad. Promise."

"Okay, but *not* the Belly Buster Burrito Salad from Blazin' Tacos."

Neal sighed. "Fine."

This was their first day back on duty after their confrontation with Rachel in the cemetery. Neal was glad to be working again. He hated taking time off, and since most of it had been spent answering questions from high-level Analysts sent by Maintenance Control, as well as being examined by doctors from both Medical and Psych Divisions, the break had been even less fun for him than usual. Gina had been forced to undergo the same routine.

But aside from a mild concussion she'd received from being struck by the frame holding the Umbral feather, and a touch of E-energy sickness they'd both contracted from their proximity to the Atrocity Engine, they were fine. A half-day's treatment in the Cleansing Chambers at Columbus Division took care of the E-energy contamination, and while Gina's concussion resulted in a headache for a couple days, it healed on its own. The psychologists had also given them a clean bill of mental health, but they cautioned Neal and Gina that they might experience some PTSD after everything they'd been through.

The psychologists would've preferred they be given at least a month off from active duty, but Deanna – who was back at work herself after undergoing surgery for her hand wound – wanted them back out in the streets as soon as possible. Maintenance, no matter the division or its location, was always shorthanded, and after so much E-energy had been released into Ash Creek's environment, there was no telling what sort of ill effects it might have on the town. Deanna wanted all her agents working and on high alert.

The psychologists settled for having Neal and Gina agree to meet with them once a week so their *readjustment period* could be evaluated. Neal thought it was a bunch of horseshit, but if it got him back out on the street, he'd live with it.

"How are things between you and Amador?" Neal asked.

"Dad hasn't stopped bragging about me to all his cronies in the DC Division and Control. It's embarrassing. And he's been pressuring Deanna to promote both of us."

"Like that'll ever happen. We broke so many rules trying to stop Rachel that we're lucky she didn't demote us to Custodial."

"You're exaggerating," Gina said.

"Maybe. But Deanna takes Maintenance's ethos of non-waste seriously. She knows I can do better as a Surveyor than anything else – even if I have a tendency toward... independent thinking. As for you, she'd rather not rush your career development."

Eleanor cut in then.

"And she wants you to keep an eye on Neal, make sure he walks the straight and narrow."

Gina smiled. "I'll do what I can, but I'm not a miracle worker."

"That stuff Brother Nothing said about your family? A creature like him lies as easily as he breathes."

"I appreciate you trying to protect me," Gina said, "but he was telling the truth, wasn't he? And you knew it."

Neal sighed. "Yeah. But your family has done a hell of a lot of good over the years too. Don't forget that."

"I know, and right now, that's what I'm going to focus on. But someday soon I'm going to have to a serious talk with my parents. My brother and sister too. And then... well, I'll cross that bridge when I get to it."

Neal nodded, but he worried how that conversation would go. He was confident Gina wouldn't follow the rest of her family and join the Black Trust, but what would happen if she threatened to expose them? The Salvadors had friends in Control – *powerful* friends – who protected them. But as Gina said, that was a problem for another day.

She changed the topic then.

"I keep having nightmares about Brother Nothing," she said. "Especially those eyes of his." She shivered.

"Me too," Neal confessed. "I'm sure they'll go away. Eventually."

"Do you really think so?"

Neal didn't reply, and after a moment, they returned to eating in silence.

They'd avoiding talking about Brother Nothing since that day in the cemetery, but he was never far from Neal's mind, and he was sure the same was true for Gina. Fighting Rachel had been hard enough, and they almost hadn't survived it, but as powerful as she'd been, Brother Nothing was on a whole other terrifying level.

I'll think I'll keep my eye on you. If nothing else, it should prove amusing.

Neal wanted to believe that it was just talk, that neither he nor Gina were important enough to a being like Brother Nothing for him to bother with. Hell, he'd probably forgotten about them the moment he left. That's what Neal wanted to believe, anyway. And if he worked hard enough to convince himself, maybe someday he would.

Maybe.

"How are you doing?" Gina asked. "About Pam, I mean."

"It was hard to see her die a second time, but she told me herself that she was only an echo of the real Pam."

"I think she was a little more than that."

"Yeah. Weird thing is, even with all the horrible shit that happened that day, it was still good to see her. It felt like we finally had a chance to say goodbye, you know?"

Eleanor came over their comms then.

"We just got a report on a Teguzilla sighting at the Clybourne Apartments. There's a large pond onsite, and he's gotten into the water and is devouring the geese that live there. Deanna wants the two of you to go confirm the sighting, but she does not – repeat NOT – want you to engage."

"Let's go."

Gina stood, picked up the tray with her partially-eaten salad on it, and headed toward a waste receptacle. Neal didn't want to go. After Teguzilla had helped them out last week, Neal had started to think of the Void Breather as a sort of unofficial mascot for Ash Creek's Maintenance Division. He was reluctant to do anything that might result in the creature's capture. But Teguzilla was still dangerous, and he and Gina had a job to do.

He took one more quick bite of his burger, then stood, grabbed his tray, and hurried to throw the rest away.

It had turned out to be a beautiful day – not too warm, not too cold, a clear blue sky. As Neal and Gina walked out of the mall and started toward their van, Gina looked up at the sun shining high in the sky.

"Do you ever wonder..." she began.

"I try not to think about it," Neal said.

They got into the van, drove out of the parking lot, and went back to work.

Twenty-Five

Fire.

Around her, inside her, burning, burning, eating away at flesh, mind, and spirit...

Feasting.

But no matter how much of her the flames devoured, she remained whole. She felt agony in every atom of her being. Light, heat, pain... These things were her gods now. She tried to scream, *needed* to scream, but when she opened her mouth, all that came out was a great gout of fire. *I'm a dragon,* she thought. *The Dragon of the Sun.*

She laughed, this time ejecting small spurts of flame.

She struggled to recall her real name, but it wouldn't come to her. Agony, Misery, Torment... these were her new names. She did remember another name, one that blazed in her mind even more strongly than the seething inferno that had become her whole existence.

Brother Nothing.

Two more names came to her then.

Neal. Gina.

These were the names of those who had hurt her, who had consigned her to this hell. One way or another, she would free herself from this prison of nuclear fire, and when she did, she would seek out the owners of these three names, and when she found them, she'd make sure they knew what it was like to burn too.

She laughed once more, and she continued laughing for a very long time.

The Custodians will return in The Book of Madness.

About the Author

Tim Waggoner has published over fifty novels and seven collections of short stories. He writes original dark fantasy and horror, as well as media tie-ins, and his articles on writing have appeared in numerous publications. He's a four-time winner of the Bram Stoker Award, a one-time winner of the Scribe award, and he's been a finalist for the Shirley Jackson Award and the Splatterpunk Award. He's also a full-time tenured professor who teaches creative writing and composition at Sinclair College in Dayton, Ohio. His papers are collected by the University of Pittsburgh's Horror Studies Program.

LINKS

Website: www.timwaggoner.com

Blog: http://writinginthedarktw.blogspot.com/

YouTube Channel: https://www.youtube.com/c/timwaggonerswritinginthedark

Newsletter Sign-Up: https://timwaggoner.com/contact.htm

www.ingramcontent.com/pod-product-compliance
Lightning Source LLC
Chambersburg PA
CBHW030354310726
48979CB00001B/295

* 9 7 8 1 9 4 9 8 9 0 8 9 1 *